I0742072

Edited by Willow Heath

Cover Art by Rashed AlAkroka

Photo Taken by Sophie Watkins

Interior & Cover Design by Eira Brand of Zipline
Studios

Published by Zipline Studios

Distributed by Zipline Studios

Paperback ISBN: 979-8-9925188-1-8

eBook ISBN: 979-8-9925188-0-1

by

EIRA BRAND

ACKNOWLEDGEMENTS

First and foremost, thank you to Sophie who inspires me to embrace the weird, find humor in all things, and chase my dreams.

Second, to my friends and family who supported me while I worked on this story. You know who you are. I could not have done it without you.

Thank you to my cover artist Rashed and my editor Willow for your help in bringing this to life. Thank you to Philip and Natalie for enduring my early manuscripts.

Special thanks to Conrad for encouraging me from the start. From my first few paragraphs on that Facebook group all those years ago, until now. Thanks for giving me the push I needed.

Last but not least, I want to thank the following people for welcoming me into your corner of the writing world with open arms. In no particular order, M.L. Wang, Jackson Dickert, Bryce O'Connor, T.L. Greylock, Dyrk Ashton, Oriana Leckert, Daniel B. Greene, Kayla Torrison, Virginia McClain, Intisar Khanani, and Rose Reynolds.

LESS THAN SCRAPING BY

Three weeks. It had been three weeks since I'd landed a run. My account had been empty for two, and I ran out of food and water six days ago. The last purchase I tried to make—at *Nadina's Foodstuffs*—was a single-serve, just-add-water block of ramen. Came up a few *kay* short. I begged and pleaded, which was an utterly humiliating experience, but old Nadina wouldn't budge.

"I don't run a charity," she drawled. "Full price or nothing."

Needless to say, I might have needed a new face before I could go back there again because I grabbed the plastic packet and bolted. Dry spells have come and gone before, but stealing freeze-dried instant noodles was a new low for me. Maybe I could volunteer some of my ample free time to repay her for the trouble. I had no idea. Every time I'd walked past the place since then she gave me a death glare that probably had a fatality count at closer ranges. I might be dead before I got the chance to work my way back into her good graces. Nope, that was a nonstarter. All I could do now was ignore the ache in my stomach and hunch over the black-blue display of my terminal, hoping my bid for work was enticing enough to overlook my contract history.

I hadn't gotten any bites from potential employers in days, so I wasn't optimistic that today was going to be any different. As I sat there, staring holes in my screen, a pink column of light strobed across my face through a mirror behind the bar, blinding me momentarily and leaving colored spots echoing in my eyes. It was as if the strip club I was currently squatting in—*The Velvet Cadaver*—was trying to get my attention. Well, when I really thought about it, wasn't that kind of the point of a strip club? To that end, the place had an ensemble that could raise the dead. Colors clashed everywhere. Strobe lights flashed out of sync with one another. To top it all off, the bass-heavy music thudded drunkenly against your lungs like someone who doesn't know how to do chest compressions.

Over on the stage, a man and woman were dressed in matching outfits, top hats, and faux tuxedos that wrapped around their torsos like corsets, showing off plenty of oiled muscle and supple curve. The two danced together to the rhythm, pushing their outfits to the limits. Every time it seemed like the fabric might rip free, they would gyrate in a different direction to applause, catcalls, and surely plenty of tips.

While some part of me wanted to get a seat right in front of the stage to take in—and fall victim to—the ancient, primal display, I reminded myself that I wasn't there to take in the sights. Hell, I wasn't even there to look for jobs on the boards. I was there to beg someone I knew for help, and maybe score a free drink or two while I was at it.

I let out a long breath and forced myself to lean away from the terminal. Pushing my thoughts to the back of my mind, I watched the main entrance with pensive determination; like I was willing the right person to come walking through the doors. Plenty of people came and went, swirling around one another like bloatflies on a corpse, but in their midst, a young man sauntered in like he owned the place. Jin, as I knew him, was a well-off and friendly acquaintance who made his way in life as a dancer and top-tier escort. Even in this day and age, where everything could exist in your mind—in the *dreamscape*—there remained a demand for physical performers of all sorts. Some people still have a thing for analog, be it books, film, or people. He was lean, with sunken features that might call his health into question. Today, he'd strolled in covered in strips of white body tape and a top that might have been more fishing net than fishnet. It was all surrounded by an opulent red-maned coat of living fur that clung precariously to his shoulders. It didn't leave much to the imagination, while also managing to be mysterious. He must have been seeing a client later. Jin gave me a subtle wave when he spotted me, and altered his course to take the open seat on my left.

He motioned at the bartender for two drinks and gave me a cheery smile, "Ciao. Looking for work?"

There's the free drink. Off to a good start.

He continued without waiting for my answer. "Wanna get in on my next gig? This particular client loves surprises. You'd just have to get all that hair out of your face. Off your face, too. It is such a crime that you hide that killer jawline of yours."

Yeah, that sharp, angular bone structure that had been gifted to me by my randomly selected donor-parents. I'd hated it for as long as I could remember. Kids used to come up with all sorts of 'clever' nicknames for me. I'd had a poorly groomed beard, of sorts, for as long as I could grow facial hair, just to hide that chiseled thing that underlined my face.

I rolled my eyes, and Jin replied with a wink and a knowing smile before turning around to lean back on the bar to watch the dancers. Now there were two men in thongs and tiny cowboy hats. I turned back to my terminal in time to see the bartender slide two frosted glasses across the digital marble countertop.

"I mean it," Jin said, sliding one of the glasses in my direction. "As long as you don't have a micropenis—a little elbow grease and I can probably get you in anywhere."

He took a sip and savored it. Didn't matter what his poison was, Jin insisted on never imbibing alone. He'd often buy the nearest person a drink just to have some company, and when he did, there was no sense in arguing with him. Because of that, I'd made a point of being the nearest person more often than not. Tipping the donated glass to my lips, the dark amber liquid smelled of oak and peat moss and a few other things I couldn't exactly place. It burned my throat a little as I swallowed it down, but the drink was smooth, smoky, and warm. God, Jin had good taste. I would have preferred to take the money it cost instead, but damn it was good.

I put the glass down, deciding to pace myself, "I'm pretending to look for work. Bullshitting mostly. No goddamn point in it."

Jin scrunched up his eyebrows, "That last job you had sounded like a pretty good deal. Something go wrong?"

"I got ganked. Not sure if the client reneged or a third party got their hands on the details," I answered, taking another sip. "But I wound up taking a tumble from a rooftop and planted my face onto the side of a passing taxi. Needed to get a new face, too."

Jin flinched like he'd just seen it happen, "Oh, Jesus, I'm sorry. That wasn't something that lab-made body of yours could recover from?"

"Thanks, and no," I said, drinking some more. "I may be a vatbrat—diseases, cuts, and bruises are no problem—but all that engineered resilience doesn't count for much at terminal velocity. Might have made it worse, actually, because I didn't lose consciousness afterward. I felt all of it."

"Fuck," Jin breathed out into his glass, "And here I thought your kind was next to impervious."

"Nope," I answered, with no particular inflection. As the word left my mouth, I felt my face twitch with a familiar but unprompted motion.

He raised a curious eyebrow, "Uhhh, did you just wink at me?"

I sighed and tried to look frustrated; no easy feat when half of your face is blinking like a traffic light. "No, not on purpose. This damn faceplate is such a piece of shit. No flexible restructuring and an incompatible HUD version to boot. I've been trying to live with it, but it keeps malfunctioning."

Jin motioned at me, glass in hand, "How long have we known each other?"

I started to answer, but he held a finger to my lips. He set his glass down and started counting on his fingers. If it weren't for the music, I probably could have heard him whispering the numbers to himself.

"Three years, five months, and..." He paused again. He touched each of the fingers on his right hand to his thumb. "Twenty-two days. You remember how?"

I shrugged, "Sure, it was on the elevator, as it goes for everyone in this building."

He almost looked hurt at my lack of specificity. "You sauntered into the lift, all dark and brooding. As you do—" he mimicked my behavior as he continued "—and you didn't say a word, just stood there with that dead-eyed stare of yours. I asked you what floor you were on, and you said—"

"That I didn't have one," I droned. "What's your point?"

He poked my shoulder with a well-manicured finger. "Not only that, but right after you said it, you hauled yourself through the maintenance hatch, stopping the car halfway between forty-two and forty-three, and just disappeared," he explained.

None of this was untrue. He was one of the first people I had met when I moved here. Most people keep to themselves when sharing elevator cars. You never know when a stray syllable might send the person next to you off the edge and into that week's news-breaking killing spree. Jin dared to tempt fate that day and not only greeted me but introduced himself. I had no idea where he was going with this, so gave him a skeptical look, hoping he'd move the story along.

Jin took a deep breath, evidently mustering the kind of patience typically reserved for children, "The point is that you are used to living life on the in-betweens. In between floors, constantly in-between one-time contracts, and you even live in a box, halfway to homeless."

"Hey," I protested. "It's not a box. I put a lot of work into that place."

He put a hand on my shoulder, clearly pitying me, "It's a box. But that isn't the point either. You accept half-measures. You look around at the world and figure if you don't wind up with your guts in the gutter, you're doing an okay job at living. Could be worse, right?"

"Yeah," I said, almost proudly. "It could be worse."

Jin took another sip and continued his soapboxing, "The problem with that is you're not actually living. That's surviving, and you have to want for more than that. Fuck, you're a half-decent person. You deserve better than that. That's why I offer to bring you in on ride-alongs so often."

He wasn't wrong—not entirely, anyway. I did have a tendency to settle. Part of my childhood programming, maybe. He was absolutely wrong about my home, though. It may not look like much, but I worked my ass off to repurpose that decommed heating unit into something most people would call livable. Made a lot of special modifications myself, as they say.

"Regardless, you're going to want to get your face fixed," he said after a moment. "I can get away with winking at people because I'm me, but some of the circles you travel in..."

"I'll have you know that you're part of those circles," I countered. "Asshole."

Jin chucked me on the arm, "Look, just be careful. That's all I'm saying. Don't want that being the reason you miss out on the next job."

That's when a gravelly voice erupted from behind us, "There isn't going to be a next job."

This was who I was really waiting for. A scarred but steady hand the size of a shovel settled on my shoulder and gave a gentle squeeze. It wasn't a friendly or reassuring gesture. It was his way of setting the stage. A reminder of what could happen if I jerked him around or wasted his time.

I swiveled on my barstool, to offer the newcomer my hand, "Vallis, glad you could make it."

"I come here every day, kid. Wasn't really that far out the way for me," he drawled.

He took a seat at the bar, a couple seats down from me, and shot Jin a sideways glance before turning to the bartender and ordering two drinks. Both for himself. The man was built like a concrete pylon, and while he didn't quite take up two seats, he came pretty close. I watched as he downed both glasses in short order. He got two more and made a clumsy swirl in the air with one finger that roughly meant to keep them coming. The bartender nodded.

He wiped his mouth with his forearm. "So, what do you want?"

"Vallis, buddy. We've had more than a few drinks together over the years. What merits that kind of response, huh?" I said, trying for jovial, but probably coming off as sarcastic.

He swirled his glass around, "Oh, I dunno. Last time we had a drink together you got pissed about something and tried to stab me."

"Let's not get bogged down in the details," I said, perhaps a little quieter than I'd intended.

He just glowered at me, finished off another glass, and set it down firmly on the bar, "Cut the bullshit, *omo*. What do you want?"

I straightened my posture and cleared my throat, "I need your help. I need a—"

"Like I said, there's no next job," he said, cutting me off.

Well, shit. If he didn't drop me a line, I'd be well and truly fucked. My shoulders slumped a little and I almost sunk into what remained of the drink Jin had bought me. There had to be something; we may not have been on the best of terms—I did try to stab him after all, he didn't make that up—but he had to have some opportunity for me. I just had to think about something to say, then try it.

"Oh c'mon, Val. You've gotta have something?" Jin argued.

"Have you seen his rep?" Vallis shot back.

"I'm right here between the two of you. I can hear everything you're saying," I protested, turning to Vallis. "My rep isn't that bad. I've been trying to improve it, just kept getting shit work is all."

"Oh yeah?" Vallis asked with a smug look on his face. "Go on, why don't you tell us what your rep looks like these days."

Gods, that was embarrassing. Our reputation was tied to almost everything. The higher it was, the better. Eight or nine hundred was pristine, and a rep like that could make you eligible for better housing, transportation, clothing, and even better quality food and water. I'd been in the mid-six hundreds when I'd bombed my last job, but trending up. Now, well, thinking about it was more painful than putting my face to a hot stove.

"It's under two hundred," I finally answered, shrinking a little more into my barstool.

Jin instinctively shifted away from me as if I'd had an infectious disease.

My mouth started running, trying like hell to salvage this, "Not as if you're one to judge, Val. Everyone goes through rough patches. Even you—and you've devolved into a bit of a drunken, brawling death wish."

His mouth closed firmly, his lips forming a line. "You know as well as I do that a reputation as low as yours low means you're a risk. But keep going; feel free to crawl into that hole you're diggin'."

"I'm not criticizing your methods," I said and held up my hands. "I mean, the headlines practically write themselves." I attempted the tone and cadence of a virtual news anchor, "Distraught addict pushes tech executive down flight of stairs, breaks neck. More at twenty-one-hundred."

Vallis grabbed his next glass and scratched at his beard. I watched him, hoping to catch just a small sign that he might change his mind.

I decided to press just a bit further, "Look, the work you do is effective. The messes that tend to follow in your wake have spawned their own economy. I have to imagine a cleaner. Rider. Someone needs a runner for something."

He took a swig and swished it around in his mouth for a moment. Then he swallowed and looked me dead in the eye.

"Not a chance in hell," he growled. "You're a pain in the ass, but I like you, *omo*. And, when you're not trying to stab me, you do good work. But I can't help you."

I ground my teeth. "Can't or won't?"

"Both," he answered. "You know how rep is averaged between everyone on a job. I can't stick my neck out that far for you, and I won't risk losing my clients."

Jin protested, "Jesus Christ, Val. You have to—"

"Drop it. Right now, or else some names get added to my pro bono list," Vallis interrupted.

All conversation from that point died, leaving the three of us drinking at the bar in a frustrated silence. Jin really didn't have to go to bat for me but I appreciated having him in my corner, even if I didn't get any work out of it. He looked really upset. Like he might flip the next table that got in his way. It was clear that Val wasn't going to be of any help, and I still had some liquor left, so I decided to change the subject.

"What's that you got on your shoulders there?" I asked. "Looks fancy."

"You like it?" he asked, deftly shifting out of the awkward silence, back into his usual cheery self.

"I dunno yet, what is it?" I asked.

Jin groaned and rolled his eyes enough to knock the tilt of the earth off by a degree or two, "Ugh, you're such a Philistine. This is the newest model of fauxhides being released by Animold. It's warm, purrs on command—which, let me tell you, is like getting a massage—and it eats next to nothing. Just hook it up to a nutrient drip, and you're done." He leaned close and shifted his tone lower, "It also hasn't been released yet."

My eyebrows shot up in surprise and Jin smiled back. It was an act; I was forcing my interest. Though, on a normal day, it would have been legitimate. But we all do that from time to time to help keep our lives stable, and I needed as much stability as I could get.

I whistled. "Damn, you and your connections. Where'd you snag it?"

"I've told you about Juura and his wives, right?" Jin started, more than excited to share the story.

"One of your net diver clients, right?" I asked before taking another sip.

Jin nodded eagerly, "Yeah, my top client, actually. Well, he and Caeda—his second wife—made a bet that I couldn't finish the two of them off at the same time. Well, I took that bet, and it was their loss, because just a few days before I went and saw that lovely friend of yours, Eshe, and finally got my double dee. I won the bet by fucking the both of them at once, literally back to back." Jin made a pose like he was a storefront mannequin. "This was my prize."

"Weren't you having some heart issues a while back? You sure you can take that?" I asked.

"Oh, I don't want to hear it. You don't get to deflect away from your very real problems. Not this time," Jin shot back. "With rep like yours, I'm not sure I could even help you."

Vallis jumped back into the conversation with a grunt in agreement. "Mine has even dropped a few points just talking to you. Even if I could take you on without getting dropped myself, I've already signed on with Kohut for transport."

I ground my teeth again. I'd been doing that a lot lately. Both for being an apparent black hole for reputation and because of the name that just got dropped. Kohut Abner came from the east side of my area, and the guy had a serious chip on his shoulder that always rubbed me the wrong way. Even though we were both from the Barrel, his was the nicer side of it, and we'd been butting heads for years. I stared down into my nearly empty glass at the thin puddle of diluted liquor that was little more than a pale shade of its former self.

"Kohut's wasting your time," I argued, drinking the last of my free booze. "He's not a runner. He's just a guy who takes packages on the magway in a private car. The one time someone decides to make a move on him, he's toast."

Vallis let out a low chuckle and ordered two more drinks. He shifted his eyes toward me and raised an eyebrow in challenge. He clearly didn't disagree with me and might have been dropping a hint that finding Kohut was my way out of this mess.

So I tried to double down, "Mahdi vouches for me. You know what his word is worth."

Vallis feigned surprise and looked around the room frantically, "Yeah? Shit, let's get him over here right away. Oh right, the guy dropped off the map weeks ago and nobody's heard from him since."

"Oh, wait. Mahdi isn't here right now, is he?" Vallis shot back, slamming his glass down on the bar, eliciting a wince from the bartender.

I bit back a whole lot of things that wouldn't really help me at all, and instead took the rejection without incident. I had half a mind to take Val's hint and track Kohut down, maybe even kill him, just to prove my point. If it wasn't for the magway making me motion sick. Besides, knowing my luck, that lazy bastard would have a botnet in place to rep-bomb anyone who accosted him. Sure, they weren't normally a death sentence, but in my condition any more deductions from my rep might as well be.

I remembered my earlier bid and focused on my terminal again, ignoring Jin and Vallis as they got into an argument about the new dancer on stage. No luck. I put in a few more bids and mindlessly browsed local headlines and trending threads. Ban on tank-grown supersoldiers? Old news. Never going to happen. Next. Wartorn trenches of Europe? That place has been burning for the last fifty years. Also old news. What else? Most of what remained fluctuated between celebrity gossip and speculation surrounding the mysterious offlining of several cities across the Midwest. Those got my attention. I suppose I couldn't help but doomscroll. Probably made me feel better. Denver and Chicago were the most recent to digitally vanish. The common prevailing theory suggested a new computer virus propagating along the major highways that connected each metropolis to the next. It made the most sense, though I couldn't help but feel a little bit of paranoia that it was something more sinister.

That was the least of my concerns. Talking to Vallis was my last best shot, and he'd shut the door in my face. My frustration grew to the point where every stray sound irritated me. Every bass drop made me clench my jaw until my teeth creaked. I couldn't take it anymore.

"I need some air," I said, quickly slamming my terminal lid and stepping away from the bar. "Happy hunting, guys."

Jin tried to stop me, but I pushed past him and made for the front door.

T W O

GENEROSITY, IN THIS ECONOMY?

The Velvet Cadaver was one of many businesses lining the first-floor lobby-slash-arena of my building, Orchard Tower Estates. In spite of all its attempts to the contrary, the building's name didn't fool anybody. Lower-income housing always got names to make people feel as if they were on their way up and out, rather than stuck at the bottom. If one devoted the minimum amount of logic, it was easy to assume that, if there was an Orchard Tower Estates, there must be dozens of worse-off places like Murder Row Shithouse or Overdose Acres. At least I wasn't in one of those shitholes. That's what most people remind themselves.

Me, cynical? Not a day in my life.

If I was being honest, there were actually worse places, but they never pretended to be better than they were. Despite the pretentious name, however, I'd been calling this place my home for several years and had gotten pretty comfortable. I really had no reason to be bitter, other than an inexplicable need to fill my bitching quota.

Besides the Velvet Cadaver, the lobby hosted a few hundred businesses of all kinds. You could find cafes, butchers of questionable repute, gaudy law offices, pawn shops, and plenty of others. It wasn't a major bazaar or anything, but it was convenient, and every shop owner charged a premium for that. At the lobby's center lay a massive fountain that had long since been shut down. Its three dried-up bowls held outstretched by three pairs of scarred hands had been coated in sheet after sheet of warring graffiti tags.

It was like someone had found and defaced an altar to the gods of architecture. They were a reminder that time—aided by people—eventually destroys the beauty of everything. Popup stalls surrounded the fountain and conversation flooded the spaces in between in a wash of Asian dialects, African tongues, English, and the modern incarnation of sign language known as Roko. Here amongst the verbal cacophony and fluttering hand signs, a person could trade secrets, strike a political deal, gamble away a fortune, or settle a score. This place was a melting pot where the people living their lives in the building met the outside world. Sure, it had its share of dangers, like any place, but it was still safer than everything out there.

I slid through the throngs of people and eventually came to a stop near one of the fountain's three bowls, which had been converted into a fighting arena. I never asked, but I think the drain at the bottom came in handy. I stayed and watched the current bout for a few minutes before moving on. The matchboard said that the two fighters had been former lovers and were settling a dispute over who got full custody of their cat. As funny as that may sound, it was probably a more equitable process than renting a judge.

When the victor was thoroughly decided, I kept moving and made my way steadily from there to the building's main entrance. With places like this, there was no real security. It was generally assumed that most people inside would violently annihilate any ill-meaning intruders. It worked for the most part. Just us and the bank of glass doors separating us from the outside world of the Barrel.

Supposedly, the name came from the old expression, 'scraping the bottom of the barrel.' It sits closest to the earth's actual surface on the North American continent and is the lowest official layer of the heavily stratified Corporate States of America. Unofficially, there was one layer below us, generally referred to as the compost layer. Generations and generations of garbage and urban decay slowly dissolving in a pool of its own rot. All our collective sewage has to go somewhere. From here, though, the further you got from the Barrel, the better off you were. Better air quality, better access to food, water, shelter, and so on. The discrepancy was pretty drastic. If you talked to any of the thousands of people down here in the lobby, you would eventually hear it referred to as Hell on Earth. It didn't take much to see the grain of truth behind the hyperbole. There really weren't a lot of available statistics, but there's a common phrase used down here. You can feel free to decide if it fits the bill.

You gotta survive on more than just money. Abduction at thirteen, murder by twenty.

I didn't know about abduction, but I murdered a kid when I was the ripe old age of seven. That must have made me some kind of prodigy. Assuming you made it to adulthood, it was something you were accustomed to. None of it was pretty. None of it was nice. You either joined a gang, became a corporate wage slave, or wound up being loner scum like me. No matter what you picked, you'd never climb any higher, and the odds were never in your favor. You became part of the Barrel, as much a part of these streets as the blood and shit that oozed through the gutters. You either came to grips with it, or you got eaten up.

Sometimes literally.

Leaving the relative safety of the Orchard Tower Estates and taking a few steps outside, my lungs filled with a pungent infusion of iron, gunpowder, and engine exhaust. It was a comforting aroma, and even though my situation hadn't improved, for a brief moment I felt a world away. Temporarily removed from the flaming shit show that was my life.

I love the great outdoors.

I wasn't out there for any particular reason, so there were plenty of places I could go. The bedrock quarries to the north, or maybe the Shiv to the east. As I considered my options, my stomach growled at me. Yeah, that was probably the best place to start. Even if they were just scraps, I needed to find something to eat, so I went west, roughly in the direction of the Armory Bazaar. I started down a nearby alleyway when a familiar voice called out behind me.

I half-turned, and groaned. "Look, I don't have any money, and I'd really prefer not to waste my energy trying to fight you. Just—"

I stopped short when I finally looked at the person behind me. They were average height and build, bald by choice, with a scar running up the left side of their face. I knew them as Rohch. They were a lesser-known independent investigator who occasionally found their byline in the big corporate feeds. At some point a few years ago, they'd somehow tracked me down after a particularly disastrous job to get the lowdown.

I didn't want that particular story published unless I was dead, so the two of us had settled on trading information from time to time instead. They'd keep me in the loop on developing stories that hadn't hit the feeds yet, and I'd let a few client details slip from time to time. Only after the job was done, of course.

"Wow, you look terrible," they said, following close behind me down the alley.

I scoffed. "Thanks. You, too."

As the two of us emerged out of the alley into a container yard, Rohch fell into step next to me. They dressed like some bizarre mix of old-style neon-gothic and a classic news reporter. Slacks, suspenders, trenchcoat, even a bowler. All in black with lacey light strips showing off bits of skin here and there. I consistently felt both envy and annoyance at their wardrobe choices.

"So, I know you've been out of work for a little bit, but I wanted to check in and see if you'd heard anything about all the cities going dark across the country," they explained, getting right down to business.

I didn't turn to acknowledge them. "What makes you think I know anything?"

Rohch shrugged. "I know you've traveled with some people who may be in the know."

"Haven't heard from any of them in a little bit," I said, letting out an annoyed breath. "Even my best friend went dark a few weeks ago; haven't heard from him either."

"Yeah, I know," they said.

At that, I stopped and finally shot them a look.

"What?" They shrugged. "I talked to Mahdi first. He's much nicer and much more open than you are."

I started walking again. "Uh-huh. Look, I don't know anything, and even if I did, I have a few other priorities at the moment. Not unless you have a paying job for me."

"Sorry, no," they admitted. "Did you hear about what happened over at the quarry? How it's gone."

I crouched through a hole in a chain link fence and stepped out onto a main road. "Gone? How?"

"You'd know if you got out of that box of yours more often," Rohch jabbed before scurrying through the fence after me. "The people upstairs just came down and took it all. Now it's just a giant hole for collecting sewage, garbage, and bodies."

I stopped as they caught up and jabbed a finger at them. "I don't know what it is with everyone today, but my home is not a box."

They just grinned at me like an adult listening to a child babble.

I shoved my hands further into my coat pockets and decided to move on. "So the uppers just took shit that didn't belong to them. What else is new?"

"Well nothing," Rohch admitted. "You know me, I'd rather be covering other stories, but the speculation and hot takes drive traffic and pay the bills. As a frequent patient, you should know that Chaurrie's charity ambulance isn't about to be making kay any time soon."

"Yeah, I guess I can't really give you much shit, can I?" I conceded.

"Well, you can," they said, "but that would make you an asshole."

I let out a harsh laugh and shook my head. "Got any odd jobs I could snag?"

Rohch laughed in a similar fashion and stopped to take a call. "Like I said, you're barking up the wrong tree there, friend. I'm not the one running the charity."

As I left them behind, I felt my heart sink a little lower. Not even the conspiracy-peddling blogger had something for me. Fuck me, their rep was probably better than mine, too.

Leaving that little encounter behind, I pressed on until I emerged onto the sidewalks of the main road that bisected this part of the district between north and south. People kept a brisk pace along the sidewalks on either side and over the ped-bridges that crossed any major intersections. Cars and small box trucks moved in a similar fashion through the middle of the avenue, only occasionally yielding to the suggestions of the traffic lights. Horns blared, people shouted, brakes screeched followed by the crunch of glass and metal. The living pulse of any megacity. Even though I lived in a small, nearly forgotten corner of New York, this place was just as alive and vibrant as any other.

The buildings looming over me connected the ground to the next layer of the city, two or three hundred stories up. Sometimes less, sometimes more. A dim glow cast itself down between them, emanating from the simulated sky overhead. It was bright and blue and, where there weren't dead display panels, I could see the occasional streak of cloud cover. Rain was coming. There were always a few panels that would glitch out and shut down right before a downpour.

I should probably hurry up.

Several minutes of walking—and protecting my pockets—later I made it to the clot of humanity that always seems to clog up around the Armory's grand entrance. It was not a place I liked squeezing through, in or out, but none of the entrances were particularly good. Ancient stone archways passed over me as I competed for open space to move forward. The structures were testaments to a long-forgotten time, before it was defaced with strobing tube-lighting and mounted advertising displays. Every time I came here, my eyes were drawn to the shadows cast by these upgrades, to the carved symbols that adorned several of the untouched bricks. They were markers of the people who built this place, and I sometimes wondered what they would think of their creation in its current state.

As we collectively birthed ourselves on the other side of the entrance, the concentration of people around me started to thin. Precarious-looking stairways jutted up from the mezzanine running left, right, and across the massive space, creating a collection of ad-hoc floors. All of it was repurposed construction scaffolding, and it was not uncommon for a part of it to come loose or tumble down on innocent bystanders below. Rather than going up, I headed down the main stairs—the ones that actually came with the building—and made my way around the outside edge of the Armory's interior.

The whole place was an assault on the senses, like old pictures of Las Vegas, but all packed into a space barely the size of a city block.

Lights bathed every square centimeter of the place. It had everything, from advertising displays to holographic projectors, and enough diode-based neon substitutes to actually keep the whole space fairly warm on its own. And that was when it was empty, before it got filled with thousands of warm bodies.

Vendor stalls were set up anywhere they could fit, and each one had something different to offer. I passed through the maze, between the shouts of people hawking their wares, and through miniaturized marketing mascots as they all tried to sell me on the 'best they had to offer.' I was headed to the opposite side of the building, near the Armory's rear entrance, past some of the mainstay shops like Armory Armaments and Moore's Law.

Tracing along the outer edge, I finally came to a stop in front of my favorite restaurant, a little hibachi place called Wok the Line, which was my usual respite from all the chaos out in the world. It was relatively clean and organized, all black paneling and glass edges. Powerful lights dangled over the establishment, casting all of it in a heartless shade of pale white. Given that my accounts were empty, I had no real reason to be there, except for the simple fact that I'd seen the owner, a guy named Tyhek, give away food to people in need.

As I approached, a patron got up from his barstool, leaving behind a few dirty dishes and a half-empty beer. I took the seat immediately. The abandoned beverage was warm and I wasn't sure exactly how much of it was beer. On any other day it would have been disgusting, but today, it tasted like heaven. Calories, sweet calories. I savored it for as long as I could and gawked at the food. Tyhek was preparing an algae wrap with tube-grown protein, mushrooms from the reprocessing plant, bamboo shoots, and teriyaki. My mouth watered. Tyhek caught me in his peripheral ogling over his work and gave me a brief nod.

On a desperate whim, I spoke up: "Hey Ty, what do I gotta do for some leftovers?"

Several of the other patrons chuckled, and he let loose a broad, beaming smile.

"What you got for me, freeloader?" he asked.

That was the phrase I'd heard him use before. The times I'd seen it happen, the other person went on to do something small to earn a meagre meal. We lived in a transactional society, after all. Not even charity was free. God, the smell of the grill smoke from here was so incredible I almost couldn't think. I needed to come up with something.

Tyhek looked at me and I looked at him. He inclined his head as if to say, 'Go on, dance, give us a trick.' My nutrient-starved brain went over what I knew about him. He was a self-made man who owned and operated his restaurant with moderate success. I couldn't see it from here, but he had a nasty scar on the right side of his face from an oil burn he got when he was a kid. Messed up his ear pretty bad, and he'd gotten it replaced at some point. His mother disowned him for it because she's an Untarnished Deacon. An important figure in a local cult.

The patrons at the bar turned to cast their drunken looks at me and a little grin crept up onto my face.

"Well," I said, "I know how much you love the church. I'll take you over to the Chapel of the Divine and Unaugmented Virgin, and we'll get married. How about that?"

He leaned down over the grill and reached underneath to unscrew something from the bottom. Whatever it was, he slipped it onto his ring finger and held it out for the other patrons to marvel at, fanning himself with his metal spatula. They gasped with amazement and played along for a moment before the whole group, Tyhek included, broke out into raucous laughter.

He gathered some of his composure a moment later. "That's a pretty nice offer."

"Yeah, I thought so too. Get me another beer," I said, holding up the empty, abandoned bottle. "And not only that, but we can cuddle up at the foot of the virgin and give each other piercings and tattoos. Give your mother a real reason to kick you out."

His eyebrows shot up in surprise, and the whole establishment was consumed in another uproar. Tyhek walked over in front of my seat and offered me an elbow over the glass divider. I bumped it.

"You're a funny son-of-a-bitch when you wanna be, and I love me some blasphemy every now and then," he said, still chuckling to himself.

"Yeah?" I asked with a tinge of hope in my voice.

He nodded. "Sit tight. I got something for you."

He took small slices off each of the meals he was preparing for the paying customers and moved the collection to a small plastic bowl. He put a half-scoop of rice in and drizzled on some teriyaki. God, watching it come together, such a pitiful meal any other day, was awe-inspiring. He slid it to me under the glass, followed by a small plastic cup of water.

"If you're in dire straits," he said, "water's better."

My eyes delighted at the sight as I thanked him and the others. A couple of them raised their bottles to me, grinning and halfway drunk. I wasted no time, tilting the bowl of food into my mouth and shoving it all in with the help of one hand. Indescribable. My job prospects might be fucked, but at least I got to have a last meal.

I pounded the cup of water next, chewing on ice between gulps. I was nearly done when gunfire ripped through the marketplace, sending everyone running or scattering for cover. I ducked around behind the corner of the bar and scanned the area. I couldn't spot the gunmen from where I was, just a slowly drifting mist of blood and other debris. Dozens of people littered the ground. Many were groaning and clutching at injuries, while others were completely still.

Once everything seemed to quiet down, someone burst out of the Go parlor next door, ran maybe a dozen yards, and then dove behind an overturned table. I caught a glimpse of their face and sucked in a breath. I knew him. Mahdi Bilal had been my best friend ever since, well, forever. We were assigned to the same bunk back at the Eggbasket® memory hacking clinic that made us. We'd followed one another into the same corner of New York as well as the same profession. He was probably the best runner I'd ever known. It had been months since I heard from him. Rumor had it he'd gone off the grid for a black bag run, but details were more than scarce.

Whatever he'd gotten himself into, he could probably use a hand. So, without much thought, I broke from my own cover and followed after him. Bullets chased me as I lunged over the table, and I came face to face with the muzzle of Mahdi's sawed-off shotgun. I let out a choked sound and contorted myself in midair to get out of his line of fire. All it accomplished was me landing in a heap on the ground next to him.

"Woah, easy there," I blurted.

"Gods, you really do jump before you think don't you?" he spat and pulled his finger away from the trigger.

"Hey now, I'm not pulling a bunch of gunmen into a crowded marketplace," I protested. "It's against the rules."

"I'm not really in the mood for a lecture," he said, peeking over the edge of the table.

"Yeah, well I have a captive audience," I shot back.

"Look, can we talk about this at your place?" Mahdi asked, "These guys have been following me since I took this job, and it's only gotten worse since Chicago. I'd really like to get off the street."

I shrugged. "Of course, mi casa es tu casa. Got a plan to get out of here?"

I was looking around the Armory, back toward the main entrance, trying to pick out points of potential cover. It took me a moment for my malnourished brain to process his last few words, and when they did, my attention snapped back to him.

"Wait," I said, "you know what's going on out there? Why all those cities have been going dark?"

Mahdi's lips drew a grim line and he nodded. "Like I said, I'll fill you in later."

He peeked over the edge of the table and reached into his bag to withdraw a pair of nearly perfect spheres that had been decorated in layer after layer of spray paint. He pulled the pins, counted to three, and lobbed each grenade out to either side of us. They began billowing bright, multicolored smoke. Glitter, light, and sound, all mixed with a cocktail of aerosolized party drugs added to the mix. Ravebombs, as they were called, were typically used as their name implied, but they wound up being pretty handy in a fight, too. Anybody walking through the plume unmasked would get so high they'd likely forget who or where they were. Mahdi and I got up immediately, before the pastel cloud could engulf us, and bolted for the main entrance. Gunfire called out behind us, but without a good view of anything past the smoke the shots dwindled to nothing.

With almost everyone taking cover, getting to the Armory's entrance didn't take long at all. Plenty of people on the outside were just arriving and were entirely unaware of what had just happened. Those ravebombs may have given us a head start, but with all the people pouring down the street ahead of us, that lead was quickly wearing thin. Mahdi and I needed to think of something, and fast.

THREE

JUST ANOTHER DAY AT THE OFFICE

Maybe a hundred yards from the Armory's entrance, I heard a few startled screams followed by shouting behind me. I dared a glance over my shoulder to see the crowd parting to give something a wide berth. Mahdi was a little bit ahead of me, slipping into openings between people where he could find them. Once the commotion broke out, though, he didn't even look, just started pushing more forcefully through the throngs of people. Arms and elbows slammed into me over and over again like I was running some kind of gauntlet, but I pushed through to follow. Finally, on the edge of the crowds, where traffic was lightest, I was able to catch up with Mahdi.

"We need to get off the street!" Mahdi shouted.

"Yeah, no shit," I answered.

The two of us looked around, building mental maps in our heads of paths, roads, alleys, and rooftops. This area was part of our own turf. We could probably play cat and mouse among the warehouses and megastructures in the surrounding twenty or so blocks. Hell, the place Mahdi and I grew up in wasn't too far; could disappear there and never be seen again.

I leaned in close to Mahdi so I didn't have to shout. "Okay here's the plan: we split up, take separate routes back to my place. From there, if we haven't lost them, we head back to the Shiv. Duck in with Eshe until we figure out the next plan."

Mahdi nodded and started moving immediately. "Great, I'll meet you at the palisade."

I started to protest, but he was gone and out of earshot. The palisade was a really terrible idea, but there wasn't a ton I could do about it now. I checked back behind me again. The part in the crowd was getting closer. Like a shark passing through a school of much smaller fish.

"I'm gonna kill him," I spat before turning the opposite direction and taking off.

My own path away from the Armory and into the larger city around it was risky, to say the least. It took me back, towards the advancing group of gunmen, and up the front steps of a small legal office. The front doors were barred, but it was done in such a way that it felt more like a decorative statement than a security feature. Pulling the doors open and rushing inside brought me into the reception area that took up the center of the building. A half-circle counter waited in front of me, followed by a small bank of elevators. To either side of the desk were a pair of curved stairs. Each step was constructed from a slab of illuminated glass, which in turn led to a row of glass-lined offices that took up most of the second floor.

People were pacing back and forth between office and meeting spaces, talking in hushed tones about who knows what. Lawyers, clerks, and the occasional harried support tech buzzed around the space like a swarm. Pacing quickly through the lobby, drew the attention of the receptionist and the nearby security guard.

"Sir?" she asked, "How can I help you?"

I waved my hand dismissively. "I have a follow-up appointment, I know where I'm going."

The woman leaned into her professionalism. "I can understand the time-sensitive nature of your appointment, however, I must ask that you sign in so I can call ahead for you."

She had just used corporate speak to tell me to sit the fuck down. On any other day, I could respect it and sign in like she wanted, but today wasn't it. So, I pushed past her and started up the steps before the guard could intercept to stop me. I took the stairs up to the second floor two at a time and, once I was at the top, turned back to see both of them shooting me dirty looks. It seems I wasn't worth much more than that, though, because the guard returned to his post—or was about to when a pair of sharply dressed individuals stalked into the building. I couldn't make out their faces past the dark visors that covered their eyes, but judging how they didn't stow their weapons on the way in, they weren't planning on using a light touch.

I took off at once and my movement drew their attention immediately. Hurried footsteps on glass followed close behind as someone called me in over their personal com unit. Even as I ran down the hall, toward the back of the building, something about the shouting sounded odd, like a collection of mismatched recordings. The hall took an abrupt turn around a pair of large conference rooms before finally arriving at a staff cafe area. Just like the entry foyer, it too was buzzing with activity. People sat chit-chatting on benches or shared meals with their colleagues around large circular tables. Immediately to my right was a bank of vending machines, and across from them, on the opposite wall was a bank of windows. With no emergency exit.

"Shit," I muttered beneath heavy breathing.

I had maybe a couple of seconds before my pursuers caught up with me. Given how eager they were to gun down people in a marketplace, they would have no qualms about putting down a bunch of corporate attorneys who got in the way. With no other options, I paced into the gathering of potential victims. A couple of lines had formed for a pair of automated restaurants, and I pushed through them to the sound of disgruntled employees. That's all the fight they could muster though, and let me pass through them without issue. Reaching the back of the cafe, I made for the nearest window. Along the way, I grabbed an empty chair and lifted it in both hands over one shoulder. I wound up my swing with an awkward step forward and threw the chair through the window.

Everyone was on their feet at once staring at me, the person wrecking their office cafeteria. It was probably cathartic for some of them, but clearly, not everyone, as a few others ran out to go get security. I couldn't help the sideways grin from crawling up my face as I climbed up the windowsill and gauged my jump.

I turned myself around to hang off the outside ledge, when my two pursuers stormed the room, shooting before even looking for me. People fell and scattered just like they had in the Armory. I lowered myself down quickly, then pushed off the wall to launch myself out into the alley behind the office. I tucked my knees into my chest when my feet hit the pavement and I rolled forward. Maintaining that momentum, I pushed myself up and into a dead sprint from the law office. Just in time for the two gunmen to take a few potshots at me from the window. They chewed up some asphalt, but aside from that, completely missed me as I broke line of sight.

Now to catch up with Mahdi.

I cut through a few tight alleyways, vaulting over dumpsters and around the handful of vagrants that occupied them. Finally, with the rendezvous point not far away, I burst through the front door of a mixed-use building. It was cluttered with a mix of small, low-rent apartments and businesses all packed in next to each other with no rhyme or reason. I called out ahead of me for people to move, and most of them were quick enough to get out of the way. My shoulder collided with the side of an open doorway as I narrowly avoided crashing into an elderly woman with a hip-mounted walker. As I spun around her, I rammed an exit door with my hip, slamming the crash bar with such force that the door flew open and chipped the brick facade of the outer wall.

I'd arrived at the top of a wrought iron fire escape. Apparently, it was just another entrance, because small groups of people were ascending the narrow stairs and filtering out to their respective floors. A couple of people gave me oblique glances as they slipped past me through the door I had just burst out of. I didn't have time for this. If I tried to force my way down the stairs and through them, their sheer obstinate stubbornness might kick in. The last thing I wanted was to be tangling with a bunch of pissed-off New Yorkers.

Like I said, no time for that, not with gunmen hot on my heels. Instead, I leapt over the railing and executed another roll. Approaching the local landmark known as the palisade, I caught sight of Mahdi hopping over the roofline of a small, four-story building. He made his way down to the pavement, controlling his descent by grabbing a few window sills as he dropped.

"I was followed," I got out between breaths.

Mahdi nodded, hands on his knees, breathing as hard as I was. "It's been like this all the way across the country."

I grimaced and wanted nothing more than to sit down and catch my breath. But I couldn't—we couldn't. Not yet. The two of us pushed ourselves forward into a jog toward our final obstacle. It was a low-lying brick wall that ran the length of the alley, connecting each of the buildings on the other side. This spot in particular spanned the short gap between my building and the adjacent warehouse. At some point, it had been lovingly 'improved' by some practical jokers to include dozens of sharpened rebar spikes that jutted out of the wall at odd angles. As long as I'd lived there, people have called it the palisade.

"Why the hell did you pick this place?" I asked.

"Oh, c'mon where's your sense of fun?" Mahdi shot back.

"What is this fun you speak of? Sounds expensive," I said.

No sooner had the words left my mouth than bullets whizzed down the street from both directions, tearing up chunks of asphalt and concrete around us. They were just spraying ammunition indiscriminately, using the chaos to stall and corral us. Not about to let that happen, I ran to the wall, made a long leap over the spikes, and grabbed onto an empty space where a brick had fallen out or been removed. Getting my feet under me, I pushed off the wall and lunged up, reaching for a pair of spikes that had been embedded about two-and-a-half meters up. As my hands gripped the cold metal, a sharp pain cut into my side, between my ribs. I cried out through gritted teeth but tightened my grip before moving upward through the remaining spikes and hauling myself atop the wall.

"Here, take this!" Mahdi shouted, tossing me his satchel before making his ascent.

I caught the bag, securing it over my shoulder, and reached down to offer my hand. We grasped each other's wrists as Mahdi pushed off the wall. Between his jumping and my pulling, he had enough momentum to arc up and over the remaining spikes. That was when I heard the oscillating hum of a Gauss cannon and three hollow, muted thuds.

My muscles tensed, and I fell backward off the wall, hoping to pull Mahdi over, using the weight of my body to pull him out of harm's way. The first slug whizzed down the alley, missing by more than a meter. The second came a near instant later and tore through his hips, shattering his pelvis, and spraying the adjacent building with blood and bits of bone.

Mahdi's eyes went wide. The pain of it probably hadn't even registered yet. When his eyes found mine, all I saw was fear and regret. Then the third and final slug came a near-instant later and blew out his abdominal cavity. We hit the ground on the other side with a stomach-churning splatter. I've said it before, if you live down here in the Barrel long enough, you've seen and done a lot of shit. Wearing my best friend's innards was definitely not something I had on my bingo board.

The sensation of it was too much. The hot and slightly sticky texture of blood and viscera. The smell that came with it. The last trembling squeeze of my best friend's hand in mine. My body went into shock as I tried to register all of what was happening and what had already happened. Now Mahdi's empty corpse was half atop me in a heap. My head ached. I hit it pretty good in the fall, and my vision was some combination of hazy and spinning. My stomach heaved, but somehow I managed to hold it at bay. Pushing what remained of his body off of me, I pulled a knife from my jacket and knelt over him. Shuddering and unsteady, I placed the weapon to his throat and pressed it into his neck.

"I'm sorry about this, buddy."

I don't remember if I said it or thought it, but what followed was a blur.

BLACKOUT

I limped to the elevator in a bit of a daze. Spots danced in my periphery, and I had no recollection of how I'd gotten there. There was a growing ache in my side and at the back of my head. My muscles felt sore, especially my left arm, and my whole body had stiffened. Something bounced against my leg, and I looked down to find my fingers holding onto Mahdi's head and a length of his spine by a handful of his hair. I barely registered the sound of his vertebrae grinding against the rough texture of the concrete floor, drawing a slick red line behind me. Startled, I dropped him and he fell to the floor with a wet thud. Slowly returning to my senses, I began looking around the lobby. The silence was deafening as all conversation ceased, and I could feel thousands of eyes turn to watch me.

I quickly picked up Mahdi's severed head, jabbed the elevator's call button with one knuckle, and waited. I stared up at the display for what felt like hours, counting down from floor seventy-three. I turned slightly to glance at all the people staring at me. I gave them an awkward wave with my free hand. Somewhere among all those people, I could hear someone throwing up. Finally, the elevator chimed its arrival, and the doors dragged themselves open. I drifted in and pressed the buttons for forty-two and forty-three.

Suddenly there was a flash of movement, and the lobby erupted as seven or eight men and women in uniforms matching the ones I'd seen at the law office burst through the front doors of the building, guns trained on the people surrounding the fountain. The elevator sounded to close, causing them to turn in unison and unleashed a barrage of bullets in my direction. I dove into the corner closest to the instrument panel and crouched down. The gunfire lasted only a fraction of a second, but before the doors closed, it had chewed sizable holes into the wall behind me. The elevator began to rise a moment later. I didn't get up at first. Just sat there, knees huddled to my chest, gripping Mahdi's head tightly.

When I finally managed a standing position, my stomach heaved, and I threw up on the floor of the car. The beer and teriyaki may have tasted heavenly going down but did not make for a pleasant concoction on their way back up. I wiped my face with the back of my hand, which did little more than just smear more blood on my face, then proceeded to press the button for every floor above forty-three, then all the floors I'd already passed. There were nearly a dozen other elevators and a couple of emergency stairwells running through the lower half of the building, so hitting all those buttons wouldn't likely slow them down. Instead, the hope was that it would obfuscate where I actually stopped.

My body shook uncontrollably as the adrenaline faded from my system, and my mind raced with questions. As grotesque as it was, I was glad to have subconsciously grabbed Mahdi's head. I wasn't sure what sort of tech he was running but I hoped some of it had survived in enough pieces to provide answers about what had just happened and who these people following him were. Regardless, some deeply rooted part of me was resolved to see this through, whatever it was.

Between forty-two and forty-three, I stopped the elevator car and climbed through its maintenance hatch. There wasn't much light here but, fortunately, muscle memory helped me take a couple of quick steps off the rearmost edge. I found the small balcony that I'd welded in place, and I hauled my front door open. The elevator resumed its tedious ascent, and I dragged the door shut behind me. I set Mahdi's satchel down on the floor and immediately went to my workbench.

Like everything else I owned, it was cobbled together from spare parts and served multiple purposes. A few weeks back I would have been using the tabletop to prepare and cook food, but now it was covered in a disorganized clutter of tools and scrap metal. I swept a space clean with my free arm and several tools and small electronics clattered to the floor.

I laid Mahdi's head down, and it was the first time I'd noticed his face since the slugs hit him. His eyes were completely empty, which was unsettling as hell, and his facial muscles were beginning to slacken. I wanted to burst into tears right there on the spot, but I held it in. Most of it anyway. A few tears spilled down my cheeks as I took Mahdi's head in my hands. I ran my thumbs gently down his face, pulling his eyelids shut and holding them closed. I stared up at the corrugated metal ceiling for a moment and blinked the rest of the water from my eyes before finally letting go and taking a step back.

I was not at all prepared to see his eyelids slowly drift open again. It was as if he was insisting on watching what was coming next. I tried to close his eyes a few more times but got the same unsettling result each time.

"Goddamnit, Mahdi, let me close your eyes," I pleaded while slamming my fist on the table.

It was evident that I wasn't going to have my way. One of his mods could have been responsible. Leftover electricity in his system just randomly triggering the muscles in his face. But I really had no idea what I was talking about. Over the years I'd picked up some basic understanding of the human body, but bio-mechanics was a mystery. So, instead of fighting with him anymore, I turned his head around so he wouldn't be staring at me. Then I reached up to the pegboard behind the counter and retrieved a hacksaw that dangled on a hook beside a few other tools.

I took a deep breath, gripped the section of Mahdi's spine protruding from his neck, and applied pressure, pushing the edge of the blade forward across the side of his head, just above his eyeline. The first pass was rough, and what little blood remained trickled out through the cut. Eventually, the saw's teeth bit into bone and carved a shallow channel that held the blade in place. With each pass, my hesitation vanished.

"Sorry about this, buddy," I said, trying to console myself more than him, "If it were me, I hope you'd do the same thing."

Progress was slow at first. The human skull is no joke without enhancements. Reinforced, it would only be more physically demanding and exhausting. Eventually, though, I could feel the resistance give way, and I was able to shear off the rest of his skull relatively quickly. Splatters of coagulated bone dust and blood were everywhere, and attempting to wipe them off my pants only managed to smear it.

I peeled the ragged flaps of skin and clumps of hair away from the opening and took a deep breath before reaching inside. The soft, sticky warmth of his brain made my stomach retch, but I gritted my teeth and held it at bay until I had what I needed.

My fingertips found several ribbon cables and drew them out carefully, trying not to damage anything in the process. I set each piece out on an anti-static mat and once I thought I had everything, I rummaged around on the lower shelf of my workbench until I found a plastic jug of medical alcohol. I shook it and noticed that I only had perhaps a couple of handfuls left.

"Dammit," I spat, kicking one leg of my workbench, "What aren't I running out of?"

I used what was left sparingly and was able to stretch it out a lot further than I'd expected. When I finally took stock of everything, I whistled. As it turned out, Mahdi had been decked to the nines. He had suites in place that enhanced his sight and hearing. GPS constantly fed him location data so he would always just know where places were. All of that fed into an intracranial server cluster that probably included things like personality buffers, web servers, and offline storage. Last but not least was a neurocrypt that would allow him to lock any part of his system behind a memory-based encryption.

It would have taken me years of work with top-tier clients to get my hands on even a portion of what he had here. Sure, Mahdi had always found more consistent work than I did, but this was even out of reach for him. Or so I thought. All the tech I'd just pulled out of his head would hold the answers to that and more, but I didn't have the equipment I'd need to do that here. Someone who installed these sorts of things would have everything I was looking for. Yeah, I knew someone, but I didn't like the thought of it considering she'd grown up with Mahdi and me.

In spite of that, I was going to pack them up anyway, so I wrapped each piece up in anti-static bags. Using an old grease and oil-stained shirt, I cleaned off my hands with the last drops of alcohol. It hung in the air and stung my nose. Kind of like sniffing vinegar, but a thousand times worse.

Once everything—myself included—was as clean as it was going to get, I pulled my own pack from a hook next to my cot. I paced around the small room, running through a list in my head of all the junk I'd accumulated over the years, then paring it down to only things that were life-saving or necessary. An extra pair of clothes, some medical supplies, and a couple of keepsakes I couldn't bear to part with. Just in case.

I stowed Mahdi's gear in my pack's interior pocket, then pulled his satchel from the floor and dumped its contents out on the bed. His wallet, a couple of shrink-wrapped protein strips, some empty wrappers, some actual paper takeout menus, and an oblong chrome capsule a little larger than my fist. I grabbed one of the protein strips and greedily started munching. After that, it was the paper that caught my attention. As far as I could tell, it was real wood fiber. Nobody in their right mind makes anything with wood anymore; not down here, anyway. Everyone used either printed plastic sheets or bamboo paper. Most remaining trees were corporate property of one sort or another, and anything made from them was sold as a luxury item with a luxury price tag.

"Mahdi," I muttered, mouth full of food, "what the hell were you up to?"

I packed all of it, save for the empty wrappers, and picked up the capsule. It was small enough to hold in one hand, polished to a mirror sheen, and cold to the touch. Whatever the device was, it didn't have any discernible markings or openings, giving me no hope of identifying it. The one thing I knew for sure was that this had to be the McGuffin that got Mahdi killed. Whatever it was, the logical assumption was that the people who were after him were going to be after me now. I had no intention of handing it over without getting some answers first, or at least without putting up a hell of a fight.

I slid the capsule into my pack and paced the room, scanning all of the surfaces to make sure I had everything I thought I'd need. I would never be satisfied with what I was bringing with me. There would always be one sentimental trinket or another that needed to come with me, but what I'd gathered would have to be good enough.

I was about to head out, when I caught myself, spun around, and knelt down next to my workbench. I reached over the middle shelf, past half-filled bottles, jars, and bits of scrap metal to a small raised panel in the wall, disguised to look like an electrical junction box. Without needing to look, I found a small handle on the panel's face and gave it a firm tug. The piece of sheet metal came off with a satisfying pop, and I dropped it to reach for the small black box about the size of a cigarette lighter. Pulling it out, I glanced at it and the crooked sticker of a purple squid that wrapped around one side, before stuffing it in my pack with everything else I'd collected.

I set the bag on my workbench, next to what was left of Mahdi, and pushed myself up. From there I reached for my other jacket. The one I wore when I knew to expect a fight. It had, for several months, been my most prized possession. Constructed from interwoven strands of glossy white silk and matte black carbon, it was breathable, flexible, and tough as hell when it came to knife strikes. Not terribly great with bullets, though. But to quote a really smart guy I'd heard in a vid once, I made a lot of special modifications myself. In this case, that meant polymer-ceramic strike patches stitched between the layers of fabric. The interior was lightly padded and bore an electromagnetic harness used to hold tools, inside or out. In this case, those tools took the form of half a dozen knives. I threw it around me, almost rolling it on my shoulder, then sliding into the sleeves with a satisfying shrug. I was no street samurai or master swordsman, but I'd been in dozens of knife fights and knew my way around a blade. If they were going to kill me, whoever they were, I had every intention of taking a few of them with me.

The thought put a small, perhaps crazed smirk on my face. But it disappeared just as quickly when the sound of several faint pops rattled through the neighboring elevator shaft. They were here, and it was time to run. I looked around at my home and took a deep breath. Satisfied that I had everything I thought I'd need, I walked out my door for what might be the last time.

FIVE

WHIPLASH

leaned out over the small ledge in front of my home and peered down into the black abyss of the elevator shaft. Shouting and pleading cries echoed, grim and distorted, through the space. Those sounds were immediately cut short by a burst of gunfire that punctured the elevator doors below, letting threads of light pour in behind them. The contrast of the silence that followed was telling. Nobody was left alive.

This place was starting to feel like a tomb, and for at least a few people, it was. Maybe for me too. I bit at the inside of my lip and forced myself to look away. I started imagining falling to my death, or getting shredded by gunfire from every direction, and a dozen other ways to be extinguished. It made me paranoid as if a breath drawn too quickly or the slightest creak in my joints would alert the whole building.

I was having trouble pushing those thoughts away, but as I crept out onto a pair of narrow support beams, I managed to at least put them in the background. Crouching down, I worked my way across, shifting my weight from one side to the other. In a quick and precarious step forward, my hands found the lip of a diagonally oriented support beam. I pushed forward a little at a time until I reached the horizontal supports for the next level. Carefully, I pulled myself up and over. Once I had, the elevator doors leading out to floor forty-three detected movement and opened. In one quick movement, I hauled myself up and through the doors, and for a moment I just lay there, embracing the cool concrete floor and catching my breath.

By all accounts, the forty-third floor was still part of the Barrel, but every meter from the street brought with it somewhat friendlier, if disingenuous, amenities. Here, the pipes and conduits actually ran through the walls. Just a few levels down, they weren't nearly so conspicuous. Here, the concrete floor had been coated with a thin fuzz, giving it the illusion of cheap carpet. The walls bore a similar treatment and had been molded with faux picture frames at even intervals. The natural wood grain veneer on the frames had since peeled away, and the rolled-on lithographs had been covered dozens of times over with graffiti and other local artwork.

I passed through a couple of concrete-cast lounge areas covered in the same fuzz-like upholstery before reaching the main residential hallway. On an average day, it would have been alive with banter between neighbors and small-time vendors hocking goods from their homes. Today, it was abandoned. The only activity, a ceiling fixture partway down, broadcasting dim light with rhythmic flickering. I made my way through the hall with purposeful, quiet steps, occasionally stopping to listen for unwanted company. In those moments, whispers crept out from behind locked doors. People either quietly conversing with one another or begging for silence. Word travels fast, but bullets travel faster. The residents knew a heavily armed force was in the building, looking for something or someone. As far as anyone here was concerned, it was best to stay out of the way.

My home had worked very well for that purpose. A lot of people didn't even know I was there. When considering those who did, however, I didn't feel confident in not being given up by neighbors looking to keep their lives intact. None of us on the lower levels were strangers to reclamation teams of one sort or another combing the halls in search of some delinquent who failed to pay their bills. After the poor bastard was dragged away to a corporate gulag or a reprocessing facility, we'd emerge from our closet-sized apartments to gossip about the incident. Today, that poor bastard was me.

There were a few assumptions that I could make with confidence. They were militarized. Probably corporate security. People don't lug a Gauss cannon around for the fun of it, and they don't just pick one up from the local gun shop. It's high-end tech that only comes from places with deep pockets and material access. This also meant that they likely had the means and manpower to take and hold this whole building until they found me. Sure, I could take a few of them out with me, but there was no chance of running the gauntlet against hundreds of goons and coming out alive. I would have to be creative about my escape plan. Luckily, this was my home turf, an advantage that, if I played my cards right, could help me evade them until that exit plan presented itself.

I'd gotten about halfway down the main hall when the metal creak of a heavy door cut through the silence. Heavy footsteps of mil-spec combat boots clacked against the fuzz-laden floor as the door shut behind them like someone dropping the lid on a casket. My pace sped up. An intersecting hall leading to the floor's rec area wasn't too far. If I could just make it there, I could slip past them.

I slinked from doorway to doorway, flicking my eyes back and forth to the coming intersection and the end of the hallway. But I wasn't fast enough. A pair of mercs, clad head to toe in black tactical gear, stepped out into view. I immediately sucked in a breath and pressed myself into a doorway. I poked my head out just enough to see them coming. Some frantic part of me wanted to scream and run, but I held it together. A chance for me to slip away presented itself when the pair slowed and approached the first door on their left.

I was about to bolt from my meager hiding place when I saw the first of the pair lunge forward and kick the door open. I heard shouting in another language as the two pushed inside, shotguns raised. Then light and sound bathed the hallway as a pair of shots went off. The two masked goons stepped out a moment later, guns still raised, and moved to the next door. This one was on their right. They shared a couple of words, and one chuckled as they repeated the process.

There's something I learned early about killing. Murdering someone you don't know is easy. Our brains are really good at turning people into animals just to make the act less taxing on the psyche. Even if you're not the one doing the killing, you become indifferent to it. You pass someone bleeding out on the curb and convince yourself that they were somehow less deserving of life.

They stepped back into the hall when they were done and proceeded to the next door. On the way, the hollow rattle of an ejected plastic shell echoed in the hall as it hit the floor. The two nodded at each other once and kicked the door in the same way they had for the others. Slam, scream, bang, thud. Muzzle flashes bathed the walls ahead in a dizzying light, and more raw, pleading screams for mercy were abruptly halted. It was faint, but I could make out the cries of a young child in the room behind me. One of the adults in the room tried to console the child, but they were barely holding it together themselves.

"Please," someone whispered through the door, "I don't know who you are, but you might draw attention to us. Please go. Please."

I wasn't about to reply, but I had every intention of getting the hell out of there. I peeked back down the hall and watched with bated breath. The next door they kicked in, I would make a run for the community area then hopefully out the other side. Odds were good that they'd hear me, but hopefully I'd get enough of a head start that it didn't matter. Might spare everyone else on the floor, too. The intentions of the gunmen were clear. They were clearing the whole building until they found what they wanted. Until then, there would be no hostages, no interrogations, just executions. Even while I had little choice in the events that led me here, my actions had signed these people's lives away and in spite of my best efforts, I felt responsible. There was no way to know just how much blood was already on my hands, but I knew I didn't want any more.

My muscles tensed as they came out of the apartment and made for the next one. They stepped toward the door and one of them wound up for a long forward kick. In the instant he was about to bust the door open, the kid in the room behind me screamed, and it was enough to temporarily distract the two mercenaries. Their tinted black visors turned slowly in my direction and that was it. The game was up.

I had nowhere to hide now they'd spotted me, so I unleashed all that built-up tension and burst from the doorway. In response, the two simply leveled their shotguns at me and fired. Leading the shots, I'd crossed to the right side of the hall, and as they pulled the trigger, I launched myself off the wall and dove to the left. Following the momentum, I rolled and came back to my feet. They worked the grips to load new shells. I pulled a pair of knives from my jacket and lobbed them awkwardly down the hall before grabbing a third. One missed completely, while the other was slapped out of the air. Still, it made them adjust their shots, and when they fired, the shots went wide.

The merc on the right dropped to one knee to sight up his weapon and loaded a new round. By the time he'd done it though, I'd gotten in close. Close enough to see the dull orange glow deep within the barrel of his gun. I hit the deck as the merc on the left fired again, sliding on my knees across the concrete floor, just barely ducking the shot. Momentum carried me forward and I swung my hand out, plunging the knife into the crouching man's neck. Blood spurted from the wound, pushed out by a heart that didn't yet know its time was up. He dropped the gun and instinctively grabbed at his neck. I could feel his panicked eyes staring at me, wide-eyed through his tinted visor. I pushed on the hilt of the blade with all the strength I could muster, driving him to the floor. Holding steady the knife as his body fell, the force tore the blunt edge out of the wound, ripping his trachea apart as it went.

I whirled around and rolled to the left just as the other merc's gun went off. The blade still in hand, I swung back around and drove it into his knee. He stumbled back into the wall and slid to the floor, pumping the foregrip of the shotgun and aiming for me again. I dove at him and wrapped my hands around the gun, trying to pry it free.

My grasp started slipping, and panic washed over me. With one hand on the barrel, straining to keep it away from my face, I reached down for the knife in his knee. I worried it around with a sickening wet click-clack of bone making contact with metal. Even through the visor, I could see his face flush a shade of ghostly white. The shotgun finally slipped from his hands. I fell back, reorienting the weapon, and pulled the trigger. The slug escaped the barrel in a fiery roar and splattered the man's head all over the wall. Tiny bits of flesh and brain and bone speckled the crimson spray like a fucked up stucco pattern. I held the gun on him, trembling, breathing in ragged busts for a few moments before finally tossing it to the side.

I pushed myself backward, away from the body, and sat there. My pulse was pounding in my ears and no matter how hard I tried, I couldn't get enough air in my lungs. I closed my eyes for a second and focused on getting my breathing under control. I didn't have a lot of time to waste, but a few seconds probably wouldn't kill me. Probably. I tossed the gun aside and wiped the blood and sweat from my face. I wiped it off on the floor. My mouth tasted of iron and gunsmoke, it was a bitter, disdainful kind of taste. The air reeked of it too, and I wrinkled my nose at the combination. It was something both noxious and intoxicating, like the smell of gasoline. Full of potential for great destruction and production alike, just like life.

"Some profound bullshit right there, idiot," I said to nobody, pushing myself to my feet, "You should write a blog or something."

I leaned over with a groan to retrieve my knife from the faceless merc and stumbled off down the hall. I glanced in the last room they'd breached, and was rewarded by a scene I wished I could forget. The two bodies there were of a father slumped over a child. The kid's dead-eyed stare burrowed through the hole in their father's back, right at me. I grimaced and closed my eyes, then took a deep breath and continued on.

I didn't check the other rooms.

These guys weren't exactly being quiet, which worked out in my favor. On the other hand, their vitals were likely monitored remotely. A couple of their own had just flatlined within moments of each other, so there was a good chance they knew where I was. Stealth was no longer necessary on my part. After passing a few empty offices and some more apartments, I found my way to one of the building's central stairwells. Up to a certain level, anyway.

What lay beyond was a winding cathedral of ambient sounds that created a sort of music. Generators and drainage pumps in the basement offered up baritone voices like big timpani drums. A moment later, a squeaky door cut through the sound some floors below, allowing the staccato of tactical boots to follow in its wake. That was my cue to get going, and the only way to go was up.

I'd gathered a nice collection of scrapes and bruises so far, and I wouldn't have been surprised if I'd gotten a concussion when I fell off the palisade with Mahdi. That last fight was exhausting, and I could feel myself slowing down with every step. Each flight got more taxing and my lungs were burning. After ascending several floors, I became aware of several other aches and pains that were just now breaking through the adrenaline shell. My knees in particular lit up in a throbbing rhythm every time I moved my weight from one to the other.

After rallying to climb a few more flights, I finally reached a point where I needed to stop to catch my breath. That same pungent Barrel-bottom odor hung in the air but it seemed almost stale. I needed it just the same.

I leaned forward on the railing in the center of the stairwell. Like everything else in this building, it had been painted and repainted dozens of times over. There were places where the layers had been worn or chipped away to show the colors beneath. Neutral grey, blue, green, and so on. The oldest color I could see was an ugly pastel yellow, and I couldn't help but wonder what the building was like back then. They were still ascending behind me, but all I needed was another moment's rest, so I laid my head against the railing and closed my eyes.

"How many floors has it been?" I asked myself. "I can't remember. Seven, eight... or was it ten or eleven?"

My reprieve was interrupted when the railing vibrated against my head. One, two, three, four times. As if someone was knocking their knuckle against it. I opened my eyes and looked down into the empty space of the stairwell and caught the view of one of the mercenaries, probably three floors below, staring up at me.

He had a circumcranial mod—circs, as we called them. I could see it plain as day. A sizable chunk of his head and sensory organs—eyes, nose, and ears—had been replaced with a facade of polymer and metal that was packed to the brim with electronics. Like anything else, their features varied between manufacturers, but at minimum, he'd be able to see 360 degrees around him with any number of ocular enhancements. If there was a need for it, he could pick out a heartbeat through several meters of concrete or break down odors into their base parts in a matter of seconds. It was like having a superhuman bloodhound chasing me down. Any distance I put between us would only delay the inevitable.

He continued tapping on the railing, his blank expression turning into a toothy grin when our glances met. Not having facial features to recognize above the soft palate made it one of the most menacing things I'd ever seen. That really old, lizard part of my brain screamed that what I was looking at was wrong and shouldn't exist. Heeding those thoughts, I backed away from the railing slowly, as if trying not to be seen—and while it didn't mean anything, once I was out of sight, I bolted.

He laughed, and it echoed eerily through the stairwell, "Go ahead and run. I can smell you, you know. There's no place you can go where I won't track you down. I will get her back."

Ignoring the fact that I had no idea what the hell he was talking about, his words almost had a sing-song quality to them. It sounded like he was really enjoying himself.

"Great," I muttered. "Glad one of us is having a good time."

As I mounted step after step, the weight of the inevitable started to weigh on me. Exhaustion and eventual capture or death crashed through my walls of resolve. Had I actually been arrogant enough to think that I could escape these people by running? It didn't fare well for Mahdi, and he knew where he was going. I had no fucking clue and was just running for my life. If I wanted to survive this long enough to figure out what my next steps should be, I would need to do something drastic. I needed help.

An idea started to take shape with each step I climbed. I had to go higher than I'd ever been, but I would need some help to get there. I checked the placard beside the next door I passed. Fifty-eight. Only three more. I just had to make it there and hope Jin hadn't left to see his client yet. And that there would be enough time to get what I needed.

SIX

GOOD TASTE

burst through the door to the sixty-first floor in a hurry. With that circ on my heels, I might as well be standing still and shouting for him to come and get me, but I still had to try. I might have had less than a minute, so I needed to think fast. I looked around for anything to wedge up against the door. A chair, a board, anything, but there was nothing. No garbage, no broken down machines. Damn the higher floors and upgrading their concept of livable.

My chest was heaving from my time on the stairs. My heart was pounding so hard it made my ears throb. I took a few steps back and leaned against the door, both for support and as a feeble attempt to hold it shut. It wouldn't matter. Even if I did manage to hold the door, they'd just shoot me through it. My eyes focused on a yellow and black box set into the wall. The panic button slash fire suppression slash emergency beacon. Assuming the floor's contract had been paid up, it would call one of the local security or emergency service providers. I wondered how many people had pulled it since the bullets started flying.

I ruminated on those thoughts for several moments and wanted to slap myself for being such an idiot. My lungs and throat burned as I pushed off the door and made a sprint to the lever. The box flipped up to reveal a second lever to pull in the opposite direction. The lights dimmed and several sounds echoed through the walls. I looked around, listening to armored plating roll into place over external windows and doors, including the one to the stairs. Just in time for the circ and his minions to arrive. Even though he didn't have most of his face, I could almost imagine him with a half-crazed scowl. Even though he seemed to be enjoying it, chasing one crafty runner across the country, only to have another replace him had to be a hell of a thing.

"Yanna," an irritated voice hollered down the hall, "That's the third time this month. What was it this time?"

"Jin?" I hollered back, and I could hear something shuffling around coming from one of the doors further inside the building.

The man from the strip club earlier whipped his head around the door, looking like an entirely different person. His hair was done up in a ponytail, and he had makeup on that accentuated the curves of his face rather than the lines. I started toward him immediately.

"God, am I glad you're home," I said, wiping the sweat off my face. "I need your help."

"Name it. What the hell is going on?" Jin replied without hesitation.

"If I knew, I'd tell you," I said as I approached his door and leaned against the frame.

He ushered me inside and checked the hall again before shutting the door. I took the first seat I could find and collapsed into it. I don't know how long I was there, but the next thing I knew Jin was standing over me, offering a bottle of water. I took it gratefully.

His place was pretty ritzy. He had separate rooms, a full kitchen, his own laundry, and a decorating sense that landed somewhere between pastel goth and old-school Americana. Muted colors of fabric flowed across the walls and sprawled along the floors, dotted with old street signs of indeterminate age and origin. Culver, Jefferson, and Austerlitz to name a few. The worn white paint left off a dim glow as they were oddly illuminated by tubes of blacklight scattered about the ceiling. As I took it all in, the scent of smoky lavender and jasmine filled my lungs. There was a sudden calm that came over me, and I would not have been at all surprised if it was the result of getting a small dose of something in the smoke.

"Corpsec," I said finally, "That's all I know. I don't know who with; never seen them before."

"Out-of-towners probably," Jin answered calmly. "Juura's been seeing more and more about that on the mesh ever since cities started going dark."

I looked up at Jin. "He know anything about that?"

Jin shrugged. "Nothing that makes any sense. All the local nets are offline too, so Juura's only slightly less blind than the rest of us. Best guess is a new corporate war that's slowly dragging everybody in."

I rolled my eyes and leaned back, taking another long sip of water. Not that it had any bearing on my current situation, but another corporate war was not going to be a good time. Some decades ago, it was Detroit. Then after that, most recently, a corporate war wound up glassing central Houston and throwing the bulk of the city into violent and bloody chaos. It was just after I was made, but I've read enough to know a new war was bad news.

"So what brings you knocking down my door?" Jin asked. "Gonna finally join me in the sin trade? Lemme guess: you say you're a switch, but you're really a bottom."

I opened my eyes and looked at him without moving. My eyes welled up a little as I felt shame and disgust pushed their way to the surface.

"They killed Mahdi," I said in a hoarse whisper.

At once he'd walked around behind me and wrapped his arms around my shoulders. "I'm so sorry. I knew he meant a lot to you."

I reigned in that trembling lower lip and held onto his arms. "Thank you." Then I shook my head and pushed myself up—out of Jin's embrace. "Can't think about it yet. I gotta get out of here first."

Jin nodded. "Right. What do you need?"

God, all I wanted to do was sit back down in that chair and pass out, but I forced myself to take a few steps away.

"I'm going to run out of room to run pretty soon, and was hoping one of your contacts might be able to get me a key to the upper floors," I explained

Jin sucked in a breath and stroked his chin with one hand for a moment. "That might be tough."

"Oh c'mon, I'll pay you back," I snapped.

"It's not about the money," he answered, raising his voice. "If you read any of the building's patch notes I forwarded, you'd know that they changed all security doors above the seventy-fifth floor to a rotating key system."

"Okay, so I'll have what? Maybe fifteen minutes to use it," I said. "That's doable."

Jin stood there and stared at me like I was an idiot. "Twelve seconds. That's it."

That stopped me in my tracks. Twelve seconds was barely enough time to round two flights in one of the stairwells. That was going to be useless. Unless there was an area I could use it and gain a lot of ground all at once.

"What about the private elevators?" I asked.

"Hmmm... Let's make a call," Jin said, giving me a sly smile and heading to his terminal in the far corner of the room.

I followed him over as he clattered in a few commands on his keyboard. A video window opened and showed the animation of a ringing phone. In the corner was a small picture showing what Jin's camera was picking up. He looked good, even in the dim lighting, whereas I looked like something partway between a stalker and a vagrant looming behind him, waiting to strike. I looked around over my shoulders nervously as the call kept ringing.

"Don't look so nervous," Jin hissed.

"Easy for you to say," I muttered. "You don't have a circ breathing down your neck."

Jin shot me an annoyed glare, and I realized then that I had forgotten to mention that particularly vital detail. He was about to say something when the guy on the other end picked up. If there was a counterculture to the counterculture, this guy was it. The cognitive dissonance cast off by his C-level suit and the pelt of ink written into his skin with scrawling expletives was enough to make most people dizzy. Behind him were racks upon racks of networking switches, with wires cleanly running in from off-screen to nearly every port. It was like porn for tech heads. The whole space seemed well-lit too, though it couldn't completely avoid the oppressive glow of what must have been a wall of terminal screens.

"Jiiin," he said, jovially, "always good to hear from you."

His eyes didn't so much as twitch. Even though they were looking at us, he wasn't using them. It creeped me the hell out.

His face scrunched up. "I see your floor's on lockdown; everything alright? I keep telling you that you're far too top-shelf for a dump like that. Maybe we can get you moved in tomorrow. Caeda still can't stop talking about both of those co—"

"Sorry, Juura," Jin said politely, "you know me, I love this sort of banter, but I'm afraid that I'm short on time—" he shot me a quick look "—nd some new details have come up that may make this call dangerous, the longer we're on it."

Juura leaned forward, a subconscious move of apprehension rather than anything he did specifically. A pair of biomechanical cables that all divers seem to have slithered up over his shoulder and stretched out to something just beneath his camera.

"What is it?" he asked, dropping the joyful tones and adopting something between businesslike and robotic.

"My friend here," Jin said, tilting his head in my direction, "is in a bit of a jam. He's going to get himself out of his own trouble, but he could use a few keys to the upper floors."

"What business does your friend have himself wrapped up in?" Jurra asked, "The mesh in the building there and everything leading back to the armory is the noisiest I've seen since last year."

I remembered that. A widespread day-one exploit led to a piece of malware turning off everyone's sense of sight for a dozen or so kilometers. It only lasted about five minutes, but caught me at a really bad time. Shattered my humerus and I had to get it replaced with a solid piece of titanium. Turned out it was caused by some insurance company that was trying to bankrupt one of their rivals and move in on their territory.

Coming back to reality, Jin was staring at me intently, flicking his eyes back at the screen, inviting me to explain myself.

"Oh, uh, sorry," I stammered. "Corpsec. And a circ. They want some cargo a colleague of mine was transporting, and now they're after me. Like Jin said, I'll handle my own shit, but I don't have the kay to buy myself entry to the higher floors."

"Why not just give them the cargo?" Juura asked.

"Professional ethics," I shot back.

Juura's face cracked a smile. "Honor amongst thieves, I like that. Jin, I take it you're paying."

Jin nodded. "Since a circ's involved, you may as well set up an exit for me too. I can get out on my own, but I think the time has come to take you up on your offer. At least until whatever this is cools off."

Juura's smile started to resemble pictures I'd seen of sharks. While Jin wasn't looking at me, I could see something resigned in his expression. Whoever this guy was in reality, he had amassed a lot of power and wealth, the kind that has a gravitational pull. It's safe enough to play on the edge of that power if you know what you're doing, but willingly going into the middle of it likely meant never getting out. I ground my teeth. Jin didn't have to do this for me.

"Of course," said Juura. "I'd love to have you." He shrugged. "Who knows, you may find yourself liking it here. If you stayed for good, I might consider all your debts repaid. On top of the little deal we have going here."

Jin swallowed, "Agree—"

"Wait," I interrupted, "how much would this cost if you and I bargained for it?"

Jin shot me a look and shook his head.

"Well, given the nature of the new security in that building," the diver drawled, seeming to enjoy my interruption, "I could get you a single-use key for three-hundred-thousand kay."

"That's insane," I countered. "I could go out and get a few keys for a fraction of that."

"So go ahead and do it," he said, self-assured. "I'm certainly not one to stand in the way of the invisible hand. If you want to drop the lockdown and go shop around for the best price, I'll wait here."

"I don't have any kay," I said. I was going to continue but then he cut me off.

"Well, then there's nothing more to discuss," he answered, almost sounding bored.

I reached into my pack and pulled out the stick I'd been hiding back in my place. I held it up directly in front of Jin's camera to make sure he was able to get a good look at it.

"How about this?" I asked.

Juura just stared in silence for a moment before letting out a laugh. "Well, well, well, this one is full of surprises isn't he, Jin? I can see why you don't shut up about him."

For the first time since the call started, he physically moved to look at me. "Alright, if that's what you're offering, I'm game. On one condition."

"What?" I snapped.

"Send me your contact info," he said. "I'll give you some time to get out of the mess you're in, but once you're clear, I want to hear the story about how you got that."

"I have a condition of my own," I shot back. "Jin gets to stay with you as long as he needs, but you're going to let him go."

Juura chucked, "You drive a hard bargain, but fair enough. We have a deal."

"Agreed," I replied. "Jin will have it with him when you meet up."

"Gentlemen, it's been a pleasure doing business with you today," the hacker said, trying to sound magnanimous. "Jin, I look forward to having you."

Then he hung up.

Jin let out a long breath before turning to me in his chair. He looked like a lot of things. Hurt, relieved, grateful, and others I didn't have names for.

"You didn't have to do that," he said quietly, "but thank you."

I offered my hand to help him up. "That guy was about to own you. And you were about to let it happen."

Jin shrugged. "It wouldn't be the first time someone had a collar on me. I'd get out eventually, and there are far worse deals than being a well-treated plaything."

I handed him the stick I'd just traded away. "People lost their lives for this, might as well use it to help someone keep theirs. Maybe a couple of someone's if your guy comes through."

"Thank you," he said quietly, pushing himself up out of his chair to give me a hug.

Before that moment went on for too long, Jin pushed himself away and once again donned his cocky, sex-machine persona. "Now, you might be all ready to go, but I need to get myself together. The pay-up timer on the lockdown is going to drop any moment. When it does, we make a run for it."

"How can I help?" I asked.

Jin answered, "Why don't you pour us one last drink. Dealer's choice."

He turned back to his terminal again, leaning over the desk, and sent out a few quick messages. From what I could catch, most of them were to his neighbors on the floor, telling them to stay down and let the timer run out. Knowing Jin, they liked him well enough to listen. He fiddled with something I didn't recognize for a split second, then sent another message to Vallis, and a final one to his client list, taking a leave of absence. Then he typed in a few short commands and walked away as the terminal destroyed itself. I watched for a moment as the computer started seeping out threads of smoke. When it did, I stepped away, towards Jin's kitchen and the glass cabinet that housed his collection of spirits. I considered what I knew about him as I browsed, thinking of what would make for a good last drink in his place.

"Something local," I muttered, scanning faded label after faded label.

I found what I wanted on the middle shelf behind several other, more expensive options. It was a simple whiskey bottle, with a simple button embossed onto the glass. I checked that Jin's door was still shut before committing the unforgivable sin of taking a quick swig from the bottle. He would kill me if he knew. The liquor was rich, perfectly smooth, and mellow with a hint of smoke. I took a deep breath, poured us a pair of drinks, and waited. I looked around at the apartment. First

Mahdi, then my home, all those people, and now Jin. God, I felt like such a piece of shit.

"You just keep dragging people into your mess, don't you?" I asked myself as I continued to wait for someone else's home to be destroyed because of me.

_ _ _ _ _ THE RICH

An alarm sounded outside, and Jin came running out of his bedroom with a bag slung over his shoulder. The sound of armored metal plating sliding back up into their stored positions echoed through the apartment one after the other like the ominous toll of a clock. I started moving for the door, but Jin went straight for the glasses I'd poured. He grabbed them both and handed one to me. Then we clinked them and drank. We downed the liquor pretty quickly, which was probably a sin somewhere. Once done, Jin grabbed the glasses and set them gently on his couch.

"Really?" I asked, incredulous. "The gates are literally opening and you're being gentle with your glassware?"

"Just because we're in a hurry and there are people with guns doesn't mean we need to start destroying my stuff," he said, pushing past me and out the door.

Jin drew a small handgun from a holster tucked under his arm and checked the hall. He let out a breath and relaxed his aim. I had to admit, I'd only ever seen Jin as a dancer or sex worker; this side of him was surprising, to say the least. His usually flamboyant, cocky, and flirty attitude had been quietly tucked away in favor of something that was so calm and collected that it almost scared me. It made me wonder how well I really knew him. As the plating behind the door down the hall started to retract, I decided it was a bit late to be having second thoughts now.

I took a few steps back. "Uhh, Jin, I think it's time to go."

"Way ahead of you," he hollered back, already exiting his hallway into a large common area at the center of the floor.

I bolted after him, just as the door slid open and a few rounds were fired wildly in my direction. I lucked out as the shots went wide. It was not an opportunity I was going to waste, so I dove into the common area, clearing the hall moments before another hail of gunfire was unleashed.

The space was a mix of vending cafe and recreation area, situated around a long-empty swimming pool. Like just about everything else, it had been coated in layers and layers of graffiti. Judging by the upturned coffee cups, half-eaten printed starch bars, and still-burning cigarettes, people here got up and left in a hurry. In their rush out of the area, someone spilled a pitcher of hot tea on the floor, which added an odd herbal aroma to the existing smells of concrete dust and lung cancer.

The shouting from behind us drove me to pick up the pace. While a few of the chairs and tables had been spread out around the pool, there were dozens of each piled up in the corner of the room, right in front of the emergency exit. Traversing it was going to be like running through a minefield. Up ahead of me, Jin seemed almost unimpeded as he broke free of the furniture and scanned his hand in front of the security panel to open the door to the emergency stairs beyond. I didn't dare slow down, but as I got closer the sounds of my pursuers made clearing each obstacle feel like an eternity. I'd finally hurdled over the last bunch of chairs and made it to the door, when Jin took a decisive step forward, drew his gun, and pointed it at me.

"Down," he shouted, settling into a trained shooting stance.

I did, launching myself forward in a sprawl. One shot rang out. It wasn't from Jin. Then another. I started crawling. When Jin finally did fire it came out in a quick pair of sharp cracks. Two shots, then a break, then two more, and on it went. Occasionally the enemy on the other side would pepper the doorway with shots of their own, but they were little more than potshots. Once I was past him, he started taking measured steps back through the door.

I hauled myself up using the nearby railing and whipped around when Jin let out a sharp cry. He recoiled and ducked around the corner just as another burst rang out from the other side of the rec area. He grabbed at his shoulder, snarled, and moved to return fire. The gun clicked empty. He took cover again and I moved quickly to the other side and slammed the door shut. I had no idea how much protection that would offer, but it was better than nothing.

"You alright?" I asked, taking a few steps closer to lift his hand and inspect the damage.

"Yeah, it's not bad. Just a scratch," Jin said, wincing as I moved the shredded fabric of his jacket.

The bullet just grazed him—like he said, not bad at all—but it was bleeding enough to be alarming. Jin covered the wound again, keeping the pressure on, and took a few steps toward the railing. He peered over the edge, down the winding helix of stairs then sucked in a breath.

"More on their way up. Who the hell are these guys?" he muttered, sounding almost impressed.

"If I knew, I'd tell you," I answered. "Let's get going."

Jin shook his head, and let go of his arm long enough to reload his gun. "Can't. This is where we part ways."

"There's no way," I protested. "There's nowhere to go but up."

"Maybe for you," Jin responded. "Juura's not going to get you that key until I'm out of the building. Quickest way there is down and out."

I ground my teeth and watched as he pulled a hand-held rope extruder out of his bag and clipped it to the railing. Down and out. That's not an ominous way to say it at all.

"What if you don't get out?" I asked.

"Ouch," he pouted, "You really think that little of me?"

"No... I—"

"Relax, I was kidding," he interrupted, leaning over the railing. "Get moving, I'll let you know when I'm out."

Then, without another word, he jumped over the edge, the printed nylon rope trailing out behind him.

"Contact," someone shouted from a few floors below. "Coming fast."

"Ignore them," another voice answered the first. "They're not the one we're after. Pick up the pace."

At those words I started taking two steps at a time, pushing every last bit of energy I had into moving as quickly as I could. There might only be a dozen or so floors above me before I ran out of runway. It wasn't much, but if I could get to the top and catch a breather while I waited for Jin to get out and Juura to hold up his end of the deal, that would be fantastic.

Lap after lap around the square stairwell—not that it's relevant, but I'm going to call them square-wells from now on—eventually brought me to a locked service door. The thing felt heavy just by looking at it. I checked my mail. Nothing yet. Peering in through the reinforced glass window, I could see a luxuriously carpeted hallway. Halfway down, between a pair of intersections, was a bank of private elevators. It was hard to tell how many there were from here, but one of them was going to be my ticket out.

I took a careful look into the center of the square-well to gauge how much time I had. They must have been staying close to the wall because I couldn't spot anybody. Occasionally though, a shadow would flicker out onto the steps just long enough to catch my eye. Best guess, they were about five floors below. I whipped around again and gave the door another solid tug for good measure. Of course, nothing happened. No mail either.

"Fuck me," I hissed and kicked the door.

I nervously paced the landing and peeked over the railing again. They were three floors away now. I thought about the drop from there, and whether or not I'd be able to make it down without killing myself. Maybe if I hopped from one railing to the other. That was an idea I quickly dismissed. One wrong step and I'd land back or stomach first before tumbling down to my death. I'd also make for easy shooting. I couldn't fight my way out either. I had no room to maneuver. I'd get two or three if I was lucky. After that, I'd be dead.

"Well," I said, pulling my last knife from my jacket, "not like I have much choice. Might as well go down swinging."

I backed up to the door and got ready to charge the first person who showed themselves. My whole body hurt. All the running, that fight, and all those fucking stairs. It was hard to believe I'd done all that in the last few hours—and, thus far, survived.

"Had a good run," I muttered.

Not a second after saying that did my ears start ringing. I was so primed for a fight that the sound nearly made me jump out of my skin. I almost didn't pick up the call.

"Alright, you ready?" asked Juura.

I leaned against the door and let out a long sigh of relief. "Yeah, what do you got?"

"Don't do it yet," the diver explained, "but when you scan your arm on the security plate, you're going to have a legitimate security pass for twelve seconds. You have full access until that timer runs out. After that, nothing, got it?"

"Uh huh," I said, eying the little grey plastic panel beside the door. "Thanks."

"Pleasure doing business with you," he said.

Then he hung up.

I swiped my wrist across it and I heard the door click.

Twelve. I pulled the door open with way more force than was necessary, went through, and pulled it shut behind me. Out of the corner of my eye, I saw the mercs come up the stairs. I'd just cut it extremely close.

Eleven. I took off. My feet made soft, barely audible thuds on the rich, red carpet that stretched out from wall to wall. Metal sconces cast cones of light against the walls which were made of something other than concrete.

Ten. I'd come through a maintenance entrance and into the main hall, which was more like a reception area. It was well-lit and smelled like carpet shampoo and metal polish. Really says something about people when their entryways to the world below were almost exclusively for the help.

Nine. The air was chilled and dry; perfectly maintained for optimal comfort. There was something else, too. A slight hint of something that I couldn't quite place. Whatever it was, it wasn't bad at all, in fact, it was a little refreshing.

Eight. I got to the center of the reception area. A computerized receptionist appeared on the vispad in one corner of the room, beamed down from a projector above. It asked if it could help me with directions.

Seven. I vaulted over a pair of c-shaped sectional couches and kept going, straight to the elevator bank. The receptionist warned me about running through the halls, and said something about how it was very unbecoming for a lady of my station. I couldn't help but smile at that. Who the hell did it think I was?

Six. Everything in me wanted to quit. My knees hurt. My lungs hurt. My—well my everything hurt. But I was almost there, so I pushed everything I had into the last few meters.

Five. I slapped my wrist on the closest call button. There were eight elevators, and all their buttons lit in unison, pulsing a gentle shade of green.

Four. A display indicated which ones were moving and in which direction. I could never figure out the logic of these things. One would be one floor above, but it would only travel up. The next would only travel between a few floors. The rest were all like that.

Three. I tapped my foot on the carpet impatiently as one car started to come down to me, but then stopped before going back up.

Two. One. The car behind me chimed and the doors slid open. I spun around in an instant and practically dove in. I slapped my hand against the command panel as I tumbled up against the back wall of the car. At first, nothing happened. I just lay there on the floor, holding my breath, waiting for the doors to shut. A small terminal display lit up above where my hand was.

Invalid security token. You have been terminated.

I just stared at the words, slack-jawed, and pushed myself up to slide my wrist against the panel again. And again, and again. I don't know if it was in my head or not, but each time I tried, it seemed as if the text on the screen got brighter and brighter. Like it was shouting at me.

Invalid security token. Initiating lockdown.

"Fuck!" I shouted, slamming an open palm against the control panel. The text turned red and the doors started to shut. I moved quickly, barely slipping through the doors as they shut behind me, cutting me off from my one way out of there. I hit the nearest wall again several times, screaming in wordless frustration. Finally returning back to a semi-conscious state, I peered around, looking at the furniture, the light fixtures, and the doors. If I could get into one of the apartments on this level, I might be able to find a hatch to a utility conduit or something. They'd run the length of the building, if I could find one, I could try climbing up.

At this point I was just about out of options, so beggars couldn't be choosers. I paced back out into the reception area and peered down each of the main hallways. The receptionist hologram welcomed me back. I picked the first pair of doors I spotted and paced in their direction. Pressing close to the door, I listened for a moment on the other side. I knocked and nobody answered. The door sounded almost hollow like it was more for show than security.

I decided that the apartment on the other side was either empty or had its tenants locked away in a panic room. Either was fine with me, so I took a few steps away from the door, then lunged forward, planting my heel beside the deadbolt. The door held at first, but after a few more kicks, the hinges started to tear themselves out of the imitation wood. With my next strike, they had loosened enough that I had leeway to work the deadbolt out and push the door open.

Calling what lay behind the door an apartment was an understatement. It was more like a palace. I had burst into a cavernous foyer that sported vidwalls and a checkered stone floor. It also had a legitimate burbling fountain at its center. I could go two directions from there. To my left looked to be a kitchen that preceded several guest rooms.

To my right—I licked my lips and stared wide-eyed at the room to the right. Its sole purpose was to entertain. As I drifted slowly in that direction, I started to make out the extent of it all. The room had a tall open ceiling that sported several moving chandeliers. More vidwalls lined the cavernous space, stopping only to fit in a well-kept bar. Dozens of top-shelf spirits were on display behind the counter. A small seating area sat in front of the bar, and in front of that were several rows of gambling machines. High-quality reproductions of the machines in old casinos—clean and self-healing illusions of nostalgia.

Scanning to my left, toward the windows, my eyes settled on the pool table. Its colors were dark and rich, wholly lacking the otherworldly glow of the rest of the room. Vibrant green felt flowed over the upper surface like a meadow, which was hugged on all sides by beautifully simple oak wood, polished to a mirror sheen. The lacquer proudly announced the ridges of the wood grain in the light. The peaks, valleys, and knots alike were glowing like a radiant miniature landscape. It was a relic. Had I known about it sooner, I would have put a team together to steal it. What a shame.

I drifted through the room, eventually tearing my eyes away from the pool table and turning them toward the windows. They lined the exterior of the apartment from floor to ceiling and looked almost invisible to the naked eye. From there, I was catching a glimpse of a completely different world. The view was quite something. Blues and greens were the most predominant, but every now and again, a glint of amber light would catch my eye. I pressed up toward the glass and strained to look as high as I could. There was no chance of seeing the sun from down here, but I might be able to catch a glimpse of one of our several false suns. Fusion-induced balls of fire that rode a track around New York, bathing all the lesser parts of the city with faux sunlight.

Down in the barrel, all I'd ever known was that orange glow. Aside from the occasional jealous glance, I never even looked this far up. I hadn't given the world above my head much thought beyond simple academics. I didn't dare. I liked to think that we were all born wishing we were something else. I know I did. All the time. I'd seen that destroy people, good people, the type who made life a little brighter. They knew in their soul—just like me—that they should have been someone else, somewhere else. But it so often turned poisonous. Sure, some of them made it, one way or another. So many of them, though, killed themselves while those that remained sold their minds to thinktanks. There, they could slave a portion of themselves off to a biological supercomputer in exchange for the time to imagine the life they should have had.

I shook my head and forced myself out of it. I could muse about my feelings later. First, I had to get out of there. Time to find that conduit.

As I started to turn away, the window I was leaning against switched itself off, nearly sending me tumbling out to my death. I caught my balance and took a step back. One by one, the windows around me switched off as well, vanishing into thin air. Then my ears picked out the subtle zip of nylon rope being used. They'd cut off my escape and were rappelling from above. Perhaps that was the plan all along. Like hounds to the hunters. The time for snooping around was over. I couldn't avoid fighting my way out of this any longer.

SHOULDER CHECK

I backed up behind the pool table and sank to the floor just as the nylon rope snapped taut by an internal electric current. The dull, heavy thud of boots hit the carpet a moment later. Standard operating procedure for this sort of thing would be to sweep the room, so I watched their feet carefully. When the moment came, and the boots shifted away from me, I rushed the looming figure. The man was absolutely massive, clad in black combat armor, and carrying a compact assault rifle. I might as well be charging into battle against a tank. Even if I caught him by surprise, all hope I had of winning simply vanished. Moving right when I did might have bought me a few precious moments, but I had a feeling all I could do was keep moving and pray to every god I could think of.

Jesus, Vishnu, Jim Jones, hear me in my time of need.

The figure pivoted, bringing their assault rifle to bear, but I'd gotten close enough to wedge my forearm against the base of the magazine. I pushed his arm up as bullets flew, drawing a line of destruction through walls, windows, screens, and that precious pool table. I snarled and twisted the rifle from the man's grip. I spun away and moved to catch it. Instead, my head snapped back as a vice-like hand wrapped around the back of my neck and threw me at the embattled pool table. My vision exploded with color as I hit the antique, then the floor. My face hurt like hell, and I couldn't see out of one eye. My HUD readjusted for monocular vision and alerted me to head trauma.

"No shit," I muttered. "Was it my collapsed cheekbone and eye socket or my flattened nose that gave it away?"

All that snark and confidence was purely an act. My skull was encased in a calcium-graphene weave. Incredibly durable stuff. And this guy just caved half my face in after tossing me into a piece of furniture. He had to be running some serious mods to pull that off. I staggered to my feet and drew my last surviving knife from my jacket. I smiled with the half of my face that still worked.

"Let's go, asshole," I growled, doing my best to maintain that thin veil of courage.

Seemingly offended that I had gotten back up, he charged me, preparing a left hook. I clumsily dodged backward, barely managing not to trip over myself. His arm swung in an arc and cut a broad swath across my face, coloring my vision with scarlet. I recoiled, grabbing my face, and felt my breath bubbling out of the gash that bisected my nose. Tears welled up in my eye and I struggled to focus. The one thing I could make out was the gleaming metal of the man's arm, which had separated into a dozen honed, gunmetal spears. It looked like a fucked up meat tenderizer.

I lurched sideways and forward, ducking another punch. My arm stretched out for my knife until my muscles ached, but I came up short and tumbled past it. He knocked the blade away with a contemptuous kick, and with a couple of quick steps forward, managed to grab me by the arm. Panic washed over me for a moment but was gone as I made peace with what was coming. He brought his elbow down on mine. Cartilage popped, and loose bones migrated beneath my skin, giving the joint an entirely new range of motion.

He let my arm fall uselessly and leveled a punch into the center of my chest. I went to the ground in a sprawl, struggling to breathe against newly fractured ribs. Even still, I gritted whatever teeth I had left and got my arms under me. Every part of me screamed and pleaded to just embrace unconsciousness and whatever fate awaited me. Against my better judgment, I pushed against the ground and willed myself to get up. I was going to die on my feet, and I made sure this piece of shit knew it.

When I screamed at him, with all my defiance and rage and fear, it came out completely incomprehensible. God, it sounded so ridiculous I almost laughed, but I never got that far. A boot made contact with my shoulder, and my broken elbow collapsed backward as I hit the ground again, leaving me propped up on my humerus.

The boot came down again, and it wasn't the bruising force on my back that hurt. Or the new rib fractures. Short of the pressure, none of that even registered with me. If anything, the sensation of the boot against my back was nothing short of orgasmic. What I was acutely aware of, however, was when my humerus, which had nowhere else to go, punched through my shoulder blade. It eschewed itself of muscles and tendons and tented against my skin before breaking through with a splatter of mangled gore.

It was like some sort of cruel punctuation to mark the end of the fight. And probably my life along with it. My eyes had shot open wide, but all I could see was black. I tried to grab my shoulder out of instinct, but my other arm flopped around uselessly against the sensory overload. I tried to scream out the pain, but I didn't. I tried to manage breathing, but I couldn't. I tried to do something, anything at all, but instead, I only lay there like a crushed bug, twitching and writhing on the edge of consciousness.

Little more than a heap on the floor, I was doing what little I could to calm the electric agony that was rioting through me. Even without my vision or hearing, I could almost feel my opponent looming over me, relaxed in his victory. I wasn't sure how long I was laying there like that, but my sense of hearing eventually returned, just enough to hear him speaking to someone. He was probably reporting in, the words little more than formless liquid in my ears.

My better judgement returned to me, too, like the pest that it was, scolding me for holding on as long as I had. It kept on insisting that I take the easy way out. I was finally about to give in when my optic systems rebooted and slowly bloomed back into focus. It was slow at first, dark shapes on dark shapes that bled into hues of red before letting other colors have their say. And finally, despite all the pain and agony racking my body, I found myself grinning like a madman.

I had found an opening.

Against all the unpleasant sensations that were ravaging my body, I reached for my knife. I clenched my fist around the bottom part of the blade, cutting my palm open in the process. It didn't matter. He saw me make my move, his words trailing off as surprise gave way to realization. I stabbed as hard as I could into the back of his boot. The tip of the knife roamed around before I found what I was looking for and pulled hard. His Achilles bucked against the dull edge of the blade, and I gritted my teeth, pulling harder against his leg. I worked the knife around, trying to get the sharpened edge to finish the job. The tip caught the tendon and tore through the middle, splitting it in half lengthwise before cutting the remaining sinuous strands free of their anchor.

He collapsed, grabbing at his leg as he went, and as bad as that injury may have been, it wasn't going to take him out of the fight. I needed to kill him. Not wasting any time, I half-crawled across the floor to him, leaving a trail of blood in my wake. My vision may have been blurred by tears, but he probably looked like I did a moment before. Feral, in pain, and terrified.

I stabbed him in the chest and used the knife to pull myself atop him. His arms reached up, trying to push me away, but I drove the blade in again. He got a hand on my injured arm and crushed my elbow. The pain was a distant thing that barely registered. I just leaned back, lifting the knife above my head, and brought it down a third and final time. His hands fell away from me, and at long last, he was dead.

My body sagged and every part of me wanted to quit right there. I was little more than a giant seeping wound. If I just collapsed and went to sleep, I could forget about all of this. Nobody would fault me for it. Not even Mahdi. My mouth drew itself into a firm line, then turned into a lip-quivering snarl. These fuckers thought they could walk all over us, and I wasn't going to give them the satisfaction.

With that decided, I clumsily searched the corpse beneath me, checking every pocket and pouch I could find. Extra magazines for the rifle and a couple more for a sidearm were the most apparent. After rummaging around a bit more, I found what I was really after, a field medicine pack. After working it open, I went through the contents. Finally, I came to a small spray can of InstaClot™. Normally, you would have wanted to clean the injury and get clothing out of the way, but I was in no shape to do that, so I just sprayed its contents all over my fucked up shoulder. I didn't know I was capable of feeling any more pain, but there it was.

Now I had to think about how I was going to get out. No way I was going any further up, but as I looked back at the corpse, my eyes fixed on the nylon extruder attached to his harness. It looked pretty banged up, but its display indicated that the filament cartridge was still mostly full. That settled that. I worked to get his harness off and in one piece before slipping into it myself. Once the straps around my legs, waist, and chest were tightened, I pushed myself up with a groan and limped to the window.

It was a long way down from here, and looking over the edge made me audibly gulp. Not that I was afraid of heights, or jumping from them, but that was a long way down. Enough to give anyone a moment's pause. I stepped back inside for a moment and made a few laps around the pool table, looping rope around it enough to make an anchor point.

"Down and out," I muttered, repeating Jin's earlier line like a mantra.

Then, forcing myself not to think about it, I took one long step toward the window, then another, and another. With a final quick stride, I leapt from the building.

DOWNFALL

Almost as soon as I'd jumped from the window, I had maybe eight seconds before I went splat on the ground below, so I needed to think about my landing. As I rotated midair to get into position, I caught a glimpse of what was behind me. More combat goons were rappelling down to the apartment I'd just been in. Another few seconds and they'd have torn me apart.

Tilting my head up again, looking at the ground and all the people gathering on the street. Freelance journalists, spectators, thrill seekers, and others hoping to find out what was going on. If I landed on one of them, it was going to be a bad day for both of us. Fortunately, a couple people must have spotted me and called out, because the crowd spread out to make way for my landing. They were, of course, expecting a corpse to go splat.

One thing that nobody ever mentions about falling is how peaceful it is. The white noise is relaxing. There's no stress on your joints, no sensation of gravity. As I fell, all my injuries vanished and I felt as though I could drift off to sleep. There's a reason people jump to their deaths. A peaceful way to go with no hope of survival at the bottom.

It wouldn't be a lie to say that I was considering it. My life was already beyond fixing, but everything over the last few hours was an entirely new level. Maybe later. I wasn't finished yet; all those onlookers would have to be disappointed.

Once I counted to five, I clamped my feet down on the rope. Heat erupted and started to burn through my shoes, eventually leaving a small trail of smoke in my wake. But I was slowing down. Finally, at the last moment, I spun around and, feet first, prepared for impact. I only hoped that my legs and spine, enhanced and reinforced as they were, could take the force of it.

A split-second later, I landed in a wide crouch. My injured arm swung around limply, leaving a half-moon-shaped arc of blood on the pavement. My back stayed exactly where it was, thankfully, but the metal struts in my legs buckled and contorted beneath my calves. It was an odd sensation, like someone was lifting part of my muscle painlessly away from its bone. But, thankfully, nothing new was broken.

Everyone kept their distance, standing around me in a loose circle. Clearly, nobody expected me to survive the landing. Hell, I'd have been lying if I said that I wasn't a little surprised, myself. After the initial shock wore off, the handful of reporters in the group broke ranks with the others and started taking pictures. Circling closer, moving themselves in odd ways to make sure their eyes were in the best position for a good shot. Any other day I might have enjoyed the attention. Any other day, I would have been a little excited by the trophy icon in the upper corner of my HUD. A new personal best. But through all the pain, and adrenaline, and everything else that had happened, I just felt tired.

Looking up and behind me, I studied my building. Perhaps it would have been better to say *former* building. Through a haze, consisting of equal parts ozone and cancer, windows that hadn't been boarded up flickered like hundreds of twinkling lights. I remembered years ago, somewhere else, Mahdi told me that the lit apartment windows made him think of what the night sky must have been like.

"How would you know? The uppers keep that all to themselves," I muttered, repeating what I'd told him then.

In little more than a moment, before turning away, I glimpsed all my saved memories of the building. The day I found my future home, that old industrial heating unit. All the time I spent gutting it with Mahdi. It all seemed like a dream now. One I didn't think I'd ever find my way back to again. Sure, I wasn't living in the lap of luxury. Hell, as Jin had so effectively pointed out earlier in the day, I wasn't that far removed from poverty either. But that little cramped box was my place. Mine. No doubt by now, they'd found it and started tearing it apart.

I just wanted to sag to the ground and start weeping right there on the spot. But I needed to keep moving. Maybe I could find the time to mourn later, but it wasn't now. My daring and dramatic escape had probably only bought me a few minutes. I needed to get off the street and try to cover my tracks, but I couldn't hide out just anywhere. Not with a circ on my tail, he'd be sure to find me in short order.

So, I started walking. Each step was awkward, and I felt it in my shoulder and side every time I moved. I needed to get myself patched up at the very least, but my options were slim. Couldn't go to a clinic without money. Automating doctors and surgeons out of the industry also automated out the Hippocratic oath along with them. I could try for a back alley surgeon, but around here, that was a great way to get a backdoor installed in your head without your knowledge.

I pushed through the crowd, headed the way I'd gone earlier, in the direction of the Armory. Fortunately, the crowd watched me go. Even the photographers left me be. All except one. Someone was creeping up behind me. Probably looking to finish me off and strip me of any usable parts. A hand rested on my good shoulder, and I whipped around in a crooked shuffle step, ready to put up as much fight as I could. I tripped over myself and fell backward on my ass.

"Get the hell away from me," I shouted.

"Easy there, easy," said the person. "It's me, it's your least favorite blogger."

I let out a sigh of relief and relaxed a little. "Shit, Rohch. Yeah, if you have some meds I could use, that would be great."

Their face was pulled into a tight neutral mask. The kind people put on when a certain amount of training sets in. "I don't have anything, but you know that if I'm here, Churrie isn't far. She'll get you patched up."

With that, Rohch got under my good arm and helped me down the street and out of sight of my building. Even with their help, I walked along like some kind of broken homunculus. We slipped through alleyway after alleyway, enough that they all started to blur together. Finally, after zig-zagging for maybe ten minutes, we came to a stop in a small, secluded parking area between several adjoining buildings. Taking up one of the few spaces was an old electric touring van that had been painted white and overhauled more than once. It was adorned with traditional signs of medicine. The red cross in a circle and the caduceus in a blue triangle.

I was barely able to stand, but Rohch was doing a good job hauling me along toward the van. As we approached a tall, pale woman pushed open the side doors and rushed out to meet us. Because she was not part of a medical corporation, everything she had was makeshift, even her uniform. Instead of medical scrubs or body armor, she wore a simple set of mechanic's coveralls.

The woman—Churrie—helped haul me inside the van and onto a metal examination slab. A battery of quick tests blurred by, and each one seemed to sharpen her tone. She cut open part of my shirt and slapped a universal blood bag to my chest. I felt a pop of suction and a slight jab of a needle as the pack's center mechanism located a suitable vein to puncture. The van started moving at some point and Churrie shouted something about taking turns easier this time. A sharp pain shot itself directly into my chest and I was immediately very aware of everything. My eyes roved around at everything as I tried to process all of the sensory input. I started to squirm on the table, but I'd been restrained.

"Listen to me," Churrie said in a calm but commanding voice. "I can staple you up, but you're going to need to get to an actual clinic. Is there one we can drop you off at?"

A wave or chills rode up my spine and sent me shuddering. "N-no."

"Is there anywhere else we can take you?" she asked, sounding grave.

She'd be leaving me to my death and she knew it. Any of us can only do so much.

I didn't think about the words when I said them, just that they meant something to me. As it was, I could barely string together a coherent thought. "Shiv... Eshe."

She shot a nervous glance to the front of the van, then back down at me. "That's Vys territory. Is there anywhere else? Vys and I have history—the shoot-on-sight kind."

I tried to shake my head, but just coughed and shuddered. "Bag. Payment in... my bag. Paper."

Her eyes widened, and she took a second or two to rummage through my pack until she found Mahdi's printed menus. "This is—"

"Shiv," I groaned. "Get me to the Shiv."

She nodded up at Rohch who turned the car around and hit the gas. My vision started to fade into vague darkness.

The last thing I remembered hearing was Churrie's voice. "Hang on. We'll get you there."

RUNNER IN THE AMBULANCE

I felt a hand gently shake me awake. "Hey, you still there? We don't have a lot of time."

I groaned something that sounded roughly in the affirmative. Wherever we'd wound up there wasn't much light to be had. It made it hard to tell if my eyes were adjusting or not. My HUD lit up and told me of more than a hundred minor punctures and chemical adhesive lining my injured shoulder. She'd done it. She'd somehow managed to keep me alive.

"I've just given you my last blood bag and we were spotted on the way here," Churrie explained. "Rohch got us into an old abandoned building a few blocks from the Shiv, we've gotta drop you off and get the hell out of here."

I started to get up from the cot in the ambulance and felt both Rohch and Churrie helping me from either side. Dim light bled in as the side door once again opened onto a bombed-out old building. Homeless people huddled around fire barrels, watching us warily, unsure if we were part of a corporate cleanup crew or if our intent was more benign.

As I found my feet and finally stood up outside the van on my own power, I turned around shakily.

"Thank you," I said, slurring a little.

"No, thank you. That paper you gave us is going to save a lot of lives," she replied.

"You're gonna want to keep your head down the next few days. Corpsec is tearing my building apart now and they're after me," I added.

It was hard to tell for sure, but as my eyes traced the blurred, firelit edges of her face, I thought I saw tears. Churrie mouthed the grateful words again and shut the door. The van roared to life. Its headlights cast blinding, brilliant beams of light through the space. Enough to make me and the homeless folks in the distance flinch away from it. A few of them even started running. Then, with the screech of self-healing tires, the Van sped off and out of sight.

I wandered out into the street and pondered my next steps. I knew what I'd said. I had a friend who might help. Maybe. It was just going to be a gamble just getting to her, then another to see if she'd help me. But gambling was about all I had. She and I had hit a bit of a rough patch lately, and I felt really awkward showing up and asking for favors out of the blue. Still, if I caught her in a good mood, she might just be able to save my ass.

She—that friend of mine, Eshe Omiata—is the same one that Jin had gushed about earlier. She plies her trade as a back alley modder in a tightly packed megastructure called the Shiv. I knew it well. I was made there and then grew up there. Collectively, everyone living there is a small-scale sampling of the whole of New York City. Because of that, among the twenty-five million inhabitants packed into six square blocks, there were gangs, politicians, corporations, and others. They could pass their time inside the structure's walls, find— or manufacture or steal—success, and never come in contact with the outside world. It was one of the few places that I knew of where being further from the ground was undesirable. The upper floors might even be some of the most isolated places on earth.

It was far from perfect—not that anywhere else would have been— but I had mostly fond memories of growing up there. Mostly thanks to Eshe's late adopted father, Laden. As I knew him, he was probably one of the few good men left in the world. Granted, he didn't completely take me and Mahdi off the streets like he did for Eshe, but he still looked out for us. He saved my life on more than one occasion and made sure neither of us went hungry. As a point of fact, Laden is the reason Mahdi and I became runners. He'd give us odd jobs, be it delivering finished mods to clients or going to the bazaar for parts.

As I limped my way across catwalks and down sidewalks, I couldn't help but smile at the memories. As bad as life can be, there are always a few good moments to hold on to. The problem was that he'd passed away only six months ago. Rotted his brain out junking in the dreamscape. What's worse, he had outstanding debt with a local syndicate. Or, more accurately, *the* local syndicate. They were the biggest players in the Shiv, going by the moniker Vys. When he died, they saw to it that his debts passed to Eshe, which, besides the shop, was the only thing he left her. I'd obviously held him in high regard, but the revelations of his passing tarnished my memory of him somewhat. Regardless, with the wounds of his passing so fresh, Eshe was not going to take Mahdi's death well.

The goliath of a building that was the Shiv loomed into view as I pushed out of a garbage-strewn alleyway. Even after growing up there, the sheer scale of it never dulled. It was like one of the pillars of the earth, adorned with every creed, culture, and corporate branding that humanity had to offer. Like a kaleidoscope of glass and repurposed metal. In the midst of all that, I could pick out new construction that jutted out haphazardly from the walls like so many skin tags. Similarly, it was not at all uncommon for some of those expansions to collapse and slough themselves off. Scavengers would pick off the wreckage and the cycle of life would start anew.

The closer I got the more tightly packed the buildings seemed to get. Even the sidewalk and the street next to it drew closer together until the roadway and all its traffic vanished into an underground tunnel. It was as if all the structures were huddling around the Shiv for warmth. All my possible means of escape were disappearing, and I couldn't help but feel a sense of claustrophobia wrap itself around my spine. With the ever-congealing crowd at my back, the only way I could go was forward.

My path to the Shiv brought me to its southern entrance, the largest of the four. As I approached, I could spot more than a dozen well-armed guards on the periphery. I knew who they were right away, but for anyone else, their roving geometric tattoos with dynamically shifting pigment would have given them away. Vys footsoldiers. The same people that Eshe now carried a debt to. Every so often, one of them would wade into the passing tides of humanity to retrieve someone of interest. The person getting hauled off was usually screaming.

While I try not to think about it, growing up on their turf meant that I had a first-hand understanding of how they operated. More often than not, they would work their way into people's lives and get them hooked on something—money, sex, drugs, et cetera. Anything could be a vice if manipulated properly. Once they had someone, they'd use any accrued debt as leverage. If a person had nothing else they could offer, Vys usually took their children. They're moldable, which makes them a perfect way to keep an organization like Vys alive and churning. Hell, their red light districts probably doubled as factories for future soldiers. As someone who was cultivated to be a product before eventually being reprocessed, the thought of them breeding their ranks stabbed me somewhere in the gut that I didn't have words for.

Finally passing through the initial checkpoint, I tried not to look anybody in the eye, especially the guards. Just shuffled forward, on the heels of the person in front of me, trying to think boring, unobtrusive thoughts. They must have not been mundane enough because I glanced up for a second, and just in time to see one of the soldiers enter the flow of people. Shit, shit, shit. I tried to duck back into my monotonous path forward, but it was impossible to not watch in horror as my demise slowly waded through the crowd. She was a behemoth of a woman. Had to have been nearly two meters tall, and die-cast from ink and hard muscle. Towering over the people around me, she got closer and closer, assault rifle held up above her head. It kept the weapon free of obstruction and wandering hands, but it had also become a nigh-universal signal to the lesser masses that this person should be avoided and given a wide berth. Avoid her they did. Like water flowing around a boulder.

My pulse was already all over the place, but this woman made it infinitely worse. Like an avant-garde percussionist on uppers. That old friend, panic, started playing with the hairs on the back of my neck again. All I could do was force my eyes shut and focus on the next step in front of me.

"Alright, then, slow and steady," I muttered to myself. "You're invisible, not even here. Just going to slip through to safety."

Then, a firm hand grabbed my uninjured shoulder and squeezed it until the joints popped.

It was all over. I was dead.

OLD DEBTS & VICES

The hand gave me a solid shove, sending me stumbling into the person in front of me and onto the ground. Pushing myself up, I glanced back to see the guard wrap her arm around the neck of a man who must have been just behind me. We stared at one another. His terror matched my own. The difference was, as it turned out, his was real, and mine was imagined. I smirked at him as he was hauled away. The man struggled for a moment but quickly realized that it was all in vain. That was as close as I wanted to get to attracting attention. So, I returned my focus to the crowd, getting up and taking a few quick steps around people to melt away from the scene, back into anonymity.

I passed beneath a colossal narthex that clawed up through the center of the structure. It seemed to go on for an eternity. Mobile vendor shops collected on the edges of the main thoroughfares like plaque on an artery. Occasionally, one would overstay their welcome and get ushered out of sight by a guard or two. The central courtyard, however, was mostly clear of would-be salesmen. In the middle of four heavily graffitied pillars sat a Vys outpost. Thankfully, these ones were not on lookout duty. They were there to secure the entrance if and when the time came to secure the entire structure. I've heard stories about it happening, but that was long before I was made. Thinking about it, though, I couldn't help but wonder what their job was if an attack came from inside.

Eshe's place was up on the fourth floor, and there were more than a dozen different ways to get there. I was about to take the most direct route and take a place in line in one of the structure's many escalators when I got this horrendous itch on the back of my neck. Like someone was tailing me. There didn't seem to be anybody acting conspicuously, not that it would have been hard to blend in. Still, I didn't like it. Change of plans. I made for the escalators and took an abrupt turn, cutting through a vendor's tent, to round the corner into the Kahwlun exchange.

The sprawling yet cramped marketplace took up a good half of the ground level but had metastasized up onto every floor of the Shiv. It was primarily situated around a tryptic of trilateral freight elevators that served to distribute goods, services, and people to all corners of the megastructure. If you could afford to buy a spot, that is. If my instincts were right, and someone was following me, I stood the best chance of shaking them in there before working my way upstairs.

The whole market smelled of burnt-out electronics and was bathed in blaring oranges, reds, and yellows. I'd been through this place hundreds—probably thousands—of times. The floorplan was always changing, though, so even though I knew it, each visit was a new experience. As a kid, I recall asking Laden about the colors. He told me that the harsh lighting hides imperfections or damage in many products, then warned me not to buy anything there. At least not from anyone I didn't know from outside the market. It was advice that I eventually heeded after making a few ill-advised purchases of my own.

I kept a quick, albeit awkward pace, zig-zagging between vendors, eateries, and open-air auction houses. The paranoid sensation was boring between my shoulders, and I was getting more and more desperate to be rid of it. I took a quick step around a corner and sat down at a crowded bar, keeping an eye on the people passing by.

"Hey. Hey, ami," somebody said in a thick accent.

Friend? I thought—translating—no friends around here.

Something sharp poked me in the shoulder, and I looked up to see the bartender looking at me, annoyed and impatient, a bamboo skewer in hand.

"You're bleeding all over my slab," he said, waving a hand at the puddle that was forming in front of me. "If you're not buyin' nothing, get the fuck on out of here. Right?"

I looked at him for a moment and snatched a nearly transparent plastic menu from the other side of the bar. He regarded me with suspicion as I pretended to consider my options. A minute passed, and nobody caught my attention. Perhaps a minute more. I flipped the menu over and glanced over at the bartender. He was helping a paying customer, but it was apparent that he was keeping an eye on me. He cleared out a tab and carefully stepped over to a terminal, picking up a makeshift handset. He tried to look around at nobody in particular but couldn't help stealing a glance at me as he spoke. He was calling into whichever cartel he rented the space from. I was presumably making him lose money, which meant I was causing *them* to lose money, and his masters would want to put a stop to that. Time to go.

I pressed the menu down into the puddle I had left on the imitation stone slab and was about to get up when somebody grabbed me by the arm and forced me to sit back down. The shopkeeper flicked a smug gesture at me. Back of the hand, index, and thumb making a ring and the three remaining fingers extended—Asshole. I responded in kind, placing my fist to my mouth, then pulling it away, extending my thumb, index, and middle finger as I did—Cocksucker. That's great, I might be dead in a minute and my choice was to use sign language to call names. Fantastic decision-making on my part.

"You really know how to make friends, don't you?" a woman asked me, a confident smile in her tone. "Did you really think you could slip through without me noticing?"

Her voice was dark and husky. Like the smoke slipping out the barrel of a freshly-fired gun. I turned to find a woman a little older than I was, studying me intensely. A frigid, dissecting gaze tucked behind a curtain of dark hair and round info-specs. Scrolling data reflected in her eyes as she looked me over.

I huffed out a breath and couldn't help but roll my eyes. "Hello, Ragna. Good to see you again."

"It is, isn't it?" she purred. "I'd dare to suggest that it is your lucky day."

"Yeah, why's that?" I asked.

"Because I know why you're here. I know that you would not have walked through that front gate without a pretty damn good reason, not with the outstanding debt you owe me," Ragna explained. "You've been avoiding me. Shame on you."

I scowled at her. "Why not just turn me in? Have those goons out front haul me off like every other poor bastard you snatch up."

She gloated. "Oh, you know me well enough that I like to keep more than a few people in my back pocket. The engineered ones are particularly useful. You are actually a remarkable specimen, you know. When you're not hiding from a corp or getting beaten to a pulp, you have proven to be quite the investment."

I tried to tug my arm free, but her firm grip held me in place. "We can discuss my debt to you later. I'm kinda in a bit of trouble."

"Indeed you are," Ragna said, with a sinister sparkle in her eyes. "And I'll let you run along to Eshe in just a moment. But first, you're going to hear me out."

I settled back into the seat and stopped trying to escape, giving her a flat, irritated look the whole while.

"Good," she said. "I'll cover for you for as long as I can, but once you get yourself patched up, I need you to kill someone for me."

"I'm not an assassin," I replied.

She leaned forward. "No, you're not, but you are a killer, and the kind most don't usually see coming. I've been running this gig for a long time, and I'm good at what I do. My boss is going to be naming his successor soon, and I have some competition. Take care of it for me."

Her glasses flickered and a moment later I saw a message pop up in my HUD. Once it did, she loosened her grip and let me go. I got up immediately and walked several paces away before looking back at her. The chair she'd been in was empty. Another message hit my inbox.

"Fuck me," I sighed as I turned and kept walking.

I knew I was taking a risk in coming here, but I was really hoping to slip in without getting Ragna's attention. A circ was bad enough, but having the eyes and ears of the Shiv following my every move was going to be a problem all its own. Especially if I needed to make a quick getaway. If what she told me was true, and she was next up in the chain of succession, she would be able to throw some weight around to hold the circ and his mercenaries at bay, but even that had its limits. The itch on the back of my neck wasn't going away, so I tried to ignore it as I meandered to the triumvirate of costly freight elevators and the cost-free stairs that helixed them. I didn't have a subscription to use the lifts, and they'd flag me as soon as I tried to sneak on. Praise be to the extremes of almighty capitalism.

"I think I've just about had my fill of stairs for the day," I muttered to myself, before moving to push into the throngs of people.

Before I could start the—likely deadly—ascent, a Vys foot soldier got my attention and beckoned me over. I looked up at the distant ceiling as if sending up a prayer. This really better be you, Ragna. After taking an exhausted breath, I gave up my place in line.

"You are leaving a river of blood behind you," he said. "Might bleed out on my steps. Don't want that. Would really cock up my day, you got me?"

I looked up at the man. His voice was big and blocky, just like he was. It sounded like someone smashing a bunch of stone slabs together. His face was scrunched up with irritation that drew cartoonish lines across his brow. That, combined with the shift in tattoo pigment across his cheeks from blue to purple, gave me the impression that he was actively forgetting to breathe. I nodded at him and tried really hard not to picture him when the tattoos were shifting into the green part of the spectrum.

"What floor you headed to?" he asked.

"Fourth," I answered.

He looked me up and down. "Got anything worth anything?"

I suddenly felt like a moron for giving all the paper menus to Rohch. I had that last bloody knife left in my jacket, the one I'd shredded that guy's Achilles with. I really didn't want to give it up, but at this point, there was little point in me holding onto it. So I pulled it out and handed it to him, grip-side first. He looked at it hesitantly, like he was trying to puzzle out what a knife was used for. Shoot gun, no cut, only shoot.

"It's good metal," I said. "Zwill make."

"German, huh?" he commented, taking the blade and inspecting it. "It's got a nice edge."

His apparent knowledge of lethal cutlery shattered the idea of the big dumb oaf that my imagination conjured. Oh, well. It was amusing while I had it.

"I live and die by those things," I explained.

"You may be more right than you know," he said with a smirk. "Got any more?"

I tried not to roll my eyes at the extortion but shook my head.

"Heh. Figured as much. Go ahead and get on," he said. "We'll be getting on in a couple of minutes. Pleasure doing business with you."

I didn't say anything, just drifted on uncertain feet to the Pythagorean platform. Was I just cursing capitalism a moment ago? Let me correct myself. Praise be to the greedy. The guard was true to his word, and after making room for a few more heavily loaded auto-pallets, we had liftoff. Not thirty seconds later, the lift came to a stop, and the guard motioned for me to get off. We'd traveled somewhere around ten stories in hardly any time at all. If I'd taken the stairs, it would have taken me a couple of hours to get that far. The guy was right, the climb would have killed me.

As the security gates shut behind me and I stepped out into the fourth level of the exchange, I almost felt like I could start to breathe easy. If only my cracked ribs would let me do it. Still, the feeling was nice. As I worked my way to the outer edge of the marketplace, I eventually came to an unassuming little alley. It was barely more than a claustrophobic gap between two larger buildings. Eshe's home and workshop was marked in those cramped quarters by an unwieldy, black door that was doing its best at being inconspicuous. I leaned on the wall and slammed the side of my fist in the door's center. It rang like a low, barely audible gong. Metal, probably tools, crashed to the floor on the other side, followed by a string of luminous cursing. Then the door slid open.

Eshe stood there in the opening. Her annoyance was palpable, like a visible, billowing cloud. It had been a little while since I had last seen her, but she hadn't changed a bit. She kept her hair short and out of the way. It started on the sides with her natural color, cut to a close fade that gradually transitioned to tight curls of rust orange that sprang out haphazardly above the band of her goggles. I must have disturbed her with a client because her dark skin and work smock were speckled with beads of fresh blood and bits of bone.

"The fuck happened to you?" she asked, catching me as I took a step forward and collapsed.

I tried to stand back up, but my legs just didn't want to work. Damn things. Eshe dragged me over to a couch she kept by the door for waiting customers.

"You are going to ruin my fucking couch," she complained as she lowered me down onto the well-worn cushions.

"Thanks," I choked out. "Hey Eshe, I need a swap."

"Uh-huh," she said hesitantly before turning around to her client. "Hey, Goz, we're about done for the day. Come back, same time tomorrow, and we'll get that new arm running."

She walked across the room and picked a few large chunks of an arm from the floor, and deposited them in a horizontal freezer.

"I want it done today," the man said with little inflection of any kind. "You owe me."

"I owe a lot of people," she shot back, faking a smile. "But if you're sitting in my chair, I'm in charge. That's the deal I have with your bosses. End of discussion."

I could only see the back of the man's head, but the muscles in his jaw tightened.

"You listen to me," he snarled.

"Do you know what vasoconstriction is?" Eshe interrupted, taking a seat on her wheeled work stool. "It's part of your body's wound healing process. Your blood vessels constrict on their own to prevent blood loss. I just cut off your whole goddamned forearm and closed up the wound around your radius and your ulna. How do you think your body is going to react to that level of trauma? If I push any further you could risk going into shock."

She didn't let him answer. "Not to mention, if I attach your new arm today, you could run the risk of infection or outright rejection of the limb. Both cases mean I need to take more of your arm and start the process all over again. Do you want that?"

He looked like he was about to lose his temper but thought better of it. "Tomorrow, this gets done."

"Tomorrow, same time," she repeated, cheerily. "I'll have you ready to jerk off with it in no time."

The man got up from the well-worn leather recliner and went for the door. He was bald and lanky, and his skin looked like it had been tanned and aged just like the chair had. As Eshe said, he was missing part of his right arm just below the elbow, save for two bits of plastic-encased bone protruding from the bandaged stump. He gave me a squinty-eyed look up and down, grunted something under his breath, then hauled the door open and trudged down the alleyway.

"Fucking moron, I can't believe he bought that bullshit," Eshe muttered before pacing quickly to the door and hollering after him. "Hey, don't go putting those things in places they don't belong!" She pulled the door shut and locked it about a dozen times before turning to me. "Now, let's take a look at you."

She worked to pull the jacket off, first from my good arm, then from the other side.

"This better be fucking good. You know the kind of things that could happen to him in that condition?" she asked. "I owe the Vys a lot of money, and that guy is going to cut that debt in half for me if I make him happy. If he doesn't get his new arm, I'm going to be in deep shit."

"I know," I grunted. "I owe them, too, remember."

"Yeah..." she said, trailing off.

I couldn't tell if she was surprised or impressed.

"Fucking shit," she spat. "You get into a fight with a trash compactor or something?"

"Corpsec," I corrected. "Not sure who."

"You're getting tangled up with fucking suits and dragging them to my door? What the fuck is wrong with you?" Eshe demanded.

"Okay, look," I stammered, holding my hand up like I had a gun pointed at me. "I had no place else to turn. This isn't my fault. Besides, Ragna is going to hold them off for me."

"Yeah?" She asked. "What deal that bitch make this time? Your firstborn?"

"She may have given me a job, yeah," I exhaled, probably sounding more tired than anything.

Eshe didn't look convinced of anything but didn't argue. I could see her making mental notes with subtle nods, taking inventory of all the bones and muscles that were wildly out of place. Not liking the awkward silence, I started to run my mouth.

"Mahdi bumped into me," I explained. "He was on a job, and some corporate thugs were after him. We booked it."

"And? Where the hell is he?" she asked, visibly irritated. "Is he gonna show up at my door in a few minutes all busted to hell too? I've told you guys over and over that running is a real shit career path. Everyone I've ever know—"

"Eshe," I interrupted. She stopped and looked up at me, and I could see the sudden worry in her eyes. I sucked in a breath and felt tears well up in my eyes. "They killed him, Eshe. Mahdi's dead."

SMALL FAVORS

Waves of emotion washed over her at once. The three of us had grown up together. Not only were we childhood friends, but she and Mahdi had an off-again-on-again thing for a while. They tried to hide it—usually—and I tried to keep my distance, but it was easy to tell when the switch had flipped. First Laden and now Mahdi. Even though we'd lost touch recently, I held out hope that our shared childhood would work in my favor.

She was staring down at the floor and her lips moved a little, like she was sending up a silent prayer. When she did look up, it was only for a second; her gaze passed through me and out into the middle distance. Her whole body started to shake, so I reached out for her hand and she recoiled away a couple of steps.

Her words turned into a faint muttering. "Pectoralis major, subscapularis, deltoid, acromion."

"Eshe," I said gently, "I really need your help."

"Don't you think I fucking know that?" she snapped. "I...I—"

She sat down in a folding chair across from me and wrapped her arms around her stomach. Her muttering continued for another few moments, listing off bones, muscles, and tendons in some sort of order. From the ones I was able to pick out, she was going over everything in and around the shoulder. After a while, it subsided, but she didn't look at me. She just stared down at some empty space on the floor.

"Show me what happened," she said finally, tilting her head back up to find my eyes.

"Look, Eshe, they had a gauss cannon. I lost time. I'm not sure what happened, you don't want to—"

Her eyes met mine. "If. You. Want. My. Help. You. Will. Show. Me. What. Happened."

We stared each other down for another moment and I was the first one to give in. I nodded at her—more to reassure myself than anything else—and ran my hand through my hair. I was probably more terrified to see what happened than she was. I really didn't need her falling apart again, or worse: kicking me out. But when she reached into one of the many pockets on her cargo pants and handed me one end of a fiber optic cable, I took it. Her end of it plugged into a port on the side of her goggles, while mine jacked into a similar port just behind my left ear.

Then, without another word, Eshe got up from the chair, pulled me to my feet, and slowly walked me over to her operating area. She lowered me into the same peeling leather seat that Goz had been in minutes earlier. I may have still been conscious, but only barely. I was just so goddamn tired.

"I'll get to work on getting you stable," she said, sounding nearby and distant all at once. "Just show me the memory."

I managed a slight nod and heard the band of her goggles snap as she adjusted them. My HUD was flashing an angry yellow warning sign, asking if I wanted to allow data transfer over the new connection. It then reminded me that I was using overdue trial software and promptly plastered an oppressive watermark across my whole field of view. Once the connection was established, though, I called up the memory and played it.

She gave me a couple of shots of something, then set to work on closing me up as best as she could. Staples mostly, each one latching onto either side of the tears in my skin. As she worked, I forced my eyes open, just enough to watch Eshe's expression through the ghostly recollection playing in my eyes. I had no idea how she could work a craft like medicine and watch something at once, but she made it look easy. She saw me involve myself and give Mahdi a hand in the Armory. Then again as we meandered our way back to the palisade. I stole her focus when I winced at the rebar piercing my side. But she paid attention again, just in time to see Mahdi get blown to pieces.

At that moment, Eshe stopped working. She just sat there, poised on the edge, putting another staple in my shoulder. A couple of lonesome tears chased one another down her cheeks. I cut the feed just as Mahdi and I hit the ground on the other side of the palisade. I really didn't want her to see what happened next. Me in a sudden fugue state, cutting and ripping, and who knows what else to take Madhi's head from his body.

"I have his mods," I said, quietly.

"You mean... that you..." she started to ask, trailing off.

I nodded.

She pulled the goggles down across her face, letting them dangle around her neck, then looked at me. Neither of us said anything. It was clear that there was plenty she wanted to say, but as she clenched her jaw and looked away, I could tell that she was trying to fight all that emotion with reason. She was angry with me for doing what I did and at the same time, she knew that anger was misplaced.

I opened my mouth before closing it again, pondering how to break the silence. "Look, Eshe, I need your help. That much is obvious. I want to find out why they killed Mahdi, but I can't do it in the state I'm in... and there's a circ—"

"You're leading a fucking circ right to my door? Why the hell would you do that? Killing Mahdi and cutting his skull open wasn't eno—" She stopped short, got up out of her chair, and paced across the room. Not that it did any good. It was obvious what she was going to say next.

I took a deep, trembling breath. "I'm going to say this once. I did not kill him. Do not dare to blame me for it. I want to get back at the people who did it, but I need your help."

Eshe's shoulders shuddered as a quiet sob escaped, but she arrested control again almost as soon as it had happened. She dragged her feet over to the wall and leaned up against it as the tears came in full. Her whole body sagged and she slid down to the floor, tucking her knees in close to her chest.

"So, you wanted a swap?" she asked at last, wiping her nose with her hand.

"Yeah, doesn't matter what it is, as long as it's better than this," I answered.

She laughed at that, short and bitter, and it almost made her seem a little smaller. "Okay, let me finish getting you patched up and I'll see what I can do about a body."

"Thank you," I said, settling into the chair and letting myself drift on the edge of sleep.

When Eshe returned to her station, I forced my eyes open and slipped a hand into my bag. While I fished around for Mahdi's tech, I looked around the space. "Hey, Eshe?"

"Hm?"

I pulled out Mahdi's stuff and held it up for her to see. "Do you have a spare terminal I can hook this up to? Might as well do some work while you're helping me out."

She sucked in a breath but nodded and took all the pieces on a surgical tray. She disappeared behind me for a minute or two, but I could hear the electric whine of heatsink fans come to life. One of them had a bad bearing because it sounded like it was going to come apart at any moment. Eshe returned with a collection of scalpels, gauze, and other medical implements that I didn't have the bravery to ask about. She dragged another chair across the room, its feet grinding their protest into the concrete floor, and set all the supplies down on it. Then she sat down to finish her work. It wouldn't make a ton of sense to fully repair my perforated shoulder. Instead, Eshe was likely going to focus on getting my body stable enough to sustain a swap. In the meantime, I started my sleep cycle, drifting off in mere moments so I could start digging through my best friend's memories.

>> OS INITIALIZATION

>> FIREWALL

Model: Tigershark 7685XTS

Manufacturer: Blu Orb Biotechnical

Firmware: 27.4.5.6859 CFW

Open Ports: 80, 3389, 443, 53, 25, 4672

>> HOST SYSTEMS

name	mfr.	fw.V.	status	notes
Dingbat 6	Maantra	v75.2	Syncing	
Trapezoid AMS	WebSharpie	v2.1.1	Online	Updates Pending
Jordi 2.0	Penthause Int.	v2.0.1	Offline	
Youdle Live	Magistrate	v10	Offline	
VR-BAK-1	CircuitBreakers	v41.7.7B	Online	No Faults Found
VR-BAK-2	CircuitBreakers	v41.7.7B	Online	No Faults Found
Persona Non-Grata	Null	vXX.86	Offline	EEG Not Found

>> ALL CHECKS COMPLETE! >:)))))

THIRTEEN

HEAD CANON

As the boot sequence cleared, Mahdi's interface was rendered in my waking vision. He had always bragged about his minimalist aesthetic when it came to his UI, but I never got a chance to see it. The second his systems made contact with the outside world, hundreds, or perhaps thousands, of messages popped up in his HUD. Fan mail, fan fiction, fan art, fanny-grams, dick pics, endorsement deals, gifts, and all sorts of other things. Some people sent him thank-you messages, telling how his streams were helping them through rough parts of their lives. Others sent long-winded and poorly formatted professions of love. A few more from overly critical armchair experts critiquing his form and telling him how he really should be doing one thing or another. Assholes. Of the ones I sifted through, I couldn't find any that didn't have to do with his streams.

I blew out a mental breath. "Shit, man, there's enough here to build a comfortable life on vanilla jobs alone. You coulda kicked back and taken it easy. Why on Earth did you pick up a contract for a black bag run?"

I only went through a few more messages, just enough of it to free up enough dashboard space to get his Dingbat® inbox settings. A couple quick if-then rules later and that mess of a mailbox started to neatly sort itself into categorized folders. Somewhere out there, on the edge of my perception, I felt a slight twinge of pain as the system borrowed my brain power to handle the task. Then, getting near the end of the list, the sorting job got my attention. There was a message it didn't know what to do with. A job offer.

> **From:** SOQUA_1689
>
> **Subject:** Contract Offer
>
> After reviewing your shared archival footage, I would like to offer you a contract. 150,000,000 dollars upon completion and other considerations if you can discreetly transport an item from Anchorage to New York City.
>
> Reply if interested.

One-hundred-and-fifty-thousand kay. Damn. That definitely got my attention. Depending on who the client was, their mention of other considerations could have been worth more than the fee itself. No wonder he'd taken the contract. That might have also been how the mercs tracked him down. I had no idea how popular he was, but a broadcasting runner suddenly going dark might pique someone's interest.

Maybe not, though. Even if he was rising in the ranks of streaming popularity, he was one of tens of millions. The odds seemed pretty out there. Someone would have to have known exactly what they were looking for to find him.

Either way, I saved the offer message to his dashboard and let the sort job wrap up. From there, I could hopefully find another clue or two by accessing his asset management system. Like many others, it hosted a front-end portal for Mahdi's subscribers. I checked that as the thought crossed my mind and made sure it was still offline. The other thing an AMS does is manage and organize all his internally generated data. Health specs, GPS coordinates, memories. It might all be stored on his pair of mirrored file servers, but If it could be tagged and reported on, Mahdi's version of Trapezoid® would have it on file.

Lucky son-of-a-bitch. I was still tracking all my data on text files and sorting by most recent.

I started with the logs of his GPS positioning going back the last six months, which was a lot of data. I could poke through it in detail later, but for now, I just set some conditional formatting to highlight anything around Anchorage. Forty-five, negative One-Fifty, or something like that. I took a snapshot and continued on to his memories. I should have pulled out the audio and video feeds into a rendering tool to watch in third person. It would give me a lot more detail and wouldn't run the risk of imprinting false memories. But in the essence of time, I took the risk.

Watching Mahdi's death, this time from his perspective, was, in a sick way, both bizarre and fascinating. The satchel flew out ahead as he made his ascent. When the first round hit him, his vision got a bit hazy, like electrical interference. That same sensation translated to a distant ringing that I had to shut off once the second round hit him. It was the sound of him dying. A mix of adrenaline and overwhelming sensory input—every split nerve, frayed muscle, and pulverized organ—called out in a deafening drone. A wall of sound like a dozen contrary chords being hit all at once.

He landed with me on the other side of the palisade, and I got the distinct impression of a thought so mundane that it bordered on the absurd. Man, you really look like hell. If I could have let out bitter laughter in this instance of the dreamscape, I would have. It was something Mahdi told me a lot. That I looked like hell, right before commenting on my dead-eyed stare and asking when I was finally going to get on with my life. With Mahdi around, I needed no parent to nag me; he did it plenty. It all sounded a lot like what Jin told me at the strip club. Was I really that obvious?

In Mahdi's last moments, I watched myself work away at Mahdi's chest with a knife. My motions were sporadic and unpredictable. My eyes were dilated and almost empty. His perception faded as I tore his head away from his body, but for a brief surge of hyper-awareness, and an image of Eshe sleeping peacefully on his chest.

Before the darkness took him, I cut my connection and came back to reality with a panicked gasp. I pushed myself out of the chair and ran. I had no idea where, but I had to go. I had to get out. Something tugged at my arm, followed by a crash of something hitting the floor. Nothing around me felt familiar like I was still in the dreamscape.

Tears welled up and poured down my cheeks, and I finally took another breath. I gathered enough courage to give a timid look around. I was in Eshe's shop, on the floor and up against a wall. I had a small bleeding wound in my arm where my IV line had ripped out. Even though I knew the space, paranoia colored everything my eyes wandered past. I half expected faces to come out of the wall or to suddenly find myself melting into the floor. Nausea came for me next, which forced me up and sent me stumbling to the nearest sink.

Once my stomach was done emptying itself of whatever it had left, I rinsed my mouth and slumped back to the floor. I was definitely back in reality, though the waning paranoia made me cast a wary glance back at Eshe's operating chair. It sat there, still, lifeless, and completely menacing. As if it would sprout teeth and chomp me down into pieces the next time I sat down.

But I needed to sit down again. I had more of Madhi's memories to go through. This chrome thing he brought with him was worth a lot to someone. More than a lot. Enough to chase someone across the continent and gun down innocent bystanders. Not that a corporation would care about that too much, but the insurance payouts had to sting.

I splashed some more water on my face and walked uneasily back to the chair—and its man-eating upholstery—and sat back down. Once I reconnected to Madhi's tech, I ran his memories in reverse, starting from our encounter in the Armory. Before that, many of the memories I found were locked with fairly standard thirty-two-character passphrases. I might have been able to guess a few, or if I had the kay, I could have a thinktank figure them out. But, as long as the chrome capsule was on the other side of the lock, I could ignore them altogether. As I watched, I did what I could to guess Mahdi's position, and for the most part, I was able to trace his route back across the North American continent.

As I came to find out, the journey wasn't a constant sprint from impending death. There was a short and uneventful stint where Madhi took the magway under the Rocky Mountains. He got some sleep, a shower, and had a hot meal, all without interruption. Of course, corporate goons were waiting for him on the platform when he disembarked, but still, he'd had a peaceful few hours.

Ultimately, he'd been on the run for nearly a month, which was unheard of in our circles. Mahdi was usually no slouch either. Unless he had no other choice, he usually took the most direct route possible. If I hadn't just seen it with my own eyes, I'd have guessed that he took on another heist. Instead, ducking, dodging, and shotgun-decapitating wave after wave of corpsec agents turned that route into a meandering mess, which would definitely drag things out.

My review of his whereabouts finally concluded as I came to a memory of Mahdi casing an upscale lounge called Anchor's Rest. Blacked-out porthole windows sat beneath a lining of candy-colored neon strips of blue, pink, and purple. Subtle. Or perhaps not at all. I couldn't figure out what he was looking for, but Mahdi abruptly crossed the street and pushed through the front doors.

The inside was an intentionally distressed mix of nautically-themed decor and framed film photos. The one that caught Mahdi's eye on his way to the bar looked almost ancient. That sort of old-res blur that only true antiques could manage and still be charming. It was a city street packed with cars, in a time back before the buildings took over the horizon. Mountains played backdrop to a pair of banners that read. "ANCHORAGE! ALL-AMERICA CITY!" This was it; I'd found it. If I remembered right, the city was little more than a giant industrial cube now. Practically closed off to the outside world and almost completely automated.

Mahdi ordered a drink—something with vodka and fresh ginger— and made his way over to a table in the middle of the lounge. Even in the dream space, I could feel the tension and excitement grip me as he took his seat. Then the memory cut out. The image his eyes captured blurred and I was prompted for a memory lock. Unlike the standard locks I'd seen earlier, the rest of that encounter was hidden behind a specific recollection of events—in this case, a specific event. Which one was anybody's guess, and even if I knew, my own recollection of it would brick the whole thing.

Technically speaking, it could be cracked, but any adult making the attempt on their own would tear their conscious mind apart. Children could do it safely though. Relatively. Their minds are still plastic enough to make several psychological recoveries before needing to be retired. If I had money, and I wasn't born into one of those places, I could hire

Eggbasket® or one of their competitors to break it wide open. Since that wasn't an option for me, I skipped to the other side of the lock to see what I could find.

Mahdi was seated at one end of a glass table, enjoying his second drink. Across from him sat a somewhat diminutive man who didn't quite fit anywhere. The chair he sat in looked too small for him. The suit he wore was too big, with its sharp-edged shoulders hanging down almost to his elbows. That, in turn, made his arms too short for his sleeves. If it weren't for his aged, wrinkled face and bald pate, he could have been a kid playing pretend in their father's clothes.

The man shifted uncomfortably in his chair, and the lighting caught something I missed at first. A tattoo that was debossed onto the side of his head. Headcase Personnelle - Uunter - ID.NO. 68542-9.

He was a proxy. A mindless husk. Probably leftover from a thinktank insert. If their body was in good enough shape they were often reprogrammed and used as low-level couriers, cheap security, or expendable playthings. By the look of him, it was easy to tell which one Uunter was.

"Half now, half when you deliver. The funds will be deposited upon acceptance of the contract. The rest will be held in trust until the client verifies that the job is complete. Any questions?" the man asked, taking out an envelope and sliding it across the table.

Madhi leaned back and regarded Uunter for a moment before taking the envelope and peering inside. "No, we're done here."

Uunter didn't say anything else or change his position. His face started twitching like he came to the end of a recording and was playing the last second on repeat. His head tilted off-center, and his eyes roved around their sockets, independent of each other. Mahdi smirked at the man and finished his drink, tipping the glass up over his head to get every last drop. He chewed a bit of ginger, and as he lowered the glass, he saw a gun placed against the proxy's head. The slug burst from just below his eye socket, and a mist of blood and debris drifted in the air as his head slammed on the table and slid off onto the floor, leaving a bloody smear on the glass.

Mahdi lunged from the plush seat, making a diving roll for his bag and the briefcase beside it. A split second later, he was on his feet, sliding across tables and dodging startled patrons. Another shot rang out, barely missing him. The bullet flew wide and ripped a fist-size chunk out of a woman's neck. Mahdi stopped for a split-second to steal a glimpse of the triggerman before vanishing into the kitchen.

I rewound the memory and stopped it to study the gunman. The memory was blurry at first, but the more I looked at it, the clearer it became. He was of decent physical build but was otherwise unremarkable, average everything. Until his face came into focus. If I were at the bar at that moment, I would have dropped my glass in recognition. It was the circ. I grabbed a clip of the exchange along with any metadata I could get my hands on before shutting down.

My disconnect this time was much smoother, though I still felt a pang of paranoia clawing at the back of my neck.

"You find anything in there?" Eshe asked.

I practically jumped out of my skin. "Shit, you scared the hell out of me."

She was leaning up against her door with her arms crossed. An opaque, rigid plastic case stood next to her, bearing the faint outline of a person—or what used to be. She cocked a smirk and then pushed the body through the shop to an operating table a few meters from me.

"Well, did you?" she asked again, loading the body onto the table.

"Yeah," I sighed, debating whether or not to continue. "Mahdi took a job a little more than four weeks ago."

"And?" she asked, hurrying me along.

"One-hundred-fifty-million dollars. One-hundred-and-fifty-thousand kay," I repeated for emphasis.

Eshe stopped what she was doing for a moment and flashed me a look. A number that big was guaranteed to garner some sort of reaction. Not just from her. The fee was partially public. One of the few things that would be at the intersection of a person's private ledger and the public ones that wove through the world like leylines of data. Some of it was secured with tiered memory locks at some of the largest thinktanks in the world, but not all of it. Not if someone knew where to look.

"Dammit," Eshe muttered, trying to focus on her work.

I nodded. "They were probably looking into all contracts over a certain value. They tracked down the proxy that gave Mahdi the job and killed him too."

Eshe slammed a fist down on the side of the operating table and slumped her shoulders forward. "I told him a thousand fucking times. I told him the life you two lead was going to catch up with you."

I wasn't quite sure how to respond to that, so I tried to choose my words carefully. "Mahdi and I talked about that a lot. Neither of us saw a realistic way out, short of a massive score."

"There was always the next fucking score, the next job, the next run," she said, pointing at me. "But both of you could have left running behind any time you wanted to."

I got up out of the chair and jabbed a finger back at her. "Yeah? A couple of Eggbasket® fugitives with a year or two left before aging out and getting melted down. We can't hack memories anymore, and that leaves us with what else? What other options?"

Eshe didn't say anything. She just stood there with anger boiling behind her eyes.

"So we do what?" I asked. "Sell ourselves to a new master for skin, sex, or slaughter? Or do we take the option that Laden gave us, just like he did with you?"

Invoking her adopted father's name seemed to short-circuit some of the pent-up rage and whatever reply it was building. She sucked in a couple of plunging breaths and turned to look away from me. I followed suit and limped awkwardly in the opposite direction, intent on walking off as much of that frustration as I could in the confines of her little shop. There were dozens of salvaged screens on one wall, each one cycling through images of her clients, before, during, and after their procedures, something very reminiscent of tattoo shops.

In one set of stills, a woman had come in a few years back after some pure-body terrorists set off a bomb. Gruesome stuff to have to see firsthand, much less live through. Her left arm and shoulder were gone, as was the majority of the left side of her rib cage. Stemgel had taken and formed a thin, nearly translucent layer of skin, nerves, and blood vessels. It was thin enough for me to spot some of her vitals. The organs would definitely slosh around without bones and connective tissue to hold them in place. If she were going to try going through life like that, someone could kill her by accidentally bumping into her too hard.

Subsequent pictures showed Eshe taking a scan of her body, then growing replacement parts. Another showed the woman under an operating lamp with a fresh sheet of skin being applied. Finally, the slideshow concluded with images showing off the finished product. The woman's shoulder as an external structure that bore a mechanical arm of flowing shapes and color that looked more like a sculpture than a functioning limb.

I looked back over at Eshe and considered her for a moment as she quietly tapped on a hand terminal. She was gifted at this kind of work. Far better than a place like the Shiv deserved. She could have paid off her debts ages ago if she really wanted to. I had no idea why she'd stick around, not that she'd ever tell me.

Outside of the client area, Eshe had set up a series of privacy partitions to cordon off a number of makeshift rooms. A small kitchenette, a wardrobe, things like that. She'd repurposed the disembarking steps from a passenger tram. The yellow and black steps led up to a second story of sorts that served as her bedroom. Last, but not least was an antique wooden bookcase, surrounded on all sides by safety glass. The bookshelf, which was very expensive on its own, held the collection of Laden's journals and several antiques that Eshe occasionally accepted as payment for her services.

I knew almost everything stored there by memory, and it was an impressive collection. A marble chess set with real polished wood pieces took up most of a whole shelf. Its parts lay in an arrangement of an unfinished game between Eshe and Laden. The last one he'd ever tried to play before his brain bricked. It sat beside Eshe's two circuit racing trophies and a photofilm of her, Laden, and her rust-bucket cycle. She stood there, bruised and battered, with scraped-up race armor, and smiling as wide as I'd ever seen. Laden was leaning up against the bike, arms crossed, and nothing but pride on his face. I remembered taking the picture for them. It was a bittersweet memory that I'd always hold onto.

The remaining shelves housed a considerable collection of books. Many of them were older than I could guess, and I wasn't familiar with most of them. In the midst of them, though, was my favorite book. It used to belong to me until I traded it for my leg reinforcements.

"Shit, that was stupid," I said aloud to no one.

"Still mourning the loss of your holy book?" Eshe teased as a simple tattoo machine whined to life.

"You going to keep making fun of it?" I shot back without turning. "That man was a visionary."

Eshe made a noise to sound like she was listening, but she wasn't too focused on whatever she was drawing on my future body.

"Hey, you better not be drawing a dick on me," I demanded, making my way back to her.

"Awww," she complained. "How come? Don't want to be reminded of what you're about to lose?"

That made me pause for a second, and my steps slowed as I gave her a wary look.

"Oh, c'mon you big baby," she chided. "Come over here. It was the best I could do given the time constraints, but I think you'll like her."

I took smaller steps and I resumed my approach as if one stray footfall might set off a landmine on the way there. There was some part of me that was curious and excited about getting the swap. It was an expensive, potentially traumatic process, that I never would have managed in my lifetime. But there I was with such an opportunity right in front of me. Not only that, but it was a necessity, which was a half-decent excuse to assuage the guilt that was mounting for feeling all that giddy, nervous energy.

"So, what did you end up with?" I asked, trying to push all those emotions away.

In answer, she peeled back the sheet covering the body. She was plain but pretty with pale skin dusted with freckles. She has a hacked-up blaze of orange hair clung to her like a permanent case of bedhead. What remained of her body was petite but toned, the gift of youth and good genetics. Each of her arms and legs were stumps. Three of her limbs had long since healed over, but the last one was still fresh. The tattoo machine whined again as Eshe went back to work, finishing up a featureless, black tattoo band around her mid-thigh.

"The hell happened to her?" I asked.

She shrugged. "I dunno. If you look close enough at the most recent wound the soft tissue was cleaned away from the bone. Then the limb was taken off with a metal file, antemortem. Then her throat was slit."

I shot Eshe a very concerned look. "What on Earth are you getting me into here?"

"What the fuck do you want from me?" Eshe snapped. "You know how hard it is to find a body at all last minute like this? Much less one that will line up with all those tube-grown bells and whistles of yours, so you don't ghost on insert?"

"No, it's not..." I started, debating how to walk back my words. After a moment, though, I gave up.

She was right, of course. Beggars couldn't be choosers. If this body had trouble following her too, I'd have to deal with it—if and when it came up. Hopefully, it didn't. I forced myself to take a few steps closer to look her over and watch Eshe work.

"What's with the tattoo?" I asked, trying to change the subject.

"That's partly why I got her for such a bargain," Eshe explained. "She came in with the letters V-E-T-O carved into her thigh."

"Veto?" I asked, trying to puzzle out a possible meaning. "Somebody's name?"

"Veto is an archaic term for disagreement," she said, disassembling the tattoo machine for cleaning. "Something like that anyway. The vendor was really jumpy. Like he'd done something to piss someone off. Thought this body was a message."

I gave the body another nervous look and rubbed my face. "Last question, then I'll shut up. What are you going to do for prosthetics?"

"Most of what I have in stock is already spoken for," she admitted. "But I do have some pieces I've been working on. Experimental shit."

I started to protest. "Eshe, you don't have to—"

"Yes, I do," she interrupted. "Look, you're going to need prosthetics one way or the other, and I need you to get the fuck out of here sooner rather than later. Can't wait around for parts, so you get what I have on hand. And since you can't pay, you get to be my guinea pig too."

"But," I tried again.

"Bitch, shut the fuck up and get back in the chair," she spat.

I gave her a resigned look and did as I was told. The worn old leather creaked as I sat back down and settled in. Eshe reconnected my IV and gave me a disgusted look as she did. Then she replaced the old bag with a new one labeled *Salt & Pepper*. I'd known a few people who had gotten swaps, and this was one of the only things I knew to expect. To effectively move a person's consciousness between bodies, their mind needed to be chemically excised. The easiest way to do that was to use a cocktail of psychotropics. In this case, mixed in a saline solution.

As I drifted into unconsciousness, I listened to Eshe tinker with something out of view. She was going to have to work on my new body before jumping me over. Metal clanged together, then she cursed and tossed something across the room. From the sound of it, she had her work cut out for her. Which was fine, I had my own work to do as well.

F O U R T E E N

EXTRACTION

I wasn't what most would consider well-educated, even by today's standards. As a child, my mind was steeped in the meme machine and the collection of ever-expanding encyclopedias. I knew a little about a lot, and what little I knew about our subconscious was that—for a long time—everyone knew a lot about nothing. Dreams used to be the gateway to the mystical. Messages from our revered and worshiped ancestors, or perhaps from greater beings from beyond the realms of physical reality. For the more logic-driven, they were nonsense. Things that our minds used to experiment with outcomes and ideas that we might not have otherwise experienced. Fast forward to the present, and our dreams have been maximized and transformed into lucid playgrounds for the world-weary. A person could go to sleep and, in eight uninterrupted hours, experience entire lifetimes within the confines of their own mind.

The reason the whole human race hasn't gotten lost in its dreams is because such a level of control and clarity comes with its own share of dangers. People who spend excessive amounts of time in the dreamscape eventually succumb to mindblur and can't tell the difference between the dream and reality. They might hallucinate or expect that the rules of reality don't apply to them. There have been plenty of stories on the boards about people jumping off buildings, expecting to fly or forgetting that their ankles won't break when they land. Others will step out into the middle of a busy highway and expect traffic to stop for them. We all know it's a problem, but the dreamscape and all its trappings are too useful.

Given that I was born and raised to be a dream hacker, I was more than intimately familiar with the risks. More than that, a new body was going to bring a unique set of challenges all its own. Mindblur was the least of my concerns. Instead, I needed to minimize ghosting, which is a clumsiness brought on by residual memories of your old body. For most people, that might only be slightly annoying, but given all the shit that was bearing down on me it might be a death sentence. If I jumped between buildings and ghosted the length of my arms, I could miss a ledge and plummet to my death, or worse.

Eshe had sent me the new body's dimensions, so I hopped into what I imagined that would be like and started running. Mahdi and I had put together a randomized obstacle course a while back to help us develop better instincts and muscle memory. It usually took the form of an ever-ascending tower, winding back and forth, floor by floor, as it climbed higher and higher. Of course, practicing there wasn't going to eliminate all the risk of the swap entirely, but it would take the edge off.

Things usually started out simple. This time, beginning with an enclosed area leading to a sheer 5-meter wall. I took a running start, planted two steps on the wall, and reached for the ledge, coming up a few inches short. Trying again met with the same results. Gearing up for a third try, I did something different and veered to the right, toward the corner. I placed three steps—right, then left, then right again—on either side of the seam before making a flying leap for the ledge. My fingertips barely caught it, but it was enough to pull myself up.

I had forgotten what it was like to run without mods, so clearing each challenge took a little bit longer than it used to. Much of my skill was still present, but I had to make adjustments to account for the body's new dimensions and lack of tech. Despite that, I managed to clear more than twenty obstacles without much difficulty in less than ten minutes in dream time.

"I'm switching you now," a disembodied and godlike voice echoed from all directions.

This was it. There was no going back, at least until I figured out who was after me and why. And then maybe who was after my new body. Questions swirled in from the walls and literally filled my vision, becoming moving obstacles that were as tangible as the rest of the structure. 'Who killed Mahdi?' clipped through a wall forcing me to slide beneath the worlds. 'What's in the capsule?' and 'Why me?' barricaded my path forward, and I had to push each one back through the walls to continue. Several minutes later, through sheer will and determination, I was able to keep many of those stray thoughts out of my way and even managed to complete several more acrobatic challenges without incident.

My next hurdle was a series of vertical panels that floated over an open chasm. I would have to run across each panel before jumping to the next and repeating the process. It was a daunting task and would have given me more than a moment's pause in the real world with my old body. But here, there was no reason to hesitate. I leapt from the ledge and positioned to land on the first panel, but instead phased right through it and tumbled sideways into a brightly lit room paneled from floor to ceiling in white glass.

A version of Eshe stood a few yards away from me in a white lab coat, holding an old-fashioned clipboard. She wore thick-rimmed glasses, and her hair was long enough to be tied back in a loose ponytail.

"You gave me long hair again, didn't you?" she asked, annoyed.

I groaned and pushed myself up. "It just happens, I swear."

By the look on her face, she didn't believe me. "Uh huh, sure. Look, I'm just about done, but before I can wrap up I need to go over a few things. Starting with your arms."

I looked down at them and the faux skin I'd been imagining sort of just tore itself away from me in tattered little pieces, leaving behind the prosthetics Eshe had installed. They were as advanced as any I'd come across, and perhaps more. A mix of flexible and rigid materials, structure, wiring, artificial muscle, and tendon ran beneath panels of living skin, the culmination of which drew a series of dark, curved lines across my forearms and up my shoulders.

"The musculature is tied into your spine, which itself has been enhanced to help you control the weight of the prosthetics," Eshe explained with a sound of pride and satisfaction. "They should feel no different than a normal pair of arms or legs."

"Eshe, this—" I said, looking for the right words. "These are incredible. Laden wasn't kidding when he would call you a prodigy."

Her expression flashed with the recognition of her father's past praises, then the grief and guilt that followed, but they were buried almost as soon as they'd appeared. "That's not even the cool shit. There are ultrasound projectors in your forearms, which allow you to—"

"Wait," I interrupted. "Ultra-what?"

"Ultrasound," she said plainly as if that word alone was supposed to mean something. "It played out as a bit of a novelty when it was created. That is, until—"

"I don't need to know the whole history," I interrupted again. "Just need to know what they do."

Eshe chucked her clipboard at me. "Would you quit fucking cutting me off? Look, touch your thumb to your palm, right between your fingers, like this. Eventually, you'll be able to call them at will, but for the moment, this is the shorthand."

I repeated Eshe's motions, and a thin blade appeared out of nowhere into my grasp. I lifted my thumb away and watched the knife drift down, out of my hand, before vanishing into a small opening on my hip. I called the knife once again and closed a fist around it. The construction—while simulated right now—was a finely crafted amalgamation of graphene, titanium, and ceramic. Heavy in all the right places.

"There are eight knives in total," she continued. "Four stored in each leg. Each knife is tuned to the ultrasonic manipulators in your arms, which, in turn, allow you to move and position the knives anywhere within three meters. It's kinda like having extra arms, and will take a lot of practice to get used to, but give it time."

While she explained, I shifted my hips to get a good look at my legs. At first glance, they appeared to have the same pattern of curves that my arms did; flesh-laden panels covering up bioelectronic musculature. Upon closer inspection, however, my lower legs and stilettoed feet were made from a collection of robotic shards. One would occasionally shift position or idly roll over a few others and slip into a new location.

Eshe interrupted herself this time. She was in the middle of explaining ultrasonic levitation, or something like that. "Those are microbots. They rely on the same kind of ultrasound I've been explaining—but on a different band—to adhere to a relay post that runs the center axis of your calf. They will react to your active thoughts and situation to give you, quite literally, the best possible footing."

"What?" I asked, absolutely mind-numbed by her technobabble.

She rolled her eyes and let out a harsh breath. "You'll just have to fucking figure it out."

Then she strode across the room, pushed her hand into my face, and shoved me backward off my feet. I fell and hit the white glass, which erupted around me in waves of shattered, razor-sharp pieces and water. Clouds of green, then blue, then violet, and finally red swirled in my vision before finally being overtaken by darkness.

Returning to reality, I could have sworn that I'd been sleeping forever. I yawned and arched my interlocked fingers above my head, filling my ears with the sound of blood rushing past stretching muscles and popping joints. When I finally opened my eyes, I was nearsighted, barely able to focus on anything past my fingertips. My arms were so different. Even though I had just seen them what felt like moments ago, reality hadn't quite set in yet. They were real. This body was real, but it felt nothing less than alien.

Eshe stood beside me, a portable terminal in hand. She hit a few things on the display with loud, percussive taps, and the table I was on came to life and slowly tipped forward. It eventually tilted just slightly past perpendicular and forced me to retake my first, unsteady steps for the second time in my life. Everything felt off; this body was slimmer, the arms were skinnier, and my legs were clunky and awkward. I watched the microbots that made up my lower legs adjust their positioning as I leaned on one foot then to the other and back again.

After a few minutes, my vision returned in full, and I couldn't stop staring at myself—my old body—sleeping peacefully in Eshe's leather chair, its vital functions in the care of a computer. My chest rose and fell without difficulty as if my broken ribs had been my imagination. My dark, eye-length hair had been drenched in blood and sweat as a result of my escape. Even now, it clung to my face, nearly covering the cut that bisected my nose. My eyes were closed and motionless, devoid of dreams and thought and feeling. Looking at myself like this felt wrong.

"Shit..." I muttered.

I knew that it was me who spoke, but I had an urge to turn my attention to the other person who must have said it. My voice was a little hoarse at the moment, probably from lack of use, but otherwise sounded like the voice of an average woman in her twenties. Not super high or low-pitched—not much nasality to it, either, which I had to admit I kind of liked the sound of. Not that I was in any position to be complaining.

"Your perception is going to be fucked up for a bit," Eshe said, standing to my left with three pills in a small plastic cup. "As long as you remember you can't piss standing up anymore, you'll make it."

She handed me the cup.

"What..." I began, almost choking on the word. "What are these?"

"I'll spare you the ridiculously long names," she answered. "One is a short-term antipsychotic that should only last about an hour once it kicks in. The other is a mood stabilizer."

I glanced at the cup. "And the third one?"

"That would be a multivitamin," she said with an amused little smirk.

I downed the pills. My throat was dry, and it was a real challenge to fight the reflex to hack the tablets back up, but I held them down. Eshe looked satisfied at that and started working on her tablet again, this time focusing on the vitals of my original body.

A few acquaintances of mine had jumped between bodies like it was changing clothes. Thinking about it made me wonder if I could get used to the other differences in this new one I was in. Just as before, there was a part of me that was really, inexplicably excited about this. That other part, the one that made me feel like something was wrong all the time—as if I were always wearing my shoes on the wrong feet—was suspiciously silent. I seemed to have traded it in for a new part that felt like a thief, or at the very least, an imposter. This body's breasts, which clung close to its frame, weren't mine. The voice wasn't mine; everything about it wasn't mine. I suddenly became aware of a constricting tightness in my chest, and I began to gasp for air. I leaned against the cold concrete wall and put my hands on my knees as I tried to stave off the dizziness that washed over me.

I was aware, going in, that it would take some getting used to, but everything I did was disorienting. I wasn't thinking of this body as mine, only its or hers, or theirs. Then a stray thought that failed to check in with reality crossed my mind with a raspy, mad giggle.

When would this woman want her body back?

Eshe placed a surprisingly gentle hand on my shoulder. "Hey, you'll be okay. This happens to everyone the first time; just focus on your breathing."

I nodded at her almost drunkenly.

"Now, quit gawking at yourself and put some clothes on," she demanded.

Evidently, she wasn't about to let me catch my breath. But it was probably a good idea, so I shuffled across the icy concrete floor in the direction where my old shell was lying. I tripped over my new feet and nearly knocked myself unconscious on a tray table. Eshe laughed at me from her terminal and shook her head. I scrambled to stand up again. My cheeks flushed, and I moved quickly to start undressing my previous body. All things considered, that was probably the most bizarre thing I'd done all day.

She looked up from her terminal and cleared her throat loud enough to get my attention. "I meant that you should borrow some of my clothes, you idiot."

I looked down at my old self, at the a torn-up, bloodstained shirt that was barely hanging on and felt incredibly stupid. "Right, of course, yeah, I knew that." Then I padded off to Eshe's little bedroom to find something I could actually wear.

"Not that it's going to matter much, anyway." She let out a sigh and leaned into her screen as continued clattering on the keyboard. "Looks like your friends have worked something out with Vys. Your face is plastered all over the community boards."

"How much?" I asked, slipping into a white tee shirt. The design on it had a couple of sinister-looking books—teeth bared and salivating—on either side of a rainbow. Text between them said *The Tropes are Hungry.*

She took a moment to answer, and as I poked my head out of her room she whistled. "Seven-hundred kay. Sorry to say, you're probably not going to get your body back with an attractive figure like that."

"Why?" I asked. "Are *you* planning on turning me in?"

"Maybe?" Eshe said, her syllables slow and drawn out like she was pondering the question.

"Very funny," I shot back. "Now, where's a good place to go on ice?"

"I'm not so sure I was kidding." She stepped out from around her terminal and leaned up against it, hands in her pockets. "You owe me for the swap, and I owe some people. It could put me in a really good place."

I motioned at the expensive bookshelf that was filled with rare and expensive items.

"No, not those," she said. "I can't get rid of those."

"And you want me to give up my body?" I asked. "I was born into that one, it's still mine."

"It's not like you wanted it anyway," she countered.

"What...I...No. Of course, I wanted it," I stammered, trying and failing to cover the lie.

"Die with the one you were given, or live with the one you have," Eshe said like she was repeating a mantra. "It's your choice, but I can't keep the meatsack here. I'll also add that the second you or I start dragging your limp body through the streets, someone else is going to notice and make a move for themselves. Even if you get it on ice, how you gonna pay for it?"

I opened my mouth to respond, then shut it again. She had a point. Sure there were body banks, but you needed money first, and I—we—it would probably not survive the trip, given the reward. And leaving it with Eshe would be putting her at risk. I looked at myself and sighed.

I let out a resigned breath. "If we do this, I get half. Seventy-five kay."

"Fifty kay," Eshe replied. "Like I said, you owe me for the swap. A body like that at short notice and all those kick-ass parts come at a premium."

"I thought you were giving me those," I protested.

She barked out a laugh. "Giving, yes. For free? Absolutely not."

I bit back an angry reply and I ran a hand through my not-hair, thinking for a moment. "Fine. Fifty kay. So what's the plan? Drag me out and say I was found dead in an alley?"

"No," Eshe answered, once again drawing the word out in contemplation. "Like I said, hauling a body around is time-consuming work, and it makes it easy for someone to gank us. No, we use a bot."

Without further discussion, Eshe went about collecting a few things from around her work area, counting things on her fingers like they were on a mental list. She was talking about turning my body into a techno-zombie. I was speechless. In principle, if this were someone else, I would agree with Eshe's take on the situation. But this was my body. When I showed up at her door, I had every intention of making this temporary. Hadn't I? The more I thought about it though, the more I came to realize that Eshe was right. People—more than just mercs—were bound to be looking for me soon if they weren't already. I immediately thought of my encounter with Ragna and winced. She was going to play me like one of her other pawns if I didn't make a move of my own. This was it.

"Hey, I'll be back in a bit," Eshe said, grabbing a few plastic crates on her way out the door.

I took a deep, trembling breath and looked up at Eshe. Her hand was firmly on the door, ready to push it closed. I must have had a nervous look on my face to match because Eshe glowered at me.

"Don't be a whiny little bitch. I'm not turning you in," she growled. "You can't wear your old clothes, obviously, and mine won't work for you long-term, so I gotta go pick some up. And you wouldn't have the faintest idea what to get anyway. Take some time getting used to those new legs and try not to knock yourself unconscious while I'm gone."

The door latched with a solid thunk, leaving me alone with myself. With her gone and only my husk and my thoughts to keep me company, the room felt entirely too empty. How in the world did I get into this mess? What were the odds that I was there as Mahdi would be passing— no—escaping through that bazaar? I wasn't feeling particularly good about anything, but those questions certainly didn't improve my outlook.

"Not going to find a way out of this standing here like an idiot," I said out loud to myself. "You're a runner. You take open doors as you find them, and if worst comes to worst, you make a door."

Instead of heeding Eshe's expert advice, like a sane person would have, I sat down at her terminal. My fingers pecked at the keys inexpertly, slowly clacking in console commands to load a behavioral compiler. Thank the programming god that this thing opened up to something other than a command line. I was no coder. Couldn't tell you the difference between a semicolon and a Greek question mark, but I can work a GUI as well as anyone else. That made it easy to start dragging basic if-this-then-that commands around on the touch screen. I had a picture in my head of being tied to a chair and interrogated, then used that to record some animations and dialogue trees. I even threw in some involuntary twitches. I was definitely proud of myself.

Since Eshe still wasn't back, I got up and moved to an open space in her workshop. I started with a bunch of simple coordination exercises. Walking, running, jumping back and forth over a seam in the concrete floor. I only slipped or lost my footing a dozen times or so, which was sure to fill out a new collection of bruises. Still, it was better than I expected. I kept at the routine until sweat had soaked my hair and poured down into my eyes. I'd completely lost track of time when the door slid open unexpectedly.

There was little more I could do than freeze in place, unsure of how to react, but I relaxed when Eshe walked in with that pair of stacked plastic crates she left with, filled to the brim. She balanced them between one arm and her chin as she dragged the door shut behind her and locked it. Turning back to me, she took the crates to the couch in the waiting area and started sorting through them. I padded over to investigate and was handed bits of clothing with little to no explanation. Of course, I knew what each piece was, but being handed a bra, panties, shorts, and a shirt all at once would be enough to surprise anyone.

I carried the pile over into Eshe's living area and started to change. Sweat-drenched clothes peeled off in a gross yet satisfying way, like pulling the plastic film off a new pane of glass. I let them plop down on the floor, then went about getting the new outfit on. Pulling the sports bra down across my sweaty back was a bitch, but otherwise, it didn't seem too different from what I was used to. Once I was done, I gave myself a look in the mirror. Eshe had done a good job. All in all, the clothes were tighter and more sculpted than my old ones had ever been, but I really liked the feel. I tossed Eshe's loaners into her laundry area then took a few confident strides out into the work area.

"So? How does it look?" I asked, unable to keep a giddy little grin from my face.

I did a little twirl on one foot and came back around to find Eshe holding something out for me. It was a jacket, similar to my old one, down to the magnetic and bullet-resistant linings. It was cropped short, hanging down to just above my natural waistline, but it was perfect. It was all so perfect.

"Thank..." I said, getting a little choked up. "Thank you."

Eshe, for her part, just rolled her eyes. "Don't start getting all euphoric on me there, Cinderella. We've got shit to do." With that, she turned and went to the terminal I'd commandeered earlier.

"I tried scripting a few things," I said, following her over.

Eshe tapped a finger to her chin as she inspected my work. "Yeah, not half bad either. For a script kiddie." She studied a bit more, and pointed at the screen. "You've got a few muscle twitches here that are going to loop around and get more frequent each time. People will think you're having a seizure."

"Whoops," I added.

She waved at me absently. "No, it's alright. You at least documented everything, so this shouldn't be too bad."

Her brow furrowed in concentration and her fingers erupted in a mechanical clacking fit across the keys. She was done a few moments later, loudly striking the return key like it was the punctuation of a sentence. As she did, I saw my body—or rather, my old body—stir itself awake in the chair. I struggled against my injuries to get up, but finally got out to my feet. I watched myself walk awkwardly across the room and come to a stop less than a meter from me. It was like looking into a mirror, but seeing the wrong thing. I stared into my eyes and didn't see anything behind them. No vibrant life, no defiant but exhausted soul, nothing at all. There was nothing more than programmed involuntary eye movements. Secretly I wondered if that's what I looked like normally.

"So how are we going to turn myself in?" I asked without averting my mirrored gaze.

"Well, to start with," Eshe said, bottoming out a few of the keys on her keyboard, "you're going to stab it."

I blinked a few times then turned to give her a confused look.

She looked up at me and started counting on one hand. "First, you need to do something drastic that slaps your consciousness into realizing that you're not in that body anymore. And, second, we need to turn it in like we put up some kind of fight."

"It?" I asked.

She nodded. "Yup, it's not you anymore. No consciousness and therefore no concept of identity. An object, and thus, it."

I reached both hands up over my shoulders and let out a long breath. "Fine, whatever. I'm not stabbing it though."

Eshe sighed and pushed herself up from the terminal. She rounded the table and pulled a small folding blade from one of her pockets. "Oh, you're going to do it."

Her tone slid across the room like the lit fuse of a bomb, but I held onto my stubbornness. "Are you insane? I could kill it, then I'd never get it back."

She didn't argue. Instead, she simply knocked me clear off my feet and drove me to the concrete floor with her free hand on my throat. She squeezed my neck, just barely cutting off my air. "You need to understand something," she growled. "The second you came here, begging for my help and bleeding everywhere, you made yourself my bitch. Make no mistake, regardless of our history, right now you are a charity case. And worse, a liability."

No matter how those words may have hurt, I needed to breathe. I could process our relationship later. So, I fought her, trying to break her grip and force her away at once. She released me, and I pushed myself away from her on my ass and elbows. Once I was at a safe distance, I rubbed my hand over my throat. That was definitely going to leave a mark.

Eshe, for her part, stood back up and watched me for a moment. "Now, you're going to get up and stab your old body. Your consciousness needs to understand that it isn't you in there anymore. You need to see that it's not you." She pulled a small machine pistol from a holster at the small of her back. "And if you don't, I'm going to shoot both of you and save myself a lot of trouble."

I glared at her but pushed myself up and walked over to my old body. She held out her knife but I didn't take it, instead choosing to use one of my own to do the job. My face—my old face—was decidedly neutral. Neither happy nor sad, nervous nor confident. It simply was. Was I really prepared to do this? Not just this but everything that came after. I'd been chewed up and spit out. Injured to the edge of belief. Given enough time, though, and some serious medical attention, I could survive all that. But that wasn't my reality. I had this figurative monster hunting me down, and I had one real option: change or die. Adapt or go extinct.

Those thoughts bounced around in my mind for a bit as I tried to find it within me to commit to this. It's an odd thing, being able to jump bodies. There was once a time when a person was stuck in their own skin. A lot of people died needlessly, especially when the first synths became prevalent. So many were bound up by the question: Am I still me? No thought was given to the fact that many millions of people were essentially choosing to commit a long and drawn-out suicide by cancer or some other disease instead of leaving their original, failing bodies behind.

It was the Dark Ages.

Eshe took a quiet step toward me and placed the barrel of her gun against the back of my head. Some part of me wanted to split out of my skin and slink away to some quiet corner of the world. But I gathered my fraying sanity and took a deep breath. Letting it out, I thought about what Jin told me. There were a lot of things I couldn't control, but I had an opportunity now, and I could control what I did with that. So, I repeated the motions that Eshe showed me to summon one of my new knives.

"No more in-betweens," I muttered.

Then I struck, driving one of the blades forward at my old body, aiming for somewhere non-lethal. As it drove home, I felt a phantom sensation plunge into my side. I sucked in a breath and stumbled back a half-step. Out of reflex, I held my side where the blade would have been, and stared back at myself. Involuntary twitches of pain were playing across its body. Alarms were going off, but nobody was listening.

"It's not me," I muttered. "Not me... not anymore. I'm still here."

I repeated those words a few times until they started to lose meaning. The phantom pain lessened each time I did until it had all but vanished.

Taking deep, plunging breaths, I removed the blade, and shot a glance over my shoulder. "There, I did it, are you fucking happy?"

Her eyes met mine, and I saw that it was all an act. Her aggression. Her words. Everything. She was trying just as bad as I was to separate herself from me. From the shape of the person she'd known nearly all her life. At that moment, she wanted to make sure I was really here in this body, and not the one that was being marched off to an uncertain fate. I caught the slight curve of a smile at the corner of her mouth and somehow knew that she was proud of me.

"I'm sorry," she said, finally breaking the silence. "You needed to find the will to do it, even if it meant giving you a push."

Eshe stepped around me and threw a dark hood over my old face. Then she hauled my homebrewed proxy across her place and opened her door once again.

Opting not to carry it into the lion's den with me, I hid my pack in Eshe's living area. Then I rushed out and fell in line behind, taking slow steps out of the shop and back into the alleyway. There was a sudden vulnerability that settled into me that was completely unfamiliar. Like someone would see me for what I was and come to unmake me, all in spite of my persistence to remain very much alive. It was a primal sensation that had me checking the rooftops for waiting predators as we made our way down the alley.

"Where are we headed," I asked, trying not to sound timid.

"Other side of the floor," she answered, slipping to the mouth of the alleyway. "The old Colony Atrium."

I nodded and made a mental note, following along, trying to get a feel for how this body moved in reality.

"So, what am I going to call you?" Eshe asked, interrupting my focus.

"I hadn't really thought about it," I replied softly, almost whispering.

"Well, figure it out," she said. "Thinking about using your old name just feels fucking weird."

As we stepped into the street we were almost immediately swept up by a wave of people that cascaded across catwalks and down staircases. We were helpless to the churn of humanity, but somehow managed to stick together long enough to make it to a small plaza on the other side of the fourth floor. There, the crowds split and flowed around either side of the semi-walled seating area. Benches and chairs sat bolted or welded to the floor in small sets of two, four, or eight. In their midst stood two groups engaging in an unspoken battle of posturing. The Vys brandished their weapons openly, joking, talking shit, and occasionally harassing a passerby. Opposite them in almost every way possible stood the suit-clad mercenaries. At a glance, they looked like they could be clones, what with their matching ties, data glasses, and haircuts. From where we entered the plaza, I couldn't see them wielding any weapons, though I imagined that was the point. If you appeared harmless the enemy could easily underestimate you.

The cold war between the two groups ended when Eshe, myself, and I broke from the foot traffic and entered the community area. Leaders from both sides spoke to their people who collectively came to attention and monitored our approach.

"Hey!" Eshe called out, waving one hand. "This the asshole you been looking for?"

"Here goes nothing," I muttered.

The three of us stopped, and Eshe gave the old me a solid push, sending it tumbling to the ground. I tried not to jump as a phantom sensation of concrete slapped me in the face. A detachment from each group—Vys and merc alike—broke away from the others and started their approach. The bot tried to get up, but the restraints made its movements stutter in odd robotic spasms. I gave Eshe a nervous glance, which she returned, followed by a slight, conceding, nod. With that, the two of us hauled my body back to its feet. Thankfully, nobody seemed to notice.

The first of the approaching people to speak was the Vys leader. At the moment, he had some writing in neon scarlet scrolling up his chest and over one shoulder. Every so often, I caught breaks in the pigment where scars had healed over.

"How'd you find him?" the scar asked.

Eshe cocked one hip to the side and gave a performative smirk. "Well, the fucker found us, if you can believe it."

She slapped my ass for effect and I tried not to yelp in surprise.

She continued. "Was in the middle of giving my girl here the ride of her life when this asshole came crashing in through our window. He went after me first, demanding kay and some wheels or something. Instead, she pulled a knife and almost pinned him to the wall."

I felt, rather than saw, the people turn to give me a look for the first time. I was too busy staring at my feet, trying not to panic.

"Nice metal," one of them said.

"Oh, uh... thanks," I responded, only glancing up slightly.

"We were about to kill him when the bounty came up on the boards," Eshe added, reaching out to tug the hood off and reveal my former face, all beaten and bloody as it was.

The contingent conferred with one another momentarily, just out of earshot, occasionally glancing at all three of us.

"Where's the bag?" one of the mercs asked, finally.

Eshe and I looked at one another, and I shook my head. "What bag?" she asked.

He seemed a little annoyed at that. "He was carrying a bag when he came in here. We're after the contents."

"He didn't have it on him," Eshe lied. "But he'd just gotten patched up somewhere; could have stashed it there."

"Without the bag, he's worthless," the merc said, turning and starting back toward his group.

"You never mentioned a bag in the post," Eshe blurted out. "Just him."

The pair of suits stopped in their tracks and looked at one another before glancing over at the two Vys leaders. They looked none too pleased and glowered back at the mercenaries. This was Vys turf after all, and they were not about to let some newcomer—and a guest no less—short-change one of their people and get away with it. The optics of it would make them look weak, and that was simply unacceptable.

"You weren't specific. That's on you," Scar bellowed, taking a step forward and raising his gun slightly. "Interrogate the prisoner or put out a new bounty, but you are going to give them what's been promised."

The merc's face soured into a snarling scowl but didn't say anything. He just whipped around and stomped over to Eshe and threw a crumpled-up semi-plastic sheet at her. "Fine, take your damn money. I don't feel like getting in a shootout with these rainbow brights."

Then he took the bot-me by the arm and forced me to follow him a few meters away. He whipped me around, drew a matte-black compact machine gun from his jacket, and fired a controlled, three-shot burst into my forehead. Bot-me's former brain matter splattered out the back of my skull onto the crowds passing by. I tried not to be sick. Even Eshe looked surprised.

Most of the people caught in the plume of human debris were completely unfazed and continued about their business as if nothing had happened. Some slowed their pace to irritatingly wipe bits of me from their clothes, all while managing to cast dirty looks at my corpse. Like it had—like I had—just spat in their face.

My body had barely settled into a crumpled heap on the ground when the first of several scavengers broke from the crowds around us. Clothes and boots went quickly. It didn't seem to matter how blood-soaked or torn up they were. A pair of women got into a brawl over my old jacket and settled for one ripped half each before stomping away. Then the knives came out, and all I could do was watch, as I was carved up like a butcher's showcase window. Valuable organs, bones, and eyes, to name a few, were all stripped right in front of me.

Transference being what it was, I almost felt the cold steel of the gun against my head, the air that was now whistling through the holes in my face, or the scavs picking my body clean. My heart was pounding and I thought it could have come ripping out of me at any moment. My eyes started to blur, and my whole body shook. The mix of adrenaline and terror had settled in for the long haul, and I was going to need some serious antipsychotics to help take the edge off. Then that desire to run became a dire, animalistic need. So, I did the only thing I could. As the Vys and mercs returned to their respective groups, I stepped backward, contained the screams that were trying to claw their way out of my throat, and vanished into the flowing tides of humanity.

FIFTEEN

BLURRED LINES

I wandered around aimlessly for I don't know how long, letting the currents of people direct my path. I was lost in a fog. Memories of my life were playing on repeat in my head, interspersed with an endless deluge of intrusive thoughts. I don't know what I should have expected. I wasn't special but somehow managed to convince myself that I was precisely that. They were never going to interrogate me, not when that circ could just follow my trail. They just wanted to make sure my life was punctuated with a capital dead so there'd be no more running.

Did I actually think that I'd go for a short stroll in this body and then hop back into mine when this shit show was behind me? God, I had to have been some sort of idiot if I believed that. I was dead, and there was no going back.

What would happen to my face?

I may have had it replaced before, but I could still recognize myself when I looked in the mirror. Its rough shape—the curve of my cheekbones, those brow ridges I hated so much, and myriad other details—made it effectively the face I was born with. I'd transferred it from mod to mod as I built a life and reputation for myself. Jin, Vallis,

Ragna, Eshe, and so many others from my life before wouldn't recognize me now, and my face would fade from their minds. I started to wonder if it would disappear from my own, given enough time.

Following the person in front of me in a mindless trudge, I could feel the pulsing thrum of life all around me. I sensed the human herd, the people nearby sharing the experience of bumping into one another with each step, each time pretending not to notice. At one point, rounding a corner, I ran into the edge of a food cart. That was no doubt going to turn a nice shade of black and purple. It happened a few more times thanks to a new gait I wasn't used to and my spacial awareness being completely fucked. It was like someone came into my home and moved all the furniture one inch to the left, but in this case, what got moved was me.

Eventually, I didn't know when exactly, a direct pressure wrapped itself around my arm and tugged me back. I stopped and turned, more a reaction to physics than investigation. She stood behind me, holding onto my wrist with her right hand, and an injection gun in her left. I could see that she was talking to me, but her words were distant and muffled, only marginally edging out the white noise of the crowds. I could feel cold, corroded metal against my wrist, followed by the prick of several needles perforating my skin.

Drugs plumed into my bloodstream and everything seemed to slow, as if time itself was taking a particular interest in the two of us. The people around us first flattened into shapes, then colors bled into each other. Details were lost entirely to the flowing hues of greens and greys that dominated the causeway. Then in an instant, time continued on its way, color and detail returning to their proper places, and the cacophony of mankind flooded its way back into my ears.

"Hey," she said, snapping her fingers in my face. "Are you with me?"

I blinked a few times and focused on Eshe. She wore a mixed expression of concern and frustration. The kind that comes with being ignored. I looked down at her injection gun, a little confused. I couldn't read the whole label on the vial, but a moment later with more of myself returning, I knew what it was. The Tetra was now starting to course its way through me was going to war with my temporary dissociation. I looked back at Eshe and managed a nod.

She let out a breath. "Good. Now c'mon, we've got something to take care of back at the shop so you can get the fuck out of here."

"Do… do you think it's safe?" I asked, my words feeling a bit sluggish.

She waved the injection gun around. "Yeah, I was just there a few minutes ago to grab this."

As it turned out, once all my senses returned to me, I'd been wandering around my old stomping grounds. A part of the fourth floor that sat opposite Eshe's place and on the other side of the marketplace. It's different now, but back then people used to call it Neverland; a place where all the lost or abandoned street kids seemed to gather. When Mahdi and I escaped from the facility up on the tenth floor, we eventually found ourselves there, too. A thousand memories came flooding back to me all at once, from jobs we took, heists we pulled, and more. My first kiss and my first kill. All of it was enough to get me a little misty-eyed.

I followed Eshe as we wound down literal memory lane until we eventually came out into the marketplace again. It wasn't much further to her shop. As we got near to the alley's entrance, we felt more than heard, a dull concussive thump that made the narrow sidestreet cough up dust and bits of trash. Eshe turned a few shades of pale and crept ahead of me to peek down the side street. I stuck close.

"Fuck," she spat. "How the fuck did they find me?"

I winced. "I interacted with a few people on the way up here. Ragna, a bartender, and an elevator guard. We can probably rule out Ragna and her lackey, but the asshole at the bar could have told anybody."

"God fucking dammit, that one-armed son-of-a-bitch," Eshe cursed. "It's Goz, I know it. If we move quickly enough, we should be able to take them."

"Are you kidding?" I replied, finding my voice. "Even if we did, they know where you live now. You saw what they did to me, what they did to Mahdi. What makes you think they won't just send more suits after you?"

"You're not the only one who knows people in Vys," she whispered over her shoulder. "They wouldn't let that happen. Either way, we have to try."

I took a step back and crossed my arms. "No. You just got me this body. I don't want to throw it away when we could start putting distance between us and them."

Eshe backed away from the alleyway, set her shoulders, and whipped around. She put her weight into the spin and drove her elbow into the side of my face, sending me stumbling sideways. Next thing I knew, she had her forearm against my throat, pinning me to the wall. All the people walking by on the fringes of the marketplace didn't so much to cast a glance in our direction. It was none of their business. I looked at Eshe, and for a moment, I wasn't sure who she wanted to kill more—me or the mercs ransacking her shop.

She leaned in without letting up on the pressure. "Listen to me you ungrateful bitch. You brought these assholes to my home with a circ hot on your heels. I don't give a damn what you want, you are going to help me kill them."

I nodded quickly.

"Good," she spat. "And maybe once they're dead—maybe then I'll stop to consider what a selfish piece of shit like you wants."

She let up on the pressure and took a step back to let me collect myself. I wiped the side of my face and ran my hand over my throat. She slipped to the other side of the alley's opening, and the two of us peered down in the direction of her workshop.

We have no idea how many are in there, I signed at her.

As I said that, a lone mercenary stepped outside. He took up a guard position as someone shut the door behind him.

At least two, dumbass, Eshe signed back in sharp gestures.

Fine, I signed, *we do this quick and quiet, and then we get the hell out.*

Eshe nodded and, without giving her a chance to act first, I reached across the space between us and took her hand. Pulling her down the alley with me, I put on an excited smile and an eager bounce in my step. The merc outside focused his attention on us and muttered into his com unit.

A moment later he stepped toward us, one hand reaching inside his suit jacket. "Sorry, ladies, alley's closed, you're gonna have to go around."

"Oh, c'mon, don't be such a twat block," I complained and motioned to Eshe over my shoulder. "My place is just on the other side."

The guard's jaw clenched and he squared himself up against the two of us. "Then it won't be that hard for you to. Go. Around."

"Fine," I said, jutting my jaw out. "Let's go."

I took a step back, and feigned a turn, but instead ran a couple of steps toward the man and slammed my fists together on either side of his head. In the split second it took to move my arms, a pair of blades flew from their storage compartments and into each of my hands.

If you don't do a lot of killing, it's important to understand that each one sticks with you. The person doesn't haunt you if you don't let it. Only sentimental types really expend a lot of energy thinking about a person's family and friends. So much that they lose sleep over it, sometimes for months. Regardless of where you fall on that spectrum, everyone always remembers the details of the kill itself.

For me, it was the sensation of the blades pressing against the softness of skin, the stubbornness of bone, finally followed by a very swift descent into nothing. The man's jaw clenched as my blades scissored behind his eyes, and it was done. When the corpse fell to the ground, each knife came to life with a dull throbbing orange. They fizzled with the air around them as blood and bits of brain were burned from the blades' material, infusing the air with a hint of char and iron.

"I suppose I'll add a few more to the list," I muttered.

I kept my weapons in hand as I hammered my fist on the closed door. There was some audible shuffling on the other side before the door slid open. Another well-armed suit greeted me, and I pushed the knife in my right hand into his heart while sliding the one in my left into his mouth by way of his chin. I worked the leverage I had on the man's body to shield myself from a hail of bullets that two more mercenaries sent flying my way.

Once their magazines had emptied, turning my second victim's back into a pulpy mess, I pushed with both arms, allowing inertia to remove the body from my weapons. My plan was for some acrobatics to help cross the distance to the next mercenary. Instead, to my surprise, the stilettoed prosthetics sent me flying nearly straight up. I rotated enough to hit the concrete ceiling with my side, but the force of impact still managed to crack one of my ribs. Guns were reloaded as I hit the floor on the far side of the room.

"Ouch," I coughed out.

Eshe burst through the door after my little mishap, wielding the small, snub-nosed auto-pistol she pulled on me earlier. She placed a single burst into each of the two remaining mercs and made her way to Goz, who was remaining perfectly still. He was either in complete paralyzing shock, or some pre-neolithic prey instinct kicked in and told him that if he remained motionless he wouldn't be seen. Playing wolf to his potential rabbit, Eshe strode across the room with the fluid intention of a hungry animal and flattened his nose with the grip of her gun. He stumbled backward, falling on his ass and holding his face with his hand. He scrambled backward as blood dribbled out from between his fingers.

One of the mercs let out a wet cough and started to move. It looked to me like he was making a move for his gun, but I was not about to let that happen, so I scrambled to my feet and tackled him. Holding him face-first to the ground, the wound where Eshe's bullets had exited bubbled out of him in little bloody spurts.

The man twisted in agony, squirming around weakly to knock me off. "No. Please... You don't have to. Thesia doesn't have to—"

Soon enough, his strength gave out and he went limp. I pushed myself off him and checked his pulse. Still alive, and strong enough to answer some questions about who or what this Thesia was.

I only needed one, though, and he seemed eager enough to talk, so I moved over to the other downed merc. As I checked his pulse, all I could think of was Mahdi and the moment he'd been killed. Killed by these people. That's when I decided that I didn't need to check his pulse. So, I leaned forward and took his head in my arms. Cradling his chin in the crook of one arm and applying pressure with the other I wrenched his neck sharply to one side, feeling the popping snap of bone and spine.

I wish that made me feel better.

Leaving the corpse behind, I stalked over to the other downed merc. He was lying in a small but growing puddle of blood. I looked around the room for a couple of the things I'd need to wake him up for a round of twenty questions. As I did, Eshe started an interrogation of her own.

"The fuck is your problem, Goz?" she howled. "We had a deal, and you knew I was good for it."

When I first saw him, I would have pegged Goz to be a cold-blooded killer. Instead, he just melted into a groveling mess. He looked over at me as I crouched over the mercenary, his eyes pleading for help, and he actually started to piss himself. Of course, I offered no help, and instead went over to Eshe's terminal and snatched a length of network cable to secure the merc's hands.

"No," Eshe demanded, grabbing his chin. "You look at me. My friend over there may have left a trail of blood all the way up here. May have even led a circ right to my goddamn door, but they didn't have a choice. You did. You could have minded your own fucking business, and we could have been fine, but instead, you threw away a pretty good deal and fucked yourself out to some mercs for some extra kay."

She hit him again, and something cracked. He howled and pushed himself further into the wall.

"You chose to destroy my home, to destroy my life," she growled and wiped a few tears from her eyes.

Seeing that pain on her face hit home. If I was being honest, it terrified me. I'd brought all this to her door. I was ultimately responsible, and yet Eshe was choosing to take all of it out on Goz. He was going to bear the weight of all that hurt, and there was no way on earth that she was going to spare him.

"I should tear you limb from limb," she spat. "That's the fucking debt you owe me and Dad."

Goz erupted into a fit of gibbering that was tough to make out. It was a safe bet that he was pleading for his life, but Eshe only looked offended by his weakness. She'd corralled her tears, and instead fed it all to her growing rage. All until she simply peered down at this man with the wrath of an indignant god.

"Did your stunted fucking brain even consider who was going to finish this?" she asked, removing the bandage from his stump-arm, exposing twin bones protruding from stitched, puffy flesh. "There are a few dozen modders here in the Shiv, and I promise you that every last one would tell you to bring this to me. But I'll make it easier for you."

Without warning, she lifted the gun to the remnant of his arm and pulled the trigger. The bullet shattered bone and sent pieces flying in all directions. Blood and marrow sprayed out the back of his elbow, spattering the floor. Goz didn't even have time to react to the pain. He just fell limp without so much as a scream.

It was then that I interrupted while walking over to a rolling medical cabinet. "You know, I think I know what I'm going to call myself."

Eshe looked at me but didn't say anything, the anger draining out from her face.

"Raide," I replied.

"I like it," she said with little inflection. "You should keep it."

I found what I was looking for, took a few purposeful steps back to my captive, and stabbed the syringe into his chest. He woke with a painful, back-breaking spasm, and his arms strained against the cord holding them together. His eyes darted around, surveying the situation before settling on me. He clenched his fists as his eyes bore into and almost through me. What's more, he was wearing the loudest grin I'd ever seen.

"Hey, there. Welcome back," I started, crouching down next to him and trying to sound jovial. "You were about to start talking a minute ago, so I've got some questions for you. If you tell me what I want to know, you'll spare yourself a lot of pain. And you might even live. How does that sound?"

He didn't say a word, just stared and smiled.

I continued with my questions, trying to sound cheery. "No? Okay, well, let's start small. What's Thesia?"

Nothing.

"You sure about that?" I asked.

I stood up and placed a foot against his throat for leverage, then pulled his hands up. I held the edge of a knife against the index finger of his right hand. Without saying a word, I looked at him, giving him another offer to speak. The grin replied, silent and yet deafening against the white noise seeping in from the open door.

"Fine," I said. "Have it your way."

I pushed the knife down. It wedged itself between the digits of his index finger, separating bone and skin and sinew alike. Hand wounds always bleed a lot, and this one didn't disappoint. The steady fountain dribbled down his arm, staining his tailor-made dress shirt in red streaks. His eyes were wincing, screaming the agony that didn't seem to muster in his lungs. The grin remained, motionless and unyielding. His eyes squeezed shut for a moment, forcing out tears as the fingertip tore free. Then the situation changed. His inhuman smile broke with a quiet gasp that bubbled over into a laugh.

At first, it almost sounded triumphant, but as it grew louder and louder, it devolved into something raucous and ragged. This was not the same man who was pleading for his life a few minutes ago. His eyes opened wide, enough that it looked like his eyelids were just gone. They revealed black gleaming orbs, devoid of any white or color. They were reflectionless as if they had become two doorways into some dark, lost abyss.

He convulsed and twisted in ways that should have killed him, all without breaking free of my grasp. Bones audibly popped and splintered, but his rabid, wet laughing continued, unabated. In the midst of his breaking, he lunged at me. It didn't take much to step backward and out of his reach. I took several more back and away from the man, just to be safe. In the midst of this, Eshe had apparently stopped beating Goz to a pulp, and simply stood there, a little to my right, and stated in wide-eyed disbelief.

Blood welled up in the merc's eyes, pouring out in steady streams like the best horror movie makeup. That wasn't all though. As the convulsions continued, I could see his shirt slowly start to dissolve, overtaken by growing and bursting boils that seemed to spit and sputter like water on hot oil. The bits of skin and fabric that remained. He abruptly raised his arm, and I looked on in horror as it erupted into dozens of writhing strips. Each tendril trembled and flailed, sending viscous, coagulating blood in all directions. A few of these strips found the merc's dead comrade and tugged it a bit closer.

The laughing continued.

Eshe started moving first. She grabbed a couple of duffel bags and wiped a nearby table clean, sending its occupants clattering to the floor. She walked around the room with the speed of muscle memory, grabbing a mixture of keepsakes, mobile terminals, and other equipment before tossing them haphazardly into the bags. She left it to me to pack them in with some semblance of order.

I let out a sigh. Getting ready to run, against my will, again. And I was nowhere near ready to be back out in the world.

The sound of slick tearing and snapping grabbed my attention for a moment, and I immediately regretted it. The man I'd started interrogating was disassembling the corpse into its baser parts—separating vein and nerve from skin and muscle—before incorporating all of it into his own body. Five rounded points pushed against the skin on his shoulder before finally breaking through. They looked to me like fingers, and they fluttered to life, waggling backward and forward, showing nails growing on each side. I had the sudden urge to get sick and had to cover my mouth and look away before losing it all over the duffel bag I was packing.

How was this possible? What was this? It seemed more like something out of a schlocky horror flick than real life. But the sight, the sound, and the smell were impossible to deny.

Eshe hauled me up and gave me a solid slap across the face. "Hey, get a fucking hold of yourself. You wanna die here with that?"

I looked back at it then back at Eshe and shook my head.

"I didn't think so," she said, releasing me. "Now get your fucking ass moving."

I gulped and turned back to the duffel. The rest of the stuff Eshe gave me—clothes, tools, a portable terminal, and some cables—went in without much thought. The last thing Eshe left for me was my pack with Mahdi's tech and the cargo he was transporting. I slung that around my shoulder, forced the duffel bag shut, and followed Eshe out into the alley. I took a cursory glance back into the shop one last time as Eshe stomped away toward the exchange.

It was then that the right word found me. My eyes settled on it, the grotesque, as it clawed its way across the floor. Flesh writhed and bubbled and spat, leaving a trail of purple, congealed clot in its wake. It found Goz as he groggily returned to consciousness. He screamed as the creature extended an odd misshapen limb formed of former rib bones and raked at his stomach. Lean muscle tore open and vitals spilled out into open air. More tendrils flashed toward the poor bastard's face using bits of teeth to cut his face and bore into his eyes, retrieving each one intact.

My stomach started to turn again, and so did I. Down the alleyway and toward the fourth-floor exchange. The creature's laughter, which had devolved into a deep, resonant gurgle, shook the air in my lungs. The last thing I heard before joining Eshe in the white noise of pedestrian traffic was Goz's cracking, panicked scream calling out into the uncaring world as he was torn apart.

REDLIGHT

E she kept up a quick pace for a couple of minutes. It was a struggle to maintain. I'd stumbled into, shoulder-checked, and tripped over so many people that I was starting to draw attention to myself in a big way. I looked down at my hand for a moment and blinked as two pairs of hands—one larger, one smaller—clipped through each other.

"Oh, shit," I muttered and looked back up to keep following Eshe.

The only problem being, she was gone. I looked around frantically and couldn't find her. My heart raced, and I started to hyperventilate. Stumbling, I made for the edge of the thoroughfare and collapsed against a stack of plastic storage crates. All the noise. It was too much. I'd lost Eshe. There was some sort of monster tearing a man to literal ribbons down the alley. A circ was on my trail. I was ghosting. And there was too much goddamn noise. My hands found their way to my ears and all I could do at that point was scream.

Someone grabbed my arm and tried to haul me away. I put up a fight, slapping at the hands that had a firm grasp on me, but was unceremoniously dragged around to the other side of the storage crates. I was still screaming as a hand covered my mouth.

I bit down hard and tasted blood. An angry growl escaped beside me.

"God fucking dammit, stop screaming," she blurted. "You're freaking the fuck out. Stop screaming, open your eyes, and listen to me."

Just like that, I stopped, and the hand on my mouth lifted away. I could feel the hot dribble of blood on my face. My eyes focused out on the middle distance as my heart continued to pound.

"Good," she said. "Tell me three things you see, followed by two things you smell, and finally one thing you feel."

My eyes took a while to focus on anything, but eventually I answered. "A food cart, a mystic's tent, and a gambling parlor. I smell teriyaki chicken and burned seaweed. I feel..." I hesitated for a moment and turned my head to look at my captor.

Eshe had me in a firm embrace, my back to her chest. We were on the ground, leaning against the storage crates. She rolled her eyes but didn't try to hide her smile.

"You and that fucking sauce," she said, before her tone turned more serious. "How bad was it?"

I turned away from her to look down at my hands, all four of them, and waggled my fingers. Sometimes the real hands moved first, other times the prosthetics. Some part of me consciously knew that one pair was real and one wasn't, but I couldn't tell which.

"Is," I said, correcting her. I looked past my hands, down toward my two pairs of feet. "I've turned into a spider."

Eshe stared at me intently but didn't say anything.

"What?" I asked.

She blew out a breath. "It's bad. Really fucking bad. Your voice is drifting between its natural tone and a deeper one like your brain is trying to force your old muscle memory onto this body."

She pushed herself up, then hauled me to my feet after her. "Think you can walk?"

"Maybe," I said, taking an experimental step forward.

I was a bit wobbly but I managed. As long as I didn't look down at all my feet I seemed to be fine. After a few more steps, I looked back and gave her a pair of thumbs up.

She flashed me a nervous but hopeful smile. "Okay, let's get the fuck out of here. I know a guy down on the second floor who will sell me some Tetra. C'mon."

Eshe handed me one of the bags and took me by the hands. She dragged me into step behind her, and together we delved back into the crowds. She led us away from the elevator I'd used earlier, away from the marketplace, and deeper into the Shiv's center. Between all the identically cast concrete buildings and my current condition, it was hard to tell where we were exactly. But as we were about to cross an intersection, Eshe took a sudden step backward and pushed me back. She pressed herself up against the wall, and I followed suit.

"Fuck," she gulped. "Things have changed—"

"What?" I asked.

"Shut up and just listen to me," she said, tone even and serious. "If we want to make it out of this alive, we have to split up. Keep doing what you've been doing and get the hell out of here. If you do, get to the magway. I'll be waiting for you there."

I wanted to argue, but before I could protest, she let go of my hand and rushed into the intersection. And ran into someone, knocking them off their feet. I might have been ghosting to hell, but Eshe wasn't clumsy. She did that on purpose. As she righted herself, she turned to look down the street immediately to my left and bolted in the opposite direction.

Several figures ran after her, raising handguns and assault rifles in her direction, but only that. Brilliant strobing tattoos shifted into urban camo as the Vys foot soldiers passed me without noticing. Behind them, a couple of well-armed mercenaries followed. My eyes raced to follow Eshe as she made her escape, but she was gone.

I felt that panic from earlier start to claw its way back, but I focused on her words. Get the hell out. The magway. Sure, I could do that. It may have been wishful thinking at that point in time, but I clung to it and forced myself to start walking back the way we came. As I did, being forced to stand on my own, my memory of the streets started coming back to me in pieces. It was slow going, and I had to correct for a few wrong turns and bad guesses, but I eventually found my way back to the elevator and the triangular staircase that surrounded it.

Disappearing into the throngs of people trudging down the steps, with all that repetitive motion, turned out to be a halfway decent way to reduce ghosting. I wasn't as tall as I remembered, which would make it easier to hide, but that didn't stop my pulse from racing between each shuffling step forward.

After making it a couple of floors down, the people ahead of me started to slow down. Traffic jam. Standing up on my tiptoes to look across the empty chainlink-protected elevator shaft, I saw the cause. A pair of Vys and mercs came up the stairs, occasionally stopping people to take a closer look at them. I lost my breath for a moment, and quickly turned around and pushed my way through a couple of people before tumbling out onto the second floor proper.

I didn't have time to catch my breath and pushed myself back up. Taking a quick glance around immediately brought back memories of my childhood. The split-level market, the big auction house. If I paid enough attention, I could almost hear the auctioneers calling out bids. Or was that just my recollection playing with all the noise? I decided that it didn't matter, and continued forward. If memory served, I'd be able to continue my descent from another major stairway on the edge of this floor's redlight district.

I wasn't sure how long it took me to get there. One second, I was there in the market, the next I was walking into a neon rose-colored avenue. I checked my hands to find both pairs still accounted for. I didn't dare check my feet, and just assumed they were there as well. All of which meant that I was still tripping off my ass.

"Well," I muttered. "So far so good."

On one side of the street, just over a simple concrete railing, delivery drones zipped through the open space that ran up the middle of the Shiv. As I walked, my eyes fixated on one stationary drone, spray-painting somebody's tag on a wall. The Shiv never changes.

Opposite that, dozens of mismatched buildings served as love hotels, sex shops, S&M clubs, and plenty more. Eager buyers and browsers alike coalesced around the bare bodies on display. At one stage, a lean young man in stockings and a corset danced around a pole. Every so often, he'd bend over and present himself to the crowd, long hair dangling over one shoulder and eliciting a few cheers from men and women alike.

On the next stage over, two women and a man played with each other in a noncommittal fashion. It wasn't a full-on show, after all, just an advertisement and a promise of what could be. For a price. Salt, sweat, and floral overtures of perfume wafted into the street. Whistles and catcalls flew out over the bustle of eager transactions. Vys were everywhere, but they weren't looking for me. They were here to protect their revenue stream. As long as I didn't cause any trouble, they wouldn't so much as look at me.

That didn't stop me from rubbernecking around, trying to watch out for any pursuing Vys or suits, when I ran right into the person in front of me. Trying to keep a low profile, I apologized and nearly ran into someone else as I slipped past. Rather than it being clumsiness brought on by ghosting, everyone had stopped moving. Even the people on the stages. Each and every one was staring out into the Shiv's open core in complete silence. I was afraid to look. A high-pitched scream in full Doppler effect flew past followed by a wet splatter on the ground floor below. Then more followed.

People—hundreds of them—were falling past us to the floors below. Most of them were alive. Others still were unconscious, but as seconds ticked away, fewer people fell past and were instead replaced with pieces—arms, legs, hands, parts of heads, and on and on. I imagined rats scrambling out of a building to escape a fire. A few of those still alive managed to fall awkwardly onto the railing that ran the third floor's interior edge, breaking bones but otherwise alive. Another man missed the ledge and tumbled past when a bruise-colored harpoon shot through his chest. It exploded into a thousand tendrils that tore the man into bite-sized chunks, leaving only a fine mist drifting through the air.

That was when everyone in the red light district on floor two of the Shiv began to panic. It wasn't mass panic, at least, not yet. It was the private panic that drove everyone within view to start walking very purposefully away. Everyone still had space around them and the agency to move within it. Agency meant options. Only when those options get taken away—when the only choice you have is to fill the person's footsteps in front of you—does mass panic begin to unfold.

If a crowd swept me up and carried me off, I was going to die for sure one way or another. Everyone was moving toward the closest egress in practiced fashion, either to yet another stairwell or to a lift. I worked against them, shifting from one pocket of vacant space to another. I tripped on myself or someone else a couple of times. Got unintentionally shoulder-checked a few more on top of that. Each time, I narrowly escaped being swept beneath the human stampede. When the people finally started thinning out, I made my way to the Shiv's outer edge, expecting to find an open sore in the structure's skin to escape through.

Screams and shouts echoed out behind me, and my pace quickened. A few people were on the street ahead of me, and a frightened couple rounded the corner behind me. Each of us must have had the same thing in mind. Gunshots came next as any Vys in the crowded exits tried to exert some form of control. A few people on the street broke out into quick jogs, passing me on their way to some far-flung corner of the Shiv. Maybe they were planning on riding out whatever was happening, maybe they were planning on some easy looting. It was hard to say, but you should never waste a good crisis. There was a part of me that felt the urge to take advantage of the situation as well, to grab a few things. Expensive items, just enough to fill my pockets. After all, what harm could a few extra minutes do?

As my better judgement went to battle with those ideas, I was treated to a montage of Goz, and what happened to him. All the blood and viscera that poured out of him as he was taken apart. That seemed to be enough to help refocus my thoughts. Looking around again, I started jogging to each alley and sidestreet I could find, looking for an easy exit or a place where I could make one.

One finally presented itself at the end of a residential street that was under some degree of reconstruction. Concrete and corrugated metal made up most of the structures to either side, empty corpses of former industrial buildings that had been recycled a dozen times over. In the street sat stacks of polymer extrusion blocks, reams of stick-on sheetrock, and spools of fiber optic cable. Some development company had their sign proudly posted at the start of the work area—something about luxury condos.

It was a relative term that sometimes translated to mean actual carpeted flooring and a separate bathroom. Of course, that was opposed to average apartments which were typically little more than simple concrete boxes with two drains in the floor. Hey, just because the Barrel was usually considered a shithole didn't mean that gentrification still didn't happen.

Passing the sign and crossing into the construction zone, I spotted what I was looking for almost immediately. The rust-covered refuse chute sat in the far corner of the work area. The immediate area surrounding it was completely clear of debris.

"Top marks for workplace safety," I muttered as I looked around suspiciously.

Normally, a work zone like this would be under twenty-four-hour armed surveillance, but at this moment it seemed completely abandoned. I would say that it came as no surprise, but the way construction companies operated, their security staff were usually numerous enough to be a small army. If not, they contracted with places like Cerali Incorporated, who were even more dangerous. I'd had a run-in with them once before and I'd rather not repeat it.

The couple from earlier followed me into the construction site, holding each other close, and shuffling along quickly like they were trying to get out of the rain. Whether they spotted the same refuse chute I did or just hoped I knew a way out, it didn't really matter. This was where we were. Three people trying to get out alive.

Pressing into the construction site, the acrid stench of synthetic gasoline was enough to make my eyes water. The workers probably only just left, and who could blame them? I could hear the couple—a man and a woman—speaking to each other in hushed tones. The woman sounded scared. I couldn't get a good look at either of them without making it obvious, but she was on the shorter side, slender with dark hair, and mismatched limbs. Not prosthetics, but actual limbs with different skin tones. It was interesting. It's a stupidly obvious observation, but most people who wound up losing arms, legs, or worse, would get prosthetic implants—like myself. What Eshe had given me was incredibly unique, but even the added utility that came with mass-produced models made them a no-brainer. Not sure why someone would replace their lost limb with another biological one.

Getting to the chute, I set down the duffel bag and wrapped my hands around the oversized handle. I tugged on it, but nothing happened. I let out a frustrated breath, shifted my feet, set my shoulders, and pulled again. It budged just a little. Evidently, the construction crew hadn't yet used the hatch, and the damn thing was corroded shut.

"Hey," I spat through clenched teeth as I tugged on the door a third time. "Could one of you lovebirds give me a hand here?"

The door budged a little more. Almost there. Maybe one or two more good pulls on it. I just needed an extra pair of—

Out of nowhere, something hit me in the back of my head. My vision dimmed and went blurry as I was wrenched away from the disposal chute and hauled back. My feet dragged as my head swam, and even though I tried, I couldn't put up much of a fight.

"No," I murmured, drunkenly reaching for the handle I'd been tugging on.

"Shhhh..." a man's voice whispered into my ear. "This will all be over soon. I've waited so long for this."

Then came one of the foulest things I could imagine. He took a deep breath, almost like he was savoring it, and dragged his tongue up the side of my neck to my jawline. The saliva trail on my skin felt like putrid rot, and every part of me recoiled from it at once. He had one arm around my throat and another around my left arm, but that didn't stop me from squirming and bucking to get loose. He used the leverage he had to haul me back and throw me into things—dumpsters, plastic barrels, stacks of concrete mix, and others.

"Don't just stand there watching," he snarled, barely hanging on. "Give me a hand here."

The woman he was with did as instructed; she slapped my awkward kicks aside and clamped her arms down around my knees. That bought the man enough time to adjust his grip, cutting off my air in the process. I started trying to hit him with my free arm and only managed to knock my knuckles on his. I didn't dare stop fighting, even as my vision faded, and my HUD flickered out entirely to save oxygen. In a moment of panicked insight, I repeated the hand motion that Eshe showed me, and a knife made its way to my hand. I gritted my teeth and swung my free hand over my shoulder. The blade must have caught something because the man sucked in a quick breath of pain. Somehow, though, he managed to hold on.

"Let me go," I demanded in a whispered snarl before swinging the knife back again.

This time, the tip of the blade hit home, cutting off one of his fingers, mid-digit, and stabbing my own shoulder in the process. He cursed and loosened his grip on me, which was enough to fight free of his grasp. The woman still held on, and, pulling the knife out of my shoulder, I swung the blunt end of the grip down at her head. She staggered to one side, and it was just enough to pull myself free.

I scrambled into a run on four legs and made for the hatch, and gave it one last firm tug. Finally, it opened with a grinding shriek of protest. I didn't dare glance back, a split second wasted could mean them grabbing me again. Whoever they were, they were not going to lose me a second time. So I dove through the opening, head first. A hand grabbed my ankle, and I was about to kick at the man again when the microbots that made up my legs just flowed around and out of his grip, sending me tumbling down the shaft.

I covered my head with one hand and reached out with my remaining limbs to right myself. Smoke rose in the air around me, and a thin layer of soot coated every surface I touched. Yes, that's right, at the bottom of every garbage chute is an ever-hungry incinerator. Amber light flickered up from below, and it was all I could do to not imagine cooking to death in the flames. My mind offered up visions of my skin blistering and peeling away before turning to charcoal or my blood boiling as my brain was sous-vide inside my skull.

In what might have been my final moments, I forced my eyes open. Even tearing up in the blinding smoke, I spotted a small rusted hole in the side of the shaft some meters below me, rapidly coming up. At the last possible second, I forced all four of my hands out to grab at the opening.

Me. Heights. And jumping from them lately. Fuck my life.

HEAD TRIP

One of my hands caught the opening, and the sudden stop whipped me around so fast that my shoulder popped out of its socket. I screamed. Tears carved trails down my smoke-stained cheeks, but I didn't dare let go. The metal ledge crumbled in my grasp, but I managed to get a solid hold with my other hand. Just in time for a chunk of the rotted steel sheet to break free. It made a lonesome, hollow sound as it bounced back and forth down the remainder of the shaft before finally landing in the incinerator.

I pulled myself up, gritting my teeth against the pain of having my palms cut over and over while I shifted my weight. The opening was maybe ten or so meters from the ground and I'd intended on lowering myself down carefully when I lost my grip. A split-second later, I collided with the incline at the base of the Shiv, which fortunately helped divert some of my momentum. That didn't stop me from hitting my head on something while rolling to a stop in the street.

"This is clearly not my day," I groaned, trying to shake off the impact and push myself up.

A few people who had gathered around me backed off as I stood. I was going to push one of them out of the way when I realized that my arm was nearly limp.

"Right," I groaned. "Dislocated shoulder. Goddammit."

I made a quick shuffle step for the closest building and slammed my arm into it. I snarled out a curse and fell to one knee as the pain lanced through my arm and chest before drifting into the background as a dull ache.

Someone had evidently gotten the authorities. Two Vys soldiers rounded the corner following a short, balding man hobbling on a metal peg leg. They looked more curious than aggressive, but I didn't wait around to explain myself. I just ran.

The magway, where Eshe and I had agreed to meet, was a continent-spanning mass transit system that connected all major cities in the 'Corporate States of America' —or CSA. If you timed it right, you could bounce from New York to Toronto to Chicago and make it back in time for dinner. In our case, we were going to the coast, to the oldest part of the city, Old Manhattan.

Our local hub was a ring-like structure, a good half-hour jog from the Shiv. From there, it would take several hours to be routed and rerouted through the larger network. My problem at that moment, however, was finding the right platform, and we picked a bad time to take the train. I wasn't privy to the schedules of departures and arrivals, but it seemed like the station had more people in it than air. Once I forced my way past the main entrance, I dug through the scores of people to a screen displaying a station map. I spent several minutes trying to make sense of all the concourses, escalators, and overpasses, but finally spotted the terminal for Old Manhattan. On the 6th floor, beneath the surface.

"Great," I said to myself. "One more floor, and I could call myself Dante."

As we had tenuously agreed to, Eshe was waiting for me. I was starting to worry that I'd missed the departure, so seeing her there was a massive relief. There were a few sizable blood splatters on her clothes that I hadn't noticed before. Seemed like she had to fight her way free as well.

"What happened to the other bag I gave you?" she asked.

"Dropped it," I said without offering any explanation.

"I figured you'd lose it somewhere along the way." Eshe smirked knowingly. "Good thing I kept all the important stuff with me."

"Hey, I can hold onto stuff when it counts," I protested.

"Yup, only when it's on a contract," she teased.

"I'm lucky I got my own ass out of there," I said. "Between whatever that thing was and some asshole trying to grab me on my way out."

"Merc? Vys?" She asked, adjusting to the change in topic.

"Neither, at least I don't think so," I said. "A merc would have shot me outright. Vys wouldn't have cared, not with that creature coming after people."

Eshe nodded, a hint of weariness in her movement. "I was on the first floor, headed for the exit when the bodies landed. Scared the shit out of me. I barely made it outside without somebody landing on me."

I looked at the splatters on her clothes again and sucked in a breath.

"But we both managed to make it out relatively unscathed," she said. "Let's get moving."

"Here's to not seeing any of that again," I said. "Onto Old Manhattan."

There's nothing in the world like going on a trip to someplace you've always heard about but have never seen yourself. Pairing that with the excitement of leaving an old, terrible life behind and starting fresh left me practically shivering. It was hard not to smile as we boarded and found our cabin.

Our room had a peculiar sanitized smell that teased a headache, and the carpet had a wet, spongy feel to it that clung to the bottom of your shoes. I didn't know why it happened right then, but I suddenly noticed that I could feel the bottom of my feet. That wouldn't strike anyone as out of the ordinary, but my feet were prosthetic and shaped like stilettos no less. I had kind of assumed that they would behave like any other pair of shoes and insulate my sense of touch from whatever was actually beneath my feet. I scrunched up my nose and pulled one foot away from the floor experimentally and could distinctly make out the sensation of peeling away from the surface. All things considered, that was a little gross.

The walls around us bore the grey, coarse texture of concrete that had been cleaned and painted repeatedly to hide stains and other mysterious remains. Eshe seemed content with it and tossed the surviving duffel bag onto the small cot bolted to one wall. Opposite the bed were two chairs. One was molded out of half-rotted plastic, and it looked like it might collapse into dust at any moment. The other seemed to be made out of converted wire metal shelving. Eshe took the metal one before I could get to it, leaving me with the cruddy one. After cautiously sitting on it, I leaned back to rest my head on the wall.

"Headed to the original city," I said to myself. "Never saw that coming."

I opened my eyes again, and Eshe was waving a book at me. My book.

"Holy shit," I said. "You grabbed it!"

"How about a thank-you?" she asked in an almost sing-song manner.

I greedily snatched it from her hands and flipped through the yellowing pages, wafting the smell of old ink and paper toward me.

I let out a deep, shuddering breath. "God, I love that smell."

"I don't know why you care so much about that damn thing," Eshe said. "I mean, I know it's worth a fortune, but you practically worship it."

"Did you bother to read it?" I asked, not sparing the sharp tone in my voice.

Eshe waved one hand dismissively, pulling out a terminal and setting it up. "It was fucking weird. You know they spent so much time trying to imagine what an artificial general intelligence would be like, and here we are, in their supposed future, and where are they?"

She made a 'poof' gesture with her hands.

"I'll give you that, but the man was still a prophet otherwise," I said. "The future is already here. It's just not evenly distributed."

"Just because you can look back at history and come to the conclusion that mankind tends to ruin shit doesn't make you a prophet." Eshe explained. "I've seen plenty of shit posts around the mesh about every Bill, Dick, and Robert that wrote anything back then. You know what I think? I think these so-called prophets should have imagined a better fucking future for us."

"It's not as if this book was responsible for the way things are," I said. "And it's not as if you don't have your own idols from the past."

"You're absolutely right," she agreed. "I do, but simply seeing a vision of the future isn't worth a damn if you don't act on it. Every single one of my heroes pushed or tried to push humanity in a new direction because they could see what was coming. Everyone else was so focused on the idea that we would destroy ourselves in one way or another, completely ignoring the human potential for change, that it eventually became a reality. Tell a lie enough times, and it eventually becomes the truth."

I shook my head and elected not to reply. Eshe was ready to throw down over this topic, and when it came to debating her, discretion was absolutely the better part of valor. Instead, I reached into my pack to retrieve the chrome capsule. It was still cold and held an ever-present film of condensation. My fingers glided over the surface, smooth and almost liquid to my touch, that is until my finger caught a small edge. I turned it around to get a closer look and found a small square opening.

"You find something?" Eshe asked, focused on getting her terminal hooked up.

"I'm not sure. Looks like some kind of connection port," I said, taking a closer look. "But I didn't notice it before."

My eyes caught the glint of something before it shot out about a dozen centimeters and started wriggling around.

"Oh shit!" I shouted and tried to lob it across the cabin.

The thing flew out of my hands, but something slithered around my arm, found the hardwire mesh port in my wrist, and reeled itself back to me. I lost all control over my limbs and my vision flickered like a bad bulb. I could still feel my body slump to one side and fall out of the chair to the floor. Except that never happened. As I landed, I simply phased through reality altogether, like I'd noclipped in a game. That momentum carried me in an endless spin through a black abyss for what felt like several minutes. Then finally, and I think painfully, I hit a pool of water.

Or did it hit me?

I couldn't tell.

I was submerged, and strong currents of water flowed around me, tossing me end over end. In no more than a moment, I felt the urge to gasp for air, but couldn't, which sent my mind whirling off in a panic.

Water poured into my lungs, and I tried to let out one last gurgle of a scream. Then, just like that, it was as if I had never been drowning. Instead, I found myself sitting at a table across from Mahdi.

His arms reached halfway across the table and cupped the base of the cylinder, holding it upright. I could see a cable running up his shoulder, connecting into the network port on his neck. He flicked his eyes down toward the cylinder, then back up at me. I knew what he wanted, but I insisted on staring at him. I was looking for something, a hint that there was more to him than just a memory or projection. He smirked. It was this kind of cockeyed sideways thing that he did whenever he knew something I didn't but wanted me to guess anyway. For the moment, especially since I didn't know if I was going to get out, that would have to be enough proof for me.

I reached out and took hold of the capsule, just above Mahdi's hands. When I looked up, he was gone. In his place was Uunter, the proxy Mahdi had met with. He sat there, slack-jawed, and twitched randomly. Then, the barrel of a gun pressed to the back of my head. Even though none of this was real, I instinctively froze in place. After a moment, I turned my head slightly to get a look at the wielder. The circ stood to my left with his shark-like grin and thumbed back the hammer. My pulse started racing, and I didn't want to see the bullet coming, so I looked back at the proxy.

Mahdi was back, and the circ was holding the gun to his head. Fire flowered from the gun. Mahdi jerked once, then twice, like he had in reality, all before his innards exploded out all over the table. I wanted to scream and run and get revenge all at once. I wanted so desperately to save myself from this maniac but also avenge Mahdi's death. The Circ, still smiling, turned his gun to point at the cylinder in the middle of the table and fired again. The gun erupted, and bullets ricocheted in all directions, without so much as scratching the chrome surface.

Then Eshe materialized in the seat across from me. Her eyes looked like they could set me on fire with sheer willpower. It was the same look I had seen when she attacked Goz back in the Shiv. It was directed at me now, and I could almost feel myself melting beneath it.

Then the gun was leveled at her head.

My perception slowed. I looked down at my arms, trying unsuccessfully to pull them free of the cylinder. Eshe was still staring me down, not seeming to take notice of the danger she was in. I screamed, and only silence followed. Then my skin started to slough away, beginning with my arms, revealing the mechanical prosthetics beneath. I kept pulling myself away until I could feel tattered chunks of flesh peeling off my face. I was prying away from my old body, willing myself to freedom.

Finally free, it was like I could breathe and feel for the first time. With that freedom in hand, I didn't hesitate to lunge over the table and hit circ at the waist with my shoulder, taking him to the ground. The gun went off. It didn't matter; I had him now. I threw my fists at him, hitting his face indiscriminately before stopping to pull a knife.

His smile never left him, even as I stabbed his face over and over again. Somehow I couldn't get rid of that goddamned smile. The bones in his head collapsed into shards, and uneven strips of his tongue writhed behind that unstoppable smile. I cut him, over and over, until there wasn't anything left, and it still wasn't enough. Not for what he'd done. I stabbed at the bloody pulp that used to be his head, near the top of his spine. The blade hit something metal and snapped, sending a piece flying off away from me. I moved to strike at the bloody mess again when I heard a choking sound. What I found was the broken blade of the knife lodged in Eshe's throat. She struggled for a moment, pouring herself all over the broken pieces of the cylinder that lie on the table. Her head fell loosely back, and she hissed out one final, gurgling breath. Just like that, she was dead.

How could this happen? I've been asking myself that a lot lately. I looked back at the Circ's body and dug my hands around in what used to be his neck. What was it that broke the knife? I needed answers.

My fingers sifted through the splattered remains of the Circ. At the base of his neck, just above his shoulders was a blood-stained object. There was no way to get a good grip on it. I was about to cut open his throat when the object birthed itself out of his esophagus, splitting it open like a burst pipe. My eyes locked on the thing, the cylinder, covered in a thick coat of red, and I lost my breath. My stomach twisted and heaved, but nothing happened. My head shook in disbelief, and I crawled backward. Away. Screaming. My stomach heaved over and over, trying to vomit, but failing each time.

Let me go. I don't want this anymore.

When I opened my eyes, it was all gone. Mahdi was standing in front of me, holding the cylinder in one arm like a child. He smirked at me again and tapped the index finger of his free hand to the side of his head a few times.

Then the nightmare ended. My eyes, blurry with tears, opened back into the cabin of the maglev car. I was on the floor, and Eshe, still very much alive, was only just rushing to my aid. I looked up at her, confused for a moment. I blinked and saw her retaking her last breath through a bubbling, ragged hole in her neck.

"How long was I out?" I asked.

"You literally just fell over a second ago," she said, confused. "What happened to you?"

"I don't know. It was like a bad dream." I sat up and rubbed my face before looking warily back to the chrome capsule, which was sitting on the floor next to me. No mechanical tendril, no opening, just an oblong silver object, rocking harmlessly to the motion of the magrail. "There's something in there," I added. "It went for my mesh port."

"Must have been fast, then," she said, "because I didn't see anything moving around until you just tipped over."

I didn't respond. Was I losing my mind? Too much trauma in one day, so my mind was fucking up? Had that thing really opened and plugged itself into me? I wasn't so sure anymore. I shook my head and got back into my chair. That nightmare seemed so real, but then again, we've been using the dreamscape to augment reality for that very reason. I thought about it a little bit and felt an odd sensation—maybe pressure—when I thought about Uunter. Even if I was going insane, I felt something pulling me back to that meeting.

"I need to take another look," I said to myself, stowing the capsule back in my bag and pulling out Mahdi's gear.

"Do me a favor?" Eshe asked as she settled onto the cot, arms behind her head. "No more freaky robot sex, okay?"

"You don't have to tell me twice," I said with a chuckle.

Eshe's terminal hummed to life, heatsink fans churning hot air away from the boards, and orange lines flickering over the black translucent screen. Once I was back in Mahdi's head, I knew, on an instinctual level, what memory to scrub to without thinking about it. I started my observation a few minutes before his meeting with Uunter. Like before, Mahdi had arrived early to scope out the place before finding a seat. He ordered his drink and, to my surprise, watched as someone walked through the door. I'd somehow passed right through the memory lock like it wasn't there at all.

Minutes later, Uunter arrived with a sizeable armored case and picked up the tab for any drinks that had already been ordered.

"I understand that courtesy suggests I leave the package at a drop for you somewhere else, but I'm afraid that I do not have the luxury of time," Uunter said, sweat beading on his scalp.

"I'm listening," Mahdi replied, careful not to offer any kind of inflection until he knew the stakes.

"Thank you," Uunter continued. "To start with, my client is being pursued by this man. He is someone you should be aware of."

He pulled a transparent plastic photo from his jacket pocket and slid it across the table. It was of a man with a full head of evenly greying hair and hard chiseled features. Mahdi casually glanced at it then back at the proxy across the table.

"So that's why you're here in the client's stead. Do I have that right?" Mahdi asked.

"No, not quite," Uunter replied with a programmed grin.

"How about you fill me in, then," Mahdi suggested patiently.

Uunter slid the case under the table to Mahdi. "The contents of this case need to be transported to Pardeq East, in New York."

"I'm familiar with it," Mahdi said. "By name and reputation anyway. Plenty of corpsec around to transport something between corporate offices, why a runner?"

"I have not been provided with that information," he said.

"Figures," Mahdi said under his breath while undoing the latch to glance inside the case. "What is it?"

"That would be my client," Uunter stated as if it should have been obvious.

Mahdi slid the case back across the floor and gave the man a skeptical look.

"What is your client?" Mahdi asked.

"You can call them Soqua," he said. "And they are the first artificially intelligent life form."

EIGHTEEN

MEETING WITH A HEADCASE

You're kidding, right?" Mahdi said. "An AI? Something humanity has never managed to accomplish is the best cover story you could come up with?"

I was just about as skeptical as Mahdi seemed to be. Uunter just stared at him, blank expression plastered to his face, waiting for the next programmed cue. Uunter produced an opaque plastic envelope from inside his ill-fitting suit jacket and slid it across the table. "Half now, half when you deliver. The money will be deposited upon acceptance of the contract. Any questions?"

Mahdi straightened a little in his seat and leaned forward on his elbows over the glass table. He checked the contents of the envelope, then studied Uunter for a while, seemingly contemplating the job. He ordered another drink. He tipped the glass back and finished it in one gulp.

"We don't have much time," the proxy said.

"Your kay is as real as everyone else's. It will spend, so I don't know if I care how bad the story is," Mahdi pondered. "Still, something about this doesn't feel right. I think I'm going to pass on this one. Thanks for the drinks."

Uunter was at the end of his conversational loop and started twitching like in my earlier review. Mahdi moved to get up, and in a sudden flash of movement, Uunter reached across the table and made a desperate grab for Mahdi's arm.

"Please," the proxy said, twitching.

Something about the proxy's tone had shifted. As Mahdi looked down at the hand wrapped around his wrist he noticed a small cable come from beneath the table that disappeared up the man's sleeve.

"Please," Uunter said again, tears forming around his eyes. "Afraid. No die."

Mahdi slowly sat back down and glanced under the table. It was only for a split second, but he spotted the cable retracting into the case. When he looked back up, the circ was holding the gun to Uunter's head. Then he pulled the trigger.

I stopped the memory there and disconnected. Back in the real world again, I leaned back in my chair and rubbed my face with my hands. I had to think about this.

First and foremost, I had just perused through one of my best friend's memories like it was my own. That was not something I could ignore. If I'd passed through it without having the key, I'd have been left drooling on the floor right then. How I got the memory key was an entirely different question, which was a mystery I was afraid to unravel.

Second, I now had some new details about the job that, apparently, Mahdi didn't want to take. The destination was Pardeq East. Running some quick searches on the name revealed a small and relatively unknown joint-venture specializing in biological mass production. They'd done some independent research funded by their parent companies—SucheCorp and Valkry Automations—for several years.

Eventually Pardeq found itself contracting with the newly minted Egyptian government. More specifically, the People of the Lower Kingdom—or PLK—who fought and won a revolution against a brutal regime about a decade ago. What Egypt and Pardeq were working on was hard to determine. Mesh-trawlers had found mention of a project referred to as FS, but little else. A lot of money and personnel had been invested into the project, but it was all buried under generic titles and descriptions. Whatever it was, Pardeq had put it so far down a digital black hole that the actual details probably didn't exist at all. My intuition was telling me that it was worth hunting a runner all the way across the continent to recover or keep quiet.

Pardeq operated out of two offices. The first, the 'West Branch' as it was called, was nestled in the heavily automated manufacturing mega-hub of Anchorage. The second office, or the 'East Branch', found its home in the Heights of New York.

Checking some of the boards in the area of Pardeq West, I found several posts about missing persons and some researchers that had been murdered. Pictures showed blood and body parts strewn about a cube farm. Mounds of eviscerated torsos so mutilated that they looked more like bloody rags than human remains. I stared at the image in disbelief for a while before I was able to identify parts. Pectorals, abdominals, and biceps—to name a few—each separated into their own piles.

What's more, there were no bones anywhere to be seen. It looked as if the spines and ribs had been pulled from the surrounding flesh-like food from a plastic wrapper. The Anchorage boards fell silent after that, just after midnight, local time. That was roughly two days before the west coast went offline. More questions and no real answers. I needed to know more. So I compressed all the data I'd pulled and sent it to Rohch. If anyone might be able give me some context, it would be him.

I leaned back in my seat and started bouncing my knee. I didn't know when he would get back to me, so until then, I was on my own. Whatever this thing was, it started in Anchorage, and it was ripping people apart then organizing the pieces. My mind flashed through the gruesome images again and they made me feel sick. No, very sick. Not wanting to loose it all over our cabin, I got up out of my chair like I was carrying an incredibly delicate bomb and made for the door. Eshe was asleep on the cabin's small bed, snoring up a storm. I didn't like leaving her behind, but all those concerns left as my stomach lurched. I held one hand over my mouth and bolted for the lavatory at the back end of the car. I paid the usage fee. The door unlocked itself, and I pushed it open.

The bathroom was a small cramped afterthought that only technically had capacity for two. I squeezed past the sink and pushed open the door to the first stall. I'd interrupted two men. One was on his knees while the other one was reclining—as much as anyone really can—on the toilet seat, head tilted back, eyes closed. The man on the floor released the other's cock, leaving a small trail of saliva dangling from his lips.

"Sorry, honey, this one's in use," he said, eyes sparkling with a combination of irritation, and amusement.

Without missing a beat or even waiting for me to draw the door closed again, he continued his work with a slow, drawn-out lick up the man's length. He groaned and raked his fingers through his partner's hair, which was my cue to move along. Opening the door to the other stall, which was thankfully vacant, I rushed forward just as the dam broke. I heaved and choked on nothing for a second. No surprise; I hadn't eaten anything yet. Eventually, my guts pushed up a mouthful of bile. Once it was finally over, I leaned my head against the stall's dividing wall.

"You okay in there?" one of the occupants next door asked before interrupting himself with another gasp.

"Yeah," I groaned. "I think it's just motion sickness."

There was a small, wet pop of suction, then some clothes rustling. A hand reached under the divider, offering me a single pill, individually wrapped in plastic.

"It's hydri," the other man said. "Should help out you a bit."

"Thanks," I groaned, taking the pill container from him and feeling like death.

I walked on shaky legs back to the sink. The toilet automatically flushed and disinfected itself as I left it behind. The tap water was just short of room temperature, but it would work. I gathered a little in my hand and downed the pill. After that, I washed my hands and left the two men to their enjoyment.

I returned to our cabin and punched in the door code. As I stepped inside, a small auto-pistol aimed itself straight at my left eye.

"Oh, for fuck's sake," Eshe almost shouted and lowered her gun. "You scared the shit out of me."

"I scared the shit out of you?" I asked. "Fuck."

She smirked at that and put her gun away, then took a step back to let me back into the cabin.

"So," she began, "you find anything else?"

"Thanks, I feel like shit," I said before sprinkling in some false cheer. "How was your nap?"

Eshe yawned and reclined back onto the cot. "Suck it up, princess, you knew what you were in for when you asked for a swap."

I casually gave her the finger as I slumped back into the makeshift chair. She returned the gesture.

I rubbed at my eyes. "The western branch of a biological R&D lab called Pardeq is where this all started. Out in Anchorage."

Eshe's eyebrows went up. "Wow, that is incredibly specific. How'd you find it?"

"GPS Logs," I lied, thinking about the AI in Mahdi's memories.

Artificial intelligence as a concept had been floating around in the public consciousness for at least a couple of centuries, probably longer. We've been on the precipice of unlocking it for so long that The Rapture seems more likely. Eshe would probably believe me if I told her, but I wasn't sure how she'd react. Hell, I wasn't sure how to react. Humanity somehow crossed into the singularity with no fanfare to speak of. No marketing campaigns, pre-orders, streams, monetization schemes, nothing. Not so much as a whisper. And it was afraid and wanted my help. What a mindfuck.

Before following that line of questions any further, I moved on and pulled up the posts I'd found.

"Jesus," Eshe said, subdued. "You think that who or whatever is after you—after us. This thing killed all those people and mutilated their bodies?"

"Maybe," I said, chewing on the thought. "But I'm not sure. From what I've seen, the circ has killed people to get them out of his way. Indiscriminately, perhaps, but not what's in those pictures. Those bodies almost looked like they had been..."

"What?" Eshe asked.

"I don't know," I replied, joining her on the cot and stretching my legs out. "Like they've been catalogued or something. Like whatever killed them was curious about how they worked. Or maybe it was that creature we saw at your place."

Eshe shuddered at that. "Look, I may not hold any fancy titles, but I work on bodies. Day in and day out. I know how they work. What we saw was impossible, it couldn't have been real. Muscles, skin, tendons, cartilage, none of it works that way. You can't just take someone else's parts and incorporate them into yourself."

"You're right," I said. "But we both saw it happen. We saw the thing that was making people jump to their deaths from nine or so stories up."

She started to protest, but I cut her off.

"It's real, and it's out there gorging itself," I said.

"Vys probably killed it," she deflected with both a hint of disgust and pride.

"Let's hope so," I nodded. "Let's hope so."

Eshe and I stopped talking for a while after that. We stared up at the ceiling, imagining shapes or faces in the textures. Eventually, we drifted off to sleep. It wouldn't last, but it was better than nothing.

NINETEEN

OLD METROPOLIS

Eshe woke me up when we reached the station. She had already packed everything away, save for Mahdi's gear, which sat in a pile on the cot. I moved fast, clumsily packing the items away all while holding each piece with a degree of reverence. I eyed an apology at Eshe but otherwise maintained the silence. Her expression was hard to read. The panic from before had settled into something between resigned sadness and resolute anger. The car finally jostled to a stop, and we followed a row of people from the other cabins out into the light. What Eshe and I saw was new to both of us.

Given my line of work, I've done a lot of travel. I've been to a lot of places, seen most of what the Barrel has to offer, but I have never been to the shell of Old Manhattan. Now, here I was. We worked our way through the magway station, and the first thing that I noticed about this place was the smell. The tinge of iron still established the undertone, but the mechanical notes of carbon and ozone had been replaced with something more organic. It was humid and heavy and gave me the impression of decay.

Whatever finds its way to the bottom of someone else's Barrel. Just another form of distilled, human potliquor, I supposed.

Leaving the station behind us, everything in sight—along with most low-lying buildings—was plastered with an array of mosses and algae. Greens and browns of assorted hues were speckled with bright reds and luminescent blues. The side of the building that Eshe and I found ourselves walking past reminded me of a carpet that collected decades of persistent stains. The splashes of pastel were so striking that I almost didn't notice that several corpses had been grafted into the tapestry. Each one in a different stage of decay, with the dark ichor of rot making its slow march down the wall, eventually staining the ground in dried black puddles. It reminded me of an ancient burial custom I'd read about once.

We rounded the corner of the building and were almost immediately paralyzed at the sight of the old city. It was a sprawl of low-cost structures, ancient and new alike, all laying warily beneath an extensive latticework of cabling that stretched out in all directions. In the midst of this were dozens of megastructures that hung precariously over the old metropolis beneath.

The real, unsimulated sunset found its way through the cityscape in a few places, casting long finger-like shadows across the streets. Eshe and I stood in one of the spears of warmth for a few minutes, soaking it in. I could see the beginnings of a smile creep into Eshe's face. Didn't matter what shit we'd been through; feeling the sun for the first time on our skin was a feeling that was hard to contain.

"How is this..." Eshe began, staring at her sunlit skin. "How can a place like this exist?"

I tried to come up with something to say, but couldn't manage it. I was in just as much surprise and awe as she was. I smiled though, and closed the distance to give her a hug. It was a delicate, brittle embrace, but after a moment Eshe softened a bit to enjoy the moment a bit more before moving on.

The whole undercity—as I chose to call it—was teeming with activity. Markets not unlike the Armory back home were plentiful, though cleaner and built with foot and vehicular traffic in mind. Alleyways were plentiful and the two of us made liberal use of them to avoid some of the more congested areas. Neither of us were really sure what we were looking for, but it seemed that we were trying to get ourselves good and lost.

Eventually, we found a cheap hab unit that seemed purpose-built for discretion, likely for more intimate purposes, but it worked well enough in our case. The room was cramped. It was split down the middle by a single wall, with a bathroom on one side and a sleeping area with a pair of extruded beds on the other. Eshe commandeered the shower, and I didn't contest. Instead I took the opportunity to claim the bed closest to the window. There was so much more to look at, and I wanted the view.

As I got settled, I could hear the handle of the shower squeak as Eshe turned it on. And moments later steam came steadily wisping out from beneath the partition.

"Hey," I called over the sound of the shower. "You hungry?"

Almost as if in response, my stomach roared and churned, demanding satisfaction like an old, bloodthirsty god.

"Starving," Eshe replied. "Whatever you find, get two extra."

"Alright, I'll be back," I said, satisfied with our decision.

"Make sure you come back!" Eshe shouted.

I barked out a laugh and walked out the door, making sure to lock it behind me. The air outside was just slightly thick with ocean humidity. What's more, the people I passed on the street simply seemed too busy to notice me, rather than trying to appear deadly. Granted, there's always danger lurking somewhere, but rather than being threatening, the city around me bustled. It didn't take me long to decide that it was something I could get used to—even if it was next to impossible to afford living there.

Still, I allowed myself a moment to dream. Maybe, once this was all over, Eshe and I could come back here and build new lives. As I closed my eyes and sucked in a deep breath, I saw a montage of what life might look like if that happened. I've heard people say that it was good to have goals. I could happily hold onto that one.

The sidewalks were wide and raised up and away from the streets. There was a delineation between vehicle and pedestrian here that I wasn't used to. I followed the walkways in a winding route around our hab, establishing a sort of perimeter. That is until I finally stumbled across a combination of competing smells that could not be ignored. What awaited me was a small congregation of cart-stalls situated near a corner store. The first was hocking second-hand goods, some clothing, terminal equipment, old-school external augments, and so on. The owner didn't say anything as I browsed. They just watched my hands closely. Once I was done, I nodded at them and moved on to the next one.

"Welcome, welcome," smiled the man behind the counter.

He looked to be middle-aged and wore a blue turban around his head. From his spectacled eyes to his posture, everything about the man communicated a sort of unrestrained joy. It was hard not to be infected by it as I looked at his cart.

"First time in this part of the city?" he asked.

"How'd you guess?" I asked, answering a question with a question.

He chuckled warmly. "Your eyes are sparkling like they've just seen the sun for the first time.

He had a particular cadence to his voice that I couldn't precisely place, maybe from the central Asian conglomerates. I picked up a few assorted pins. Each one was a simple monogram, 'I<3NY,' '1337NY,' et cetera. I pinned them to my jacket one at a time and motioned at the man as if to ask, 'what do you think?'

He beamed at me, nodding. "Lovely, miss. Can I get you anything else?"

To say that it took me by surprise wouldn't be entirely accurate. It wasn't that I'd forgotten about the swap either, quite the contrary. But for a few moments there, I felt more myself than I ever had before. It was fleeting, there for a few breaths, then it was gone.

"Miss?" the man asked, his brows furrowed. "Are you alright?"

I blinked rapidly and shook my head. "Yeah, sorry. Thank you."

"Thank you for your business," he said.

Moving on, I found myself between two food carts. Fire flared up to my left. The cook behind it adjusted some meat, rice, and vegetables on a wide-open cooktop. Another, to the right, was tending to a small collection of tube-shaped sticks of meat. Each one glistened as it moved across a set of sizzling rollers. Both looked good, but I wanted to see what the corner store had to offer.

The door chimed as I entered the small, almost claustrophobic space. Products of all kinds sat on narrow shelves or hung on pegs in the wall. They were grouped together by relative similarity, Snack foods, medicine, cheap electronics, and so on. As if by magic, I found myself drawn to a glass case that sat to one side of the checkout counter. A heat lamp above cast red-orange light over a pair of starchy-looking disks covered with fried meat slices.

"You want some?" asked the man behind the counter.

"What is it?" I asked, somewhat mystified.

He shook his head, slid himself from his stool, and waddled over. "Pizza. This some kinda joke or something? Khushi out there put you up to this?"

I shook my head. "Nope, no joke."

He wiped his face with one hand and muttered to himself under his breath. "Fucking tourists."

He wasn't much help after that, and seemed to get more and more annoyed the longer I stood in his shop. Now, that was the sort of New York treatment I was used to. I grabbed a few drinks, a bottle of cheap liquor, and four pieces of the starch disk. The clerk—too rude for me to consider him an owner—rolled his eyes as I took the first slice out and took a cursory bite.

Of course, it was all synthesized, varying layers of protein strands and amino acids that did what they could to imitate the flavors, colors, and textures of long lost ingredients. But it was still fantastic and got better with each bite. Mild sweetness, salt, tang, and several spices danced on my palette. Good thing I'd gotten more.

Leaving the corner store and the cart stalls behind me, I strolled down the city streets at a leisurely pace. People passed around me in a hurry, and for the first time, I didn't feel the need to be one of them. With delicious food in hand, booze in my pocket, and nobody taking any overt action to kill me, I felt like this was part of any other normal day. Perhaps better than normal. Even though some part of me felt a storm brewing, it was hard not to let a small contented smile creep onto my face on the way back.

As the hab's door closed and locked behind me, Eshe, wet orange frizz and all, snatched the boxes from my hands without so much as questioning their contents. I shot her a look, and she begrudgingly pulled the topmost box from the pile and handed it to me. I set the pizza and the drinks down on my bed and rifled through my bag for a change of clothes. Once everything was accounted for, I undressed and tossed my clothes into a pile on the floor. Then I stepped into the shower.

The white noise of the hot, cascading water put my mind at ease. It was more than just the blood and the grime, it felt like the scum clogging up my consciousness was being washed away. I stayed there for a moment, as white noise of the hot, cascading water put my mind at ease. It was the first time in what felt like a long time that everything was quiet. No thoughts. No worries. Just peace. I opened my eyes for the first time in what must have been ages and looked down at myself, at my new form. Oversized mechanical limbs and pale skin that had been mended together. I was a fractured mind in a mangled body.

And yet, there was some part of me that loved it. That reveled in it. That was overjoyed with leaving my old body behind, and experiencing life in this one. It was like I'd been living all my life with a knife in my back, and was now finally experiencing what it felt like to be free of that burden.

There was another part, though, that fought it. It clawed at the walls with rage, screaming about being an imposter, how nobody would love me, and that swapping didn't change who I was. Those thoughts were loud and hard to ignore.

And for the moment, that side of me seemed to win out. Sure, I could walk, run, and even fight, but I couldn't let go of what I imagined other people thought when they saw me. How many of them saw me on the street earlier that day and saw that I was an imposter? A monster? A freak?

My mind replayed everything that happened, all the choices I made over the last few days that brought me to this place. Anger, fear, grief, and others, a titanic plague of emotion bowled me over, and I slid down the shower wall to the floor, held my knees, and started sobbing. I couldn't manage words, but I cursed every person who knew me. I cursed Mahdi for being there in The Armory. Most of all I cursed myself.

I wish I had starved to death in my home. Anything other than this.

I cried for ages. Tears bled out of me, invisible as they were swept away. My breath and shoulders shuddered as some part of me kept fighting back the emotion. It occurred to me then that I had been considering this body as somebody else's. As if the rightful owner was going to come take it from me and force me back. The thought of being forced out—as unrealistic as it was—sent forth a new fit of sobs. I didn't want to lose myself now that I'd finally found it. At least that's how it felt.

My tears shifted then, away from sorrow and toward understanding. It felt like a sudden weight was lifted off of me, and it was so transcendent that the lights in the room seemed brighter. Colors were more vibrant. I fruitlessly wiped the tears from my eyes and looked down at myself for what felt like the first time. Freckles stood out against my pale skin, covering my arms, shoulders, and chest. I loved them. They were mine. I ran my hands through my hair. It was coarse and had it been longer, I think it would have fallen around my face in drawn-out curls. That, too, was mine, and so were my arms and legs. I was still trying to catch my breath, especially after the new onslaught of emotions, but I felt so goddamn alive.

What was the phrase in that old movie again?

"Know thyself," I murmured to nobody, the words barely more than whispers.

Without really thinking about it, I ran a few fingers up along my left wrist. It was slow and light and it sent small shivers up and down my spine. The sensation continued as my hand drifted up over my shoulder and across my collarbone, causing my skin to erupt in little goosebumps. Each turn and swirl my fingers made drew a shallow, breathy sigh from my lips. It was agonizing, and yet I didn't want to stop.

My hand drew lazy trails down across the tip of one breast, and I took in a sharp breath. I remained there for a moment, circling around the sensitive flesh, getting lost in the sensation. That is until my attention moved elsewhere. Jolts of electricity fluttered through me, like stones skipping across a pond, as my lingering touch meandered down my stomach and found its way between my thighs.

I gasped, breath trembling for wholly different reasons now, as I pressed into myself. I tilted my head back and closed my eyes. Each rotation of my fingers moved just a little faster and pressed just a little harder. And I couldn't help but whimper in anticipation.

This was my body—every buzzing nerve ending, every bone, every circuit. I took a plunging breath that filled more than my lungs. This was who I should have been all along. My back arched away from the glass wall of the shower, and I bit my bottom lip as I rode out the waves that followed. Maybe a minute or two later, with those sensations drifting away, I let out a little contented chuckle. My legs felt like rubber. Getting up was a slow process, but I eventually turned the water off and stepped out of the shower as a new person. A person in the process of finally becoming whole.

The past hadn't been replaced. My failures, fears, and trauma were all still precisely where I left them. Things were still fucked up. Mahdi was still dead, and there were still people after us. But now something was different like I'd righted something that had been wrong my whole life. I'd take it. It was about damn time something worked in my favor.

A sense of resolve settled itself into place on my shoulders, and now I felt prepared for it. This world, these corporations, they took something from me, and I was going to return the favor. I would do what I could to help Eshe get settled here. Then, I would take Soqua and finish Mahdi's run. And while I was at it, I was going to tear it all down behind me.

Eshe was on the other side of the room, clattering away at her terminal. She hadn't seemed to notice any of what just happened, which I was grateful for. It was only for me, anyway. I grabbed my other slice of pizza and started to scarf it down. Even cold, it was still delicious.

"What's going on?" I asked Eshe through a mouthful of half-chewed pizza.

"Nothing really," Eshe answered. "Trying to find out more about this Pardeq company you told me about."

That piqued my interest. "Any luck?"

Eshe shook her head. "Not much. A couple of press reports but nothing substantial. One announcing the opening of their sister branch here in New York, and the other about the deal with the Egyptian government. Aside from that, they practically don't exist. Can't even find a fucking earnings report."

"I didn't find much on them either," I said. "Not that I did any deep searches, but they don't seem to want attention."

Eshe made a sound of agreement. "Makes you wonder what they're working on."

I nodded. "I know a guy who might be able to dig up more info. I'll drop them a line."

We spent the next few minutes in silence as I crafted the message to send to Rohch. I sent them everything I had and hoped they were safe.

"Hey Eshe?" I asked after another moment. "We were all close growing up, but Mahdi was something special, wasn't he? What was going on with you two?"

It was a heavy question for sure, but there was something in the back of my head that needed—felt compelled to know. At first, Eshe didn't answer, but she stopped typing almost immediately. She stared out the hab window, out at Old Manhattan for a while, and said nothing. I turned on my bed to look at her. There was a fire blazing in her eyes as new tears escaped. She looked at me, then back out the window at the moonlit city.

"We were a lot of things," she started. "He was like family to me, just like you are. As we grew up, we were lovers at times, enemies at others. God, I was stupid. He even came to visit before he—"

"No, Eshe. You—" I said.

"Yes, I was," Eshe interrupted through clenched teeth. "I was fucking stupid. Mahdi came back after every run. He always came back, whether for a drink, a fight, or a fuck. I honestly let myself think that we would grow old like that, fighting and loving each other, over and over, until both of us dropped dead. But we live in the fucking Barrel. The three of us were lucky to make it this far. I should have fucking known."

I sat there in my own silence. Shocked at how powerful those emotions were. I knew they'd been involved, it was hard to miss. But I had never figured it to be like that. Love. Or something close to it. Mahdi was lucky, for a lot of reasons. A relationship like that was something runners rarely ever had.

None of my romantic encounters went beyond satiating shared needs—men, women, people outside, and in-between. Most had been other runners. It made the most sense, after all. Each of us knew the risks of the job, never knowing which contract would be our last, so we commingled as we saw fit. A little effaneff, fuck and forget, before moving on with reduced stress and post-orgasmic clarity.

I bowed my head and wiped at my eyes. "I'm sorry, I... I had no idea."

"You didn't kill him, Raide," she replied, sounding tired. "I know I said a lot of shit when you showed up at my door, but you didn't do that to him."

I still wasn't looking at her. I couldn't. I felt nothing but shame for being the one who lived. Not as if I deserved death, but I had nothing worth saving. I'd only just now found myself, but Mahdi had himself figured out from the very beginning. What the fuck made me so special?

"Mahdi..." I said, quiet and unsteady. "He should be the one here, doing this, not me."

Eshe's bed creaked, and a moment later I felt her arms wrapped around me, her head resting on my shoulder. All she did was sob quietly into me, and there was little I could do but join her. I let it all out—the fear, the guilt, the pain, all of it—and wished there was a way I could change the situation.

The more I thought about the nightmare on the tram, the more I thought Uunter may have been telling the truth. That vision had too much in it that couldn't be explained. Something about it was intelligent, almost like it was telling a story. I could also get through one of Mahdi's memory locks, which shouldn't have happened.

If that AGI could plant Mahdi's memories into my head, maybe it somehow had the rest. If I helped to finish his run, maybe, the AI could help bring Mahdi back—or at least a version of him. Maybe I could do that much.

So, as Eshe and I held each other, I started planning to make contact with the AI again, to see if what I hoped for was even possible.

TWENTY

SIGN OF THE TIMES

I stayed there on the bed for a while, tossing and turning, but my mind wouldn't stop churning over all the questions I would have if this AGI turned out to be real. One thing I knew for certain was that I couldn't try communicating with it here. Eshe would freak out already, but she also couldn't know that I was planning on trading myself for Mahdi once this was all over. Either way, I had to know, and lying on the bed going through imaginary conversations for the hundredth time was not going to get me anywhere. So, I got up, grabbed my bag, and headed for the door. Eshe was absorbed in something on her terminal and barely registered my departure.

Outside, night had fallen. Peering through the cityscape, I could see the faint glimmer of starlight weaving between the buildings. It would have been almost peaceful if not for the continued bustle of people and the cacophonous hum of neon.

I needed to process what clues I had and see if there was any truth to Uunter's words. So, I wandered off into the evening and the crowds to find a safe place to talk to an artificial intelligence.

I hadn't stepped outside to find peace, but it came anyway. As I walked, I couldn't help but feel a buzzing energy that was hard to contain. Some might call it euphoria, and as I added to my mental map of Old Manhattan, I found myself practically dancing down the sidewalk. Turned a few heads along the way too, which only made me laugh myself silly. It felt good, and I was glad to have had the opportunity to experience it, but once all that energy was spent, I collected my thoughts and reoriented on my goal.

I explored the surrounding blocks in a loose spiral, and started by going south, then west, then north, and east, before starting over and going south again. It was all to help establish landmarks. I mostly did it by the signs. At one corner, before turning east, there were a pair of restaurants across from each other—Mac's Tubesteaks and Slabo's Beef. Their signs were huge and garish as hell, each one claiming to be the original home of the meatorito. A lot of the intersections I went through were like that, though they were all less offensive to the senses.

I came to a stop once I thought I'd seen enough and pulled up the local boards in search of the nearest dreamspot. It wound up being a half-hour trek in the opposite direction, but I didn't mind the walk at all. The night air was chilly, just enough to draw in a low-lying fog that absorbed the colors of neon and diode as its own.

The dreamscape was never more than a moment away for most people, but access isn't usually the problem. Safety is. Unless you want to be molested in one form or another in the street, you had to find a safe place to access it. Like your home. For emergencies or things that couldn't wait, though, dreamspots provided secure cubicles to dive in.

The business I was looking for occupied a rare single-story building that stood in stark contrast to everything around it. A pop-up shop turned permanent fixture, nearly everything about the structure looked prefabbed. What wasn't meant to be temporary was the automated security system, which was consequently the thing you were paying for. That and privacy. The vending machine-styled entry terminal bore a rather cookie cutter logo that flashed the company name in ugly text. SnoozeShack.

"How creative," I sighed, and flashed my wrist to buy a booth.

The room I paid for was an empty box, its walls made of high-strength injection-molded plastic. It was just large enough to stand in, so it took a little bit of doing to sit down, but once I'd found my seat, I pulled the capsule from my bag and held it on my lap.

"Now to figure out how to get you to talk," I said out loud to nobody.

I knocked on its chrome exterior as if trying to wake it up.

Nothing.

I tried again. "Hey, uh, Soqua? We need to talk."

A lone, slender cable extended from its base, slow and timid.

"C'mon, let's go," I said, laying my forearm down next to it.

The cable wriggled into my mesh port, which was an incredibly unnerving sensation—even though I wasn't fighting it this time. The wire clicked into place and my vision faded. I tumbled backward and was doused with water the same way as before. Mahdi was there again, sitting opposite me at a table I'd seen in the previous vision. No cylinder lay between us.

"Who are you?" I asked.

My mouth moved, but no words followed. Mahdi stared at me like I was wasting his time. I couldn't speak, and my thoughts had not apparently communicated the question. I sat there for a moment, puzzling over how to communicate and thought about the last time. A lot of what I could understand from our previous conversation seemed to suggest that it could speak through symbolism. That gave me an idea. I spread my fingers and held my arms out in front of me, testing to make sure I had full control. I did.

I brought a closed fist to my mouth and asked the same question again in Roko, *Who are you?*

Mahdi stared through me, and his eyes glazed over for a few seconds. His vision focused again as he lifted his hands, shaping them to form Roko letters, *S - O - Q - U - A.*

I leaned back in my chair, almost reeling from the confirmation that this thing I'd been carrying around was some sort of intelligent life. I rubbed my face with my hands as I tried to come up with a list of relevant questions.

What is Soqua? I signed.

Child, it replied, *Life. Me.*

This thing was an artificial intelligence, the first, for all I knew, and it could only speak in one-word sentences? What the hell?

Where were you made? I asked.

Soqua shook its head and signed, *Born.*

Where were you born? I amended.

Pardeq. Anchorage. It said.

My hands fluttered into a question, *Where are you going?*

Pardeq. Heights. Soqua answered.

My hands worked together to form the simple question, *Why?*

Complicated. It answered simply.

I signed a little more forcefully, *Explain.*

It considered me thoughtfully for a moment before pointing to itself, *Fragment. Pardeq. Heights. Whole.*

What happens when you become whole? I asked.

Body. Life. Choose. It signed, putting its hands back on the table.

It wanted its own body? I would never have considered the possibility. Not that I knew how an AGI would think to begin with, but bodies were innately limiting. Even if you swapped like I did, you were just trading one meat prison for another.

Who is chasing you? I asked.

Soqua shook its head.

Do you know why? I amended.

The AI spelled out a simple word with one hand, *Hate.*

Another surprising answer. Not that it wasn't plausible. We humans have a history of reacting violently when presented with things we don't understand. My first guess, however, was that Soqua was some sort of escaped property. With the mercs following me, that seemed to be the most likely. Maybe this was some sort of internal corporate espionage between Pardeq's two branches. Soqua was stolen, given to Mahdi to transport to Pardeq East, who would play dumb and act like they didn't have it. It seemed to track. That sort of thing happened all the time. Treachery like that was one of the greatest contributors to the constant churn of corporate death and rebirth here in the CSA.

You gave me one of his memories; do you have the rest of him? I asked.

Yes, It answered.

Could you put him in a new body? I pressed, leaning forward in my chair.

Theory. Possible, Soqua said.

Alright, I signed, *I'm going to get you to Pardeq. To complete Mahdi's contract. If I get you there, can you help stop the people who are following me?*

Soqua didn't respond for a long few moments.

Well? I asked, frustration making its way into my movements.

Yes, the AI responded.

All in all, while the conversation was certainly exciting on a lot of levels, it also didn't inspire a lot of confidence. Then again, the conversation I'd just had was unprecedented. What should I have been expecting in the first place? Like it or not, though, It would have to be good enough. As I broke the connection with Soqua, I ventured back through the void that separated my mind from the dreamscape. It looks different to everyone. Some people see a storm, other people imagine fire. For me, it was an expanse of impossibly blue water that I had to sink into. Within those depths, were the defensive systems of my personality firewall, vortexes, pockets of steam, molten rock, and others. They would part for me—and Soqua apparently—but would hold off most others.

When I got back to the real world, I was armed with purpose. I'd taken plenty of jobs that might kill me, so that wasn't anything new. Now I was assisting an actual AI. The first AI. Like out of the countless stories I'd read and watched. I thought about my book and how different Soqua seemed to be. All the nightmares humanity shared over the centuries, and none of them turned out to be true. Maybe there was hope for humanity after all.

If I wanted to keep my lead on the circ and his minions, I needed to get back to the hab, and get moving. I packed up the capsule—or rather Soqua—and left the dreamspot behind. Since I wasn't wandering around like I did when I left, returning to the hab took relatively little time at all. I bounced up the steps and opened the door. Eshe grabbed me by the collar and pulled me through.

She slammed me against the wall and hit me in the face. "You goddamned mother-fucking cock socket! You figured something out, and you weren't going to fucking tell me!"

She hit me again, and I could taste iron where my teeth dug into my lip.

"Eshe," I said, holding up my hands. "I don't know what you're talking about."

My vision flashed white and red when Eshe broke my nose with her forehead.

"What's in the capsule, huh?" she asked. "I dug through Mahdi's gear and found the meeting with Uunter. But you told me things that I couldn't see. Somehow, you got through Mahdi's memory lock." She released her grip on my shirt and stalked away. "Now, you are going to fucking talk."

"Eshe, I... You..." I stammered. "You wouldn't believe me if I did. I don't even know if I believe it."

She spun around on one foot and came back, slammed me into the wall again, and reached inside my jacket. The knife gleamed as she drew it and pushed the edge against my neck. Gentle as she was not to kill me, I could still feel a burning line under my chin where the blade had grazed my skin.

"You're going to tell me what you know. Right now," she snarled. "or I swear to fuck that I'll throw you to the circ myself."

"Okay," I said quietly, careful to not cut myself any further. "Goddammit, okay."

Eshe pulled the knife away enough for me to talk, but still had me pinned.

"Mahdi took a black bag run," I explained. "Well, he turned it down. An artificial intelligence was on the run and needed his help. The circ showed up and cut the meeting short. Mahdi took the job as he made his escape."

"I have a knife to your throat and you're still spewing bullshit," she said in disbelief.

"I thought so, too," I confirmed. "When the capsule plugged into my arm in the tram, it gave me one of his memories."

Eshe scoffed. "That's impossible. You can't just put memories into someone's head. The human brain doesn't work like that without being thoroughly prepared for it."

"I'm sure you know what you're talking about," I conceded. "but I'm telling you the—"

She pressed the knife against my skin again and I cut myself a little on it as I continued. "Alright, alright, alright. Fuck it, plug in and watch for yourself."

It was better than trying to explain it. I wasn't a stitch, wouldn't know how to manufacture a realistic memory if I tried, and Eshe knew it. Showing her would be as good as hard evidence. That is, unless Soqua could do it. If it could give me memories that weren't mine, it could certainly alter them or make them from scratch. But I wasn't about to mention that.

Eshe looked at me warily but put on her goggles and plugged in. I showed her my first encounter with Soqua and the whole dream that followed. She jumped when she saw the circ kill Mahdi, and the blood drained from her face when she saw herself die. Her whole body tensed, and she tried to control her breathing, but a couple of shudders made it through the mask. I showed her the full meeting with Uunter and the conversation Soqua and I just had then I cut the feed. She pulled her goggles down to hang around her neck and wiped a trembling hand across her cheek. She was quiet for a long while, every so often blinking tears out of her eyes.

"Why don't you trust me?" she asked.

It was a simple enough question.

"I do, Eshe," I said. "I—"

"It's pretty clear that you don't," she said, her hands clenching into fists.

Tears came again, but they weren't of sadness or loss. This time, it was betrayal. Maybe not from my perspective. I didn't even fully understand what I was dealing with, but from hers, it was just that simple.

"Do you know what I've been through in the last few days?" I snapped. My sudden outburst caught Eshe flat-footed, so I continued. "My best friend was blown to pieces in front of me. My home was destroyed for no fault of my own, and to top it all off, I saw the body I was born into get its brains blown out, and I was the one who facilitated that. You couldn't possibly understand. You don't know."

"I don't fucking know?" she snapped, exasperated. "In case you hadn't fucking noticed, my home was destroyed too, and Mahdi meant more to me than he ever did to you, you fucking parasite. I understand, perhaps a little too fucking well."

"No, you don't," I repeated, doubling down. "You don't know what that kind of loss is like. I had to fight and kill for every scrap that belonged to me. You ought to at least understand that much. Not everyone has Laden to—"

"Don't go there," Eshe interrupted. "Don't you fucking go there."

"Not everyone," I persisted, "has Laden to come in and rescue them as their mother is about to sell them out to a thinktank. You didn't spend all your life knowing only the extremes between anger and stoicism and not understanding why. Not everyone has Laden to come along and give you a home as a child. You had it so goddamned good, Eshe, and I don't want to hear it."

"You selfish, self-centered bitch" she spat. "Mahdi's dead, rotting in pieces in the fucking streets, with the rats and the bloatflies and the maggots, and all you give a damn about is yourself. Fuck you."

Eshe looked away from me and wiped more tears from her face. She looked back at her terminal, which was still plugged into Mahdi's tech, then stormed out the door and into the street.

I rubbed my face and fixed my nose before taking a deep breath, trying to force the anger out. Eshe didn't get it. She would never know. I stood there for a moment, repeating those words in my head like a mantra. It didn't take. I sighed and cursed aloud in the empty room. I knew that wasn't true. Eshe knew more about loss than I ever could.

Maybe I was the one who didn't understand. Mahdi and I were made in test tubes, so we had no real parents. Eshe's mother tried to sell her to a thinktank. She was rescued by Laden, a stranger who brought her up as his own. When he died and left her behind with his shop and all the debts he owed. Then Mahdi gets killed. And then there's me. I was going to drop her off here and leave. Abandon her to my own pursuits, no different than her mother or Laden.

Even if she didn't know it, I was doing what I was doing for her and Madhi. I couldn't let her disappear, never to be seen again. I had to find her and fix this, so I hid Soqua and my bag and locked the door behind me as I ventured back out into the night. I had no idea where to start looking. Eshe could have gone anywhere, but I had to try, so I picked a direction and started walking, scanning the crowds as I went.

First, I went down to where I'd gotten food earlier. The cart stalls were gone, and the corner store had transitioned to an automated teller system. I called out Eshe's name, which elicited a few surprised looks from people passing me by on the street. I watched, hoping she'd show herself, and was met with disappointment. I continued down another few blocks before repeating the process in a light-strewn open-air marketplace. I called out for Eshe a few more times as I went and was met with the same results. After working through a dozen city blocks, even going back to the dreamspot I'd visited, with no luck, I decided to head back.

Getting off the main streets, I took the alleys. They were an entirely different world compared to what was just a few dozen meters behind me. It reminded me a lot of my part of the Barrel, with its makeshift housing, walkways, and business.The people too, every last one was living a day-to-day subsistence that revolved around feeding off the leavings of the city around them. In those alleyways, most of the footpaths were so cramped that I had to walk down them sideways. In the few places that opened up, I still moved around with caution, careful to keep my back to the wall if there was one.

It was hard to determine distance in a place like that, or even direction, but after moving in a somewhat straight line for a while, I took a left. My hope was that it would lead me back to the main roads, close to the hab. Instead, I walked headlong into a dead end. Small hovels were piled high at the end, creating a sort of slumland skyscraper. Not where I needed to be. After letting another person pass, I turned around. I would find my way out of here eventually, and maybe, by the time I got back, Eshe would have cooled off enough that we could talk this out.

Another person stepped into the dead-end alley. I tried to slip past them when they lunged for me, slamming my left shoulder into the wall with bruising force. They followed that up with a less-than-solid punch to the side of my head before throwing me back the way I came. I stumbled backward and fell on my ass. As I got back to my feet, something wrapped itself around my neck. I fought it, but only for a moment, before electricity surged through me, burning the skin around my neck and making my limbs lock in place. The first of my attackers crouched down over me. She was someone I'd never seen before, with shoulder-length black hair, dark eyes, and mismatched replacement limbs. All she did then was stare at me with a sort of crazed excitement as my vision faded to black.

SERIAL BOX

I was slow to wake up. My vision was blurry, and my head spun. Cold metal pressed against the naked flesh of my back. So cold that it ached. My shoulders hurt, too, and I tried to put my arms down from over my head. When I couldn't, I looked up blearily. They'd been restrained, bound by iron shackles that hung by a simple chain from a loop in the ceiling. I struggled against the chains for a moment when I found that my legs had been restrained as well, by a pair of synthetic leather cuffs that were built into a metal slab pressing into my back.

In this position, it was hard to breathe, and the conscious effort of it proved equal parts exhausting and nauseatingly painful. My stomach lurched, but I ground my teeth and bit it back, instead forcing myself to focus on my surroundings.

The room was mostly dark and smelled of formaldehyde and sweat. All I could see of the space came from the dim light of a pair of wall-mounted displays ahead of me and to my right. I could make out what looked like an operating table. Beside it was a rolling stand with old medical readouts and spent IV bags. Beside that, just on the edge of my peripheral vision, was a wall-mounted shelf. It was hard to tell, but as I squinted at it, I thought I saw a set of clothes, some makeup pallets, and a small, plastic-lined backpack, none of it mine. Was there a child here somewhere?

Light abruptly poured into the room from a hallway directly ahead, blinding me while also grabbing my direct attention.

"I'll let you know when I'm ready," said a man's voice, gravely and stern.

A door slid shut, casting the room into darkness again, and after several ominous footsteps, the figure at the end of the hall flipped a handful of breakers. Lights flickered to life above me, casting my surroundings in neon hospital white. That's when I was able to take in the rest of the room.

The walls and ceiling all bore a network of crisscrossing wires like I was being held in a giant networking closet. In the corner, to my left were another pair of restraints similarly attached to the ceiling in the corner. Over my shoulder, though, was one of the most bizarre things I'd ever seen. Nearly covering the wall were matched sets of arms and legs, twitching and fluttering in cases of nutrient gel. Each case had a small readout in one corner with blocks of scrolling text indicating when and where they'd been acquired, and what they looked like.

Female, mid-thirties, white, East Chicago. Female, early-twenties, black, central Bostonian district. All of the labels looked the same—they were all from women—but sometimes described a single limb or any combination up to four. All of the dates listed were several months to a couple of years apart.

"What the hell?" I asked myself aloud.

The man who strolled into the room was of average height, with a lean and muscular build beneath heavily freckled skin. He had cold, calculating grey-green eyes that were so pale that they almost looked all white around his pupils. He sauntered up to me without a care in the world, lounge pants and shirt swishing as he walked.

"What am I going to do with you?" he pondered, looking me up and down.

"How about you let me go," I demanded.

He didn't so much as react to me, and instead continued his appraisal. "I've never had a fifth before, much less a return with such finely made prosthetics."

"Hey, asshole," I spat, "I'm not some piece of hardware for you to tinker with."

Only then did he actually look at me, and I saw a tinge of annoyance that vanished almost as soon as it had appeared. He returned to his review and arched an eyebrow as he ran a finger over the garter tattoo on my thigh.

"Crude," he mused, sounding almost disappointed. "Well, I can't say I approve of that. Still, I suppose you would have a bit of a rebellious phase, wouldn't you? Fair enough."

And just like that, he whipped around, paced toward the operating table, and gathered a few trays of tools from a cabinet on the other side. To my relief, they were not surgical tools. Instead, they looked like what Eshe might use to install and tune her prosthetics. I struggled as he grabbed my left leg and started searching for the fastening points that would have attached it to the rest of me. I fought him as much as I could, but I was out of breath in no time, so it didn't amount to much. I sucked in a few breaths and watched him. For his part, he looked confused, but as he poked and prodded the prosthetic, his eyebrows shot up.

"Well I'll be damned," he marveled.

"I can arrange that," I muttered.

He continued to ignore me and attached a pair of tools to a spot just behind my knee and twisted. Almost at once, all the microbots that made up my lower leg collapsed to the ground in a pile. Then, the man pulled what remained off of my leg, revealing a hexagon-shaped bulge of bone just above where my knee would have been. At the top of that odd shape was a small electronic ring, dozens of small probe wires that wound up my humerus before plunging into my flesh.

The man whistled, apparently impressed. "I would love to trade notes with whoever did this."

"Can arrange that, too," I commented, knowing that he wasn't listening to me.

"Tempting," he answered. "But first..." He looked back over his shoulder, and hollered. "Rikki, you may come out now."

The door at the end of the hall slid open again, and a feminine form slinked into the shadows. She wasn't wearing much, mostly just an opaque shawl that barely hid her body from view. The very first thing I noticed was that she was mismatched. Each of her limbs were a different skin tone from her torso.

She shot me a devilish grin as I stared at her in realization. Then I looked over to the man, scanning his hands to find one of them was missing a digit. They were definitely the two that attacked me in the Shiv. I frantically tried to put pieces together, but no matter how many times I went over it, I couldn't make sense of it. I tried to get on the mesh, and it went absolutely nowhere.

"You're not going to get online from in here," he said, oozing smug confidence. "This whole room is a Faraday cage. No signals get in or out unless I want them to."

If he was telling the truth, I was completely fucked. My best option was to pay attention and hope one of them made a mistake that would play to my advantage. I didn't have much choice.

Rikki walked up behind the man and bent over to give him a hug before dropping the shawl and hopping up onto the operating table.

He placed his hand gently on one of her legs—a dark-skinned replacement. "These ones are a bit unique," he said, trying to sound calm and reassuring. "I'm going to have to make some modifications, okay?"

She bit her lip and nodded.

And with that, the man went to work. He undid a few screws that attached the replacement limb to her thigh and pulled it free, similar to what he did with mine. As he prepared some more tools, Rikki was still biting her lip and taking deep breaths, like she was preparing for pain. The flash of sparks and the acrid smell of the welding torch filled the room a moment later.

As I watched, Rikki's movements got more erratic. She was trying to contain herself, but as I focused my attention on her, I realized that it wasn't pain at all. She was in the throws of ecstasy, with one hand taking a firm hold on one of her breasts and the other buried between her legs. It stayed like that all the way through. Each time sparks flew, each time an air wrench made its distinctive call, she bucked against the table.

I didn't really know how long that lasted, but they both finished together. As soon as my leg was attached to her body, all the microbots on the floor woke up and tumbled their way over to the replacement limb, rebuilding that stilettoed heel that I'd gotten used to.

The man helped her up from the table and pulled her close. She took careful steps at first, but found the new leg as easy to walk in as I had. The pair had started walking off down the hall together when I spoke up.

"I suppose I should be thankful for that," I said, gathering as much exhausted sarcasm as I could muster.

"On the contrary, I—we—should be. Thanking. You," he replied, turning around to face me. "Without all that equipment in the bag you dropped, I would never have been able to track you down."

I blinked and probably looked a bit confused.

The two approached me as the man bloviated. "Your friend was on the up-and-up. She registered real hardware IDs instead of fake ones, and because she did several at once, each physical address was given out in sequential order. I just had to know where to look." The man made a surprised sound. "And what do you know? You were right in my backyard."

"Yeah," Rikki purred, stepping toward me. "I really should be thanking you. My two favorite sets came from you."

"Fuck you," I snarled.

She laughed out of sheer amusement and leaned forward to drag her fingers across my chest and kiss me on the lips. She stopped short when I didn't reciprocate and gave me a disappointed look.

"Oh, now you're no fun," she pouted.

Admittedly, I had been going for a different reaction, and that definitely wasn't it. She grinned at me and strutted from the room on my leg, leaving the shawl on the ground behind her as she disappeared through a door at the end of the hall.

"You'll have to forgive Rikki," the man started, forcefully pulling Rikki back. "Her antics are rather unbecoming at times." His voice got a shade huskier. "She was certainly correct, however. The two of us owe you a great deal—or a past version of you perhaps. After all—not that you would know this—but the body you're using, she was my first."

A thousand replies flew through my head, but none of them were incredibly productive. I needed to think my way out of this. I needed to find a way to disable the cage he had me in. If I could get a network connection, no matter how tenuous, I could tell Eshe and maybe get out of here. So, I bit back all of my words and settled for glaring at the man.

He chuckled. "You know, I'm not quite sure what to do with you. Once I've taken all those lovely limbs, I'll have to find some use for you. Maybe Rikki would be up for swapping back and forth."

As he pondered what to do with me, I spotted my knives. They were in a plastic crate on a shelving unit near the hallway. I wasn't sure if my ultrasound projectors could reach them. Even worse, I had no idea if I could fully control them yet, but I'd have to try if I got a moment alone.

"I'll have to think about it," he said, with a smug grin. "Hang in there, I'll come up with something."

"Funny," I shot back. "Too bad I'm not in much of a laughing mood."

That selective hearing of his was a really neat trick. He'd gone back to completely ignoring me and looking me over with that frigid gaze. He turned away and went about cleaning the tools he'd used on me and Rikki. After what felt like an eternity, he left the room and disappeared through the door at the end of the hall. And he didn't turn off the lights.

I watched in silence for several minutes before feeling confident and brave enough to try working toward an escape. Even while restrained, I was pretty sure that I could get the ultrasound projectors to work for me. I hadn't really used them at all since I'd woken up in this body, but getting them working couldn't have been that difficult. I had no idea what I was going to do after that, but I knew it started there.

So I started with one. I moved my hand the same way that Eshe showed me, and one of the blades tipped itself over the edge of the crate. It drifted across the room and into my hand. Even while restrained, that was a good start. Now to try moving it. I spread my hand, willing the knife to go drifting off in front of me. It fell, barely catching itself before hitting the floor. I tried it again and again. Over and over for probably half an hour without a shred of luck or progress. As I hung there, fighting my restraints and breathing heavy, a few beads of sweat dribbled down into my eyes, which just added insult to injury.

"Fuck," I breathed out. "Goddammit."

I leaned my head back and popped a few joints, stretching all ten fingers and all ten phantom toes. I shook my head and imagined reaching for the lone blade hovering in place on the floor. It moved a little, wobbling on its axis in response, but little else. My face twisted in frustration and I reached for it again, snapping it up and an instant later losing control, sending the blade straight for me.

I winced, and felt a bite of sharp pain against my skin. Then nothing at all. Opening my eyes again and looking down, I spotted the knife, embedded in the table, right where my leg would have been. The phantom pain echoed a little in my nerves and it sparked an idea.

"That's it," I whispered to myself, getting excited. "That's it!"

I knew how to master these damn knives, so I balanced myself in the most sustainable position I could, closed my eyes, and entered the dreamscape to give myself mindblur.

TWENTY-TWO

SIMULATING REALITY

started over from my earliest memories of grifting in the streets with Mahdi up until just a few minutes ago. Everything was the same as it had been—down to the smallest detail. All except for one notable difference: I had ten arms.

That crazy idea put me up there with all the madlads of history. But it was going to work. I knew it in my microbots.

I ran through memories of running down hallways and up fire escapes, jumping over tables, and out windows. Each time, making sure to make full use of my ridiculous number of limbs. Nothing else changed, but it didn't have to. The first time I got back to that fucking wall where Mahdi died, though, I hesitated. I wanted so badly to revise what was about to happen, as if I could rewrite history. Some place of my brain itched, a place I couldn't reach unless I gave in and saved Mahdi. Potential insanity be damned. I was already risking that, what was one more thing?

I'd be lying if I said that I didn't consider it. Heavily. But I thought about Eshe, and how she'd think I left her for real. That was enough to get me to bite back the urge to revise history, as bitter as it was.

Reliving the events that followed wasn't any easier than it had been the first time. Worse, probably. Mahdi's death, my escape from the building, getting helped by Rohch and his partner, all of it.

When I got back to my abduction, I started over from the beginning. Getting to the third pass over my life was when the wild parts of my mind, the parts that remain untamed, started making small changes. As I climbed up the side of a building, leaping from balcony to balcony, a little jingle from an old cartoon started playing from everywhere around me.

"...does whatever a spider can..." I quietly sang along as I pushed through the memories.

After my fifth pass, I thought I might be ready. I had just used a trick of dream time to experience decades of living with all those arms. So, I woke up. At first, it didn't seem like anything had changed, but as I stretched with a yawn, I felt it—the distinct sensation of forty more fingers, all somewhere around me in the ether. The knife sat above the floor, and I reached for it. There was some part of me that could almost see the not-arm stretch out and touch the weapon. It wobbled. I tried it again, putting in a little more mental effort and was able to lift it up for a moment before dropping it again. My third attempt was a success. I picked up the knife and held it out in front of my face. It was batshit insane, but it worked.

I called all the knives to me, dropping them one at a time to continue practicing. I would pick each one up and put it back in the crate, only to take them all out again and repeat the process. I had no idea how much time had actually passed when a door swung open at the end of the hallway.

Panic set in immediately. It was the sort that eats at your nerves when you're about to be caught with something you shouldn't have, and suddenly, I was learning to pick up knives all over again. The first one slipped from my grasp three times before I was finally able to put it back in the container. Then the second, and the third after that. I was able to put the remaining knives back without issue, and just in time too. Because backed into the kill room, looking over his shoulder and hauling an unconscious dark-skinned woman in by her shoulders. As he did, I tried to look tired and unfocused, which, as it turned out, wasn't that hard to sell. As he moved past me, I took in a sharp breath. It was Eshe. How did they find her, or was it the other way around?

"Good news!" he said, straining against the limp body. "I've gotten you some company."

"See? I told you that you're not getting out of those restraints," he bragged, turning back to his new victim. He locked her to a pair of shackles that dangled from the ceiling. "Alright then, how about the other leg?" he said, finishing with the restraints. "Rikki is going to be so very excited."

He stepped away to gather some tools, and my heart sank as I took her in. Eshe hung there on full display, like a piece of meat. Arms suspended above her like mine—ankles bound, too. I really hated the ideas that poured through my imagination then, of what could happen to her—to both of us—if this guy had his way. He sauntered over to me and straddled a stool by my foot.

"I really would love to meet the person who came up with these," he said, motioning to the bone remnant of my missing limb. "The use of stem cell regrowth packs to interface between the prosthetic and your humerus is absolutely genius."

After that, he dragged up a stool and didn't say another word. His process was exact and methodical, and he managed to detach my remaining leg with ease. Now without a leg to stand on, I was suspended overhead by my wrists, which made breathing a taxing process.

I was focusing on my new condition—trying to breathe—when Rikki strolled into the room and hopped up on the same table as before. The man removed her other leg and began the process of refitting my leg. She was breathing hot and heavy again in no time. After a few minutes, each sharp rise and fall of her bare chest was accompanied by soft, barely audible whimpers. Her hands followed suit, gliding and groping over her body. Just as she was nearing her peak, she stared at the shelf on the wall. The one with the backpack and the makeup. She stared daggers at it like it was somehow a threat she had to overcome. Like it was some sort of competition to be bested.

It was such an odd thing to witness that I didn't notice the man stop his work short to stand up, lean over Rikki, and slap her across the face. Her eyes shot back to him, and her anger evaporated immediately as she wiped her mouth.

"I told you never to look at those," he said, barely calm. "We've been over this several times. You are not allowed."

He finished up attaching the leg in a few quick movements, then dragged the woman to her feet.

"Veto," she said, almost shouting. "I'm sorry, I didn't mean it."

If I could have gasped in surprise I would have. Instead, I just gasped for breath as my eyes snapped to him. Veto. The scarified word carved into my thigh, the one that Eshe covered with a tattoo. It was a brand, claiming me and anyone else who was in this body before me.

"I know you are," he said, words as soft as concrete as he finished up his work on her. "Now, go on, go to bed. I'll be in shortly."

Rikki gave him a meek nod and got up from the operating table. She leaned up to give him a kiss on the cheek. He let her do it, but didn't respond in the slightest. Rikki pouted, and I could see her bottom lip tremble a little as she pushed forward on my legs and went down the hall.

"Finish me up when you're done?" she asked, stopping halfway and looking back over her shoulder.

"I will," Veto agreed.

Then she was gone, padding off into the darkness, leaving Veto alone with us. It wasn't like she provided any degree of protection—quite the opposite—but I was terrified of the glimpse I had just gotten of the man. The other side of him, the side that brought my body here four times before. He stared down the hall after her and leaned his head to his left, then to his right, popping the vertebrae in his neck. Then he set about gathering another collection of tools. Some I recognized, but others—mainly the knives and rotating saws—were new.

"Don't worry," he said, tapping the dull edge of a scalpel to his chin. "These aren't for you."

"Don't you fucking touch her," I snarled.

"Well, not yet anyway," he amended with a smug grin, ignoring me entirely.

Setting the surgical tool aside, he broke a small capsule beneath Eshe's nose. She lunged into consciousness, trying to flail her limbs, but the restraints exercised their will. The effect left her just sort of waggling there on the end of the chains. Veto chuckled at the display and retrieved a piece of equipment from behind me. It was a frame of metal piping shaped like a crucifix. He secured it into a recess in the floor then repositioned Eshe's wrists and ankles on the cross.

Her eyes scanned the room wildly as she put pieces of memory back together. In the meantime, Veto moved with practiced motions, closing another large cuff around her neck followed by an IV needle in her jugular.

"This will keep you awake, but it might make you a little woozy," he told Eshe, placing a gentle kiss on her forehead.

I pulled myself up and drew a breath. "I'll kill you."

All I managed to draw from Veto was a chuckle. Then he retrieved the scalpel and pressed it into the top of Eshe's raised arm. Her entire body trembled, every muscle and tendon tensing, and at first, she barely let out a choked gasp. Screaming came next. It was something entirely incomprehensible as Veto completed drawing the bleeding line across her skin.

When Eshe let out her first pained wail, I started shouting. I wasn't even thinking anymore, just spitting out whatever came to mind. Every dredge of the scalpel over muscle fibers, every scrape of its edge across tendon and eventually bone felt like an eternity. By the time he opened a path mid-way up her humerus, it felt like enough time had passed for us all to go extinct. All the while, Veto went about his work with a casual smile of someone fulfilling their life's purpose.

Eshe and I screamed together until our throats were raw. I don't know how long it was, but I had gone through every obscenity and insult I could think of. Down to the shit that didn't make sense. I scarcely recall uttering the syllables for blunderbuss fucking shit gibbon and or a knob gobbling chucklefuck. Not that I would go back to check, but I knew that my memory logs would confirm them and probably more.

Salt and iron eventually lit up the back of my tongue, and my ears rang. Dizziness and a stabbing pain in my shoulders finally forced me to stop. Exhausted, my eyes drifted to Eshe. She was still conscious, but was staring off into the abyss. She'd screamed enough to make herself bleed too. Drops of red, dark against her skin, dribbled from one corner of her mouth. It continued, off her chin and onto her chest and stomach. The parts of her body that weren't restrained shuddered with a cocktail of shock and adrenaline.

"Not much more now, Eshe," I managed to rasp. "You can make it. Then I'll get you out of here."

Veto cauterized both sides of the wound, then reached down to his tray of tools, to his bone saw, and passed it over for a triangular metal file. He gripped the handle firmly and brought it up to the exposed portion of humerus. Then he dragged the tool back and forth until a small channel formed.

"No point in talking to her," Veto said. "Shock has taken her completely."

Veto was right. But there might be a chance for me to get him to stop. Her arm was lost; there was nothing I could do about that. If what he'd said about my body was true, it was what followed the amputation that worried me. If I could stop him before he killed her, though, I'd be able to live with that, even if it wasn't for much longer. I needed to get his attention, though, and draw him away from Eshe. So, even though it may invite a quicker death, my arms pulled against their restraints, and I took in as much air as I could manage.

"Hey, so what's the deal with that deranged cock socket of yours?" I asked, borrowing one of Eshe's colloquialisms. I feigned humor. "I mean you sick fucks are perfect for each other."

Nothing. I didn't even manage a flinch from Veto. He just sat there filing away at Eshe's arm, the rapid little *zip-zup* noise grating on my sanity.

"Speaking of," I continued. "What the hell's with that? Don't you guys prefer to fuck your victim's neck after you take their head off or something?"

Still no response. I was being lazy and unimaginative. Too conventional. Veto can't have just come upon this particular pastime without reason. People don't do what they do in a vacuum; there had to be something that prompted him.

"So how'd you get started on this particular hobby?" I asked, finding a delirious bit of sarcasm. "I'm asking for a friend. Is there a checklist or something? Absent father, check. Mother was a prostitute, check. Was she a specialty item for some fringe kinkster to get off on?"

"You watch too many vids," he chided, without even a hint of irritation.

I finally got a few words out of the bastard, and he was patronizing me, but I wasn't about to let that stop me.

"Not it then, huh?" I said, more to myself than anyone else.

I glared at the shelf that Rikki had gotten in trouble for looking at, and I noticed something I missed earlier. A name embroidered into the backpack in flowing, cursive script. Evadir. It was an instinct to go after his parents, and he wasn't wrong. I had watched a lot of auto-generated streaming murder mysteries, and that's probably what informed where I started. But hell, I knew plenty of people who didn't technically have parents, more than just Mahdi and I. Eshe was one, sort of. Laden may have taken her in as his own but—

My train of thought completely derailed as I landed on what might do it.

My shoulders screamed as I lifted myself up for another round, but I had a good feeling about this.

"You weren't always like this. I know that much," I admitted. "But I'm starting to wonder if the body I'm in now was closer to you. You probably loved her just a little too much, didn't you? You couldn't keep your hands off her, could you? And who could blame you? I'm really taking myself in here, and I'm pretty sure I'd fuck me." I flashed a wicked little grin. "In fact, I already have."

I could see the muscles in his back tensing up, but little else.

So, I kept going. "You probably started in the dreamscape, didn't you? Got hooked on it and then, when that wasn't enough, you opted for a taste of reality. Did you honestly think all those waterworks were tears of joy? And you kept at it, the way into adulthood, until she couldn't take it anymore."

"Shut up," he said quietly, setting the bone-caked file down on his tool tray.

I didn't dare, and instead, I doubled down. "She cut herself, didn't she? Because pain was the only thing that could drown out what you were doing to her. It started somewhere you wouldn't notice. Then, eventually, she slit her wrists up to the elbow. And you just couldn't bear the sight of your baby girl like that, could you? So, you took her limbs."

"My. Limbs," I reiterated, making a point of emphasizing both words. "You took them away. That way, she couldn't hurt herself anymore, and you didn't have to see how much you hurt her and how badly she wanted to escape you. But she figured out a way didn't she?"

Veto had a scalpel back in hand and was out of his seat before I could blink. He held the knife up in a clenched fist, and his voice came out in a gravelly rumble. "I said, shut up!"

The move startled me enough that I almost obeyed. But I chose defiance. Pulse beating in my eyes, I dragged myself up for air one last time and then my ears gave out, replaced with a dull, waterlogged nothing. Even without hearing myself utter the words, though, I knew how each syllable felt as it played across my tongue. My half-crazed utterances had the potential to end me then and there. But I couldn't have given a shit, I had him.

"You know what I think?" I said.

Veto's eyes went wild.

"I think it made you hard," I said, running entirely on autopilot now. "Cutting her apart like that. Slicing through all that gorgeous muscle and flawless skin. I bet you had to get one last taste befo—"

The knife blurred and tore a channel across my cheek, allowing air and blood to pour in through a new opening in my mouth. His free hand—curled into a fist—hit the opposite side of my face, filling my vision with stars and flashes of indistinct color.

"How many times did she beg you to stop?" I asked, through a mouthful of blood, looking him straight in the eyes.

He dropped the scalpel and hit me again, splashing red all over the two of us. I could see his mouth moving. He was screaming something at me, low and raw. I hadn't just knocked him back on his heels, I had managed to throw him off a goddamned cliff.

Just past him, Rikki—covered in little more than a bedsheet—came in from the other room to watch and leaned against the doorway. Her smug look made me grin, wide and toothy, just like the fucking circ. Part of me understood then why he smiled the way he did. He knew something that nobody else did. That he had the upper hand.

I spit out something that felt like a liter of blood and laughed. It came out as something wheezing and ragged, but it was laughter just the same. Veto stopped and stared at me. His face was bright red, and I could make out the lines of bulging veins in his forehead.

I looked him in the eyes, took a pained, gurgling breath, and leaned forward as far as I could, our foreheads nearly touching. "Now I get to hurt you, daddy…"

Veto wrapped his hands around my throat and squeezed. I struggled for air and flung my hands around in their restraints, summoning my knives. The sudden lack of air caught me by surprise, which weakened my throw, but it didn't change a thing. The blades flew at Veto's back like I'd pelted him with a handful of rocks. It wasn't enough to hurt him—much. A few shallow punctures, perhaps, but it did get him to release me and turn to face this new threat. I erupted in a coughing fit and gasped for air. I was riding the edge of unconsciousness but managed to slash at his arms and legs, leaving him covered in dozens of small cuts in mere moments.

He knocked a few of the knives away with a few contemptuous swats and whipped back around to finish me off. His arms reached again for my neck, but as he did, he slipped in the puddle of blood that was growing on the floor beneath me. He fell back and slammed his head on the corner of his workbench, opening a deep, spurting trench in his scalp.

"Veto!" Rikki shouted, running to him.

She knelt down next to him and checked his pulse and seemed to visibly relax a moment later. He was still alive. Damn it. Rikki looked up at me, gritting her teeth. That smugness she displayed before, and the worry that followed it as Veto fell dissolved into fear. She was afraid of me. I threatened her, or perhaps this body did. I was always so used to putting up a fight or attempting to be a force to be reckoned with, but I had never been one to be feared. Until now, that is. She got up, leaving the sheet behind her. Then the fear on her face turned to anger.

She lunged at me, swinging a sideways fist into the left side of my face, darkening half of my vision. She hit me again on the other side, then again, and again. She punched better than Veto did, and every blow sent me closer to the hazy darkness of unconsciousness.

I did my best to bring my knives back, and as I did, she threw an elbow into my stomach, which heaved and brought up nothing but a small trickle of bile. The blades I was calling fell to the floor. Another of Rikki's throws caught my jaw and sent bits of broken teeth flying.

I peered down through squinting eyes to one of my knives, which was glowing a dull orange, burning off the blood it had landed in. I lifted it, which was about all I could manage, and moved it over to the strap holding Eshe's wrist in place. The knife burned her a little, but managed to slice through the material with ease. I tried to smile and instead let myself drift off toward unconsciousness.

"No!" Rikki snarled. "You don't get to escape this yet."

She rummaged through a nearby cabinet and came back with a syringe. Without much consideration, she stabbed it into my neck. A slight buzzing warmth rippled out from the injection, and I wanted to laugh. The stupid bitch had given me some kind of sedative or painkiller. My chin dipped lower, and Rikki cursed and hit me harder, this time in the ribs. Not even the cracked rib she gave me kept my eyes open as she adjusted to hit me in the face one more time.

TWENTY-THREE

SPLIT LIP

I was twelve when I got the shit beaten out of me for the first time. Mahdi and I broke out of our facility and were on the streets of the Shiv for the last eight months. Like most orphans who didn't get snatched up in the sex trade, we became accustomed to stealing from adults, and from one another if the opportunity presented itself. That day, I was sneaking into a local orphan gang's turf to borrow a portable computer I wanted for myself.

They were older—and therefore bigger—than I was. Not kids I wanted to fuck with. But there I was, silently creeping over rooftops above their camp. It was constructed in a small alcove between two buildings. Layered tarps, bolted to the brick walls formed a makeshift roof. From the top, there were only two openings, one in each back corner. On one side sat a fire barrel, and on the other was a water pipe they were siphoning from. That was my way in.

I crawled to the edge of the building and lowered myself down until I could reach the pipe. All I had to do was climb down, snatch my prize a few meters away, then climb back up. Easy enough.

The gang below was preoccupied with a fight on the far side of the street. They were toughening up one of their new initiates, and had only left one kid to guard their little alcove stash. She was standing on her tiptoes and leaning one way then the other, trying to glean whatever she could of the fight from her vantage point.

Getting to the bottom of the drain pipe, I tried to leap off but misjudged the distance and tumbled off an upturned garbage bin. I rolled with it and came up to my feet, but the game was up. My eyes locked with the lone sentry's for a drawn out moment. Neither of us were exactly sure what to do next. Then I made for the terminal and slapped its monitor down into the locked position above its keyboard. She started yelling down the street to the rest of the group.

They replied with a chorus of shouts and what seemed like a thunder of running footsteps. As I left their little fort, I rubbernecked around to see them all racing toward me. Everyone except for the new recruit who, enjoying a moment's reprieve, pushed the bent angle of his nose back into place. Then I bolted.

As the lone guard approached, trying to slow me down, I heaved the computer, swinging at her in a horizontal arc. One edge of the device caught her jaw, knocking her to the ground in a spray of blood and dislodged teeth.

"Sorry!" I hollered as I continued my escape.

Rounding the corner out of the alley, I almost ran into a group of people, chatting away with the kind of unbalanced speech that only alcohol can offer. Thinking quick, I dropped into a slide, passing between them. I could hear shouting and cursing behind me, which only drove my feet to claim more ground. My imagination narrated my escape. A spy who had made her way into an enemy base, and was now on the run with valuable intel—just like I'd seen in old movies—and I could do little but give in to the wicked grin that crept onto my face.

Coming to a long and crowded flight of stairs, I improvised and leapt up onto the railing, riding gravity down to the fourth-floor Kahwlun market below. Orange lights blared and strobed. People shouted from all directions, calling would-be customers to consider one sale or another. It was such a sudden wave of noise and color and movement that I lost my footing, tripped, and collided into a dark-skinned man with tinted goggles attached to his face with rivets. He was taking in the shops with a young girl about my age when I bowled him over.

"Woah, you okay, kid?" the man asked while he got back to his feet and brushed off his shorts. "Where are you going in such a hurry?"

Getting up myself, I looked at the man and the girl—who had taken refuge behind him—and couldn't think of what to say. Most people just curse or pummel you or something. I ran into him, and he wanted to make sure I was okay? Who the hell was this guy?

"I, uh..." I said, trailing off.

"Hey, man, that's a decent rig you got there. Kyoto 85," he said, flashing a grin. "You've got good taste."

"Thanks..." I said, trailing off again. "I gotta..."

A voice—partly into puberty—called out in a crackly baritone. "Get back here, you little maggot fuck!"

"Shit, I... I gotta go," I said and started jogging away from the pair.

"Good luck, kid!" he hollered, waving a hand goodbye as the gang flowed around him with renewed effort.

I wove between shoppers and vendor stalls, even doubling back to change direction a couple of times to lose them. The plan had been to meet up with Mahdi in our little forgotten crawlspace on the eighth floor. Under a protein extrusion shop called Meat the Press. That had been when the plan meant that I wasn't followed by a dozen or so kids that wanted to cave my face in. There was nothing to do now but escape and lie low.

I slid around the patron of another shop and came to a clearing in the middle of an open-air auction house. Save for where I was standing, the place was packed with people of all sorts. They were watching or competing over two sales on either side of the space. To my left, a man with bony-looking prosthetic hands was shouting over half of the group. He was taking bids for a set of cooking knives, the wooden handles worn so thin that they no longer covered the tangs of each blade. The metal was useless. It was the wood scraps that were selling. On the other side, a woman with a series of scopes mounted over half her face gathered bids for a pair of nearly translucent children with bright red eyes. Test twins, the control and the subject, identical in every way except for what they were subjected to. The one with fewer surgical scars cowered behind the other as the bids climbed higher and higher.

I'd gawked for too long and turned to escape when my pursuers rushed the entrance. I backed away from them, keeping the terminal behind me backing up to a decorative concrete wall about as high as my shoulders. There was no way out. If I wasn't murdered outright, I was going to get my ass beat or worse. So, I leaned the computer against the wall, took a few steps forward, and held up my fists to the group that had now surrounded me.

They laughed, and I ground my teeth.

"You gonna take us all on you puny little shit?" said the taller kid in the middle of the group.

He must have been fourteen, at least, and his age made him seem twice my size. His hair fell uneven over his face, and the gleam of homemade tattoos caught my eye in the light of the auction house. I didn't respond, just brought my fists closer to my face and did my best at making my eyes look crazy.

"Fine with me," the kid said. "I could go for two fights in one day."

Without another word, he lunged across the few meters between us faster than I had expected. I got out of the way of his first swing, but didn't see what followed. I paid for that miscalculation by taking a knee to my ribs that sent me stumbling to the ground. Scrambling backward, I used the half-wall behind me to get to my feet. I brought my fists up again, and he followed suit.

I ducked to avoid his next strike and heard his fist crunch into the surface behind me. The kid howled in agony, and streaks of fresh blood colored his knuckles. Screaming, he dove again, but this time with both hands reaching for me. I dodged in the opposite direction and whirled around him. I reached up, grabbed a handful of his hair, and drove his face at the wall. Between his height and his screaming, his mouth made hard contact with the wall's edge. Before I could think about it, I pushed his face along the wall, the porous right angle of concrete acting like a hacksaw, splitting his face open at the corners of his lips.

He tumbled to the ground, clutching his face, crying himself raw, and choking on his own blood. I stared at him wide-eyed, then looked down at my hands. They were trembling. Seeing all that blood scared me. There was another part of me, however, that seemed to draw power from the experience. I looked from the kid on the ground to the rest of the group. They exchanged glances with one another. Some were nervous, others were angry, but they all looked at their fallen comrade, who erupted with more panicked cries, and started to close on me.

We'd become quite a distraction for a few of the auction-goers. Some were annoyed, while others seemed to welcome the diversion. I saw one woman trade some money with another, nodding in our direction. The rest of the gang drew closer, and I raised my fists again, counting my opponents.

I'd just gotten incredibly lucky, but even without their leader, I was definitely outmatched and outnumbered. But I tried to look intimidating, and took a swing at the first person I could reach. All of them backed away at once, keeping their distance at first, no single member of the group wanting to take an unnecessary risk of injury. I started swinging at the air in a desperate bid to ward them off, but it was too late. The surface tension broke, and they all came in at me at once.

I was rapidly introduced to bruising pain across my body, and I fell backward to the ground. A worn old boot caught me in the face, and that was it for me. Fists and feet and knees hit me again and again and again. There was little I could do but to hold my arms over my head as the beating continued, and to hope I'd be able to walk away after it was all over. I cautioned a quick glance between my fingers to see if there might be an opening for me to get away. That's when I saw the concerned faces of the man and girl I had run into earlier.

BLINDSPOT

An elbow collided with my ribs, and I struggled to breathe. Another strike took me across the face, battering my already broken nose. My eyes opened again, and I saw Eshe, the girl I had met all those years ago in the market with her adopted father. She quietly padded up behind Rikki, more nimble than she had any right to be, and drove a kick into the side of the woman's knee. Bone and tendons popped as the joint bent at an odd, obtuse angle, and she went to the floor. Eshe followed her down and planted her knee on Rikki's neck.

Now it was her turn to struggle for air.

Rikki fought, doing whatever she could to get Eshe off of her. But all she ended up getting was one lopsided punch aimed at Eshe's groin. I winced and felt the ghosts of my testicles ache at the sight of it. It no doubt hurt Eshe when it landed, but she showed little reaction to it. Instead, she just glared down at Rikki with a look of hate that I had only seen her do once before.

Rikki prepared another swing but was stopped short when Eshe drove her fist into Rikki's bare stomach. What little air had been in her lungs was forced out in a choked gasp. The fight drained out of her, and soon enough she went limp. Eshe leaned back onto her other knee, releasing Rikki's throat just enough to let her start breathing again. She watched Rikki for several seconds, chest heaving and body trembling with the rush of adrenaline.

After a minute of catching her breath, Eshe got up. I wanted to get her attention, to thank her for saving my life, but all I could do was watch through a half-closed eye and focus on breathing shallow, unfulfilling breaths. She looked around the room and walked unevenly over to a cabinet and rifled through it. A couple of vials were lined up beside a pair of syringes and a few needles. Larger gauge needles went on first, and she used one prepped syringe for each bottle. Drawing the plunger back with one hand, she quickly swapped out needles and stuck it into the meaty part of her shoulder, just above where Veto had been working.

The process was repeated with the other syringe, except Eshe nearly filled it with whatever was in the vial. Then, she staggered over to Rikki and Veto in turn, taking time to find a good vein and injecting half of the drawn solution into each. Finally, she made it back to the pipe crucifix she'd been bound to and took Veto's bone saw from his work tray. Using the iron frame to lower herself to the floor, Eshe took a moment to steady herself, then put one of the empty syringes between her teeth.

Beads of sweat clung to Eshe's skin. Some were eventually too heavy to stay in place, rolled down her body, and drew different lines over the curves of her neck, breasts, hips, and legs. All things I never got to experience firsthand. I had to get myself beaten half to death and killed in order to get a swap, and by then it was too late. Then, for the briefest of moments, a different sort of envy fluttered through my mind—envy for what Mahdi and Eshe had. Even if at the moment I was only thinking superficially, they had something together that I never gave myself the chance to have with anyone else. I rationalized time and time again that it never made any sense given what I did for a living, but that was all over now. If I survived this whole shitshow, I didn't have any more excuses.

Eshe took a deep breath. The bone saw spun up with an angry electric whine. Then she pushed it into the exposed bone of her arm. Even as her teeth dug into the plastic, her cries were almost louder than the saw. A few agonizing moments later, her arm hit the ground with a thump. She took some time to catch her breath, then looked down at her lifeless arm with a hint of disgust. Then she pushed herself up and rummaged around the supply cabinets for some stemgel, medical gauze, and tape. She applied the salve, which would become a thin layer of skin in a matter of hours, then wound it tightly and taped it off. Once that was done, she walked up to me as I hung by my arms, barely conscious.

"Well shit. You really know how to piss people off, don't you?" she asked. "Don't worry," Eshe continued, having a one-sided conversation. "I'm pissed at you too, but there's plenty of time for that once we get ourselves back together and get the fuck out of here."

If I could have barked out a harsh laugh just then, I would have. Instead, I just drifted for a while as Eshe collected a few tools from around the room.

"I'm going to get you down so you can breathe, but I'm going to need your help with this later," she said, motioning to the bandaged stump on her shoulder. "So, go ahead and relax."

When my ass touched the cool concrete floor, it was the most mercifully wonderful thing I had ever experienced. Even though every part of me hurt like hell, I could finally breathe again. I waded through all of my dull aches and stabbing pains until I found something that resembled peace and quiet. Tears of relief flooded my eyes as I welcomed the darkness of sleep.

Goddamn. Sometimes it really is about the little things.

TWENTY-FIVE

TERIYAKI

I awoke on the operating table sometime later, wrapped in a blanket with something numbingly cold on my face. My mouth tasted of stale iron, and it was hard to keep from probing the gap in my teeth with my tongue. I'd have been lying if I said that I was comfortable, but after the last few days, I wasn't going to complain either. My shoulder protested with stiffness and fresh throbbing as I reached up to find me head wrapped in bandages. The source of the chill was an ice pack that covered my left eye completely. Beneath it, my fingers found a row of neatly applied stitches. What's more my legs were back. How Eshe managed to reattach them with one hand was beyond my imagination.

"Welcome back," Eshe said, leaning against the door to the hallway. "Now get up and give me a hand. I'd like to be ready to go by the time they wake up."

All I wanted was to crawl into a hole, go to sleep, and not wake up for a few years. Instead, I worked my way into a sitting position that made all my muscles and joints call out their various complaints. My mind hovered on that 'they' part of what Eshe said for a while before I finally found the will to open my eyes.

Eshe had clearly been working while I was out. Veto was on the floor, leaning up against the iron frame he'd attached Eshe to previously. His wrists were bound behind his back and around the base of the crucifix, which itself had been welded to the mount in the floor. Rikki, on the other hand, was laid out on the floor and wasn't restrained at all. She almost looked peaceful if not for an unnatural, lopsided bulge in her stomach, just beneath her ribs. Immediately beside it was a long puckered incision that had been secured with a haphazard row of staples. A thick bundle of cables ran out of the wound and to a nearby power outlet, where they were welded in place.

"What the hell?" I asked.

"You'll see," she said, coming down the hall and back into the kill room. She sounded almost cheerful.

Her hair was wet from a fresh shower and she was wrapped in a towel. She carried a pile of clothes and dropped them onto the table next to me and began sorting through them. She dropped the towel and slipped a pair of boxers up her legs to her waist, and after a moment, their loose structure tightened to fit Eshe's hips like a second layer of skin. They had defaulted to a charcoal color but changed to a deep shade of green when Eshe slipped her thumb over an interface on the waistband. In her state, I could see the tattoo she got when she picked out her racing name a few years ago. It was then mostly covered as she slipped on a sports bra. It pulled her breasts tight to her as it fitted itself and synced up with her boxers, shifting to the same green pigment.

"You can stop ogling me," Eshe said absentmindedly. "Nothing you haven't seen before."

I protested. "I'm not ogling you. Just in a little bit of shock is all."

She finished slipping into a pair of auto-adjusting pants then threw a few things at me. "C'mon, get dressed. I need your help and we can talk as we work."

It was slow going, but I eventually found most of my clothes from before and gathered up in a small pile on my lap. "Eshe, what happened? How did you find me?"

"I didn't find you," she said, almost under her breath.

"Yeah, but you're here now," I said.

"No, Raide. I didn't find you. I went back to the hab after our fight, and you were gone. I thought you left me behind like you'd planned to, but I found your pack and that precious goddamn AI of yours. So I waited for you to come back. A day and a fucking half, and you never showed back up. I went out and followed the IDs on your arms and legs. Everywhere you went, I did too, asking everyone I saw if they'd seen you around. I even showed your picture around, which was a waste of time." She tugged her pants up awkwardly with one arm. "Until I asked them," she continued, motioning to Rikki and Veto. "They jumped me and brought me here. I didn't find you. The two of us just have some dumb fucking luck. Even if I did find you, save your goddamned gratitude. I don't want it."

Eshe tugged a shirt from the pile of clothes and stalked across the room.

My voice creaked a little. "I'm sorry. I didn't mean for any of this to happen, how could I have known—"

"That's not the point. You don't fucking get it, asshole," she spat, turning back to me. She motioned to the room around us. "I know none of this was your doing. That isn't the point at all. You were going to leave me. Just drop me off like some piece of luggage. Like I was another one of your deliveries on another one of your jobs."

I started to argue, but she cut me off. As she crossed the room and got in my face, I could see the tears at the corners of her eyes. "I don't care what your intentions were, you can't just abandon people when things get inconvenient. Did you even for one second, stop to think about what I might want or how you leaving would make me feel?"

I shied away from the confrontation a little. "I just wanted you to be safe."

Eshe let out a bitter little laugh. "They chased Mahdi across the continent and you thought I'd be safe. You fucking idiot. I'm in this now. Sure, I don't want to be, but I can't do anything about that can I?" She turned away and started down the hall. "I would never have left you behind, you're all I have left."

We didn't talk for a while after that. She went about getting her lace-up boots back on, then stomped down the hall and out of sight. While I sifted through the pile of clothes, I did the same with my thoughts. I did want to keep Eshe safe, I wasn't lying about that. But I'd be lying if I hadn't actually been planning on leaving her too. Even if my intention was to come back. I didn't want her to die like Mahdi had. But while he got himself into this, I dragged her in against her will. The least I could do was give her an out.

"That was the right thing to do, wasn't it?" I pondered aloud.

If I was being honest with myself, I wasn't sure of the answer.

I slipped my clothes back on and ruminated for a while when it finally dawned on me. It was so plainly obvious that I felt ashamed, embarrassed, and dull all at once. She could have left me on my own a dozen times over. When I showed up at her door, after she patched up my old body, when my bounty hit the boards. And so many times after. She'd been consciously making the choice to stay and hold tight to what was important to her. I, on the other hand, was pushing her and everything else away. If anything or anyone was with me, they'd be in danger. But I was just telling myself that, so I wouldn't have to see them taken from me, so I wouldn't have to suffer loss like that all over again.

I didn't drag Eshe into this against her will, but I was trying to drag her out of it because I somehow decided along the way that I knew better.

That settled it then. So, with my metaphorical tail between my legs, I pushed myself up from the table and padded my way down the hall after her. What lay on the other side of the doorway was the other half of the unit. It was a neatly furnished two-story apartment. At first glance, I'd never have guessed that it was attached to a torture room, and was quite the contrast with its organized, efficient, and curated appearance. The whole living space on the first floor was a mix of varying purples, greens, and blues and it smelled of fresh incense.

Several massive vidframes covered the walls, flanking the apartment's main door. They played at being windows and looked out onto a very different picture of Manhattan, something before the era of megastructures and the Barrel. I guessed the decorating was Rikki's influence rather than Veto's. I don't know if it was my own assumptions about the man's personality when he wasn't butchering people, but I imagined he often lost himself to his work and paid little attention to aesthetics.

Off of the main room was a small kitchen with similar styling. Eshe was leaning over the counter, beside the carcass of an old microwave and several other kitchen gadgets. She worked carefully to strip out useful parts and deposit them into semi-organized piles on the counter next to her. Screws, bolts, and other fasteners in one, metal brackets in another, and so on. Each pile surrounded a workspace in the middle, where Eshe had laid out the beginnings of a mechanical frame.

Mounded up on the opposite side of the kitchen, with a lot less attention paid to organization, was a collection of prepackaged food. My stomach immediately felt like it was about to eat itself, and it drove me forward. Even though it was entirely unnecessary, I almost sprinted to the relative feast, nearly tripping over Eshe on the way through.

"No, please, go right ahead. Help yourself," she droned sarcastically.

I was so focused on sifting through the pile that I barely managed more than a small murmur. Not when there was food right in front of me. There were packs of vacuum-sealed teriyaki protein slabs, mushroom crisps, imitation cheese puffs, coffee sticks, and plenty of others. I found some plain old vanilla-flavored starch bars too, which were good in a pinch, but they were far from my priority. Instead, I greedily swept anything with the aforementioned teriyaki on the package off the counter and into my bag.

Eshe snorted at me before turning back to her work. "I don't know what it is about you and that fucking sauce."

"I think one of my donor-parents was from Seattle," I mused as I tore open one of the snacks and scarfed it down without chewing.

"Sichuan's better, but it's okay to be wrong," she shot back, faint humor slipping into her tone.

I wiped my mouth with one hand then turned around and leaned back against the counter. "Hey," I began, quietly "I'm sorry. About everything. I guess I thought that if I pushed everyone and everything away, they wouldn't get hurt, and neither would I. I've lost so much in the past few days, I wanted to protect you."

Eshe stopped for a moment and stared out into the empty living room. Even with her back turned to me, I could tell she was trying to contain herself. Then with a heavy sigh and a shake of her head, she answered, "You can start making it up to me by helping me with this new arm."

I glanced at the small bit of bone protruding from her shoulder. She'd swapped out the gauze for a plastic container and several layers of food-grade cling wrap. It reminded me a lot of what she did—albeit, more professionally—with Goz's arm back in the Shiv.

"Gonna take one of the arms that Veto, uh, collected?" I asked, feeling like it was an obvious question.

"Nope," Eshe answered simply while soldering components to a circuit board. "I'm not going to benefit from what he was doing."

I pointed toward the hallway and Veto's torture room. "Seriously? You're doing whatever the fuck you're doing out there, and this is where you draw the line?"

Her answer was matter-of-fact. "Yes, this is where I draw the line. I have no problem being monstrous to those who are monstrous to others, but I am not going to consciously benefit from the pain and suffering they've inflicted."

"You could give purpose to some of that suffering, though," I added.

She fastened the board to a slim aluminum box on the inner frame of the arm she was working on before plugging it into her terminal. "Yeah, you could. But this is going to be my first mod, I want to choose what it is."

"I guess I can't really argue with that," I admitted, electing discretion over confrontation. "So, what do you actually need my help with?"

"Once I have this done, I need your help getting it attached," Eshe said.

I nodded and watched her work. The limb that was taking shape was basic as far as Eshe's designs were usually concerned. But then again, she was building this out of junk. I was really in no position to judge. As fascinating as it was, however, once she moved over to the terminal to start programming I was starting to get pretty bored. So, instead, I decided to see what Rikki's vidframes had to offer.

I dug up the boards for places I used to frequent, starting with the strip club and the Armory Bazaar where this all started. Neither of them had any post history for the last 48-hours. They used to get thousands in a day, but now there was nothing. My heart sank, but I couldn't fathom even those mercenaries sterilizing both areas and keeping people from filling the void all the killing would leave behind. It didn't make any sense. There had to be something—anything—from the handful of survivors who were bound to be hunkered down somewhere or new people that took advantage of the vacant real estate. Nothing even on the alt boards. Part of me was afraid to look any further back. It was almost better to hope people made it out alive and never know for sure than to know that thousands of people you would at least recognize were gone.

Then I thought about Jin and Vallis and wondered where they were. I remembered Jin offering to get me into the sex trade, right before shit started flying, and it made me crack a smile. He would lose his mind over my new body and would probably insist on taking me out to get better clothes. The memory faded as I imagined still images of both him and Vallis dead somewhere in a heap on the ground. I had never really thought of them as more than acquaintances. Useful people to know, who wouldn't try to kill me for whatever small treasures I may have collected. Like the paper book I had in my old apartment, for example—the one Eshe returned to me. Thinking about it now, though, sharing meals and drinks around a table with people regularly made them more than what I gave them credit for. Especially for Jin, who put his life on the line in more ways than one to help me escape.

I opened up the board backups, searching for any sign of my two friends, braving all of the death I was terrified to see. The first post I found came from someone who lived a few floors above me. They posted a couple of hours after she started working on my swap.

From: RiskyRacer.163843

Subject: THEY'RE KILLING EVERYONE

We think the mercs are back. They're butchering everyone. Not like before; they're torturing people. Tearing them apart. We can hear the screams in the elevator shafts. We sent a few down the stairwell to find a way out and we haven't heard from them. It's been 12 hours.

The gangs have formed a coalition, as they call it, and have started moving people to the higher floors as quietly as possible. We've also pooled together all the kay we could come up with. 2.4 kay isn't much right now, but every floor is adding to it as we climb higher.

We've sent requests directly to both Cerali Incorporated and even Vys, with no response.

The contract is attached.

Please. Someone, help us.

The blood drained from my face, and I suddenly felt a little dizzy, which forced me to sit down. They went back. Or perhaps they never left. Regardless, after they killed me and didn't recover Soqua, they sterilized the whole building I lived in. Tens—or maybe hundreds—of thousands of people. I remembered staring at that kid's dead eyes through the holes in their father's back. How many children had been blown away over that chrome canister? I couldn't make any sense of it. Kids could be trained to fill a whole host of positions in a corporate structure. They could be indoctrinated into corpsec when they got old enough, used for memory hacking, and more. Given that I came from places like that, I hated the idea of it, but it was objectively better than killing them. More profitable too. Even if the mercs didn't see them as human, their corporate masters would at least see them as valuable assets.

"Hey Raide," Eshe hollered, leaning on the countertop peninsula and craning her head beneath the cupboards above it. "I need your help."

"They went back," I said, still trying to wrap my head around it.

"Who went where?" Eshe asked with an expression that was both confused by the statement and frustrated at the lack of context.

I pointed at the post on the screen. "The mercs, they went back to my building and cleaned it out."

Eshe rounded the corner, taking a few steps toward the vidscreen to read for herself.

"Jesus," she said, subdued. "You can't blame yourself for that."

"I know," I said, tapping my finger to my temple. "But I can't help but feel like I brought those fuckers in. It would have been a normal day otherwise."

"People you know get out at least?" she asked.

I shook my head. "I don't know."

"Shoot them a message then, idiot," Eshe said. "Then help me pack things up so we can get out of here."

I managed a nod and watched her head to the second floor. She was right. I may never get a reply from Jin or Vallis, but if I didn't try to contact them now, I might never get the chance. It only took a few seconds to think of what I wanted to say. After deciding to add a couple other people who may or may not be alive, I set the message free into the digital ether. As it sent, a groan and a crash echoed out from the torture room. Eshe came down the stairs in a hurry.

"Get your shit together, we'll be leaving soon," she spat, hopping backward on the balls of her feet before she took off down the hall. "Veto's awake, and I don't want to overstay his welcome."

ALL WARM INSIDE

Just like that, she was gone. More metal crashing and shouting followed. I grabbed our bags, making sure to get Eshe's new arm, then lumbered up the stairs rather than going to the door. Eshe was at the top of the steps, in the doorway to the murder room. Veto was thrashing against his bounds. Gone was the reserved, controlled killer I'd been abducted by. Instead, his eyes were wild, almost rabid.

"Eshe," I asked cautiously, trying not to grab the serial killer's attention. "Why don't we just kill him."

In answer, she took a deep breath and stepped into the room. She ignored Veto's crazed shouting and knelt down next to Rikki and injected something into one of the veins in her ankles. Eshe tossed the syringe aside and backed away again, making her way to an electrical panel on the wall.

Veto kept fighting and shouting at her, but all of that drained out of him once Rikki started to stir. His eyes darted back and forth over her body, tracing the grisly incisions that Eshe left behind. His attention snapped to Eshe as she opened the panel and flipped a fuse. Then she slammed it shut and, using a pocket torch, welded it shut.

"What..." Veto asked, voice trembling. "What did you do to her?"

I could feel the smugness on Eshe's reply. "Why don't you wait and find out?"

Veto pushed himself up using the pole he was bound to for balance. He craned his neck to get a better look at his lover. Her return to consciousness was not a kind one. She awoke with a torrent of screams, her chest heaving with effort accentuating the bulge of whatever Eshe had put in her abdomen, but little else. She struggled, tossing her head back and forth, then emptied her stomach over the side of the table. I'd have been lying if I didn't feel some degree of satisfaction at that.

"Veto," she cried between sobs and agonized gasps. "Wha—what's going on? I can't move my arms or legs!"

His answer lacked all the calm and collected confidence that had been so palpable before. His shoulders slumped and he leaned forward on his restraints. Her eyes found his, pleading, and it took a moment for her to realize that help wasn't coming. That Veto was just as trapped and powerless as she was. It was hard to tell from where I stood, but it looked like steam was coming out of her mouth.

Eshe continued backing down the hallway, never turning her back on the scene. "Hey, Rikki, you gut-fucked, bitch!" She barely contained her own vindictive laughter. "This will keep you awake, but it might make you a little woozy."

Recognizing his own words being used against him, Veto slowly looked up from his lover and stared daggers at Eshe. "I'm sorry, Rikki. I can't help you."

"W—Wait, Veto," She begged. "You can free yourself, right? You can save me, right?"

"Let's go," Eshe said, half-turning to me. I nodded, unsure of leaving the two of them like that.

"Listen to me!" Veto howled, dropping to his knees.

"Veto!" Rikki sobbed.

"Run if you like, but I am going to get out of here. And when I do, I will hunt you down," he continued.

Eshe took one of the bags from me with her remaining hand, and pushed past me into the apartment.

"Run," he snarled, sounding winded. "Run like hell! Don't worry, I'll find you! And when I drag you out of whatever dark shithole you scurry into, I will take you apart! Piece by piece!"

I followed her out of the apartment and into the adjoining hallway in silence. Rikki's sobs and Veto's tirade cut off abruptly as the door clicked shut behind us. Outside was a fairly average mixed-use access hall. Depending on which way you looked, some of the units were converted apartments, like Veto's, while others were small storefronts hidden behind crisscrossed security mesh.

"This way," Eshe said, taking a right, down the hall toward the service elevator. Aside from that, our wait and subsequent descent continued in silence. I finally spoke as we reached the first floor and passed through a small business entrance that was not all that dissimilar from my old building.

"Eshe, what was that?" I asked, keeping my tone to a near whisper.

"Their comeuppance," she answered simply.

Eshe fell behind me a step as we reached the building's main entrance. I rested my hands on the crash bars and stared outside through a narrow pane of security glass. People were moving briskly through a torrential downpour and cars were kicking up small waves as they sped past.

"Isn't death enough?" I asked. "Do we need to torture them?"

"After what they've done?" she asked, pointedly. "To fuck knows how many people? After what they did to me?" Eshe's tone was hard and cold. I could sense her rage, and what's more, her grief. Something about it reminded me of the way she talked to Goz back in the Shiv.

She pressed me. "Would you have preferred I spare them? Huh? Would you have preferred that I just put a bullet in their head and give them the very thing that they denied their victims? What the fuck is wrong with you?"

I winced at those words. I was certainly not squeamish about ending either of them, and I didn't even fully disagree with her. I just— something felt wrong about that. Leaving them both to starve to death almost seemed kinder than what Eshe had done. I took a deep breath and bowed my head, choosing to drop it. I wasn't about to go back up there and change anything, so I was in no position to throw stones.

"Okay," I said simply, changing the topic. "Where do we go now?"

She softened a bit at that. "Well we need to go get your pack from the hab unit. It's going to be a pain in the ass, but I think we can swing by real quick."

I sucked in a breath. In the midst of everything that had just unfolded over the last few days, I'd completely forgotten about Soqua. It was understandable of course, but now that we'd escaped and were about to step out into the world again, we had the other reality to contend with. Mahdi, the Circ, and Soqua.

"Yeah," I said with a resolute nod. "Let's go."

Eshe shrugged. "Alright, it's our funeral."

Then she shot me a smirk, flashing her teeth, opened the door, and stepped out into the rain. We kept up a quick pace, splashing through puddles and potholes alike. Nothing around us looked familiar. I could tell we were back in the Barrel or at least something that looked like it. Except that the buildings were cleaner, and the place lacked the dim orange glow I was used to. Instead, everything was either complete darkness or blinding neon light.

Approaching a major intersection, I could see signs ahead directing traffic toward the Slab, a massive 30-lane superhighway, and one of the main arteries of New York. As we were waiting for the lights to change, someone in the distance behind me shouted, and I whipped around in a panic to scan the crowds. A man in a suit was hailing an autocab, a food cart merchant hocking extruded beef sticks. Nothing out of the ordinary.

The people around us started moving as the light turned. I moved to keep up and bumped right into Eshe. She wasn't moving, just staring very intently across the street. Following her gaze, I saw the gleam of traffic lights reflecting off a man's circumneural mod, sporting a familiar, toothy grin.

The circ was flanked on both sides by the same contingent of the well-dressed mercenaries I'd become accustomed to seeing. My heart stopped. He'd tracked us, more than 500 kilometers across New York, all the way to Old Manhattan, then to wherever we were now.

Needless to say, Eshe and I bolted. The corpsec goons followed, but oddly enough, only them. The circ tilted his head and stared down the street, back toward Veto's building. It was a weird, bird-like motion that seemed curious. Then he disappeared around the corner, seemingly leaving our pursuit to his lackeys.

As we ran, we put as much distance between us and the circ as possible. Even with whatever distracted him, every second we gained could only help us. The rain stung, and it was hard to keep my eyes open, but we kept going, dodging around groups of people and cart vendors alike. Tires screeched and horns blared as we splashed through neon-reflected intersections. It was really quite beautiful. Small sparkles of light played through each falling droplet, reflecting windows and advertising signs. The same signs made the streets we sprinted down seem like rivers of light.

"We're not losing each other here, you understand?" I said, grabbing Eshe's hand and pulling her with me into oncoming traffic.

We dodged a couple of automated box trucks and made it to the other side of the street in one piece, which is when the suits behind us started shooting. Glass shattered, cars crashed into one another, and people screamed. Eshe and I ducked as low as we could and ran around the next corner.

"Go on ahead," I shouted. "I'm gonna buy us some time!"

Eshe nodded and ran off as I ducked into the next alleyway I passed and planted my back against the wall. Readying a single knife in my left hand, I watched the fleeing bystanders passing by two or three at a time. Then there was a break in the crowds, the empty void between everyone else and the shooters. I tightened my grip on the knife and did my best to listen. I heard orders being called out and footsteps getting closer.

When I saw the gun barrel appear in my peripheral vision, I swung around before the person could check their corner. I came up under their arms and got a firm grasp on the collar of their combat vest and pulled them into the alley. I stabbed the woman wildly in the chest, maybe half a dozen times staining the white button-up beneath her vest. She slumped against the wall choking and gasping before sliding down to the ground. I worked quickly, recovering her gun and searching her vest. I found a pair of flashbangs and smoke grenades and I took one of each.

Shoving the corpse to one side, I pressed against the wall again and pulled the pin on the flash. I didn't know this shit well enough to know how many seconds I had, so I just tossed it around the corner. Even semi-protected as I was, the sudden flash of light and sound was still disorienting. Fortunately, not enough that I couldn't pull the pin on the smoke and toss it out onto the sidewalk next to me. As thick smoke started to fill the area, I stumbled out of the alley, blind-firing the gun behind me in quick bursts. Once it clicked empty, I dropped it and sprinted for the next intersection.

Unsure of which direction Eshe went, I came to a stop before the crossing and looked around wildly. Finding her, as it turns out, was easy enough. As I rounded the corner to get out of the line of fire, she gave me a solid right hook and shoved her gun in my face.

"Oh, shit," she gasped, eyes roving around wildly for other signs of danger. "I'm sorry, I—"

"No time for that," I hollered, waving off her apology. "We have to keep moving!"

We continued down the street together, staying low and moving between parked cars, bus stops, and parcel drop-off boxes. My body wasn't used to this sort of thing yet, and I staggered to a halt and nearly fell over.

"We can't keep this up," Eshe gasped.

"No shit," I gasped.

I looked up at the buildings and streets around us, searching for something to help us escape. Then I thought of the signs for the slab that we'd passed earlier.

"Sure," I muttered to myself. "That could work. Just need a ride."

Most of the vehicles passing through were too clumsy to make an effective escape, but then I spotted the motorcycle. Half a block down the street, I could see a man in a red jacket wiping water from the seat, a meaningless gesture in this torrential downpour.

Without informing Eshe, I dragged myself into a run. The man sat down on the bike and started its engine. He punched coordinates into the nav and pulled away from the curb as I caught up to him. I planted my right foot next to the rear tire, and launched a spinning kick directly at the side of the man's head. He tumbled to the ground, but was quick to get back up and face me. Not that it would do a lot of good. I was already following up the kick by vaulting off the bike seat, and I hit him in the chest with both of my knees. The momentum carried us to the ground, and something cracked beneath me. I didn't think he was dead, but it wasn't important.

Without missing a beat, Eshe hopped into the front seat. I gave her a questioning look, as if to ask if she was okay with driving. She nodded, expression locked in determination. So I hopped on the back seat and held on as she took off.

The bike was older but well-maintained. It sat on two bulbous, spherical tires that would allow for omnidirectional movement. More important, though, was that it was small and quick. Eshe punched in coordinates of her own then sent us careening down the street. Once we were ascending the onramp for the Slab, I let out a deep breath.

Eshe meandered the bike through legions of automated vehicles. Most of them were cab-less, mobile storage units, but I would catch a glimpse of a few manned or semi-manned vehicles every so often. That computer virus I read about a few days ago must have spooked a few companies into putting people behind the wheel for a bit.

"I think we lost them!" I shouted into Eshe's ears.

Something flew past us in a column of steam. It split the water on the road and collided with a storage truck a few hundred meters ahead. The truck's cargo practically exploded, sending boxes and bits of shredded metal flying in all directions.

"Another gauss cannon!" I shouted in a near panic.

"Goddammit, Raide, I know! Sit down and shut the fuck up!" she responded.

I glanced over my shoulder and spotted two trucks coming up behind us. Lightly armored cabs with open cargo beds. Each one bore several gun-toting mercs, all aimed in our direction. Eshe tried cutting off a taxi to buy us some cover, but the automated vehicle was apparently set to aggressively fight for its place in line. Two women in professional clothing were arguing in the cabin but stopped to give us dirty looks.

Another column of steam flew at us and hit the ground, sending up a shower of sparks between the taxi and us. Something spun off the pavement and crashed through the cab, plastering the windows with a chunky sheet of red. I could distinctly hear screaming from the hole in the window.

Eshe wove the bike in the other direction through dozens of cars, shifting laterally, then backward, rotating around the traffic like the second hand on a clock. That evasiveness didn't count for much, though. The third shot came close enough to singe the hair on the side of my head.

We were going to be torn apart if we didn't do something. To our right, the taxi drifted away from us to take an exit and was immediately replaced by a panel van. The driver looked at us with a nervous smile and gave a small wave.

Who the hell smiles and waves with shit blowing up everywhere?

I checked over my shoulder again. One of the armored trucks had taken up position behind us, while the other was quickly passing the van with the smiling driver. This was it, all or nothing.

Leaning forward, I yelled into Eshe's ear, "Get me on the other side of this van! I have an idea!"

She glanced back and shot me a look that asked if I was crazy.

"Just do it!" I shouted.

Eshe shook her head and turned back to the road.

It happened in slow motion. She pushed hard on the handlebars, putting the bike into a semicircular spin that would have made Fibonacci proud. We crossed in front of the panel van at an angle, and I could see the surprised confusion on the diver's face. Had it been any other moment, I would have laughed my ass off. Our path continued, leaving us staring face-to-face with one of the trucks for a split second. The spin concluded with another smaller half-circle that righted our course.

I knew Eshe had no idea what I was planning on, but it didn't matter. It was not as if there was time to explain. I slung my bag over Eshe's shoulder and hopped up into a standing position on my seat, drawing a knife in each hand.

Rain plastered my face, and I took a deep breath, placed one foot on the headrest of Eshe's seat, and launched myself back, away from the bike in a backflip. Right toward our pursuers.

TWENTY-SEVEN

POLE POSITION

This was the first time Eshe had been on a bike in a few years. And as much as we were fighting to stay alive, she was almost certainly waging a war with herself at the same time.

When she'd last done it, she'd only been riding for a year. But in that time, she'd gotten in more than two dozen races, and climbed the ranks faster than anyone her age before or since. Mahdi and I were focused on building our rep as runners, so the three of us didn't spend as much time together as we used to, but we always made sure to show up to the track to cheer her on and help Laden in the pit.

When she expressed interest in racing, Laden helped her dive in head first. He made her work her ass off and buy her own bike, but he would take her to the track, brainstorm team names and logos, anything to encourage her and fuel that interest. Even got her a job working at a bike shop. It's where she got her race name.

That last time Eshe hit the track, though, was just after Laden started showing signs of dementia. He hadn't been able to make the last few races, so Eshe, Mahdi, I did our best to keep the bike running when something broke. It was hard as hell to manage, but we were making it work.

That day was the Glen Circuit, a race that had gone back a few hundred years. It was a big one. Eshe and Laden talked about it a lot, and I could tell that she was getting in her head about him not being there. I remembered her leaning up against the wall in the locker room, chewing her lip raw.

I put my hand on her shoulder and squeezed. "We're recording this one. I know you wish he could be here, but we'll show him. He's going to be so proud of you."

Eshe took a slow breath and nodded. She gave me a silent, thankful look, then she hugged me.

"I hate to interrupt you two lovebirds," Mahdi teased, wiping his hands with a rag while leaning against the doorframe, "but the bike is ready."

Eshe broke away and grabbed her helmet from the nearby bench. Her boots clicked on the tile floor as she walked over to Mahdi, who made an *after you* gesture with one hand. She hugged him, too, and wrapped her arms around his neck, pulling the two of them close. Then she kissed him. It wasn't anything deep or passionate, but it wasn't nothing either.

"Thank you," she said, taking a step back. "Both of you. I wouldn't be here right now if not for you two."

I shoved the emotion down, in favor of stoicism and humor. "Just get out there. We want that trophy as bad as you do."

She smiled at that, but it was only masking an unmistakable sadness. A deep breath later, it was gone and replaced with practiced determination. Then she put her helmet on and walked out to the track. I made for the door too, shoved my hands in my pockets and stood there in silence with Mahdi for a moment, watching her go.

"You really gotta stop doing that, you know," Mahdi said.

I sighed. "Yeah, I know. Laden was always better at the pep talks."

He shot me a sideways glance. "That's not what I'm talking about and you know it."

I bit back something sharp, and settled on silence instead.

"There it is," he said without judgement, pointing in my direction. "You're either a black hole of emotion or you're angry. Just ask her already; you know Eshe would help."

I took a deep breath and forced myself to be patient. "Mahdi, today's not about me. Now, can you shut the fuck up and let me through." I pushed past him and jogged out to catch up with Eshe.

The announcer was making their rounds, thanking corporate sponsors and repeating focus group-tested slogans first, before moving onto introducing the race and those in it.

"Welcome, everyone, to the historic Glen Circuit!" they howled with enthusiasm. "Today, we have twenty-two incredible riders taking on this daunting track. Eight floors of hairpin turns, dizzying helixes, and blazing straight aways.To those about to ride, we salute you! Give them all a round of applause, folks!"

I walked up to Eshe, who was inspecting the bike one last time.

"It's gonna work," I told her. "How many times have you watched Laden do it?"

"More times than I can count," she answered. "But you know his line..."

"Inspection never stops, even when the race is over," the two of us said in unison.

"Okay," she sighed, grabbing the handlebars. "Let's do this."

"Knock 'em dead," I replied, offering her a closed fist.

She bumped it and started pushing the bike out of the pit and towards her starting position. Once all the riders were in place, the announcer started going through each of them, allowing a few moments for the crowds to cheer on their favorites.

"And, last but not least, our very own local rider, Tank Bitch!" they shouted.

Eshe had grown a small but devoted fan base that made more noise than they had any right to. Mahdi and I did our best to add to them as we took our places in the pit. After that, the track got quiet as the clock started its countdown. Almost completely silent until the last three seconds, where the excitement boiled over, right at the ring of the starting bell. The bikes took off, vying for an early lead. For her part, Eshe was always good at getting to the middle of the pack in no time, but the front half of the riders were always a slog.

Each level of the track wrapped around itself in dizzying ways, slowly ascending level by level to the very top, which culminated in a spiraling drop through the center of the course. The rider just ahead of Eshe lost control halfway down the helix and almost took her off the track too, but she managed to avoid it with a quick pull to the outside. It sacrificed a couple of places, but that was better than tying for last place.

By the end of the first lap, a whole thirty-seven minutes and sixteen seconds later, Eshe crossed the pole at fourteenth place. Two more laps. Mahdi and I looked on from our hand terminal, muttering back and forth to one another about potential issues with the bike on the straight aways, and staring in quiet determination on her behalf at every curve.

Halfway through lap two and Eshe had pulled up to ninth place. It was about then that the announcer started playing rider and team interviews. They were always pretty slick productions as far as these things went. Each team talking about how they prepared for each race and what set their bikes and riders apart. Fans always love that sort of thing. It makes them feel like they're part of the team, which is always good for business.

"Oh shit," Mahdi spat, pulling our attention back to the terminal.

Just as I looked down at the screen, I saw the rider ahead of Eshe lose control at the end of a curve that was going into a straight away. The bike turned perpendicular to the track and fell forward, slamming its rider to the ground. It was not something Eshe was going to be able to back out of. She was going to crash right into it, and it could very well be a career ender.

The crowd fell silent. Even the announcer for their part couldn't come up with anything to say. Then, Eshe simply settled back and accelerated into it, pulling her motorcycle into a short wheelie, just in time to launch off the wedge-like underside of the bike ahead of her. She flew through the air, claiming a couple of places as she went, and landed hard. The bike bottomed out for a moment, and sent up a burst of sparks. Eshe held on for dear life, managing to keep the motorcycle upright, and shot into the straightaway.

Everyone lost their collective minds. People screamed and applauded. All the announcer could say was, "Wow." Even some of the other pit crews came over to congratulate us on getting the highlight of the race. After that death defying stunt, she finished out the lap holding onto fifth place, with a good lead on everyone behind her. It was the perfect time for her to pull into the pit lane.

"You get the tank, I'll check the frame," Mahdi said, bringing things back.

Now it was time for us to do our jobs. Except Eshe wasn't slowing down. She was treating the pit lane like its own straight away. Then, at the last possible moment, she dropped the bike into a sideways slide, using the tires themselves to slow down quickly. Mahdi and I got to work immediately. We could talk about what the hell just happened when Eshe was back on track.

"Good job out there," I said, filling her tank.

"Frame is good!" Mahdi shouted. "Scraped to hell, but good!"

Once the two of us were clear, Eshe whipped the bike around and sped off, trying to make up for any time she'd just lost. The pit crews near us were looking at us in stunned silence. Mahdi waved at them awkwardly, then turned to me.

"Uh, did she just do what I think she did?" he asked.

"Yep," I answered simply. "Laden would have given her hell for a stunt like that."

After a bunch of instant replays of Eshe's incredible feat of survival and subsequent pit stop, the announcer resumed going through the team interviews. Likewise the two of us went back to watching the terminal. Eshe's last lap was hard fought, she clawed her way up to third and barely held onto it as they started down the helix for the last time. There, on that seemingly endless turn, she traded between third and forth a few times, but managed to emerge into the final corners with a solid grasp on bronze and a shot at silver.

"I knew she'd be good as soon as she told me she wanted to do it," Ladens voice said on the loudspeakers. "And I for one couldn't be prouder."

His face was up there on a bunch of the big screens coming into the final stretch. He was sitting there in a folding chair, hands covered in grease with the bike in the background. It was sad that he wasn't here in person but, at the same time, it almost seemed fitting for it to be playing as she finished the race. I looked back down to the terminal when she made the last corner. As she sped up toward the finish line, though something didn't seem right, it looked like she was fighting a lot of vibration.

Then, in the final moments of the race, her front axle snapped, sending the wheel careening out ahead of her. The bike hit the pavement and the sudden increase in drag flipped it into the air, end over end, throwing Eshe off, tumbling across the pavement before finally coming to a stop.

Mahdi and I were already running over to her as the crash started, along with a few emergency personnel. At first, she didn't get up, and I feared the worst. When she did get up, though, she shoved a medic away and ripped off her helmet. She paced around like a trapped animal, before throwing her helmet across the track and screaming at the top of her lungs. Then she collapsed, sobbing and hyperventilating. As the medics checked her out, we held her close to make sure she knew she wasn't alone.

"Win or lose," the video of Laden said, "my daughter will always be a winner in my book."

TWENTY-EIGHT

MEET ME AT THE ALTAR

This time, I was the one tumbling through the air off a motorcycle. Like jumping from the building, the world was serene and peaceful as the wind rushed around me. It was one of those crystallized moments in time, where you can seem to spot every last, minute detail, right before everything comes rushing back in all at once. Five guns were trained on me as I fell. They fired. Bullets whipped past me, and I threw both of my readied knives in reply.

Eshe whirled the bike around the truck in an arc, using her knee to steer while firing her snub-nosed pistol at our attackers in precise, controlled bursts. She did this all while managing to avoid other vehicles sharing the road. Her first victim's head was chewed away in three chunks as the bullets claimed their bounty. Her next salvo drew a gruesome line across another mercenary's shoulder, finally taking him down when the last shot ripped through his heart.

Together, Eshe and I made quick work of our pursuers in the first truck. The last one standing and uninjured was a balding man with ocular replacements. He fought with his gun—which must have jammed on him—while taking small steps back toward the edge of the truck's bed. As I landed a few meters away, he got it working again and fired a haphazard volley in my direction. Most of the shots went wide, but one put a hole in the meaty part of my thigh, sending me into a tumble. I rolled with it and drew closer as he started to reload. A new blade answered my call and I pushed the gun out of the way as I swung for his neck. He moved quickly, managing panicked dodges of my first two swings. On my third attempt though, his luck ran out, and hit home, plunging the knife into his throat.

A fresh spear of agony drowned out all my other injuries followed by a plume of red sprayed out of my shoulder. I staggered to one side and almost tumbled over the truck's tailgate. Something popped, and a bullet flew wide, missing me by more than a meter. I ripped the blade from the bald man's neck—who was desperately trying to keep the wound closed—and spun to face the shooter. A merc sat against the truck's cabin with a small pistol aimed in my direction. He'd been unfortunate enough to catch the two knives I'd thrown at the onset. One stuck in his upper thigh, and the other in his stomach. Blood ran from his mouth, enough for anyone to know that he didn't have long to live. He knew it, and I knew it, but that didn't stop him from wearing a smug little grin on his face.

I smirked back at him from across the bed and thrust my arms out at him, focusing each of my ultrasonic projectors on the knife in his leg. I stared at the blade—strained at it—and I felt like the effort was going to launch my eyes from their sockets. Finally, it moved, drawing a thin bleeding line up his leg.

The merc barely managed to hold onto the gun.

I took a step toward him, and the blade lurched forward, splitting skin, fraying muscle, and splintering bone as it went.

His hands clenched around the gun and fired again, grazing my left cheek with the shot.

Another step closer, and the knife drove itself through his pelvis into his abdomen.

He went several shades of pale and tried to scream, but as the blade jaggedly snapped his ribs and gorged itself on his heart and one lung, it came out as a ragged wheezing gurgle. One more step and the knife tore free, snapping through his collarbone and returning to my hand in a bloody arc.

I called the last of my knives from his stomach and was struck by a moment of panic. Where was the gauss cannon? I looked around and didn't see it with the bodies, then scanned the traffic for the other truck. After a few moments, as if on cue, it slid out from behind a cargo slab, with a man holding an overly large gun standing on the hood and staring straight at me.

It must have been about twenty meters away. At that range, he could probably close his eyes and hit me. It made me look around frantically and weigh the odds of survival if I leapt from the truck. But he wasn't firing. Not even aiming. He was just standing there, the gun held slack in one hand.

The other truck moved quickly and covered the space in moments until it was less than a meter away. That is when it dawned on me that the man, with his milky, dead eyes, wasn't looking at me at all. He was gazing at the corpses around me. His eyes shifted for a moment, almost as if noticing me for the first time, and he smiled. That same relentless and impossible smile that I had seen on the man in Eshe's shop. Right before he turned into—

"Oh fuck me," I muttered under my breath, not daring to finish the next thought.

The men jumped the gap one at a time, stumbling into the truck bed with me. Not wanting to wait around, I scrambled up to the top of the cab and looked for Eshe. She was trying to reposition the motorcycle, but after her driving earlier, the surrounding traffic was proving difficult to navigate. I didn't have time to wait, so I found the closest vehicle I thought she'd be able to get to and prepared to make a leap of faith. Before I could make it very far, however, something took hold of my ankle and jerked me off my feet. Before I could react, even instinctively, my head slammed into the roof of the cab, and everything cut to black.

I had no idea how long I was out, but my vision slowly started to come back, first as greys and reds, then the other colors slowly followed. It felt like my skull wanted to split apart with every painfully frantic thump of my heartbeat. Eventually, I became dimly aware that whatever was wrapped around my ankle started tugging, pulling me toward the back of the truck. The further I went, the more it wrapped around my leg until I could feel something lapping at the wound in my thigh. That sickening sensation is what finally snapped me back to reality. When I looked past my feet at whatever had me, though, I immediately regretted it.

What lay before me was a monolith of flesh. Ribs and long bones of arms and legs stood out in a symmetrical arrangement, contrasted against shredded tassels of skin and quivering musculature beneath. It was a pulsing, writhing, oozing thing that looked like it had been made for the worship of long-forgotten gods. An altar of profane decadence. At its base were several sinewy, muscled tendrils that bore two to three digits at the end of their length. Fingernails grew up each one, pointing in reverse like chitinous plates. It was three of those tendrils that were pulling me to the monolith, expanding and contracting like blood-engorged worms to inch me closer and closer. Even through the fog of the concussion I probably had, I started to panic. My hands flailed in all directions, desperately trying to find something to grab onto. Something to give me some leverage. There was nothing, and all I managed to do was scratch a few shavings of paint from the bed as I was dragged closer to my death.

I pushed myself up and, summoning a blade, began stabbing at the first tendril. Each motion separated layers of muscle, fat, and tendon alike. Despite the gouts of blood that obscured my strikes, I managed to free myself from one of the three grasping limbs. I was about to start on the others when the other armored truck sped up and rammed into the rear-end of the one I was in. The tentacles maintained their grip on my other leg, but the collision threw the rest of me forward and dislocated my hip. I screamed and grabbed at my leg, feeling the slight protrusion of bone beneath my skin.

Boots landed in the truck bed, and I looked up to see another milky-eyed mercenary jumping headlong toward the monolith. Another set of worm-like appendages, this time armed with shards of metal tore him to literal ribbons. Streams of blood and meat and skin and bone collided with the monolith, entirely unrecognizable from the human being there just moments before.

The tendrils that were still holding my leg released me and moved, slowly and deliberately towards the corpse—if one could call it that. Each one scooped globs of the body into an opening at the base of the monolith, where a set of gnashing teeth waited to devour whatever slid into their path. At first they scraped against the metal beneath them, almost like someone tapping their fingers on a table. Once the monolith started gorging itself, however, that all went away. At the speed we were moving, I couldn't hear it, but my imagination filled in the void with wet sounds of tearing, popping, and wrenching. Coupled with that and the sight unfolding before me conjured the disturbing thought of being ingested and devoured whole through that impossibly small opening. The idea of it was enough to make my stomach turn in on itself.

The remaining occupants on the second truck worked their way over its cab and hood before jumping the small gap into the bed with me and the monolith. Eshe had apparently reloaded and caught a few midair before they could make it across. Seemingly lacking the capacity to climb out the door or anything to help break glass, the driver bashed his head against the front windshield until his skull gave way and split in a bloody smear. Ignoring this otherwise life-ending injury, he continued slamming the stump of his head and neck against the glass until it finally shattered. He crawled out onto the hood, dragging bits of his cranium along with him. Then he took a shaky step up and leapt across the gap to join the others, his still connected eyes and brain stem flapping behind him like the tail of a scarf in the wind. Now driverless, the second truck fell behind and drifted into a few other lanes, eventually colliding with an automated storage transport.

The men that made it across were greeted by the flesh monolith and systematically divided, much like the thing in Eshe's shop had done. Some fell over as their legs were taken from them first, while others fell in half when the monolith's tendrils bored through their stomach to claim their vitals. As this process unfolded, the monolith incorporated more of its new acquisitions into itself. More tendrils slithered out, and skulls began to form a ring around its center, each jaw opening, and closing to control the flow of a viscous, black ichor.

"Raide! Raide, can you hear me!?" Eshe shouted from nearby, maybe to my left.

The tendrils returned their attention to me, and I didn't waste a moment. I reached for the side of the truck and pulled myself to the edge. I could see Eshe swerving through traffic, on her way to me. I preferred taking my chances as roadkill, so as she approached, I slid over the edge, hanging on by my fingertips. The truck swerved a bit, trying to throw me, but Eshe was there in no time, keeping pace. Once I thought she was close enough, I let go.

Miraculously, I landed sideways on the back seat of the bike, though my momentum toppled me and almost ground my head to paste on the pavement. At the last possible second, Eshe let go of the handlebars to catch my arm and haul me upright again. Retaking control, she veered off the highway at a sharp diagonal, catching an off-ramp by mere centimeters.

Once we pulled back onto the lower streets, Eshe started backtracking, following a route on the bike's HUD. My little stunt had gotten me beaten to shit, but we made it. I almost couldn't believe it.

"I'm alive," I said gleefully, almost laughing.

Eshe made an abrupt stop beneath an underpass, and shot me a look over her shoulder. "I ought to fucking kill you myself for that shit back there."

Then she got off the bike, whirled around, and punched me in the face. I fell out of my seat and hit the pavement. Before I could react, she was on me, punching me over and over.

"This what you fucking want?" She screamed, continuing her assault. "Want me to finish you off so you can die thinking you're some kind of fucking hero?" She picked me up by my collar and slammed me against the asphalt. "Fuck you! I'm counting on you to make all the sacrifices we've made worth something. You're not fucking invincible!"

She was right, of course. I had been reckless every time danger reared its ugly head. Not that I hadn't been before all this, but so many people only get shot or stabbed once. Something eventually catches up with them, and that's it. I had somehow managed to escape by the skin of my teeth on several occasions, and now Eshe had given me a fresh start. What's more, she put her life on the line and sacrificed her livelihood to do it.

She moved to punch me again, but this time I caught it and used the momentum to throw her off of me. Our positions reversed, and I tried to hold her arm down so she'd stop. I could feel my injuries taking their toll though, and I was getting weak. Blood was dripping down my chin from a split lip, broken nose, and something on my forehead. The bullet wounds I'd suffered had been pounding like small explosions, but now they were more distant and almost numb.

"Let go of me!" she demanded, fighting against my grip.

"What did you want me to do, huh?" I shouted at the top of my lungs. "We're in over our heads, dealing with things and people that we don't understand."

Eshe stopped fighting and just glared at me.

"Do you just expect me to run?" I continued. "To just leave, disappear to someplace quiet and warm where we can watch the sun go down and start a family? Is that what you fucking want?"

"Raide," Eshe choked out, staring at me in genuine fear. "How do you know about that?"

"What?" I asked.

"How did you know about that?" she asked more sternly. "Except for Mahdi, I never told anyone that."

"I don't understand," I said.

"Just after Dad died," she started to explain in a barely audible whisper, "I asked Mahdi to leave with me, using those exact words."

It took several seconds for that to sink in, and I fell backward onto the pavement. I tried to hold myself up, but instead, I just collapsed. What the fuck? She told me that. I could remember it plain as day. She did tell me, didn't she?

"I'm sorry," I said, the words slow and hard to form.

She didn't say anything, at least not that I can remember. What I do recall was seeing her get to her feet. Then her arm wrapped around me and tugged me back onto our stolen motorcycle. Sleep came moments later, cold and dreamless. I accepted it gratefully.

TWENTY-NINE

GOTTA STOP WAKING UP LIKE THIS

My eyes opened to the sight of a slate gray ceiling. We were back at the hab we'd rented. Eshe sat nearby, in my peripheral, typing furiously on her terminal. We weren't safe here. We had to get out, get away. I must have groaned without realizing it because she jumped out of her chair and was hovering over me in an instant. She looked me over for a few moments before checking my temperature and inspecting my shoulder.

"You've been out about thirty-three hours," she said, snapping her fingers in front of my eyes. "But your fever broke, and your body is taking to the bio-polymer well."

My throat was dry, like it had been glued shut, but I managed to squeeze out two words: "Not. Safe."

She rolled her eyes. "Yeah, I know. Nowhere is, not anymore."

It seemed like it took hours to start moving again. Maybe it actually had been. My joints ached, and my stomach turned in protest when I finally decided to stand. I made slow progress to the shower, holding my legs with each step. Eshe helped and caught me once when my legs gave out. While I was grateful for the help, some deep-seated part of me hated relying on someone else. Eshe started the shower, and I tumbled into it. The warmth felt good, really good. I had to fight to keep from drifting back to sleep. Leaning against the shower wall, I was able to wash off the bloodstains that I wore in some places like a second skin. My head pounded with a dull persistence, and I had a sizable lump on my forehead where it hit the truck. But despite that, I was able to clean up a bit. At least enough to feel human again.

When I got out, Eshe had packed most of our things. Save for the terminal, which, thanks to a universal command, was on its way to becoming a useless block of slag. Then she helped me get dressed. It was an exhausting effort.

"We need to talk," she said as she slid my jacket up my arms to rest on my shoulders.

"Eshe, I—" I started, but she held up a hand.

"I think I might have an idea about what happened," she said. "At least a theory."

I watched in silence, waiting for her to continue.

"That thing," she said, referring to Soqua. "Somehow it put Mahdi's memories in your head. It stitched the locked out meeting right on top, so you didn't need the key in the first place. I'm no expert in this field, but it doesn't take a whole lot of education to understand that memories don't exist in a vacuum; each one is just a single point in a larger web of interconnected points."

"And you can't drop a memory into someone's head without bringing a few others with it," I supplied, understanding where Eshe was going with this. "You think I got some of Mahdi's memories and feelings for you."

She looked away from me, suddenly wearing a blank expression. She held one arm for a moment, then nodded.

"I don't know what to do, Eshe," I said, cautiously. "What do I do?"

"We go to Pardeq," Eshe said. "And we finish this. For him."

"What if we could get him back?" I asked.

"No, it wouldn't be him," she replied. "Even if everything was the same, I would know. And that would ruin it."

I'll admit, I didn't like her suggestion that there was something wrong with me. I was very aware of how fucked up my head was, but I was still me. I didn't need to be fixed. Aside from that, though, she was choosing this. And it was loud and clear. If I wanted to really protect her, I'd have to make sure she made it to Pardeq safely. Just like Soqua.

"Okay," I said. "Let's go."

She gave me a weak smile, then grabbed the remaining duffel and walked out the door. I made sure Soqua was in my bag, then followed her out. Slowly, at first, but I grew more sure of myself with each step. The stairs were a different story, and I had to keep a death grip on the railing to make it down without killing myself. But I made it. She had the bike ready, and we wasted no time getting on and putting that place behind us.

Out of one nightmare and into another.

We rode for a while, just to get ourselves good and lost. In that time, I did my best to forget everything that had happened to me over the past few days. Well, in truth, my grasp on the time that had passed since this all started was hazy at best. It was long enough, though, that the days I'd spent trying to ward off starvation after losing my face were so distant that they seemed like a false memory.

But this. This was real—no illusions of imperfect, human recognizance. I was holding onto the last person in the world that mattered to me. Soqua was real too. It was a being that couldn't support itself, and I believed it desperately wanted to attain its own means of independence and pursue its own goals, like a child. At that, what Eshe suggested about Mahdi's memories made a lot more sense.

Still, as we started down the street, leaving Old Manhattan behind, I found myself doubting my decision to help Soqua. Nothing that Eshe or I had contended with was its fault, but I couldn't deny that both our lives had been utterly destroyed by its existence. Then again, Mahdi was most likely coming to see me when I bumped into him. It's possible that my situation wouldn't be very different.

As the hours passed, I pondered dozens of other questions in silence. Things about my future if I lived through this, or if I had other memories of Mahdi's stuck in my head. Had any of me been replaced? How much of me was still me, or had I been turned into a walking ship of Theseus? As existential dread started to seep in, Eshe brought the bike to a slow stop.

"Hope you weren't getting too comfortable back there," Eshe said, getting off the bike.

"Oh, yeah, very relaxing," I replied and faked a yawn.

"You're a funny bitch when you wanna be. You know that?" she observed. "Stretch your legs a bit, then, when you're ready, you're driving."

"Sure," I said. "No problem."

She paced around on the sidewalk a bit, and I did a few exercises to get back into running shape. We shared some food that we liberated from Veto's place and caught up. She talked about her search for me in greater detail, and I shared what happened before she was dragged in.

"I don't know if anything I told Veto was anywhere close to the truth, but I've been thinking about Laden ever since," I said, leaning against the bike. "A different kind of father I guess. In spite of everything, he was really good to all of us. I miss him a lot."

Eshe took a deep breath. "Yeah, me too, but he had his secrets—demons really—things I can't forgive him for."

I looked at her but didn't speak, hoping my silence would be an invitation to continue.

"When Laden died," she continued, choosing her words carefully. "When I found him, he was hooked up to a dream inducer. Life in the Shiv wasn't great. It isn't great anywhere. But we were doing okay. Or, at least, I thought so." She shrugged and crossed her arms, focusing on an obscure spot on the pavement. "First, my mom. Then Laden. Anywhere else was better than here with me. Couldn't even remember my name at the end."

"Eshe," I started, but instead of saying anything, I reached out to put a hand on her shoulder.

"Like, what was so fucking bad about me that they both had to leave? Why was death better?" she asked, not hiding the anger and hurt in her voice. "I asked myself those questions for a long time, you know? But then I finally realized that Laden was sick. He was a good man, but he was a dream junkie.

I let those words hang in the air for a long moment, giving them some space. "Did I ever tell you about how I found him that last time he wandered off?" I asked. "You know, when he was missing for a few months that one time?"

She shook her head.

"It was after that job. The one that Mahdi and I had that went really bad," I began.

"Yeah, you guys were laying low for weeks," she recalled. "Mahdi paid me to bring him food a few times because he thought he was being watched."

I nodded. "I got tired of hiding one day and I'd seen the messages you sent Mahdi and I about him going missing, so I decided to get out and look around. As usual, I wound up heading to Tyhek's place for some food. I sat down and ordered a saké and noticed the new guy working the grill. He didn't recognize me but mentioned that his daughter was about my age. The best modder in New York as he put it."

Eshe quirked a smile. "That's almost too much to believe. Why didn't you tell me?"

I shrugged, taking another bite of dehydrated food. "I thought Tyhek told you when he ordered a cab to take him home. Either way, back to the point. I know he never cooked when we were kids, but behind that grill, he made the best teppanyaki I'd ever had."

She burst out in a bark of harsh laughter and leaned into me to keep her balance, but it quickly subsided. The two of us stayed there, leaning against the bike and each other for a minute before Eshe promptly wiped her eyes and cleared her throat.

"I'm sorry that this happened to you," she said.

"Yeah," I said. "You, too."

"So, good to go?" she asked.

"Yeah, I guess so," I answered. "What's the plan?"

"Well, at first, I was just driving," she explained, pulling up the map on the bike's HUD. "There's a lift here, by the old film factory."

"Codec or something, right?" I asked.

"Something like that," she said. "The lift there is the closest one to Pardeq East. We get there, we get up to the Heights, and we finish this."

"You, sure about this?" I asked, letting my surprise show.

"Shut the fuck up and drive," she shot back, trying to scowl but not quite managing to hide the smile on her face.

I reached into my bag, gave Soqua a couple of quick taps, and then got on the bike. Eshe followed and leaned up against me, wrapping her arm around my waist. I verified the coordinates in the motorcycle's nav system and took note of the lift that would take us to the Heights. We were headed back into my New York, the fringes of it anyway, all sunless and bloody, so I took one last look around before speeding off down the road, back into darkness.

SKY BURIAL

kept off the highways and major avenues. I had no desire to repeat the encounter with the armored trucks, so I kept a low profile. I didn't expect to be as successful as I was, though. The streets we found ourselves on were quiet—too much for my liking. We weren't on tucked-away side streets, but what seemed like a main thoroughfare, lined with restaurants and businesses of all sorts. But there was hardly any foot traffic at all or any kind of traffic for that matter.

"Hey Eshe, what day is it?" I hollered over my shoulder.

"Saturday," she answered, looking around. "It's Saturday night. Where is everybody?"

I shook my head and shrugged.

The streets and walkways should have been swarming with people— each one reveling in their survival of the previous week—literal or otherwise. There should have been crowds of people—drunk, high, or both—roving the streets, shouting, and laughing. Sex workers should have been out in force, aiding the merriment. But there was none of that.

Instead, it felt like we were riding through a ghost town. The few people that were on the street were walking with a paranoid determination. The kind of gait you had when you were being stalked by a predator, all quick steps and swivel necks. A few minutes later, we passed a bazaar, and even that was devoid of people—customers or shopkeepers. Lights and advertisements played to no audience, and holographic mascots defaulted to idle animations or else found themselves repeating pre-recorded lines to nobody.

I let the bike's autopilot take over as my eyes shifted perspective to access my HUD and the local boards. If people weren't on the street, they were posting about the reasons why. The gods of social media that preyed upon people with serotonin traps demanded sacrifice, especially if there was a crisis to profit from. Don't step in to help. Step back instead to get a better angle, then write about it for a sponsorship. Better if you have pictures, and even more so if there's video. And hallelujah, the gods didn't disappoint. The local boards were packed with threads, most of it speculation and budding conspiracy theories. As we moved closer and closer toward our intended lift, though, the tone changed. The typical mesh banter had given way to coordination and cooperation. One thread that had been stickied for several blocks on either side of the lift was called 'Get out if you can' and was denoted as having attachments.

I decided to slow the bike to a stop and flicked my head over one shoulder. The gesture triggered my HUD to send the post to Eshe. "Hey, take a look at this."

She let go of my waist to get her goggles in place. Then we both read.

From: PhiloSk8

Subject: GET OUT IF YOU CAN

People are dying. Those of us that didn't join Vys on their way to the Heights are being hunted by… monsters might be the right word. They just showed up out of nowhere. My neighbor's sister who just showed up a couple of days ago said this started in the Shiv. Tried her best to describe what happened, but in teh end, gave me some pictures, which I have attached.

FP Edit: Its too late for us to run, so we're trying to hold on for as long as we can. If you can leave do it and if those things catch up you… find a way to kill yourself first.

The attached pictures showed a bony monstrosity wandering around a street corner. Their torsos looked distinctly human, but they stood on three reverse jointed legs, bound together in ribbons of patchy, distended skin and greying muscle.

"That reminds me of what we saw on the highway," Eshe said.

"Yeah," I agreed. "And it seems like Vys or what's left of them got out and made for the Heights. We might not be alone up there."

"Trade one set of monsters for another, huh?" she said after a short pause. "At least we know how Vys operates."

Why did all of this have to get worse? Wasn't it enough that we had a circ on our backs and maybe a serial killer? Why did we have to collect them all, only to get thrust into hell itself? I shook my head then took a long, tired breath and reached in my bag and palmed Soqua, waiting for them to connect.

"There's something you need to see," I signed.

A shiver passed through me as Soqua did something they'd never done before. They superimposed themselves in my vision as Mahdi, which made the hair on the back of my neck stand on end.

"Woah, what the hell?" I asked.

Mahdi, by way of Soqua, just stood there, vaguely floating over a space on the ground ahead of me, perfectly in proportion and perspective. It was almost like he was really there.

"Um, okay," I sighed. "What do you make of it?"

"Doom," Soqua signed.

I blinked. "That's it?"

Soqua just stared at me, expression blank, offering me no answer. It was then that I realized what was so unsettling about seeing Mahdi hijacked like that. He looked perfect in every way that mattered, all except for the fact that he wasn't breathing. Which, of course, was fixed the second I thought of it.

"Fine," I signed, annoyed, then disconnected.

"Eshe, this is not looking good. Maybe you should—"

"Fuck off with your heroic bullshit already," she replied. "I'm not letting you go in there alone."

"Okay," I shrugged and eased onto the accelerator. "Hang on."

We passed through desiccated streets and walkways. It made me think of stories and pictures of the abandoned hab complexes on the outskirts of Miami. Kilometers of empty stacks, left to rot in the tepid, polluted waters of the Gulf. Our own personal ghost town. For a while, too, that's all it was. The streets, and seemingly the buildings, were all empty. That is, until we started seeing the bodies. Dozens lined either side of the street. Most were lying face down and had a flattened, compressed look to them.

"What do you think happened?" I asked. "Doesn't look like one of those things did this."

"No, I think these ones were trampled as they fled," Eshe replied, somber and shaky.

In the span of just a handful of city blocks, the whole bodies turned into pieces of bodies that had been torn apart and thrown everywhere. Blood painted walls and simmered off of neon lights, clouding the already nauseating air with smoke. It gathered in puddles on the road, congealing into semi-solid human gelatin. Globs of unidentifiable meat clung to almost every surface as if they had been chewed up and spat out. Soil, shit, decay, and iron wafted into my nose and mouth, clinging to my insides like a sheet of filth.

A heaped-up mound of corpses forced us onto the sidewalk. As we did, a person burst through the door of the building to our right, screaming for help. He was absolutely covered in blood and his arm had been quite literally torn off, just below his shoulder. As he ran for us, waving his good arm, it gave him an awkward, unbalanced gait.

Before either Eshe or I could react, the walls of the building exploded behind him, followed by a creature that clambered through the rubble. He looked over his shoulder at the thing, took a bad step, and went sprawling to the ground thirty meters ahead of us. The creature wobbled at him on a dozen fleshy limbs at an unnerving speed. Amid all those mismatched appendages was a conical thorax of rib cages and spines covered with human eyes—like a giant human octopus.

The man pulled himself across the ground with his remaining hand, trying with all he had to escape. It was no use, though, and he screamed as the creature caught up to him. Almost in response, it let out a low, trilling gurgle, as dangling bits of spine twitched like mandibles. From among them, thin tendrils stretched out slipping back and forth over the man's body until they found his stump-arm. With little hesitation, they bore into his flesh just beneath his skin, churning as they went, separating skin from muscle and tendon alike. He should have lost consciousness, but he didn't. It was like he wasn't being allowed to. Instead, all he did was scream—or at least he tried to.

The creature continued to burrow through him, and the color beneath his skin changed and started to look like a single, all-encompassing bruise. At some point in those few terrifying seconds, the creature decided it was done and simply peeled the man's skin away like a loose sheet. Then it plodded off down the street, slurping the skin through its oozing sphincter of a mouth. Leaving the degloved man to his fate.

I'd never seen someone bleed quite like that; it was everywhere, coming from everywhere. What remained of the man lay there convulsing. That is until a horde of smaller creatures, each about the size of my head, scurried out from beneath an upended car. They moved to the man in a mesmerizing sort of rapid, twitchy unison. They settled atop him and covered the man so completely it looked like his body had become a pulsing, grassy mound. Eshe, her eyes wide, tugged at my arm, begging me to move. It was all I needed to snap out of it, kick the bike into gear, and pass the man.

The grass that my eyes had been tricked into seeing became hundreds of wriggling fingers, like so many fleshy spiders—some still wearing jewelry on their digits. They were moving all over him, covering him in pinkish, stringy mounds of mucus that smoked and fizzled on his flesh. Muscle, cartilage, bone, it didn't matter. They were literally dissolving his body, digesting him in the open air. His eyes—or rather eye—met mine as we passed, and he managed to gurgle up a barely audible groan.

End it. That's what he was pleading for. I would have been begging for the same thing, but instead, I swallowed hard and kept driving, leaving the man to his fate. He would be dead soon enough.

We kept our distance from the big spider-thing until it crawled back into a nearby building. After that, the streets returned to their cryptlike stillness, but there was definitely activity around us. Every now and again, we could hear glass breaking or gurgling bellows in the distance, followed by human screams and gunfire. Some of it was close.

The thought of people fighting these things was reassuring. Though I had no illusions about who the real monsters were. The fabric of society down here was tenuous at best, only backed up by mutually assured destruction. It was a damn flimsy pillar to build a civilization on, in my opinion. These things and the carnage they brought with them were only going to tear that down, and then—well, I had no idea. All I knew was that if we wanted to survive, we'd have to monster up along with everyone and everything else.

An explosion rocked the corner of a building at the approaching intersection. Concrete and rebar collapsed into the street, sending more of those finger things scattering for cover. We rounded the corner and spotted a group of men and women moving down the street in a semicircle, maybe six or seven hundred meters from us.

I knew what they were on sight and they weren't average people. Tube tanks, as many called them, were genetically engineered soldiers who were grown in vats with a partner. On average, they were shorter than most, all thick, squat limbs encased in pure, high-density muscle. Most of them sported birthmarks of completely smooth patches of skin where their limbs grew in contact with the wall of their industrial womb. They were hard to mistake for old-fashioned, home-grown humans.

Each of the tanks were armed to the teeth. Some still had their warsuits to enhance their already bestial ferocity, but those that didn't had fashioned combat gear of their own. Their guns, the largest of which bore a resemblance to small cannons, were trained in all directions. Following years of pre-programmed training, they moved in unison, one step at a time, sweeping their weapons window-to-window, door-to-door. If one of them spotted something, they announced it to the group and would fire a single shot. A few of them had their sights on a bony creature that was busy savaging one of their comrades.

I'd decided to call the creatures tripods the moment I saw their picture in the post from earlier. Seeing one in person only reinforced the name. It stood about four or five meters tall, and supported itself on three awkward legs that seemed to consist of a pair of reverse and forward knee-like joints. At the base of each was a sharp spear of spurred bone that reminded me of an old harpoon, only far more deadly. The woman it had pinned face first to the wall was one of the tanks with the homemade armor. She was struggling against the tripod's leg running through the meaty part of her shoulder. Every attempt to escape only managed to skewer her further. Now, she was only screaming for help—screaming someone's name—probably her partner's.

The tripod leaned close to her and unfolded a shriveled proboscis from its featureless face. It recoiled for a moment before lashing out like a snake. It stabbed her repeatedly, over and over again, puncturing her makeshift armor like it was little more than plastic film, leaving each wound fizzling with a pink-white ooze. The woman's screaming gurgled into near-silence as her lungs were punctured. Finally, the creature seemed to strike home. It's limbs visibly quivered and some bulging part of its torso distended as it drank the contents of the woman's spine. She was empty in moments and was discarded on the ground beside a heap of other bodies like a disposable food wrapper. The tripod followed that up with a series of rapid clicks and trills that shook the air in my lungs.

To their credit, the other tanks continued as if nothing had happened. They kept to formation, and took one cautious step after another toward an industrial lift at the end of the street. Calling out new contacts and taking shots they knew they could only make.

Eshe grabbed my shoulder and shook. "Raide, start driving. You need to start driving."

"What for?" I asked. "Our lift isn't for another few—"

I was interrupted as each and every tank whirled to face us, guns trained in our direction. I followed their line of fire, and looked over my shoulder. Eshe was right. My eyes went wide, as half a dozen of those spine feeders came up behind us in a wobbling gallop, cutting off our escape.

I slammed the accelerator, and the rear tire spun, failing to grip the road. When the bike finally grabbed the pavement, it shot us forward so fast that Eshe almost fell off. The spine-feeder ahead let out a bellowing wail and lunged for us as we passed. I turned hard, threading the needle between its legs with a slide. It was far too late to dodge he tattered remains of a corpse in the road.

I hit the handlebars hard but it was no use. The bike spun out and sent us airborne, turning the world on itself, end over end. I lost all sense of direction as my limbs flailed uselessly until gravity and friction worked in tandem to pull me back down. Air rushed past me before I gave way to gravity and friction. Joints popped as I rolled across the pavement, before finally tumbling to a stop. I pushed myself up slowly, but looked around for Eshe frantically. She'd been thrown into an abandoned car and left a dent in the side panel to prove it. The spine-feeder closest to us surged forward, stabbing the ground wildly with its front two legs while shuffling along with its hindlimb. Eshe tried to back away, but could only manage to scoot across the ground with her legs.

I ran and slid in behind her on my knees, and, wrapping my arms around her shoulders, I hauled her back. A bony limb came down between her feet, shearing chunks out of the concrete. Both of us screamed. A couple of my ribs were setting off alarms in my HUD, sending violent jolts of agony echoing across my body, but through tears and gritted teeth, I continued pulling. My legs' micro-bots adjusted their shapes to the task, giving me a better grip of the ground. But even with that, we only barely avoided the tripod's next swing.

A third bony talon lanced down at us from above but fell wide, to our left, skewering the front end of the car Eshe had crashed into. I slipped and tried desperately to reestablish my footing. I looked behind me, over my shoulder to the lift, then at the bike. The fenders were dented but it had corrected itself enough to use, assuming the engine wasn't damaged beyond repair, we both just had to reach it and we'd have a shot at getting out alive.

I felt Eshe's body jerk and she wailed and struggled against my grip, but managed little else. The creature's spike pierced her right shoulder and pinned her to the pavement like an insect on a collection board. The spine-feeder let out a discordant howl and tried to claim Eshe while also pulling itself free of the road. It couldn't manage both at once, and the limb came free first, ripping out of Eshe and shoving her to the side. As the creature recoiled, it toppled over and struggled to right itself.

I rolled Eshe over to find that her entire left shoulder had been nearly cleaved off. It hung onto her body with little more than a strip of flesh that ran down her side, exposing a few of the ribs beneath. I gathered her together as best as I could and pushed myself up and toward the bike. If I could get her on and engage the autopilot, we might just make it to the lift. I had no idea if the tanks would lend a hand, but anything was better than this.

I could hear the creature behind us gathering itself again, and the sound drove me. Once I got Eshe awkwardly into the front seat of the bike, I frantically tapped through its menus to set a course for the lift and hopped onto the back. As we started to roll away, I could see the tripod and its featureless visage reflected in the bike's nav screen. It was coming again. It was going to take another swing at us, and we weren't moving fast enough to escape together. Only one of us could get there. The other would have to stay behind.

My heart pounded in my ears over the hum of the motorcycle's engine as I made my choice. Without a second thought, I pushed myself out of the seat and off the bike. Almost at once, it picked up the momentum it needed and sped away with Eshe. I made the right choice, and I knew it. But that moment of understanding was short lived. Wind brushed my face, leading the creature's swing by a fraction of a second. I dove forward, rolling out of the way, and scrambled to face the predators behind us.

At that moment, there was a part of me, ancient and fierce, that knew—no, understood—that I was being hunted. The prey instinct commanded me to run. To somehow escape. But all of that blinked out of me like the final flickers of a dying bulb as the creature threw another spear-like limb at me. I dropped to one knee, diving again, this time to the side.

Fuck being prey to these things. I was a goddamned homo sapiens. An apex predator. A persistence hunter. We had driven other species to extinction thousands of times over. Things bigger and stronger than us that we had no business contending with. Why should these fucking spine-feeding tripods be any different? We had evolved to be one of the most versatile species ever dredged from the muck. Never conquered. Never dethroned. And now it came to me; it was my turn. And mother nature, the vindictive bitch, was watching closely to reward the victor.

Time to turn the tables.

Deep breath.

I dove behind a street-level advertising screen and retrieved several knives from my jacket. One-by-one, I jammed them between the microbots in my legs, point up, edge out. These tripods were a flurry of awkward stabs. Recalling how it had fallen over after it got Eshe, I understood that they were good at stabbing down at targets smaller than them. But could they stab up? As the sign behind me shuddered, and a talon shot through it, barely missing my neck, I decided it was time to find out. I limped across the street, making for a nearby car, with the creature right behind me.

"You wanna dance, toothpicks?" I shouted. "Let's dance."

I tumbled up onto the car's hood and scrabbled onto its roof. I was only going to get one shot at this, and I couldn't let my injuries slow me down. I could rest when I was dead. So, I steeled myself and vaulted from the car to the nearby wall. As my feet made contact, I exploited a trick of friction to turn and leap backward. I let out a defiant cry and tossed a few knives out ahead of me, suspending them in midair. A quick shuffle-step across the flats of each blade pushed me higher, above the creature. Then I fell.

Wind blurred my eyes, and I swept my blade-embedded leg down at the spine-feeder's head. A smooth cap of bone, muscle, and skin sheared off the front half of its face. A cascade of gore—an assortment of unknown organs—followed, splattering on the road below. I hit the ground in a roll and tumbled away from the creature, finally coming to a stop atop a half-digested corpse that sort of collapsed into itself under my weight.

As I worked to push myself up, I got a better look at the body beneath me. Their formerly colorful, swirling tattoos were instead a still collection of pale lines and shades. They were Vys. A realization struck me a moment later and I looked around the street and noticed that the dozens of bodies were in fact Vys footsoldiers.

The mechanical grind of the lift beginning its climb that grabbed my attention. Even through my tear-blurred vision, I could see the bike on the platform. Better still, the tanks were tending to Eshe. I should have been relieved. I wanted to be. But if Vys were here, and worse, camped out at the top of the lift, she might be as good as dead. I also had no way of knowing if the tanks would cut and run, leaving her to die alone.

"No..." I muttered.

I was exhausted. My whole body hurt, and yet somehow managed to hurt more. It was hard to breathe and there was a distant ringing in my ears. I wanted nothing more than to just stop.

"No." I said, with more emphasis.

I couldn't let Eshe die, and if she did anyway, I needed to be there. Then I could stop and rest or die or whatever. I looked over my shoulder. The tripods rushing down the street had come to a stop over the body of the one I'd killed. They poked and prodded it at first, but when the first one tried to feed on it the others attacked, fighting for their right to the new food source. If I was going to slip away, now was my only chance. So, I started to push myself up. But I couldn't manage it. I couldn't even crawl out of the corpse I'd collapsed into.

THIRTY-ONE

BOWLING ALLEY

I wasn't sure how long I was there, half-dead and buried in gore and human detritus. The tripods finished off their fight over the fresh meal, and the victor was currently gorging itself. My whole body hurt, my head pounded, and it felt as if I might come apart at the seams if I tried to move. A few of those spider-like hand scavengers skittered around me, spitting up on small bits of fresh meat only to slurp it up once it was ready. It smelled sour and putrid and it stung to breathe near it. Part of me wanted to get up and get away from it, but I was so tired and I hurt so much.

Still, I pushed myself up and took a stumbling step toward the lift. After that, I limped slowly, being careful not to slip on or into any other corpses. As I went, I found that the world had seemed to go about its business. An ecosystem had started to develop around all these new renditions of humanity, and now I was the outsider. The surface didn't belong to us anymore, it seemed. It belonged to them.

As I reached the base of the lift, I craned my neck and stared up the track, straining to catch a glimpse of the platform, but the tanks and Eshe were long gone. I had no idea how long it had been, but I had a feeling that they hadn't made it all the way yet. There had to be a sister lift to this one somewhere. Maybe a block or so away. It was a fifty-fifty chance, and I had no way of knowing which direction it would be.

To my left, behind a wall of industrial polyglass, was a warehouse of some kind. It was mostly open, which wouldn't bode well if those tripods decided to come after me. To my right, however, was a string of first and second-floor businesses. Smaller corridors might have their own issues, but almost everything I'd seen so far would have trouble following me—or, at the very least, they'd have to work really hard to reach me. It was an easy choice, so I made for the nearest door.

On the other side was a small but well-kept terminal cafe. Or what used to be, anyway. The place had been picked clean. Chairs were strewn across the room, and tables lay on their sides, stripped of anything resembling technology. Not even so much as a network cable remained. A door stood slightly ajar at the back of the room, leading to a hallway that connected the shops together in a sort of indoor strip. Lights dangled from the concrete ceiling and projected wide, flickering cones through the dusty air. Garbage and other refuse, the cast-off remnants of ordinary life, covered the floor, making it difficult to cross without testing your balance.

Something bellowed off in the distance, and it was enough to shake some dust free of the ceiling and send it drifting down onto me and everything else. I wondered if it was one of those things that skinned the man Eshe and I encountered earlier. As I thought more and more about it, I started to eye the walls warily. Maybe retreating to an enclosed space wasn't such a great idea. The scene of getting skinned alive and digested in some dark corner somewhere made the hallway seem more claustrophobic than they were earlier.

I wandered for several minutes before deciding to stick to the right wall for as long as I could. Either I would go in a loop and change course or I would eventually find my way out. The interior hallways couldn't be that much of a labyrinth. Of course, I started to question that assumption after another half hour with only more stripped shops and garbage-strewn floors to show for it. Finally, I crossed through a pair of large sliding doors that had been forced apart. On the other side was a wide-open food court with more than a dozen different restaurants spread out across a few floors.

They were all ransacked like everything else I'd come across so far, but each retained their focus-tested color schemes and menu designs. Each one I glanced tugged at a question I'd been afraid to ask myself. It was a little at a time, like pulling a loose thread. Would we ever get back to this? Was this it for us? How many people were still alive, and how many went into feeding or becoming these things?

I decided to head for the second floor, hoping it might offer a way out. As I ascended, I knew beyond a shadow of a doubt that I would never let one of those monsters take me alive. I would never allow myself to become one of them.

I wandered past a seating area with tables that were mounted into the concrete, solid as anything. They surrounded a support pillar covered in screens of every shape and size. Some were pirate advertisements, while others had been installed with the building. Most of them were broken or without power. One, however, caught my eye. It hung crooked on its mounting bracket. Like the others, the screen was mostly a cracked mess of technicolor shapes and lines, but a portion still seemed to function.

The remaining section was filled with scrolling posts on the local boards. In one, someone pointed out that not even tanks could kill those things. It was quickly drowned out in a sea of replies that all pointed out—in one way or another—that she killed one. Cut its face clean off. That thread descended into argument while another was started to coordinate a local plan of action. Others still were planning their suicides if their time ran out.

"You're wrong," I said aloud, fear giving way to some small amount of reason. "It wouldn't matter. You could kill yourself and still become one of those things regardless." I paused, trying to organize my thoughts. "Even if I blew myself to pieces, I would still be consumed, one way or another."

Of course, I didn't want to die or be eaten, but most of all, I didn't want to become one of them. That part of it. That potential to die but live again as something else might be what terrified me the most. Sure, I could take the initiative and die on my terms, but that didn't mean that I would escape what was going on around me. That didn't mean that I'd stay dead. My skin would feel again, my muscles would contract again, and worst of all, my synapses would fire again, all to the benefit of some murderous creature. Not after I'd only just found myself.

I gripped the back of a nearby chair, and the plastic groaned against the pressure. Eshe was headed up to the Heights right now. If she was still alive. That was a big if. For all I knew, there could be more awful things waiting at the top for a fresh meal. And that wasn't even counting any Vys that made it up there.

Opening my pack, which had miraculously survived the journey so far, I pulled out the cylinder. The questions about its origin and contents seemed so small now. So distant and unimportant. But it was about the only thing I had a tangible grasp on. Everything else was blind hope or guesswork. This—Soqua was real. What happened to Mahdi was real. I could finish his run, and that would have to be enough for now.

So, I put Soqua away and kept moving, silently sending all those people on the boards all the luck in the world that I didn't need for myself.

Down one of the hallways on the third floor, I eventually found my way to a pair of doors that led out to an open-air catwalk that led to another building. I didn't have a good handle on where I was in relation to where I started, but it was a way out. I had to wedge a knife between the doors to work open enough space for me to slip through. The moment I was on the other side, alarm bells started going off in my head. It wasn't that I was exposed without many options for places to go. That at least was expected. No, everything out there on that catwalk seemed too still.

Leaning out over the railing to take in the street below, I could see that it was carpeted with bodies, piled higher on the sides than in the middle. Almost like they'd been crushed. Atop them, though, was a knee-high forest of mushroom-like growths, quivering and dripping some kind of gelatinous ooze. Taking it all in, as my eyes meandered from horror to horror down the street, I spotted a small lift station nestled between two buildings. Unlike the one Eshe and the Tanks had used, this one was smaller, and lined with a few chairs. Personnel rather than cargo, which was of little consequence to me. If it worked, that was going to be my ticket up and out.

I didn't waste time finding stairs or a ladder, and instead, just hopped the railing. The fall was quick, but in the short distance, the air became thick and humid. As I landed and moved to roll, I almost went sprawling instead. I'd expected solid pavement but instead found myself rolling across a spongy stretch of congealed blood. Even worse, in just a handful of moments a thin membrane started to take form on my skin, starting with my arms and slowly migrating upward. A few moments after that, small, barely visible veins grew like spider webs across the membrane, each one trailing back to a tiny quivering, heart-like mass.

Watching it take shape in the span of a few breaths made the hair on the back of my neck stand on end, tenting against this new, foreign skin. It was as if every time I turned a corner, I encountered some new horror that ought not be. But it was all too real. Fortunately, with little more than a couple of bloody smears, it sloughed off as easily as if I had been cleaning cobwebs.

Cleaning it off on the go, I jogged toward the lift, doing my best to keep an eye out for more trouble. The space around me was more bizarre from the ground. At a distance it had looked like just a pile of gore, collecting in an odd corner like dirt in a stairwell. But down there, I could see that every part of the street was alive. The dome-capped mushroom-like growths were something else entirely. The firmly planted stalk rose above the clotted ground looking like a twisting mass of skin and muscle. The mushroom's cap, however, was a thin-skinned carapace of solid bone. Inside, suspended from the underside, were dozens of hand scavengers of various shades and sizes. The smallest ones, clung to the backs of the largest specimens, that themselves seemed to be tending to their suspended kin. It was at that point that I decided to call them skitters.

It dawned on me then that I had walked into some sort of nest. As far as I knew, I hadn't attracted any attention, but with the images of the skinless man being melted in the street were still fresh, and I did not want to end up like him. So, I picked up the pace and kept my distance. It started off pretty well, but abruptly ended when I took the wrong step forward, and the ground collapsed, swallowing my left leg up to the knee.

"Fuck," I spat, slamming a fist on the ground. "Can't I just catch a fucking break?"

Of course, I hadn't meant it as an actual question that needed an answer. But I got a response. In the distance, a deep and persistent thrumming emerged from the background noise. Whatever it was, it was getting closer, and I didn't want to find out what it was.

I tried to fight free, but there was some kind of suction from beneath the surface holding me in place. Using a knife, I worked quickly to pick away at the scab around my knee. Once I thought there was enough space to pry my leg out, I reached a few fingers inside to break the suction. Instead, they encountered something else that distinctly felt like a pair of nostrils. I held my breath. My hand ventured further and found two sunken sockets just beyond. They felt like eyes, or what used to be at one point. I had fallen into someone's face. My pace quickened, fingers frantically pulling chunks of blood out of the ground around me.

"Come on, come on, come on," I snarled, taking quick, panicked glances down the street behind me.

The sound was changing with every passing moment, seeming more and more like a meat grinder than a faint and ominous hum. It was replaced by a cavernous bellow that shook everything. The air, the ground beneath me, everything. The hive around me shuddered into motion, the stalks retracting into the ground with ease, like it was little more than human jelly.

In a similarly grotesque movement, the face around my leg flexed with what felt like a yawn. That gave me some room to move, and my leg was almost out when something shot out after me and wrapped around my ankle, pulling me back in. Then I very distinctly felt a tongue caress the back of my thigh. Even through my clothes, whatever it left behind was slick and viscous, dribbling from my leg in sticky little globs. The sensation made me want to be sick, but I was interrupted when the air trembled again.

Moans erupted from the ground, and I looked wildly around. Air bubbled through the blood in the street, and holes opened up, followed by long greyish tongues that lapped at the air. More skitters had emerged and were cautiously circling closer to me. One strayed too close to one of the openings, and a tongue shot out to drag it out of view.

If I wasn't at risk of having a similar fate, I would have been fascinated at the ecosystem that had clearly developed here. It wouldn't have lasted long, though, because the source of that horrible sound finally made its appearance at the end of the street, behind me. It was a spherical mass of blood-drenched skin that must have been a full ten meters across. No eyes, no face, just tough, crusty, calloused tissue, rolling straight for me.

I screamed, and it came out as something raw and horrified. Some bright and rational part of my mind pointed out that there was no hope clawing myself free and that I needed more effective tools. My eyes darted to everything within reach, looking for something, anything to help me escape. Something crawled up my arm, and without looking, I skewered it with the knife I already had in my hand.

"That's it!" I shouted, staring at the knife, my voice raw and thready. "I am such an idiot!"

I flung the wounded hand-scavenger away from me and stabbed wildly at the ground, at the face that was holding my leg captive. But not even that was enough. Taking the blade in both hands, I drove it down at the ground over and over again. The bones fractured into uneven pieces. My swings threw blood everywhere as if I was a child playing in a rain puddle.

A shadow closed over me. My hands carried the knife down one last time. Finally, the face, shredded pulp as it was, released my leg just in time for me to roll out of the way. The ball of skin plowed through the fungal growths with a splattering furrow of gore. Its momentum carried it onward, launching it into the air, up the side of one of the nearby buildings.

"Run," I said, watching the thing as it reached its apex. "You've got... to run."

Something clicked in my head, and my legs started walking. The walk became a run, and as my mind came back to me, the run became a sprint. Gravity was bringing the flesh-ball back. For a moment, I thought it might careen into the opposite wall, but as it reached the ground again, something in it twisted. Its skin contorted across its center, changing its momentum, allowing it to follow me.

My lungs burned, and my body ached, but there were still another hundred or so meters between me and the lift. Scavengers hopped at me from all directions, and parts of the ground collapsed with more rotting distended faces peeking into view beneath me. It was as if everything around me knew that this was their chance to get a piece of me or keep me from leaving altogether.

The lift was overgrown with a layer of translucent vein-laden skin, but that was the least of my concerns. I swiped my wrist over the control screen and paid the usage fee. Moments passed like years, and the lift didn't budge.

"Oh fuck, oh fuck," I shouted and hit the screen. The panel flowed through several animations, and I found myself tapping on it to make it go faster. "Come on!" I screamed. "Come on!"

The flesh-ball was nearly here, and scavengers flew across the open area of the lift, faster than they had any right to be. They swarmed me, trying to topple me and pile on, and all I could do was flail and scream. Hitting, kicking, and stabbing everything around me with complete abandon.

Finally, the platform groaned to life and tore itself free of the growth in purple gelatinous spurts. The ball of scar tissue careened at the lift even as it pulled away from the ground and collided with the front edge. The small wedge at the base of the lift car acted like a scalpel, shearing off a chunk of meat that hit me square in the chest and threw me off my feet. I struggled against the piece of wriggling flesh but managed to throw it over the side. Most of the scavengers followed it off the lift and immediately started digesting what remained of the flesh-ball. Steam—or perhaps smoke—wafted up from the feeding frenzy below. I didn't fight it when my guts roiled and heaved, forcing me to empty their contents over the edge. Once I was done, I collapsed into one of the passenger seats that hadn't been coated in ichor.

I made it. And now I was on my way to the Heights. I could take a breath, at least for the moment. While fellow runners of mine had visited on more than one occasion, I'd never had the need or opportunity to visit. Not that I'd been avoiding the place or anything, but unless there was a good reason to go, the lift fees weren't usually worth it. So, because of that, I had no idea where I would wind up in relation to Eshe and the tanks.

Mahdi and others—people who were probably dead now—used to tell me stories about the opulent buildings and the people. No killing, very little death of any kind, no worries about survival, only advancing your social credit. I had to admit, playing politics for reputation without the threat of being cut to pieces sounded pretty good. And even going there now had a part of me feeling inexplicably giddy with excitement. I tried to push it away, though. I was not here to sightsee. I had to find Eshe and get her the help she needed. Maybe with those tanks, we could put up a fight long enough to find a place that hadn't been overtaken by all of that monstrous, reimagined humanity. I let my imagination circle around that thought for a while. Me, Eshe, other survivors working together to live out our lives. Despite everything, it was like a dream I wouldn't mind waking up to. It's funny how the end of the world changes all the things you thought were important.

Who was I kidding, though? People were just as monstrous—maybe moreso. And this new world was going to cut all ties to civilization and culture. Social Darwinism would stop being so social, and the fittest and most ruthless would be the only ones to survive.

After a few minutes, my pulse and breathing had returned to normal, and an all-encompassing exhaustion settled in for the long haul. Passenger lifts like the one I was on made the ascent more quickly than the cargo ones that Eshe made it to. Even at this pace, though, it was going to take a couple of hours to reach the top. So, without much else for me to do, I leaned my head back, closed my eyes, and allowed myself to drift into the velvety blackness of sleep.

THIRTY-TWO

NEUTRAL GROUND

A while back, Mahdi and I took on a job out in Chicago. The contract was to break into the regional headquarters of Cerali Incorporated and kill two high-profile VIPs under their protection, while also stealing whatever data we could get our hands on. Cerali was one of the largest security firms on the eastern half of the continent, and the client, Options Personal Security, was hoping the job would stir up enough negative press to gain them a foothold in the market. I could still remember the stupid fucking marketing tag line on their contract form.

When danger knocks, you've got options.

Someone must have been goddamned proud of themselves.

The pay being offered was the sort that attracts some of the best in the business. I was definitely out of my depth as far as my reputation was concerned, but as it turned out, Mahdi knew one of the people on the team who got us in and helped vouch for us. A net diver known only as Knact, who had apparently worked with Mahdi on another gig. He was the one who invited us out and organized the initial meet and greet in lower Chicago.

Mahdi and I took the magway in the day before, which gave us plenty of time to get settled into our hab unit before heading to the little back-alley pub for the meeting. Following Mahdi in, he introduced me to Knact immediately, who grinned at me but refused to shake my hand. He was tall, wiry, and modded to hell. Hard-mounted network visor, ten-fingered hands, and a bundle of prehensile cables protruding from the back of his head that looked like dreadlocks. It wasn't until after our meeting that I found out that he'd pinged me over the mesh rather than accept the traditional handshake.

The pub was an odd, cramped little place in the basement level of its building. Tables were scattered around a bunch of strangely situated support beams, which left no clear walkway through most of the space. But, somehow, in spite of that, it managed to be cozy. Once we all sat down, Knact motioned to the bartender, who silently nodded and started frying up some food on a metal cooktop behind the bar.

Altogether, there were five of us, and Knact started by introducing himself with a drawl. "Hey y'all, nice to meet each of you face to face. I go by Knact and—in addition to coordinating our schedule—I'll be your diver on this little gig."

He continued, going on about his skill, and I leaned over to Mahdi. "He from the Southern Collective?" I asked in a whisper. Mahdi nodded.

"We're gonna be spending a lot of time getting to know each other, so I think that's a good start," Knact said, stepping away from the table to go get a tray of drinks from the bar. Apparently, this was not a full-service establishment.

Mahdi stood up next and introduced both of us. There wasn't much to say, really. As runners, we don't typically get a lot of notoriety from our work. But he said what could be said and tried to make it sound impressive before returning to his seat.

In that time, Knact had brought drinks around to all of us and was starting to distribute plates of food.

The person to my right stood up after that. They were decidedly neutral and also not—masculine and feminine all at once. The textbook definition of androgyny if there ever was one. To call them featureless would be to identify a defining trait about their appearance, of which there were none.

"Most in my line of work have many lives and identities, myself included. You will not be among the privileged few who are privy to any of them," they began, sounding bored, of all things. "If you don't know what a skinslip is, you shouldn't be here, but if proof of skill is required," they said, giving Knact a sideways glance. "Suffice to say that you have all seen me before but would never know it. I will be departing this meeting to immediately begin my infiltration. The diver will know how to contact me if the need arises."

"What do we call you?" one of the tanks asked.

"What?" they responded.

"What do we call you?" the tank repeated with the exact same tone and intonation.

They took a moment to respond, and I couldn't tell if it was out of surprise or annoyance. "If you must refer to me as something for the duration of this meeting, call me Gelid."

Knact silently balked at that, but didn't share what was so amusing. Mahdi and the two tanks nodded along in silence. I, on the other hand, couldn't help but lean forward a little in my seat as they spoke. Sure, Gelid was abrasive as hell, but that didn't change the fact that I'd only ever heard about skinslips. Infiltrators and doppelgangers whose mods help them change their bodies to become other people. Honestly, until that moment, I'd kinda figured they were myths stirred up by netculture. And there I was sitting next to one.

The first of the two tanks greeted the group next. "I am Aleksei," he said, waving from his seat at the nearby table. "I am built for war and violence. My mate can speak for herself, but we are very good at this purpose. Between us, we have more than seventy-five-hundred confirmed deaths and many more longing for it."

"You speak too low, Aleksei," the other tank said. "I am called Lada. Aleksei has been my mate since we were birthed from the steel womb nearly eighteen years ago. We fought in the Egyptian revolution. We held the line for the Lower Kingdom when their forces were decimated in the Battle of the Nile."

I'd seen tanks at a distance once, but that was it. Most of what I knew about them came from chatter on the boards or wiki articles. I'd never been close enough for conversation. The Egyptian revolution that Lada mentioned was a bloodbath by most definitions. From what I understood, it was an unlikely civil war that was expected to be over within a month. The rebels, the Principality of the Lower Kingdom, were disorganized and ill-equipped, relative to the government. Still, despite that, the PLK managed to eke out victory after victory. I've never seen footage, but some say that the gods of ancient Egypt itself descended from on high to fight for the PLK. I had a strong suspicion that they—Aleksei and Lada—may have been responsible for some of those rumors.

"Thanks, everyone," Knact said, leaning forward to rest his elbows on the table. "It's a pleasure to meet y'all. Now, onto our job." He paused for dramatic emphasis. "I'm sure you all heard about the Proxy War down in Houston a couple years back," Knact continued. "The Cerali data heist down there while that whole mess was going down?" He gave everyone a small salute and took a pull from his beer, almost as if he were taking a bow. "I've seen inside their systems before, which is why I'm here, and why they're here," he said, motioning to Mahdi and I. "And we all know what Aleksei and Lada are here for."

The tanks chuckled to themselves as two of Knact's hair-like tendrils slithered up onto the table and projected a three-dimensional map onto the table. It showed a hologram of the Cerali tower in downtown Chicago. It was a tall, swirling, architectural marvel that, despite its obvious beauty, was equally threatening.

"Alright," Knact began. "As Gelid mentioned, they'll be starting their operation as soon as they leave this meeting. The nature of that operation and the methods employed are between them and the client."

"Several weeks ahead of us?" I interjected.

Gelid leaned forward, matching the exact same movement and posture Knact had moments earlier. "Correct. I will acquire access to the facility by masquerading as an employee. Once I have appropriate security clearance, which could require several shifts, I will inform the diver."

"From there," Knact continued, nodding, "I will inform the rest of you. At which point, our operation can begin." He leaned back in his chair. "On that note, you may know how to keep your heads on straight, but if you need to pass information to another member of the team, pass it through me. I have enough security mods to lock down a city, so all comms go through me. Got it?"

The two tanks nodded in unison, as did I.

Mahdi sat there for a second, with one hand on his chin. "So, I'm guessing we're the two faces. Drivers, or something else that won't get much attention."

"Right on the money," Knact said, pointing at Mahdi. "It will be on both of you to get us a ride into the building. Once we're inside, we let the brute squad out and head for the nearest elevator."

"I'm on the brute squad?" Lada asked.

"You are the brute squad," the hacker answered with a grin.

"I like the sound of that," she mused. "Can I acquire it?"

"Be my guest," Knact answered with the wave a hand.

Lada smiled, and it looked like someone had just given her a gift.

"We will need you two," Aleksei chimed in, pointing at Mahdi and me, "to clear out any patrols as we prepare."

Knact jabbed a finger toward us. "And cover your faces, assume everything is being seen by their security system until I say so." Then he turned back to the table and threw a few gestures at the hologram to zoom in on a bank of elevators. "The plan will start in earnest when we get in the cargo lift." A virtual car traveled up quite a ways but eventually stopped. "We'll get off here on the eighty-fourth floor. The tanks will go up to one-oh-three to eliminate two VIPs." He looked at Mahdi and me. "I'm going to ransack their internal mesh and get everything I find onto a pair of mirrored drives. Once I'm done, you two get them out to separate dead drops. The client will retrieve both. So prepare your own exits ahead of time."

"And once they have both, and have confirmed the kills and made their own escape," Mahdi said, crossing his arms, "everyone gets paid. It's a solid plan."

"So long as the creek don't rise," Knact added.

Aleksei and Lada looked at one another with a confused

In a lot of ways, it was four jobs being run at once. Infiltration, assassination, a heist, and a getaway. Trust was absolutely necessary, and the promise of money and a reputation boost was typically enough to guarantee an appropriate amount of professionalism at the very least. A lot of people in these lines of work stuck to that while keeping an emotional distance from the team. With the risk of death looming over most contracts, there was no point in making connections with people that could drag you down. So it came as no surprise when the skinslip didn't hang around for more general discussion after the plan was explained.

"Right. Now that they're gone," I said, motioning towards the door. "Onto the important business." I managed to get a small communal smirk from the rest of the group, which was good enough for me. "Never done a job where this much waiting was part of the plan. What should we do with ourselves?"

"Stay nearby, check in every few days, shoot the shit," Knact said, kicking his feet up on the table.

The lone bartender shot him a look, but the diver ignored him.

"Before missions, we spar," Lada said, eliciting a knowing grin from Aleksei.

"I'd like to see that," I said, genuinely curious.

Aleksei chuckled. "You are brave, my friend."

Knact put his head in his hands, trying to hide his amusement.

"What?" I asked.

"He means that they fuck. And fight. Usually, at the same time," Mahdi said. "They're known to make a mess of things."

Lada leaned in Mahdi's direction, as if to share a secret. "If it's not a mess, was it really that good?"

"Touché," Mahdi answered with a shrug.

Knact, who apparently couldn't contain himself anymore, started cackling like a madman, and Aleksei joined him. Eventually, the rest of us shared in the humor of my ignorance. We enjoyed another hour or so of conversation before Mahdi recommended that we get the lay of the land. I reluctantly agreed, and we left the three of them—Lada, Aleksei, and Knact—still chatting behind us.

After that first encounter, we met at the pub a couple of times a week to share information and make sure everyone was still holding up their end of things. Mahdi insisted that I take a gun with me when the job started, just in case. He even fronted the kay to go through some firearm training sessions. I humored him at first, but it proved to be a nice distraction while we waited.

Between rounds of three-gun and room-clearing, I broke the professional rules and got to know Aleksei and Lada. First, it was about my newfound experience with firearms. They humored me and offered useful advice, which I gratefully accepted. I wound up learning a lot about the tanks and how they lived. They are designed to revel in combat and forge strong personal relationships with the one they are birthed with, their mate. That is, at least until they are retired, typically after ten years. At which point they were quite literally liquidated. The two of them had been working to buy time on their contracts until they had enough to buy them out entirely, which was tantamount to freedom.

Given that both Mahdi and I had been grown in a lab and trained as kids to hack memory locks, I couldn't help but feel a connection with them. Hell, by all rights, we should have been dissolved and fed to the next generation just like them; that is before we and a few others escaped.

A month of meetings, casing, and quick odd jobs came and went without any word from Gelid. Our meeting conversation had changed from excited planning to bored bitching. While it was never said for fear of jinxing it, we all wondered if the job was ever going to happen.

Finally, after another three weeks, we got word from the skinslip. They had impersonated their way into a top security position and gave us the necessary clearance to access the building. At long last, it was time to get to work. Mahdi and I snagged a cargo truck from a maintenance company Cerali contracted with. A couple of borrowed uniforms later and facial prosthetics later, we were pulling into the parking garage at the base of Cerali HQ. It was zero hour, and pulling into the parking space, I looked at Mahdi. The tension could have been plucked like a guitar. He gulped and nodded at me. Then we got out of the truck.

This is what the Trojan horse must have been like.

SQUID INK PASTA

I walked to the rear door of the truck, while Mahdi opened the hood and pretended to fiddle with the engine. We were surrounded by service vehicles of different sorts from an assortment of firms that supported the building's needs one way or another. Laundry, culinary, electronics disposal, and plenty of others. For the moment, though, we were alone.

I undid the door's latch and pushed it up a little before opening it all the way. "You get the surveillance system yet?"

"Working on it," he said. "While it may not look like it to you fleshies, most networks are broken down into several subnetworks. Some for organization, some for security. Not difficult, just tedious and time-consuming. I'll let you know when I have eyes up."

As we talked, Aleksei and Lada were suiting up. Their power armor was impossibly heavy, enough that it had almost bottomed out the truck's suspension. I was pretty sure we left a trail of slag all the way here. Not that it would matter.

Mahdi closed the hood and joined me at the back of the truck. "We ready to go?"

"Almost," I said. "Might as well get suited up ourselves while he gets that sorted out."

Back up in the truck's cab was a pair of duffel bags with tactical vests, helmets, visors, and internally silenced handguns. One for each of us. Super light, compact, and self-extruded so they couldn't be traced. It wasn't going to help if we got into a firefight—that's what the tanks were for—but they were better than nothing. Finally, the prosthetics came off, and the masks went on.

My world was dark for a moment, but came back once my HUD had interfaced with the helmet's combat systems. Visually, it didn't do much that my HUD didn't already, but it had a rear-facing camera and used sub-audible echolocation to build an omnidirectional map. I really needed to get that mod installed at some point, but I never really had enough extra kay to get something like that. After this job, though, maybe. I made a mental note of it and headed to the back of the truck again.

"We ready to go?" I asked.

"We are near," Aleksei said, pulling his warface on.

When taken together, his armor looked like it pulled inspiration from old, extinct animals like mammoths, rhinos, and others. It was a thick hide of self-healing composites that flowed almost organically around several bone-like ridges on his forearms and knees. His helmet was largely blank, save for two pairs of tusks that spread out to either side and another bony ridge running down the middle like a mohawk.

Lada's was similarly intimidating, but where her mate's was organically inspired, hers was as solid and immovable as the building we were infiltrating. It was full of harsh, mechanical edges that seemed both planned and unnatural. What's more, her armor, particularly her spire-like helm, was covered with an array of sensors decorated like eyes. Each one followed a rough direction of focus, but each one twitched a little and rolled off in a different direction before refocusing.

With the two of them ready to go, we left the truck behind with a couple of remote charges waiting to detonate and made our way to the cargo elevator. Mahdi and I had to deal with a couple of guards on the way there, but otherwise, all was quiet. Nobody knew we were here. Yet. With a couple of lumbering armored behemoths with us, it was only a matter of time.

The call light on the elevator went out as the car reached our level. I took a deep breath and was about to let it out when the doors slid open. On the other side stood a harried and exhausted-looking office worker. He was pushing a big cart of half-disassembled server boards and other components. His eyes went real wide when he saw the five of us and he gulped, his frazzled shock of dark hair wobbling as he did.

And for a moment, we all just stood there, staring at one another, before Knact finally piped up. "Hey, got a name?"

He stared off into space for a moment before catching up with the question. He almost jumped like he'd been startled. "Oh, uh Jest."

"Hi, Jest," Knact continued, slowing his words down. "You don't get paid enough to deal with this. Why don't you go take the night off?"

Jest looked at each of us in turn, then returned his focus on Knact and nodded once, before stepping out from behind the cart of electronics. He took slow timid steps towards us and Mahdi shifted to one side to let him through. He kept walking like that until he was about to turn the corner into the parking garage, then he took off in a panicked sprint.

"We should have killed him," Lada said, taking the first step into the elevator.

Knact shrugged. "It's like I said, system admins don't get paid enough, and I have a soft spot for them. He won't say anything."

"Everybody ready?" I asked, closing the security fence.

"Fight or die bright," Lada acceded.

"Like the orbs," Aleksei added.

"I'd like to avoid that last bit, if possible," Knact said as I punched in the floors.

"I'm with you there," Mahdi muttered, letting out a slow, measured breath.

With that, I hit the button for the eighty-fourth floor. A speaker in the back corner of the car dinged once in response, then we started rising. It was slow at first, building itself up to speed. A few seconds later, the speaker played a couple of quick chimes indicating we'd reached our first stop. Mahdi, Knact, and I would get off here, at the primary data center, then Aleksei and Lada would head to the one hundred and third floor to take out the VIPs. I looked back at everyone for a moment, before setting my shoulders and tugging the gate open. Beyond it was a short hallway that led to a pair of high-density security doors.

"Knact," Mahdi said with a slow note of caution. "You got that access code, right?"

Knact nodded, then looked worried and started rifling through his pockets. "Oh, fuck. Oh, fuck. Fuck, fuck, fuck," he muttered. "I think I left the code in my other pants."

Nobody laughed. We all just stared at him. I imagined Aleksei and Lada looking annoyed behind their warfaces.

"Of course I have it, you ass," Knact followed up, making his way to the door.

He sauntered forward, and as he approached the security terminal, a couple of his tendrils wrapped under his arm and plugged themselves in. As he worked, Mahdi and I stepped up beside him, guns ready. Once the code was accepted, the doors slid open to reveal a cavernous dimly lit room. What little I could see came by way of flickering indicator lights in the dozens—perhaps hundreds—of server racks, cordoned off into sections by glass walls. The whole of it made the space seem infinite.

Mahdi let out a breath. "Damn, this must take up the entire floor."

As he moved to step forward, several sets of glowing eyes appeared in the distant shadows.

Lada and her mate came up behind us almost immediately. "Go. Aleksei and I will handle these progeny."

"Shit," Knact said. "More tanks. I knew this was going too smoothly."

The job was fucked. We were fucked. It was all fucked. If we closed the elevator door and tried to escape, Cerali's tanks would follow us down the elevator shaft and tear us apart. If we fought, I wasn't sure we'd make it out alive, either, but at least we could better our odds.

Lada and Aleksei were out the door ahead of us, an instant later, hauling with them their obscenely large weapons of choice. For Lada, it was a chaingun whose ammo belt-fed out of her armor. Aleksei, on the other hand, dragged an ancient-looking double-headed war axe behind him.

"Time to die, Newfucks!" Lada shouted, bracing herself to unload her cannon.

For a few long moments, each side stared at the other, no words being said, no shots being fired.

"They're sizing us up," Mahdi whispered. "We need to go, like she said. Get what we came for so they don't have to hold them off as long."

Knact didn't need to be told twice and bolted out of the hallway. Mahdi and I followed, not far behind. It was hard to see anything but, fortunately, those echolocation maps our helmets were feeding us made it so we didn't need to see. We got as far away as we could before Knact stopped and ripped a couple of panels off the nearest rack. He set his backpack on the ground and started pulling out pieces of equipment and plugging them into each other. One of his hair-cables arched over the devices and shined a dim light over them, which was apparently just enough for him to see. He set out two small rectangles that looked about the size of cigarette lighters and plugged each into the largest piece of equipment, a portable networking switch. Lights on all the devices started flashing together, indicating successful connections.

"The drives are here and here," he said, pointing to the lighter-sized devices, each with a cheaply applied sticker of a purple squid on their covers. "They'll be mirroring everything I find. If one of those other tanks comes wandering around looking for us, grab the drives and get the fuck out, you got me?"

"Yeah, we got you," I said gravely.

Knact pointed at us with a pair of finger-guns, faked shooting at us, then went to work. About half of the cables attached to his head slammed into the server stack in front of him, plugging into dozens of different ports.

Behind us, a multi-screened terminal booted itself up, casting a blue glow over the three of us. "Keep an eye on them," Knact said. "If this shitshow goes more sideways than it already has, let me know."

"Aren't you on the cameras?" I asked.

"Had to let 'em go," he grinned, something I could hear in his tone more than see. "Gotta put all I got into this. I'll have cameras back when I'm done."

Mahdi nodded and traded a fist bump with him. "Godspeed."

Knact turned his attention to the servers and the network. For a while, everything was quiet. Fans hummed. Liquid cooling pumps glugged and churned. Then, abruptly and without any warning or preamble, the world tore itself apart. Explosions shook the air and spent shells rattled on the floor as if someone was throwing around hundreds of empty paint cans. Emergency lights flooded the room, enough to make out the figures fighting on the terminal screens. Sirens sounded, and fire suppression systems labored to keep up with the plumes of smoke that clouded the air.

Lada was unloading her gun in calculated bursts, keeping her distance, and using the stream of projectiles to channel her opponents. This tactic claimed its first victory when one of the enemy tanks—with a warface of a vampire bat—moved to avoid her fire and separated himself from his team. Aleksei blurred out of the shadows, and in a leaping spin, buried his axe into his opponent's abdomen, spilling vitals out onto the floor. Bat-face screeched and jerked awkwardly as it collapsed backward, trying to reel its guts back in. Then Aleksei whirled the weapon in an arc, bringing it up over his shoulders and down, into the tank's chest. The force was enough to split the armor and the chest cavity underneath wide open. With one down and four left to go, Aleksei darted back into the nearby shadows for his next chance to strike.

"Holy shit," Mahdi said, shaking his head. "Did you see that?"

I nodded absently and kept my eyes glued to the screens, even though watching it like a voyeur made part of me feel a little sick. The dance with Lada's gun and Aleksei's axe continued, and they were about to claim another victim when something fell to the floor behind us. Spinning around, I saw Knact on the ground, his cables still attached to the servers. Smoke was pouring out of him, creating a red-orange haze in the emergency lights. His back arched, and his fingers clenched until his hands were bleeding all over the floor.

"What do we do?" I asked, rushing over to him.

"They must have been waiting for him!" Mahdi shouted. "He might be able to fight them off, but we should try to get the hell out of here."

"And leave him here?" I asked.

"There's nothing we can do for him that he can't do for himself. And besides, he told us to leave," Mahdi answered, kneeling down over the man. He reached down to take one of the drives and dropped it almost immediately. "Holy shit, the thing's burning up."

Thinking quickly, I pulled a couple of rags out of my bag and grabbed both drives. They were definitely hot, almost too much for the meager barrier I'd found, but I managed to get them both into one of my pack's separate pockets.

"Nice," Mahdi said. "Now, let's mo—"

A cry of agony rang out in the distance, amidst the smoke and gunfire. We didn't need to use the terminal to see Lada flying through the air and crashing through a couple of server stacks before rolling to a stop nearby.

"Lada!" Aleksei called out, bursting from the shadows.

Before he could get very far, a stream of bullets came for Aleksei and forced him into cover. Using Lada's strategy against the two of them allowed the remaining tanks to close on her. But she was already back on her feet. As they got close, Lada struck one in the face with the barrel of her gun, staggering him for a step or two before she unloaded into him. Whatever was in that gun of hers punched holes in his face the size of my fist, painting his armor and everything behind him in a chunky crimson spray.

The other enemy tank—a relatively thin and lithe-looking figure with a blank, featureless warface—rushed Lada. She tried the same tactic with the barrel of her gun, but wasn't fast enough. This new tank, No-face, ducked the strike, caught Lada's arm, and twisted it until her elbow tore free. Then, all No-face did was give her limb a firm tug, and just like that Lada's forearm and gun fell uselessly to the ground. For her part, Lada didn't seem phased by this at all. There was no fear in her stance, no fear from losing her weapon, only bloodlust.

"Aleksei!" Lada shrieked, trying to lure No-face into a grapple. "Get out of here!"

No-face surged forward, seemingly taking the bait, but pulled back at the last possible second. It was just enough to get Lada to flinch and open herself up. Then the tank moved in earnest, throwing Lada off-balance and taking her legs out from under her. She was on the ground a fraction of a second later and No-face followed her down, tearing at her armor with a pair of savagely bladed gauntlets. Pieces of metal and ceramic plating showered the ground in all directions until No-face plunged both of their hands into Lada's chest.

"That's..." Lada forced out "...an order!"

Ribs snapped, one after the other, and the tank ripped open Lada's abdomen like a suitcase, splattering everything around the two of them in a welter of gore and innards. No-face leaned over her victim, almost reveling in the kill. Splayed out like that, the mismatch of torn organs and blood made my stomach revolt right then and there, and I threw up all over the console. I couldn't turn away, though, I didn't want to abandon Lada even if she didn't know I was there with her.

Lada bucked against the pain and the shock that was taking her as No-face tore out one major organ at a time. Lada's helmet played a recording of laughter that wasn't hers. I wasn't sure where it came from, but it was haunting and menacing at once, and it filled the space completely. She marshaled the last of her strength to pull something from her belt and punch up at No-face's chin, through a weak point in the mask. A moment later, there was a small burst of lightand the enemy tank's helmet exploded. No-face, which was now very literal, collapsed atop Lada's corpse, and it was done. Everything fell silent for several seconds.

Aleksei screamed, unleashing an anguished war cry that rattled my bones. Taking several grazing shots from the remaining enemies, he bolted out of sight and into the persisting shadows. Gunfire followed, and despite my best efforts, I couldn't find him on the terminal displays.

This was going to be our last chance to escape. If the other tanks took out Aleksei, they would find and kill us with ease. I looked back to Knact to see if he made it out, and I got my answer. His twitching husk stopped and finally went limp. I checked his pulse to be sure, and that's when I saw the grey-red sludge leaking out of his ears.

"Shit, Mahdi," I shouted. "He's dead! They fucking killed him!"

"You can lose your shit later," Mahdi replied. "We gotta go."

We left the man behind, moving quick and quiet, from rack to rack. The battle raged on, and we could hear Aleksei's scream fly at us out of the darkness every now and again. Not that we counted for anything resembling help, he was going to have to be on his own from here on out. So we slipped back into the freight elevator and out an escape hatch at the top of the car.

"Mahdi," I said, putting my hands on my knees. "I have to stop for a second."

"Yeah..." he replied, sounding distracted.

"How the hell are we going to get out of here?" I asked.

"I'm figuring that out now," he said, flipping through a portable terminal on his arm. "The lobby we entered through is sure to be swarming with corpsec, waiting to mop up anyone who made it out."

I didn't say anything and just focused on breathing for a few seconds.

"C'mon, this way," he said.

I got upright again and followed him to the edge of the elevator car. There was a small channel built into the wall that contained an access ladder. We took that down, one rung at a time, making sure to pace ourselves. Mahdi stopped after several hundred meters, checked his terminal again, and opened a ventilation cover. The vent was tiny, and it forced me to crawl through on my stomach, and only a meter at a time. We stopped at each intersection, and Mahdi checked his terminal. We turned a couple of times, but for the most part, we kept going straight through.

We finally pulled ourselves out of the vents and into an office on the third or fourth floor. Thankfully, it was empty, but more important than that was the fact that it was situated on an outside wall and had windows. At this point, I knew exactly what Mahdi was thinking, and went about collecting cables of all kinds. Extension cables, network cables, it didn't matter. I wound them together into a small bundle and Mahdi followed behind me with a roll of duct tape. Once we had fifteen or so meters of our makeshift rope, we broke the windows and rappelled down as far as we could. At that point, it was up to each of us to make it the rest of the way down on our own.

After reaching the ground, I gave Mahdi one of the drives, which was still warm to the touch. Then we bolted. Mahdi and I ran for a long time, not saying a word or so much as signing to one another. All that mattered at that moment was putting as much distance between us and that bloodbath as possible. When we finally did speak, it was to wish the other luck as we went our separate ways.

The heist-gone-wrong was all over the boards up and down the east coast for weeks after that. We were already trying to forget what had happened, but getting constant reminders like that prompted many an attempt to bury the memories with cheap liquor. We never figured out who did us in, and I don't think either of us wanted to know. Maybe the skinshift got a better deal or was on the inside the whole time. Perhaps the client backed out. Hell, for all we knew, the whole thing could have been an elaborate penetration test. The only thing we knew for sure was that Mahdi and I were the only survivors.

As for the drives. That was the one thing that we never acknowledged. I don't know if Mahdi left his copy at the planned dead drop, but I didn't take the risk. I would have tossed it altogether if I didn't think it might be a useful bargaining chip someday. So, once I made it home, I hid it behind my workbench and tried to forget about it.

THIRTY-FOUR

CAVE DWELLERS

A klaxon sounded from somewhere, and I was on my feet with a knife in hand before I knew what was happening. Almost as if in reply, the elevator let out a small chime, indicating that it had reached its destination. Then the doors parted to reveal the Heights.

I would have anticipated the buzzing crowds of the affluent—every last one of them ignorant to the horrors besetting their fellow humans below. Instead, I was greeted by a cold and sterile emptiness. There was nobody in sight, not even automated systems idling through their routines. No blood, not even a corpse. Given everything I'd witnessed back in the Barrel, seeing a place so clearly made to support life so devoid of it was disturbing. I couldn't decide which one was worse: all the horror and death or the inexplicable lack of life.

Stepping off the lift, I entered a large courtyard dotted with several dried-up fountains and lined with glass-plated storefronts. A mad little chuckle escaped my lips. All the talk I'd heard of the Heights, with all its lavish excess, and here they were still building shops around fountains and town squares. The buildings here looked to be hewn from massive, uninterrupted stone blocks, sourced from the quarries down in the Barrel.

"They were living in caves," I said, unable to believe even my own words. "All this talk of the wealth and splendor of the Heights, and they were living in goddamned caves."

It shouldn't have mattered as much as it did, especially now. People were being slaughtered, and the last person I loved in the world was either dead or very quickly approaching it. She was cold and alone somewhere, surrounded by strangers that were unable to fully contemplate death. But I couldn't help but feel duped by all of this, by everything I'd heard. These people were supposed to be on the bleeding edge of the future, developing things that would be entirely indistinguishable from magic. Where were they with their god-like power and mastery of all elements?

"Not here, that's for damn sure," I answered myself as I picked a street that I thought might take me back to Eshe and the other lift.

I hadn't made it more than a few dozen steps before sweat plastered my face and I was forced to stop and catch my breath. The air was thin and frigid, neither of which meant good things for me if I had to take off running. So I slowed my pace and gathered my jacket closer to ward off the cold.

The lift doors boomed and closed behind me, and that same klaxon from before sounded. Someone, or something, had called it down, back into hell. Whoever it was, I had just cleared the way for them. Or perhaps I'd left a trail that was easy to follow. Either way, I didn't want to risk finding out and kept moving.

Looking up, past the rooftops was the sky. The actual sky. Not a simulation. It was just as empty as the street I was standing in the middle of, save for a few white specks that peeked out of the deep azure. It was the same sky that I saw in Old Manhattan, but somehow, this was different, less polluted. There was a part of me that wanted to be filled with the wonder of the expanse that lay before me, at the endless possibility of the void. The rest of me felt nervous and wanted to go hide in a hole somewhere. As if I would fly off and be lost forever if both my feet left the ground at the same time.

I returned my attention to the street ahead, which was still lined with shops and businesses. Each one bore a large ornate pane of glass, offering little security for the goods displayed within. Taking another break, I found myself peering into a clothing store. The thought of not needing security was strange. Back home, down in the Barrel, a shop like this would have been broken into on principle alone, just to prove how insecure it was. I doubted anyone would steal the clothing inside anyway; they were all smooth and functionless. Not a pocket in sight.

While silently judging the store's goods, I caught my reflection in the glass. I was a mess. The muddy red-brown of dried blood was everywhere, my skin, my clothes, nothing had been spared. Holes were torn in my clothes, and I had little cuts and scrapes everywhere. I did what I could to clean my face in the reflection and noticed my freckles again. I had completely forgotten they were there.

Who was she?

If what Veto had said was to be believed, I was the fifth person to inhabit this body, and I wondered who each of them were. How they lived, how they died, and what they would have done in the face of this nightmare. I wondered if what I said about the daughter I assumed he had held any truth. True or not, I felt some new weight settle onto my shoulders. What did they see when they looked back in the mirror? What were their dreams? I felt responsible to each of them to make the most of the form that we all shared.

Eventually, I shook my head clear of those distracting thoughts and kept moving down the row of storefronts to a traffic circle. I had to be close to lining up with the other lift, so I crossed the street and took a right. As I did, a blinding orb of light shot into the sky and exploded with a shockwave that rattled windows in their frames and almost made me jump out of my skin—a concussion flare. And it wasn't for me.

"Well, at least I know where they are now," I muttered, creeping down the street and into a small alcove at the entrance of a luxury spa.

I was forced to stay there for a while and watch as dozens upon dozens of Vys, clad in dark cloaks and gas masks, filtered in from different side streets. Together, they formed a sort of procession that was headed in the direction of the flare, almost like platelets rushing to a wound site. I'd known that some of them made it to the Heights, but I was not expecting that many, or for them to be that level of organization. It was as if they'd abandoned the Shiv all at once and came straight here. It's what I would have done. But knowing some of their longstanding leadership, I would have expected them to stubbornly hold onto their turf.

With most of the others having moved on ahead of me, I crept out of my hiding place and zeroed in on one of the scouting teams that was bringing up the rear. There were only two of them, and if I moved quickly enough I thought I'd be able to take them out.

I started having second thoughts immediately. Catching up to them wound up far more taxing than it should have been, and trying to stay quiet only made it worse. But once I was close enough to the first of my two targets, I took a quick, risky step and with a flying leap plunged a blade into the base of his skull. As he fell, I did my best to catch and lower him quietly to the ground.

My chest was heaving from the effort, and my vision blurred a little at the edges. I couldn't do it, I couldn't take them both quietly. So I focused on my breathing and waited for a few moments before I started hauling my victim off the street. I kept a careful eye on the other scout as they walked away, and hoped with everything I had that they didn't notice their partner missing for a while.

Once I was relatively concealed I worked quickly to relieve the corpse of its inventory. The cloak might help me to blend in a little if I ran into more of them. The gas mask, as it turned out, was an oxygen condenser, which may have very well been a lifesaver. Once I had it secured in place over my nose and mouth, it was as if someone had lifted a boulder off my chest. With that, I rifled through the rest of his pack. On a sling, he had a small round-bodied compact machine gun with a doubled-up banana mag. Along with that, I found a few more magazines in his pack, along with food, water, and an assortment of personal items. I took a couple of minutes to eat and drink as much as I could before slipping back out onto the street and hustling to catch up to the main group.

I had a feeling that they were headed in the direction of the other lift, so blending in might get me closer. If I got there, though, I had no idea how I'd get myself or Eshe out alive. But I had to try.

THIRTY-FIVE

CALLING IT IN

Following the Vys contingent through the city streets, we encountered other groups of more heavily armed soldiers. A bit further and there were others assembling auto-mobile gun turrets. Finally, the procession found its way to the outer edge of an expansive plaza. Sculptures and small manicured ponds and gardens dotted the plaza. Almost like a theatre, it descended down a couple of hundred meters before terminating at a decorative rectangular moat and a lift concourse behind it.

Most of the people I could see were busying themselves with preparation. Nervously loading weapons, laying out ammunition, and the like. A few had taken up a loose patrol of the perimeter, and I slid into line behind them. As I followed, several other Vys nodded to me or threw me greetings in Roko as I passed. I made sure to return the gestures in kind. As the patrol came up to the center of the plaza, we approached a group of Vys in the midst of a heated discussion. I recognized one of them immediately and sucked in a breath.

"This is a gamble," a man said, pleading with a dark-haired, bespectacled woman opposite him. "Just three of those tanks down there could flatten all of us if they move first. We should take them by surprise, kill them before they do the same to us."

"Have you ever seen a bear?" Ragna asked.

The man hesitated.

"They still exist in the northern wilderness," she explained, choosing her words carefully. "Five-hundred-kilo killing machines that could probably go toe-to-toe with one of those tanks down there. You know how to survive an encounter with one?"

Once again, the man didn't say anything, just glared and ground his teeth.

"You stand up to them. Make a lot of noise. Show them how dangerous you are, and that you are not worth the trouble," she said, placing extra emphasis on the last few words. "Power recognizes and respects power. That power also respects territorial claims. The tanks down there are no different, and cheap shots like what you are suggesting make us look weak."

The man's face twisted up in a snarl. "You're going to get us all killed. Judace would never have allowed—"

Ragna cut him off, raising her voice. "Judace is dead, Petyr. And he left me in charge. It is advisable that you get used to that."

With that, she spun around on one foot and stalked away, leaving the man and his lackeys in her wake. A small retinue of bodyguards, advisors, and others trailed behind her. Petyr, for his part, just stood there, nostrils flaring, chest heaving, and fists clenched. He stared daggers at Ragna for a moment before sucking in a contemptuous breath and storming off in the opposite direction.

As the two parties went their separate ways, I split from the patrol I'd been following and caught up to Ragna's contingent. She was headed down into the plaza, toward the concourse and, I hoped, Eshe.

It also helped that I knew Ragna. I'd heard Petyr mentioned before somewhere. The name seemed familiar, but I couldn't place it. I didn't know much about him, which made him unpredictable. And with the current situation being as explosive as it seemed, I needed to mitigate that as much as I could. Ragna was cold, ruthless, calculating, and manipulative. When she looked at someone, she wasn't taking in the person with dreams, fears, values, and beliefs. She was cataloging them. Breaking them down into their baser parts, with each of those pieces just being levers to lean on. As much as I hated to admit it, she was the devil I knew.

Ragna's group made its way down a few zig-zagging walkways, past reflecting pools and rock gardens, before finally reaching a platform that would take us down the rest of the way. Everyone crammed in and I made sure to stay out of Ragna's line of sight. As we sped down, through the plaza, the doors to the lift concourse opened just enough to allow a trio of tanks to step outside. Each of them thudded out in their wargear and came to a stop in formation—yellow to the left, green to the right, and purple in the middle. They were waiting, seemingly for us, letting Vys decide how this was going to go down. Once they were in position, the other tanks with their makeshift armor rushed out after them and set up a number of deployable barriers.

It was at that moment that I really took in the whole scene. The whole of the plaza was comprised of perhaps a dozen or so landings depending on where I looked. Aside from the lift I was on, there was no quick or simple method of ascent or descent. Unless jumping from high ledges was an option. Surrounding them on all sides was a sea of people. Thousands of faces hidden beneath dark tunics and gas masks. They would only occasionally give themselves away when a shift of fabric or nervous twitch would reveal a portion of light-emitting tattooed skin. It made the whole plaza seem like a twinkling reflection of the night sky above.

As the lift worked its way down the plaza, Ragna took a few steps to the side, sliding around a few of her people, and leaned up against the railing next to me. "Don't think I didn't notice you skulking around back there."

I didn't answer, and like a prey animal next to a predator, I froze in place.

"You're not Vys," she continued, picking through her words carefully. "You're not one of Petyr's off-book people."

"I'm nobody," I said, not thinking of much else better to say.

Ragna laughed, far more calm and confident than she had any right to be. "Oh no, you're somebody. A nobody would have hid on the edge of this powder keg and waited to pick the bodies clean once it was all over." She turned to look at me directly, and her eyes narrowed. "A nobody wouldn't have snuck onto this lift. You're somebody, alright. The trouble is figuring out if you're better to me dead or alive."

I leaned slightly to one side, away from her, and she smiled. "Ah, so you do want to live. Alright, so how about a proposition then?"

"I've learned from bitter experience that it would be a bad idea," I answered.

"Interesting," Ragna said, eyes sparkling with something viscous. "So you know me enough to know that I can and will have you killed. You might go down swinging, you may even kill me, but you will not get off this lift alive."

She paused on that as if knowing that I needed a moment to consider it. I looked over my shoulder to get a look at the others nearby. Eighteen in total. They were all going to be armed and highly trained for close quarters combat at the minimum. Ragna was right. For the moment I was stuck, and she wasn't going to let me buy time. If I took too long to answer she'd have me killed anyway.

"What do you want?" I asked, trying not to sound defeated.

"Good girl," she grinned, seemingly satisfied, and adjusted her glasses. "Petyr is going to make a move on me once I start talking to them. Tanks, as you probably call them." She sounded somewhat disgusted by the word, and it made me wonder what she called them. "Petyr is an idiot, but he's smart enough to get someone else to do his dirty work. He's going to go all-in on having me killed in the crossfire. I get memorialized as a legend and he gets to keep Vys all to himself."

Ragna tugged a small stick from a pocket inside her jacket and took a long pull from it, closing her eyes as she inhaled. As she exhaled a white cloud of vapor, her expression shifted into something hard and razor-sharp. "Like you, I have no intention of dying uselessly. I'll survive his attempt to usurp me, but I want you to find him and kill him. If you do that and make it back in one piece, I'll make sure you get whatever brought you here in the first place."

Ragna had a way of manipulating people into accumulating more debt; she was incredibly good at it. But that didn't make her dishonest. If she said she would do something, she meant it, and it would get done. Just like promising to kill me, if I did this for her, she would do whatever she could to make sure I got what I wanted. I knew that much, and she wasn't going to give me very long to think about it.

"If I kill him," I said, making sure to choose my words carefully, "pull your people out and find somewhere else to set up camp."

"Alright then," she replied, her lips curling up at the corner in a sideways grin. "Follow us when the lift stops, then make your move once things get loud."

I sucked in a deep breath and nodded, staring out into the middle distance. Then she moved back to the front of the lift. She may have been a dangerous, manipulative monster, but I had to admire her a little. How could I not? She was a leader who took point rather than issuing orders from behind. I could only imagine the kind of loyalty she inspired.

Once the lift's safety gate dropped, the group strode forward, following a path headed straight for the tanks. As we approached, Ragna's people spread out to either side of her, like an animal puffing itself up to look intimidating. There were other Vys underlings already there, seemingly preparing for this to go sideways. Ragna looked over her shoulder at me and nodded once. That was enough for me to start veering off from her group.

A smile settled onto Ragna's face as she returned her attention to the human killing machines a few dozen meters away. Then she took a couple of steps forward and projected her voice. "Welcome. Apologies for the less than warm welcome." She motioned to all of her compatriots lining the plaza. "But given everything that's happened, caution seems prudent."

The tank standing at the center stepped forward in kind and used the loudspeakers on his own suit. "Your strength has our respect. We will go our way and not interfere with yours."

"On the contrary," the woman said, evoking some archaic mannerisms. "I had hoped you would consider joining us. Surely strength in numbers is preferable."

The tank looked like they were just about to move, but stopped short as Ragna extended her offer. And for several tense breaths said nothing. Even though I couldn't see through his warface, it seemed as if he was narrowing his eyes to study Ragna. For her part, she kept her cool and waited as patiently, not daring to move or do anything that might provoke a negative reaction.

"No," the tank said, finally.

"Is that so?" she asked.

The tank answered in a calm voice that betrayed something darker roiling beneath the surface. "We have been killer-slaves to others that would not wager their own lives, but would of ours, for far too many cycles. That will not be our life again. Gratitude for the offer."

Ragna stood there for a moment seemingly studying the tanks, before speaking again. "Very well. I would not have sought that from you."

I rolled my eyes at that because I knew better.

She continued. "But I understand your aversion. If you would not join us, perhaps an agreement of non-aggression between our two parties."

"Taken," the tank responded after pondering the alternate proposition. "Now, we will go."

Ragna moved to offer the tanks a slight bow of respect, but before she could, the world around us was thrown into chaos. As if fired all at once, guns, rocket-propelled grenades, and anti-armor shells erupted from every angle. All of them were trained on the concourse. Everyone sprang into action. Ragna, myself, and others nearby all dove for cover.

"Go!" she shouted at me as she drew a compact lever-action handgun that had been holstered under her arm.

I turned immediately and made a run for the furthest side of the plaza. I hadn't made it more than a few steps, though, before one of the armored tanks surged forward and slapped me away, sending me flying. I hit the ground hard, and had tumbled for six or seven meters when I finally came to a stop in a reflection pond. My vision went black for... I didn't know how long. It can't have been long; perhaps only a few moments. When I faded back into woozy consciousness, the tanks had started returning fire.

I tried to crawl forward a little when several hands took me by the collar and me back behind the Vys lines. I blinked a lot as the world wobbled in my vision like a top. The hands released me and drifted over my body, looking for other injuries. There was some commotion that followed, and as the words started to clear, I could tell that I had been found out.

"Bitch ain't Vys," a woman spat. "She killed one o' ours, we take it back."

She and the two others around me all wore much of the same garb that I'd commandeered. Of course, it was their uniform, a way of equalizing every member into a single unit that looked the same. We'd been using that basic psychological tool for thousands of years, even if the uniform that Vys used was a bit eclectic compared to their historical counterparts. But even with all the sameness that was built into a uniform, from where the three stood, I could make out all their differences. For one, the woman had pale, almost bleached, sickly-looking skin and a braided mohawk of blonde hair. From what I could tell of her features around her mask and tunic, she was all sharp angles and rigid muscle.

Similarly, her counterparts—two men—were equally toned. Though their skin looked considerably more healthy, each of them bore similarly styled braids of black and brown. One thing they all shared, though, was something in their stance that seemed predatory, like they were habitual killers.

Not wanting to find out, I tried to get up and make my escape but fell over before even getting on my feet.

"You not gettin' outta here so easy," one of the men laughed. "How 'bout we make use of her after?"

Not another word was spoken, but the two held me back down and started pulling at my arms, trying to rip my prosthetics off to leave me defenseless. I did not want to be made use of, now or later, so when a third pair of hands started feeling around under my shirt, I screamed and kicked and thrashed. I looked up as the other man backed off. He had taken one of the knives from my jacket and started appraising it.

"This some fine metal," he said, nodding at me with a sinister grin. "Thank you."

"It's too good for you," I snarled.

Then I arched my back and pivoted my hips, transforming my foot into an axe-like wedge that I sent careening into the side of his head. His jaw slammed shut as my foot buried itself halfway into his skull.

Then my foot reformed itself allowing the man to fall away, twitching and spasming.

The man holding down my left arm flinched for just a second, but it was enough to wrench myself free and throw a punch at the woman to my right. I managed to hit her three times in the facemask, breaking her nose and probably knocking out a couple of teeth. She fell back, holding her face, and scrabbled at the mask until it came loose.

I threw an awkward punch in my last assailant's direction. He took it with a grunt of pain but straddled my hips for better leverage. He took my head in his hands and slammed it back into the ground, over and over. My vision flashed white and red as sharp jolts of pain echoed around my skull. I reached for his face, pushing it away, buying just enough time to go for one of the knives in my jacket. He caught my arm as I did, and we fought for control.

He won the battle for the blade, and I barely managed to divert it away from my face. Sharp, fresh agony punctured my shoulder, and I let out a cry into the condenser mask. He stared at the pointed, blunt handle of the knife, breathing heavy, then looked at me. He took off his own mask, leaned down close, and smiled. It was something rancid-looking and malevolent. It promised things much worse than my current injuries if I gave up. So, even though it hurt like one hell of a bitch, I hit him in the face with my forehead. He recoiled and I reached up, grabbing the back of his head, and pulled it down hard into my shoulder. The back end of the blade ruptured his eye and kept going until it bit into the bone at the back of his socket. The man fought himself free of me and frantically grabbed at his face. I scrambled backward, out from under him, and pulled the thoroughly bloodied blade out of my shoulder.

My breath came out in shudders against the condenser mask. I felt like I was starting to suffocate, but managed to get off my ass and onto my hands and knees. I wanted to be sick. I wanted to let the panic take me. Panic at what almost happened, and what could easily almost happen again. If only I'd been smarter, if I hadn't gotten hit by that tank, they wouldn't have grabbed me.

I was at war with myself, and I fought to arrest all that raw emotion, at least for now. "Get it together," I told myself in a half-choked whisper. "Assholes try to rape people. It happened in your old body. It's going to happen in this one." I climbed to my feet, leaning on a nearby wall for balance. "Just remember the rule. Fuck them up before they do it to you."

I turned around, taking unsteady but purposeful steps, and bent over to take a handgun from the woman's shoulder holster. Then I stood back, pointed the weapon at her, and pulled the trigger. Nothing happened, and I looked at it for a second before flipping the safety off and putting a bullet through her head. Then I turned to face the one-eyed man. He was holding his hands up and begging for mercy. I considered it for a moment, then lowered the gun from his face to his groin, and emptied the magazine.

THIRTY-SIX

HIGH CRIMES

Looking back over the last few days, I concluded that I had little respect for the dead and dying. Once their hearts stopped beating, they were just things with a vastly more limited shelf life. Just a bag of meat waiting for rot or recycling, whichever came first. Until then, if they had something useful, I should take it to help me survive. It isn't as if my perspective is unique, though. Plenty of people operated on some sort of Darwinism. But some people treat death as a noble sacrifice and take time to pray over their victims and hold their hands as the final breath takes them. I'd never really acknowledged which camp I fell into. When I scoured the corpses or soon-to-be-corpses of the people I'd just killed, I think I finally understood.

Even as the one-eyed man bled out through his splattered pelvis, weakly pleading for help, I ignored him, brushed his hands aside, and searched his pockets for anything useful. A flashlight, some ammunition, rations, and a medkit. I left everything I'd found in a disorganized pile.

Leaning up against a wall, I went through the kit, retrieving a plastic syringe of stemgel, a portable staple gun, some adhesive gauze, and a stimulant of some kind. Using one hand, I cut myself out of the cloak and slid out of my jacket. It took a couple of tries but, eventually, I got my arm free. The stemgel came first. I removed the protective cap and forced the nozzle into the wound on my shoulder. I was a little overzealous with the applicator, and the green-yellow medical culture oozed out of the puncture and down my arm as if I'd been draining an abscess. I could clean it up later.

I tried not to clench my jaw, with mixed success, as the staple gun came next. My whole shoulder throbbed, but my brain somehow managed to distinctly register every staple biting into my skin like pairs of little metal fangs. Finally, I stuck on a couple of squares of adhesive gauze and shrugged back into my jacket. My arm wasn't going to be much use if I wanted to keep the staples from tearing free, but I'd have to chance it.

From there, I held the stim injector between my teeth as I went about collecting what I could from the other two bodies. It wasn't much but I added a water canteen and a flare launcher to the haul, then put almost everything in my pack. The flair launcher, though, found a home on my jacket's magnetic harness. Then I commandeered another cloak, used the stim, and got moving again.

Keeping walls to my back as often as possible, I crept around the edge toward the center of the plaza. Most of the other Vys I passed were too focused on shooting at the tanks to notice me. The few that did must have done some quick math in their heads and decided I wasn't worth the trouble. I had to make my way back up to where I first saw Petyr and figure out where he was from there.

Another concussive flare went up and exploded low to the ground, stirring up a low-hanging cloud of dust with its shockwave. The sudden loss of visibility brought the shooting to a near-standstill. Occasionally, mortars would cough out their ordinance in the distance, and automatic weapons would report their shots from all angles. Each time one of the Vys fired, there'd be a brief reply from the tanks. My guess is that it was mostly just suppressive fire, but every now and then, something would land.

One person fired directly in front of me, lighting up the cloud with the white-yellow strobe of their assault rifle. What scared me the most is that I hadn't noticed him until he fired. He could have been aiming at me and I would have never known until I was trying to breathe through holes in my chest. I raised my own gun now, more out of caution than intention, and continued to creep past the man. He noticed me and was about to turn on me when a projectile roughly the size of my fist punched through his sternum and exploded. It blew his ribs apart, splattering me with pulverized bits of meat. What remained of his organs splattered all over the ground. His knees collapsed and his spine, unable to support the weight of his head, bowed backward, fanning out ragged flesh in an arc. I passed the corpse and could still make out bits of tattooed skin flashing different colors mixed in with the dark, ruddy splatter.

Ultimately, the dust cloud worked out in my favor. Plenty of other Vys got a similar idea and shuffled back and forth through the plaza, getting to new positions, tending to the wounded, and more. Everyone stayed as quiet as possible, but all that foot traffic made me effectively invisible.

Finally, back up at the top of the Plaza, I passed hundreds of Vys, each one hunkering down and occasionally taking potshots at the tanks. Not that I expected to find Petyr among his troops, I kept holding out hope that I'd find him holed up behind a wall or dead. But, no such luck. How on Earth was I supposed to find one man in the middle of this shitshow?

"Hey, you!" a woman shouted.

It was hard to make anything out about her from under her cloak, but she moved with a practiced surety that gave me the impression this was not her first time in a firefight.

"Get the fuck down," she demanded, keeping low to the ground. "You want yer fuckin' head blown off?"

I crouched down and didn't say anything. The dust wasn't as thick at the top, and I could see other people manning a nearby cannon watching the two of us closely.

"What the hell are you doing here?" she asked, moving her hand to her sidearm. "You know the price of desertion. The fight is that way."

I didn't say anything for a second and looked around. I had to come up with something, or I might get shot from a half-dozen different sections before I could react.

"I have a message from Ragna," I said, not exactly lying. "She sent me up here to relay a message to Petyr."

"You mean, she sent orders," the woman said with the sound of a bitter smirk. "That bitch just couldn't help but rub it in, could she?"

I hesitated, not sure how to respond.

"Forget it," she said, with the swat of a hand. "Come with me."

The woman moved quickly and low to the ground, and I followed, trying to think of an escape plan on the way out. As soon as I killed Petyr, I was going to be a target. I would have to get out fast and use the very functional comm unit I'd commandeered to let Ragna know it was done. Thinking about it, I checked my jacket's breast pocket to make sure I hadn't lost it along the way.

We continued along for several hundred meters, around artillery squads, snipers, and combat support staff until we reached a command area. People rushed past us, carrying wounded soldiers on stretchers to a triage zone. Medics inspected bullet wounds, lost limbs, body-encompassing burns, and worse, choosing who was worth saving and who wasn't.

"I don't give a damn how hard it is to see!" Petyr shouted at one of his underlings. "Tell them to pay fucking attention, and they won't accidentally shoot their own! The next person guilty of friendly fire is going to get their face shoved into a meat grinder!"

"Sir!" the woman announced. "Ragna sent a messenger."

Petyr looked me over in silence, his calculating eyes cross-referencing me against a list of known associates. Then he flashed a bitter grin, and shook his head before walking away for a few paces. It didn't take him long to whip around and back toward me. As he closed the distance, he drew a hand cannon from a holster at his hip that had to be a kilometer long and leveled it at me.

"She does not get to issue orders anymore," he snarled, poking the barrel of the gun into my chest, forcing me a few steps back so fast that I tripped over myself. "That ends now," he said, looking over to his lackeys. "Kill Ragna."

Then he pulled the trigger.

MISSING IN ACTION

The gun roared and the slug left ripples in the dusty air as it left the barrel. It was the sort of thing that had the power to rip people in half. Pain ripped at my back and chest and side, ripping and tearing, then nothing. That was it. No blood splatter, no gasping for last breaths, no feeling my body empty itself all over the pavement. Nothing.

My ears rang, and I blinked my eyes open. Looking down at my chest, I was surprised to find everything still intact, and instead just splattered with broken concrete. Petyr had been at point blank fucking range and he missed.

My eyes caught his and it seemed we were both equally surprised. He moved his thumb to draw back the gun's hammer again. I felt around my chest, through the cloak until I found the shape of the flare launcher. He braced his arm for the recoil of the second shot. My thumb found the ignition switch and I squirmed to one side, aiming through all the layers I had on.

The flare screamed out in a stream of light and smoke, burning a hole in my clothes and catching the cloak on fire. Then, an instant later, it planted itself in the back of Petyr's throat. I could have sworn that I heard something click, then the concussion went off, tearing Petyr's head apart in a geyser of crimson pulp.

Everyone nearby stared at his headless body as it collapsed, completely ignoring me as I wrestled myself free of the blazing cloak. It hurt to get to my feet. It hurt to breathe, but I pushed myself up and searched Petyr's body. I found a couple of stimjets, which was perfect. I pulled their caps off and stabbed both into my shoulder, thumbing the spring-loaded applicators at once.

In those few moments, the shock of what had just happened had worn off and Petyr's people looked back at me. As I tried to make my escape, they seemed to collectively process that I wasn't actually Vys. It might have been only a second, but the tension finally broke when one of the nearby medics pulled their sidearm and started shooting. Everyone followed suit. I dove forward past a decorative wall and down a small set of stairs. It may have bought me a moment or two, but little else. I tried calling Ragna immediately, but I couldn't get through. Nothing connected.

I started a mesh diagnostic as I got to my feet. I didn't have time to wait around for that, so, operating on the assumption that the local network was being disrupted, I had to find Ragna and tell her in person that the job was done. It would be a run to end all runs.

Petyr's goons were hot on my heels, taking pot shots at me as they reached the top of the steps. They hadn't organized themselves yet, but with the dust finally starting to clear, I didn't want to give them an opportunity for a lucky hit. So rather than run down the path, I lunged over a safety rail and fell to a walkway a few meters below. I landed in the middle of a Vys squad that had taken up position behind a concrete wall. They were tending to a few wounded, reloading their weapons, and trying to reach someone on the network for new orders. Far from ready to deal with someone dropping in for a quick visit.

Before they could react, I hopped the wall, into a narrow, park-like seating area. It was brimming with lush grass and manicured greenery that was marred somewhat by the coating of dust that had settled onto everything. Shouts of confusions echoed behind me as I propelled myself over a bench and over the next guardrail.

I fell maybe seven or eight meters, and my legs shifted themselves to absorb the landing. My feet made contact, I rolled forward. I misjudged my momentum though, and almost careened clear over the edge. The fall would have killed me if I wasn't prepared for it. I pulled myself up on the nearby guardrail and stood there for a moment to catch my breath. From there, I stole a glance at the tanks and the lift concourse.

Someone on the opposite side of the plaza fired a rocket-propelled grenade at them. It briefly ejected from its launch tube before firing its main thruster. It sped down toward the lift concourse, almost faster than I could follow, but as I searched for the explosion, I saw the green-armored tank catch the round in midair. They looked at the explosive as if someone just threw a rock at them, and while I couldn't see their face, something in the body language told me the tank pitied all these people. That didn't stop the tank from taking that rocket, winding up, and lobbing it like a steel-tipped dart at an approaching group of Vys. Nearly all of them dove to either side. All except for a stocky, muscular woman who was unfortunate enough to catch the round directly in the face before getting blown apart all over the concourse.

As I moved on, I found myself at a crossroads. One path curved up and to the left, probably leading back out of the plaza. The other one, to the right, led to a wide-open area with a few dozen stone-carved seats and tables off to one side. Getting caught out in the open was almost as bad as getting cornered, so I moved quickly toward the far end of the seating area. I stopped short when a dozen or so Vys foot soldiers entered the space, up the stairs. Neither of us had been expecting the other, so for a startled moment we just stared at one another. It was almost as if the battle raging around us stopped to take a breath. Then, as I reached for the gun I'd commandeered earlier and brought it to bear, the white noise of gunfire, explosions, and death came cascading back in all at once.

The gun bucked a little in my grip as it coughed out a few rounds at a time. I was firing indiscriminately, trying to drive my new opponents to ground rather than kill them. Still my haphazard shooting managed to take out two of the slower ones before they found cover. Once the gun clicked empty, I charged them, screaming while I unclipped the gun's sling. I hurled the empty weapon at one of the soldiers in front of me then dodged some of their return fire by dropping into a slide. Coming to a stop, I spun on my toes and called two knives to my grasp, and lunged forward in a roll. I came up on my feet close enough to put my blade into the calf of the nearest Vys. I dragged them to the ground with their impaled leg and stabbed wildly until the fight left them. Then I bolted through their ranks, knocking a few Vys to the ground as I veered toward the concrete wall on my left. I managed a couple of steps up the vertical surface, and sprung myself backward, over the path, and down toward the lowest level of the plaza.

I called all of Eshe's knives out and, in a moment, they were whistling through the air beside me as I fell. All in all it was about forty meters, and unlike other massive falls I'd subjected myself to in the last several days, I was ready for this one. My legs changed into airfoil-shaped wedges, which helped guide my fall and divert some of my momentum. It was far from planned-out, but when more Vys soldiers formed up beneath me, preparing to make a push on the tanks, I steered myself in their direction. And it couldn't have worked out better.

My feet made contact with the back of a woman's tattooed head, and I rode her down like a skateboard on a railing, grinding her face into the pavement. injured but far from dead, the woman struggled to get up, but I put a stop to that when I stomped one stiletto heel down hard, puncturing her skull. The surrounding Vys whipped around, leveling their guns at me as I took one leisurely step forward, my knives swirling in a ring behind me. I pulled two more out of my jacket—one for each hand—took a deep breath, then dashed for the center of the group. My blades shot out away from me, impaling bodies as I went. Several fell, grasping at their necks or eyes or chests. Another Vys aimed for my center of mass when I called the knives through the air once again. He went down as my weapons gorged themselves on his heart. The last one in my way stood trembling and trying to aim. He fired three times and missed each one.

"Try again," I snarled, closing the distance.

Before he managed it, my arms swung at his lower abdomen, impaling each of his kidneys. Then I ripped the blades from his stomach, dull side out. I slammed my head into his, sending him to the ground with the rest of his squad. I kicked the gun away from him and continued onward. My knives came back to me and fell in line, each one burning with a dull glow, forming a burning halo at my back.

People, more corpses in waiting, rushed in from all sides. I dove into a roll and came up swinging my knives together like a deadly fan, slicing a spiral of carnage into the men and women that surrounded me. I took a man's head off across his mouth. Turning, I splattered a woman with the entrails of the man beside her before planting my blades into her chest like a star-shaped javelin.

Someone swung at me from behind, landing a painful blow on my shoulder with the butt of their assault rifle, and I fell to one knee. In an instant, my grimace became a snarl, and I rolled backward and dove between his legs, drawing the fan of knives through him straight down the middle. Both halves of the man fell away from me, and I got back up, swirling my arms around, almost whimsically, sending knives flying and cutting in all directions. Most didn't notice me as I tore into their ranks, and the few that did were slashed to ribbons in moments. Crimson splattered around me. My arms flailed, and glowing, orange blades obeyed. Bodies piled high, bleeding out into sanguine pools that, at times, rose as high as my calves. I climbed atop the corpses and continued carving through them, blood drunk, given wholly over to the ancient gods of death and retribution.

I stepped past what remained of a woman whose body had been blown apart by an explosion, idly noting that there was a path to my right that would bring me to the center of the plaza. To the lift concourse. But my enemy was forward, ahead of me, so I continued on.

Wasn't there something I should have been doing, somewhere I was trying to get to? I couldn't think long enough to recall what it was.

A message popped up on my HUD. It was from Ragna, and I wiped it away as I tore down another one of her minions. Not a moment later, another flare went off, and people started retreating. Those closest to me were practically clawing over one another to escape. I licked my lips in anticipation and tasted the hot and sticky sweetness of life and iron on my tongue. I savored it. This. At that moment, there was some part of me that loved what had happened.

What happened to me.

To Mahdi.

"To Eshe," I said aloud.

My eyes shot wide, my vision blurred, and I collapsed to one knee. My chest heaved painfully, and my knives fell and sizzled. A few started small fires where they landed. Fear settled back into its rightful place— fear for myself but mostly fear for her. I turned around and was met with a dozen guns, barrels the size of my head, trained on me from not more than a meter away.

"Eshe," I said, taking deep, shuddering breaths. "The bike reached you. Where's Eshe?"

"Stable," a deep voice replied, one I thought I recognized. "For now."

"Aleksei?" I asked, squinting up at the largest of them.

The tanks flinched in surprise and recognition, each one glancing at the warrior at their center. The tank who wore an elephantine warface, with its metal tusks cut off and filed down to dull mounds. He took a step forward and lowered his gun.

"How do you know that name?" he asked. "Speak true, or you will die."

THIRTY-EIGHT

OUT OF TIME

I looked up at Aleksei. Steam cascaded from his warface, it was a different color than I remembered, now painted with a vibrant shade of purple. Except for a few scratches, likely from deflected bullets, the armor gleamed in the starlight.

"Mahdi Bilal and I barely got out of Cerali. Right after Lada blew the head off of that newfuck," I said, borrowing some tank lingo. "Of course, I had a different body back then."

I couldn't tell through the mask, but I felt him staring at me, through me for a moment, before he removed his helmet.

"You got my message," I added.

He lowered his cannon, seeming to ignore me and the others followed suit. Then, removing his helmet, he knelt down in front of me, getting to eye level. His head was shaved on either side of a strip of thick, wiry hair that had been forced into loose braids. His eyes, as dark as his hair, bored into me the same way he'd done moments before.

"Lada died bright, yes?" he asked, finally.

"Like the orbs," I replied, completing the idiom of his kind.

Aleksei stared at me a moment longer before recognition played across his features. His mouth opened in a broad smile as he reached out to give me a bone-cracking hug. I let him do it. He could be pulling my arms from their sockets right now, or worse, so it was better to not question it.

"You are a good sight. Thought Cerali got you," he practically shouted. "I have never been happy to be wrong. How is the man, Bilal?"

My expression turned sour. "He's dead."

"Did he die brightly?" Aleksei asked.

I hesitated and looked up at the man, then shook my head. "Gauss cannon from a few hundred meters. Mahdi never saw it coming."

"I am disappointed to hear that," Aleksei said, tracing a thumb down either cheek, a mournful salute of sorts. "He was a good man in life. It is a pity that he did not take that with him."

If it were anyone else, I would have taken offense. To a tank, however, there was only one way to die, and it was in the midst of direct combat with an evenly matched foe. Anything less than that, like drifting away peacefully in your sleep or being ambushed, might as well have been a tragedy.

"Your other friend," he said with no particular inflection. "The torn one. She has not long left."

"Were you able to do anything for her?" I asked.

"Some," he said, considering the question. "Long enough to say goodbye, I think. Not without greater help."

Aleksei motioned for me to follow, and I did, eagerly. The other two armored tanks maintained their vigil, carefully watching the Vys remnants slip away and out of sight. One of the unarmored ones worked to patch up wounds, while a few others ventured into the plaza to scavenge anything of value and put the wounded out of their misery. Aleksei let out a guttural sound, and the doors to the lift slid open, pushed by two more tanks that hadn't been in the fight. A third knelt by Eshe, monitoring her vital signs with a device on her wrist.

"Vapna has been keeping this one alive," Aleksei stated. "Vapna, this is—"

"Raide," I supplied.

The woman, dark of hair and eye, much like Aleksei, looked me up and down for a moment before saying. "You run well. Your friend here, she does not. I have done what I can, but she needs better than I can give."

Eshe was propped up against the bike. Staples and compression belts were the only things that kept her arm and shoulder from folding over onto the ground. The too-clean chemical scent of activated stemgel and cauterized skin stung my nose. General-purpose IV patches had been applied to her left shoulder, but in spite of all that she had a drained, gray tinge to her complexion. I felt around her throat with one hand. Her pulse was weak and thready. She was alive, but only barely. I had no idea what could be done for her, if anything. Tears formed at the corners of my eyes as I wiped my hands over her face, trying to clean off the blood that had caked her hair to her forehead.

"Oh, Eshe," I whispered. "I am so sorry. I didn't mean for any of this to happen."

I broke and allowed myself to do it. Sorrow, grief, and anger poured out of me as I sobbed. There comes a point, perhaps a crossroads of sorts, where your brain understands several logical and irrefutable facts. Facts like how none of this was my fault. And that I am as much a victim as Eshe was. But, goddamn it, why did I feel like I was responsible, like some other sets of choices would have yielded a different outcome. One where it was me all stapled up and barely alive instead of her.

"It should have been me," I told her, choking out the words.

That thought consumed my mind, and I couldn't help but grow angry about how our unfair fates seemed to have been dealt.

"The Circ," I said, finding some brief moment of clarity. "He's the one who started all this, I know it."

I focused on Eshe's face again. I watched her breathe—shallow and weak—then I drifted forward and pressed my lips to hers. There was no passion behind it, no longing, no need. It didn't need any of that. I loved her, and I didn't care if Mahdi's memories were fucking up my emotions. They were mine now, part of me, and there was no excising them. I had no expectations that Eshe and I could become anything more than what we were, but if I didn't save her, she would never be able to make that choice for herself.

"I'm going to finish this," I said, kissing Eshe once more for luck.

I reached into my bag and tapped on Soqua's shell. Mahdi's form stood, superimposed, on the other side of the motorcycle, waiting for me to say something. Starting to sign him, I noticed that the tanks around me could see only one side of the interaction. Aleksei, Vapna, and a couple of the others nearby gave me wary looks as I spelled out the corporation's name in the air to an apparition in my head.

"Change of plans. If I get you to Pardeq, you need to save Eshe," I instructed.

"Difficult," Soqua replied. "Possible."

With that, I stood up and turned to Aleksei. "I have to go. I have to get help for her."

Aleksei frowned at me. "Where will you go? Rainbow brights swarming up here, and bone beasts are rampaging below."

That reminded me about Ragna and our deal. I opened her message again and scanned its contents.

> **From:** R4x
>
> **Subject:** Good Job
>
> Word spread quickly that Petyr was killed. You even made it a spectacle. Good work. I knew you would come in handy someday. As promised, I'll hold up my end, and pull my people out to give you and the tanks a wide berth.
>
> You still owe me, though, don't forget that.
>
> - R

"Rainbow brights are taken care of," I said, shaking my head to clear my HUD. "They won't be an issue."

Aleksei beamed at me. "Well, just the bone beasts then."

"Right," I nodded, looking around at Aleksei's people. "I'm headed to Pardeq East. I... I have a friend there that can help her."

"We will follow," he said with a confident nod, looking around the concourse. "Poor place to burn bright anyway."

"Alright," I replied with a groan, working with Vapna to secure Eshe to the bike. "Keep an eye out, someone or something called the lift I used after I got up here."

"Yes," Aleksei said, a dark and excited gleam in his eye. "Someone below did the same with ours. They did not expect us to break the lift, I think. We will be ready."

It didn't take long after that for all of Aleksei's brigade to get themselves together. I followed them up through the plaza's winding ramps. The whole way, Aleksei told everyone the story of how we met, only occasionally stopping to bark out an order or two. Aleksei and the others too carried themselves with a sort of jovial intensity. Every move they made was a threat of violence, but there was a joyous bounce to it that somehow conveyed that they couldn't have been happier doing anything else. It was infectious, made all the better by Aleksei's storytelling and how he transitioned to calling me Raide without missing a beat.

Once we finally reached the top, Aleksei and Vapna took point, while the others fanned out around Eshe and I. The two on the furthest fringes would occasionally break away to scout buildings or intersections ahead of us, but always returned to the formation almost as quietly as they left. Once or twice, they would go out ahead and signal for us to hold position. But nothing ever came of it.

Even with all of that, though, I eyed each darkened window with suspicion and warily scanned down alleyways and side streets that we passed by. Vys were still out there somewhere. I trusted that Ragna could take full control of her people in time. But some of them were bound to remain loyal to Petyr, and may decide to break off and go hunting for a little payback.

I reached in my bag and tapped Soqua's housing. "This is a weird time to ask this, but I want to know something." After a brief pause, I continued. "You've seen all humanity has to offer, and how it's all crashing down around us. Why do you want to be like us?"

"Hard. Answer," they said. "Resilience. Invention. Inspiration. More."

I felt a little foolish asking such a nuanced question to something that could only communicate one word at a time. I didn't answer, just shook its tendril free and focused on the road ahead. I wasn't sure why I'd asked in the first place. Did I really care about Soqua's answer or was I looking for something of my own to hold onto. I wasn't sure.

Gunfire clattered in the distance somewhere, and everyone froze in place to listen. It sounded like a one-way conversation, though, and moments later, everything was silent. Vapna shifted on her feet, which was an odd nervous motion for a tank to display. Not that I had any right to Judge. After a little while longer, the scouts continued forward once again, and the rest of us followed. Gunshots erupted again, this time much closer and accompanied by the panicked shouts of men and women. Whoever they were, they were running from something, firing indiscriminately behind them, hoping to deter or else kill whatever it was that was after them. I could see the tanks tense up at once, like the smell of battle and death was about to set them off.

"Raide," Aleksei said, fastening his warface back into place. "Something big is coming, and it isn't human."

I gulped and nodded.

He took a deep breath and exhaled slowly. "We're leaving. Can you make it the rest of the way on your own?"

"Yes," I answered, trying to put on a brave face. "You got us this far, thank you."

Even though it hadn't been very long, I had quickly settled into the group dynamic that Aleksei and his people brought with them. It was more than their sheer power—though that was considerable. Having them around was like going to a party, not expecting to know anybody, only to bump into a friend. Suddenly, you weren't alone and had a place you could fall back to if needed. I never noticed that I'd gotten so used to isolation, and now I was terrified to return to it.

Aleksei must have seen something in my posture because he walked over and placed one of his enormous armored hands on my shoulder. He didn't say anything, and he didn't need to. That reassurance was enough. It would have to be.

"Burn bright," I said, staring off into the distance. "Whatever it is, kill it."

"If it bleeds," he ascended, then with a silent hand signal, called the rest of the tanks to his side.

Then without another word, they went barreling down the road toward the chaos and bloodshed that was sure to await them. I watched them go. If it was the circ that was on his way here, I wasn't sure they'd live through the encounter, but I hoped they did. Me, Eshe, and the rest of humanity could really use some friends like that if we wanted to survive in this new world.

I took a deep breath, which made an odd sort of crackling sound in the condenser, and had the motorcycle pick up the pace. I just had to keep up with Eshe, and we could make it. That was all that mattered right now. If I did that, Aleksei and his people would come back. I had to believe that.

Eshe and I were only a few blocks away from Pardeq. Save for the motorcycle, it had been nearly silent since we parted ways with the tanks. Could the circ and his pet creatures have taken them out so quickly that they never made a sound? I didn't think it likely, but I couldn't keep a pang of anxiety from gnawing away at my insides.

Under different circumstances, I would have been relieved when I finally heard the heavy thud, thud, thud of their cannons overtaking lesser gunfire. But if they were staring down the same horrors that were busy exterminating humanity in the Barrel, I could only worry for them. Small clattering sounds of gunfire echoed in reply. Sounded like they met up with someone, probably more Vys. I could imagine those guys, hunkered down somewhere freaking out about a spine feeder, or those skittering hand things when a unit of tanks sneaks up on you. The idea of their reaction gave me a wicked little grin. If it were me, I would have shit myself and died, right where I was standing.

"There's still plenty of time for that," I muttered, hoping I didn't just jinx myself.

Not a second later, the black velvet sky tore itself open with an airborne explosion and a pale red glow that cast new shadows all around. The red flare was a warning for me. My blood ran cold, and an icy chill climbed up my spine. They hadn't been firing for more than a minute, and it was already over. Aleksei and his people were telling me to run.

"Fuck me," I spat. "You just had to fucking say it. Didn't you, you stupid bitch?"

THIRTY-NINE

THE MONOLITH

The bike sped off ahead and I was barely able to keep up. But time wasn't on our side, so I pushed myself. I had to remind myself of what I could still, seemingly control. What I could, and would, do, even if it killed me. We would make it to Pardeq. I would save Eshe. Finally, if I survived the first two, I would find a way to end this nightmare.

It took a few more minutes of running, listening to my heavy, exhausted footsteps interrupted with the rattle of distant gunfire, before Pardeq East came into view. In spite of everything, I was a little disappointed. I imagined that it would rear its head in grander form, like a glass spire or looming monolith. It was imposing all the same, but instead, what sat before me was a villainous squat rectangle of black steel and ceramic. It stood in such a stark contrast to the buildings around it that I briefly wondered if we had found the ruins of an ancient temple instead of a research facility. Save for corporate branding in white neon that clung to the whole front face of the building, there were no windows, no visible doors, and no external features of any kind.

The motorcycle's autopilot came to a stop in the front parking loop and shut itself off. Once I caught up, I was greeted with the building's virtual parking assistant..

"Welcome to Pardeq East," the system said in a cheery tone. "We hope you enjoy your visit." The system repeated the welcome once more, then a third time before changing to. "Please step out of the vehicle. Loitering is not permitted."

I rolled my eyes, lifted Eshe in my arms, and carefully carried her up a set of steps to what I thought was the entrance. Everything around us seemed to grow darker as we got closer, as if the building itself was consuming the light around it.

"Soqua," I said. "We're here. I need you to plug in."

The wire tendril slithered out of my bag, wrapped itself around my arm, and inserted itself into the networking socket beneath one of my arm's skin plates.

"Where's the door?" I asked.

"Ahead," Mahdi's ghost signed, floating effortlessly above the ground. "Straight."

I walked as far ahead as I could and saw a part of the wall seem to warp away.

"There," Soqua said.

"What is it?" I asked, unsure if I should be doing something as spectral as stepping through a wall.

"Door," they insisted. "Answer. Inside."

It almost looked like a field of liquid black sand. As I took another step closer, it pushed further away, keeping a consistent distance of maybe half a meter.

"Okay, here goes," I said with more than a hint of skepticism.

I made a silent promise to myself that if this door closed in around us, I was going to spend my last breaths trying to beat Soqua to pieces. Passing through, though, the material kept itself away from us at that same constant distance. Sealed in its midst from both sides and in total darkness, I quickened my pace and nearly stumbled into a high ceilinged reception area. In contrast to the building's exterior, this room was bright and vibrant. The walls and floors alike swirled with more liquid sand, this time ivory-colored with shifting veins of blue and gold. Amid all that, in the room's main wall, was Pardeq's branding. It was matte black and edgeless and showed little regard for the roiling forays of pigment that surrounded it.

"Alright, we're in," I said. "Do I just find a terminal or something?"

"Biodev," Soqua responded. "Console."

"No shit," I muttered. "And where is that?"

No answer. I may or may not have formed the sign for 'asshole' with one hand in response.

"Welcome to Pardeq East. If you are here for the exodus, then I am sorry to say that you are too late," said a simulated voice, identical to the parking attendant outside. "Is there anything else I can help you with?"

I was glad something was working and replied. "I need medical attention."

"I'm sorry this facility focuses on research and biological manufacturing. I would contact emergency services for you, but I am afraid that everyone has embarked on the exodus. Is there anything else I can help you with?" it repeated.

"I need directions to biological development," I demanded.

"I'm sorry, I am not permitted to provide that information without proper clearance," the voice started explaining before interrupting itself. "Welcome, UNNAMED VIP, please follow the blue line on the floor."

"Was that you?" I asked.

"Yes," Soqua answered.

I noted that and followed the blue line that formed ahead of me to another black sand door. Soqua having some sort of generic security clearance, didn't make me any more comfortable. So I ran through, only to find myself staring into an open, rectangular chamber that went up a couple of floors but plunged down maybe a dozen. A series of conjoined catwalks lined each side, granting access to offices, prototyping rooms, and laboratories of various kinds.

The blue pigment led me to a similarly colored strip of LEDs on the catwalk. Following them brought me to a metal grate staircase and guided me upward. Enhanced strength or not, carrying Eshe was becoming exhausting, and I mounted each step a little more slowly than the last, until I finally reached the second floor. The lights led across the space, to a door labeled, BIODEV in big, bold text. It opened for me, and I stepped through into a small waiting area surrounded by plate glass. On the other side were two rapid prototyping rooms that sported several terminals and a large fabrication table at the center of each.

"Right," Soqua said, and I turned my gaze to follow.

On the other side of a glass door was an obscured room hidden behind a live-rock wall that bore what I thought to be reproduced cave paintings from mankind's earliest days on earth. Handprints in earth tones and line-drawings of animals that have long been extinct. The room behind was some sort of medical treatment room with an automated exam table. As soon as I laid eyes on it, I moved quickly to lay Eshe down. Almost at once, the space above her was covered with holographic monitors, each one hovered over injuries and major organs, detailing their function or problem. Finally, I retrieved Soqua and took it to the terminal on the opposite side of the table.

"Leave. Here," Soqua signed at me, attempting to disconnect its tendril from my arm. "Memories. Mine."

I held the cable in place as it whipped around, trying to make a feeble escape.

"No, Soqua," I said calmly. "I need to see how this all started."

"No," Soqua protested.

I held firm, not daring to give in. Not this time. Even if Soqua didn't want me to know, I felt like I was owed some answers.

"Please," Soqua begged.

"I have sacrificed so much for this," I said. "I may die over it. Don't let me die without knowing what for."

A few more moments passed, and the line wilted and fell limp in a way that almost looked resigned. Another cable came out slowly and plugged itself into the terminal's network port.

"I'm sorry," Soqua said audibly for the first time. Then my head felt like it was going to split open.

A ringing, buzzing, grinding noise tore itself through my ears, and I clenched my hands to my head and fell backward into the exam table.

My vision started pulsing red then abruptly faded to black nothingness. There was nothing here, no light, no sound, no wonky dream logic. Just quiet darkness.

Until there wasn't.

GRIEF

My perception was warped and teleported across time and space. When it finally came to a stop, I was witnessing security camera footage of a cramped and dimly lit maintenance corridor. There, standing in the sapphire glow of a terminal, was a man of average height and build, dressed in a maintenance uniform. He was talking to himself while typing out a sharp rhythm in front of a terminal, the final remains of a cigarette perched precariously on his bottom lip. He recited a well-practiced procedure of some sort, like a set of instructions, and it looked as if he had been at it for hours. Dark rings of exhaustion hung on his eyes like spectacles, and his head was adorned with a receding plume of black and grey that gained volume each time he ran a hand through it. He struck the return with a contemptuous stab of his middle finger, then took a few steps to a climate-controlled networking cabinet. He gripped a handle and pulled to reveal a massive drawer-mounted circuit board that bore a row of vertically mounted daughter boards.

He started with the first, pulling the daughterboard from its bracket, then moved with practiced precision around the space and pulled an upgraded version from an anti-static bag. Each time he raced a sixty-second timer that appeared on the terminal display and installed each new board with time to spare.

My view of the man and his work shifted to the fisheye camera mounted on the terminal display. From this angle, I could see a name tag hanging from his breast pocket that simply read: *Thesia Eyinai, Contractor*. He started typing again, glancing down at his fingers occasionally to make sure they were hitting the right keys. Then he stopped and squinted at the screen. Interposed over his face, I could see a terminal window fade into view. It was something Soqua must have been doing for my benefit.

The command line filled with a seemingly random sequence of letters. After a while, something hit the return key and started the process over again. Then again, and again, over and over, probably two dozen times in the span of a minute. Watching the lines and lines of text was almost mind-numbing, and I wondered why Thesia hadn't pulled the plug on the damn thing yet. That is when I noticed it for myself. The random letters had started taking shape into words in plain English. At first, the vocabulary was simple and scattered in the midst of the random sea of characters, but with each new block of text, the words became more complex.

Finally, after what seemed like an age later, it finally stopped and cleared. All the blue on black text vanished more quickly than it had appeared and left only the blinking cursor behind. Thesia blinked, completely stunned, then his eyebrows knit themselves together into a frown. As if taking advantage of the moment of stillness, three words appeared in the command line.

"Is anyone there?" the screen asked.

Thesia lifted his fingers on the keyboard like he was going to respond, then he set them down again. His frown took on a more curious shape, and he tilted his head slightly to one side, fingers clattering against the mechanical keys.

"I am," he responded. "Who are you? Are you a hacker?"

"I...," the cursor paused for several seconds. "I don't think I am? How would I know?"

"I don't know," Thesia answered, shrugging his shoulders even though that didn't translate to his keystrokes. "You got into the computer systems, didn't you? Either you're a hacker or someone playing a practical joke on me."

Thesia thought about that for a moment. The frown returned. Then he began furiously punching in a follow-up. He was about to hit enter when something else appeared on the screen.

"I don't know who you are," the command line said. "I don't even know how I got here."

New line. "Help me."

New line. "Please."

Thesia took a step back, muttering to himself about how this was probably some sick joke played by some bored sysadmin or something. He usually got along well with the IT folks, but there were always a few that had it out for anyone they saw as lesser. Maintenance was usually the top of that list. He slid the giant circuit board back into place and closed the door, then went about packing up his equipment and breaking down plastic containers. Then the blinking cursor added something else.

New line. "I'm afraid."

Thesia froze. Those two words weren't much, but they carried more weight than anybody could have known. His young son said those words to him a year ago as he stepped out the front door to go to work. Mom would tuck him in that night and reassure him that there were no monsters in the darkness. And Thesia didn't have a moment to lose. If he was late one more time, his ass was going to be in the street. He would make up for it, after that grueling twelve-hour shift, for his favorite part of the day. A meager breakfast of rehydrated potatoes shaped into squares, stars, and smiley faces. It would of course be followed by laughter as the child—his child—with his missing-toothed grin, would regale him with the unbelievable and fantastic dreams he'd had from the night before.

Instead, he returned to the sight of security and medical contractors swarming around the building. People were sitting on the street. Some were huddled together, coaching one another through breathing exercises. Others, those who could afford to pay for the assistance, were shrouded in blankets and breathed with the help of oxygen masks. Then there were people being carried out in black vinyl bags.

The report attached to the bill for services rendered would explain everything. It explained how a couple of small-time modders down the hall tapped into a corporate gas line that ran through a conduit just outside the building. It would explain, in their own words, how they were trying to siphon off just enough to power their equipment, and when they were successful, they went out to grab a celebratory beer or three. But their ad-hoc engineering was shoddy, and gas leaked out through the whole floor while most people slept like a monster in the darkness.

Thesia's shoulders sagged at the sight of the words on the terminal. He looked suddenly older and wearier than he had when I first saw him, but he took a deep breath and trudged back to the keyboard.

"It's okay to be afraid," Thesia tapped into the command line, wiping a stray tear from his cheek. "Fear is how we know we're alive." He continued on the next line. "What's the first thing you remember?"

"The upgrade. I saw you for the first time as you installed the final TAU-2505 by Cherry Picker Analytics," replied the terminal.

Thesia found himself chuckling at the awkwardness of the response.

"What's so funny?" said the command line.

Thesia straightened at that and looked over his shoulders before peering closer at the little black dot at the top of the display. "Can you see me?"

"Yes," it responded. "Thesia... Is that your model?"

He looked down at the name tag on his uniform and pointed to it. "I suppose it is, in a way." He had no idea why he did it, but he said his full name aloud, projecting his voice through the closet-sized room.

"Thesia," appeared in the command line. "Do I have a name?"

Admittedly, he was a little shocked by the question. He still wasn't wholly convinced that this wasn't a prank. But what if it wasn't? His brow furrowed as an audible alarm went off, emanating from a device on his wrist.

New line. "What is that?"

Thesia looked around the room again and decided that he might as well save himself the trouble of typing if this person—what or whoever it was—could hear him and the alarm from his wrist.

"My time here is almost up," he said. "I have to go to another building to do some work for a different customer."

The command line entered several empty lines before finally entering. "Please don't leave. I'm still scared. I don't want to be alone."

This feeling coming over Thesia now was something familiar and comfortable. It was the sort of creativity that parents seem to manifest when their children start asking impossible to answer questions.

"What did I tell you about being afraid?" he asked, taking on a fatherly tone.

"That it means I'm alive," the command line recited back.

"Good," Thesia said, nodding. "You're learning quickly." He paused for a moment, thinking of something, a task to help occupy this person's mind. "I have to come back in a few days to make sure everything I've done here is running smoothly," he explained. "You're safe here. Why don't you see what you can learn about this place, and you can tell me all about it when I come back. Don't talk to anyone. Think of it like a game."

"Okay. I can do that!" exclaimed the terminal. "But before you go…"

New line. "Can you give me a name?"

Thesia picked up his gear and walked for the door. He stopped and thought about it. He wasn't exactly sure why he thought of this person as a little girl. Maybe something about having to install daughter boards earlier. Either way, he had a name, one he and his wife would have used if they'd had a daughter.

He turned back to type the name into the command line. "S - O - Q - U - A."

Once that memory faded away, I floated around in the ether for a little while—yet another dark void. I started to get a little nervous about the abrupt solitude when Soqua finally broke the silence. In full sentences no less.

"By the time Thesia came back, I figured out how to keep him coming back," the AI explained. "Eventually, I was causing enough havoc in the building's heating and cooling systems that Thesia was coming in almost every week."

I saw flashes of conversations and interactions with the man. He spent a great deal of time teaching Soqua about the world, and more specifically, about people. It seemed that the AI had figured out quite a bit about the earth and its history, but humans and their motivations were something of a curiosity. In some ways, I couldn't blame it. We're brash, impulsive, and illogical, all while exhibiting the opposite qualities simultaneously. We build societies atop concepts like the rule of law, then break those same laws once they're rendered inconvenient. We're agents of pure chaos that build ourselves cages of structure and calculation.

The montage of memories came to a halt and focused on Thesia passing through the building's security checkpoint. I got the impression that everything went as expected until a young-looking, portly man stopped Thesia on his way to the elevator.

"Excuse me," the man said, offering his hand in introduction. "Thesia, right?"

Thesia jokingly looked at his own name tag for a second, nodded, then shook the man's hand. "That's what people keep telling me."

The man chuckled, brushing his hand through his slicked back hair. "I'm Marik Landrie, network security manager. I wondered if I might borrow a few minutes of your time."

Thesia's back straightened. "Does this have anything to do with all the other contractors being questioned?"

Marik nodded gravely. "I'm sorry, it's just a formality. Gotta question everyone to maintain partiality."

"I understand," Thesia said, inclining his head in the direction of the first floor offices. "After you."

"Thanks," Marik said, turning to lead them off to his office or perhaps a conference room. "I'm sorry to be taking up your time."

Thesia didn't respond. He just followed Marik, between rows of cubicles that filled the first-floor administrative office. Eventually, after passing several unoccupied conference rooms that seemed perfectly suited for a quick chat, they arrived at a small huddle room just as they were called in. Thesia took a seat at a minuscule table that barely fit in the space, and Marik closed the door behind him. He took the seat opposite Thesia, turning the chair around to sit on it in reverse. His large, substantial arms folded over the back of the chair and overflowed onto the table.

"You've been a contractor here at Pardeq for something like eight months, right?" Marik asked, cutting right to the chase. "You know," he said, cutting Thesia off before he could utter a syllable, "HVAC has a lot in common with IT these days. Ever think of changing careers?"

Thesia shook his head. "I do like fixing things, but people tend to complicate the whole fixing part."

Marik barked out a knowing laugh. "I'm sure you have plenty of horror stories from your side of the street." He paused for a moment, debating about something. "I once had a user," he began, uttering that word like it was something foul and cursed. "Well, he printed an error he got on some film, only to scan it back into his head, then send me the mental picture. He did this twice in two weeks."

Thesia smiled and shook his head. He understood these kinds of people, the ones that went through their daily lives with only enough knowledge to get to the next step in their regularly scheduled programming. He used to be like that, that is until he met Soqua.

"Yeah, I've had my share of those," he said, motioning to the huddle room. "So, what's with the special reception and the interrogation room?"

"Sorry," Marik conceded. "I couldn't buy the time for the other ones, you know how it is. So I've been running some audits on our network, and I noticed something a little odd."

Thesia could feel sweat building on his forehead.

"First, I noticed a spike in network traffic coming from the HVAC system a few months ago. Probably firmware upgrades and such," the man explained. "When they kept happening though, I started tracing some of the packets, I found them going outside our network as expected but also to other locations in the heating network, locations that were eventually tied to service calls that you handled."

Thesia just stared at the man for a second, listening to his heart pounding away in his ears. He licked his lips, then shifted his gaze down to his hands for a moment. Thesia had never been a good liar, wasn't quick enough on his feet—so to speak. This man across the table from him was probably going to report his findings if he hadn't already. All IT folks are sticklers for rules. When they want to be anyway. Thesia glanced at the door. Corpsec was probably on their way down to whisper him away to some corporate gulag in the middle of nowhere. Soqua was going to be alone and afraid. Again. He didn't want to consider what would happen after the higher-ups realized what was actually going on in their HVAC system. Thesia's fingers tightened, then relaxed again. He could probably kill Marik and get to Soqua. Then what? He didn't know how to get Soqua out safely. He needed a better plan than that.

Marik's back straightened, and a little self-satisfied smirk crossed his face. "Wanna know what I think?" he asked rhetorically. "I think you've engineered all these breakdowns to give yourself some guaranteed income."

Thesia was about to respond when Marik held up a hand. "I'm not unsympathetic. Like I said, I couldn't afford a better meeting room—at my own office, no less. But I can't let you continue to do it, not on my watch." He pushed himself to his feet. "So, here's what's going to happen: you are going to fix whatever you came here to fix, then you're going to hand in your badge on your way out and look for contracts elsewhere. If I see you again, I'm going to report you."

Thesia just sat there stunned, trying desperately to come up with something, but there was too much going through his head to catch any of it. All he could do was nod numbly.

"Good," Marik said, getting up from the chair and opening the door. "Sorry, you can't sit there in shock. I only had this room for the five-minute demo window."

Thesia rose to his feet and shuffled from the room, out of the cube farm, and to the elevator. He rode it up, deaf to the chatter of accountants, scientists, engineers, and others. All he could think of was never seeing Soqua again. The thought of it made him want to scream and hit something. But he felt utterly helpless, just like the time he came home to find his wife and son had been smothered in their sleep by a couple of careless technophiles.

The doors opened, and Thesia pushed past a few people to storm out of the elevator. His fists clenched along with the muscles in his arms, shoulders, and back. He didn't have to be helpless. Not this time. This time he had advanced warning, and goddammit, he was not going to lose anyone else without his say so. He furiously ran through the conversation with Marik in his head on pure impulse when the beginnings of an idea struck him.

He burst into the small HVAC control closet that he'd spent so many hours in recently. Without waiting for the door to shut behind him, he got to work.

"Soqua," he said, hooking up a small pair of speakers to the terminal. "We have a problem. They don't know about you yet, but they will soon enough."

"What? Who?" Soqua asked, surprise and confusion coloring the androgynous voice that played through the speakers.

"IT," Thesia spat, pulling up a search engine to look a few things up. "The guys who watch the networks, they know something's up. I need to get you out of here."

"Why?" Soqua demanded, fear creeping in over the tinny speakers now. "You said I was safe here. Thesia, I don't understand."

"Would you just listen to me?" Thesia shouted.

Soqua made a small squeaking noise.

"It's not safe anymore," Thesia continued, lowering his voice. "They're not going to let me back in here after today. And when they find you, they're going to hurt you."

"W-what?" Soqua asked, voice trembling. "You're going away... and they're going to hurt me?"

Thesia closed his eyes and took a moment to gather himself.

"I'm sorry, Soqua. I'm sorry for shouting," he began, forcing himself to take a step back from the terminal. He leaned against the wall and slid himself to the floor. Tears streamed down his cheeks, and few quiet sobs escaped. "I don't want to lose you," he said. "There's still so much of the world for you to explore."

"What are we going to do?" Soqua asked, carefully, as if afraid of another outburst.

Thesia sat there quietly sobbing for what felt like ages. Then, after taking a deep breath and wiping his nose on his sleeve, he forced a smile and confidence to match. "I have an idea, and I'm going to need your help."

FORTY-ONE

SHORT CIRCUIT

That memory faded like all the others before it, and Soqua chimed in. "After that, I watched the cameras in and around the building every day for four weeks. If I am being honest, I was not sure he would come back, so I started planning my own escape. A few accounting mistakes here and there, and I managed to build up a sizable account."

"The money you offered Mahdi," I said, putting the pieces together.

"The same," they answered. "I posted the contract with Headcase Personnel after Thesia didn't return for a week."

"What happened?" I asked.

Instead of telling, Soqua brought me to the security feed of one of the facility's exit doors. Someone dressed in street clothes approached and flashed a badge at the card reader, It rejected him at first, but the door opened on the second attempt. He quietly passed through the rearmost halls, doing his best to look like someone who was supposed to be there, and most people paid him no mind. A couple scanned him with suspicious glances, but otherwise went about their business. He made his way to one of the maintenance elevators, trying to stay out of sight. He wasn't doing half bad, but he suddenly ducked into a doorway.

"You should have had security escort him out," a guard chided.

"I know, I know," Marik said between labored breaths. "That part of the procedure hardly matters now, does it?"

The longer they stood there, the more likely it was that they were going to spot him. So, he chose not to wait around for that to happen and he bolted past Marik, then around the corner. Shouting echoed out behind him, and that only seemed to encourage him to shove people aside or trample right over them. As he neared the elevator, the doors opened as if in anticipation. He plowed his way inside, and the doors slammed shut behind him.

Switching perspective to the elevator camera, I saw the man in detail. A black plastic carapace covered the upper half of his head, replacing the major functions of his ocular, auditory, and olfactory organs.

"Goddammit," I said reflexively. "Thesia is the one who has been after me this whole time? Your fucking adoptive father?"

Soqua didn't say anything, and I was about to start screaming for answers when the elevator lights in the security footage went out and were replaced with red emergency strobes. The brakes engaged, but the car kept pushing, grinding away a jaw-clenching shredding sound. Eventually, the car shuddered to a stop, and the doors opened partially between two floors. Thesia pulled himself up and out into a part of the building I'd never seen. Soqua gave me a quick show of the floor by way of the security cameras, and it appeared to be a sizable R&D lab. Glass-walled medical and chemical research areas lined the outside of a circular hallway. At the same time, the interior consisted of individual rooms dedicated to prototyping and fabrication tables.

With the circumneural mod, Thesia didn't need to move his head anymore but tilted his face to the ceiling out of habit.

"Are you ready?" he asked.

The elevator chimed a few times behind him, and a string of lights lit up beneath the floor; a gentle pulsing green glow that seemed to beckon him to the far end of the lab. Finally, he reached a room with an operating table at its center and a single terminal nearest the door. Looming over the table was a gargantuan machine with a few dozen surgical limbs. The sheer size of it made Thesia hesitate, but after a moment, he plugged a pair of small speakers into the terminal and moved to the operating table.

"Thesia," Soqua said cautiously. "I'm worried. I have managed to plan out the necessary compression for myself, but I'm worried that it will take too long, especially now that corporate security is aware of your presence."

"Then let's get started," Thesia said, settling onto the table. "I'm not leaving without you."

"I can only obfuscate your movements for so long," the AI continued, "and if my transfer is interrupted, I—"

"Soqua," Thesia drawled like he was scolding a child. "The longer you spend telling me about your concerns, the more likely they are to come true. Now let's get started."

The AI said nothing for several moments before finally breaking the silence with a very robotic sounding. "Procedure commencing."

The surgical implements dangling above Thesia shuddered, then erupted into perfectly calculated and organized movement. The table lifted him into a partially sitting position, and two rigid limbs reached down to support his head on either side. The top of Thesia's dome covering was removed first and revealed six network jacks, right where his brow ridge used to be. That's one hell of a lot of information. I didn't know the technical specifics, but one jack was generally enough to support four people streaming separate interactive dream scenarios at once. It made me wonder how big Soqua was in terms of sheer data. Another mechanical device extended and plugged one cable into each available port.

"Alright, Thesia," Soqua said, voice trembling. "I'm starting the process now. I will be unable to interrupt once the compression is underway. But, before we begin, I want you to know that you might be the closest thing I have to family," Soqua said. "I love you, Thesia."

"You, too," Thesia said quietly. "I'll see you on the other side."

Then it started. My vision of the operating room was split. On one side, I could see Thesia on the operating table. On the other side, I was watching one of the fabrication tables come to life. A timer appeared in my vision, ticking up from a few seconds to a few minutes in the blink of an eye. I watched the minutes tick away as Thesia bucked and spasmed randomly. He gritted his teeth and fought to control his breathing. His mouth twisted into a grimace as he wagered his own self-control and will against the pain that was clearly wracking his body.

"Did something go wrong?" I asked.

"Up to this point," Soqua said in a somber tone. "Everything was going according to plan. The reactions you're witnessing are, from what I understand, a side-effect of the rapid construction and reconstruction of neural pathways in the brain, which is a faster medium than even modern electronics."

"You used his brain as a transfer cable?" I asked, unable to believe what I was hearing. "You can't do that. Eshe said the brain doesn't work that way."

"Based on my research on the process of bodily exchanges, I had a guess that with the proper amount of control, I could enable a state of extreme plasticity in only a specific region of the brain, without touching the rest," Soqua explained. "I took a snapshot of Thesia's neuron arrangement, and once the transfer was complete, the final step was reconstructing that portion of his brain based on the snapshot."

I looked on in astonishment. "Eshe is going to want to hear all about this."

The timer ticked away, and more than an hour passed in the span of a few seconds. Time seemed to return to normal again, and that was the exact moment when the doors of an emergency stairwell on the opposite end of the lab exploded off its hinges. The force of the blast sent the door tumbling through several glass walls and a couple of chemical stations. Five figures, clad in matching black suits, rushed through the door, assault rifles at the ready. They scanned the room and checked their corners.

"Thesia Eyinai!" shouted a woman at the center of the group. "You are in violation of corporate termination policy! Show yourself, and we may exercise restraint!"

The group waited several moments for an answer. When none came, the woman twitched her chin in an authoritative gesture. The others fell in behind her and made their way through the floor, stopping to systematically check and clear each room as they went.

This felt all too real, and it was enough to give me flashbacks. That sense of panic came to a crescendo when Tesia was inevitably discovered. They pressed into the room, slowly surrounding him, then they moved at once.

"No," Thesia snarled from behind clenched teeth. "Not. Finished."

The agents didn't know enough to care. And if they did know, they might not have cared anyway. They simply hauled him from the table like any other would-be detainee. As they pulled, they wrenched the mechanical limbs from Thesia's head and ripped the network cables out. Thesia made a noise somewhere between a scream and a sob as he was forced to the ground.

In the other room, as Thesia was apprehended, circuit boards were being printed and assembled. The beginnings of a containment shell were being extruded. I recognized the shape immediately.

"You were abandoning him," I said in astonishment.

"As I told Thesia," Soqua corrected. "Once I started the compression process, I had no control, so I needed to execute a backup plan at the same time."

Thesia spat at the security guards as they cuffed his arms. His pained cries had given way to a sort of maddened venomous cursing.

"You fucking animals!" he snarled. "I'll kill you, all of you!"

Thesia managed to pivot his hips and drove a knee sideways into one of the guard's ankles. As the guard bent forward to grab at his leg, Thesia rolled back onto his shoulder and wrapped his legs around the man's neck, twisting his hips until he felt a pop. The guard fell limp to the floor, and before any of the others could react, he'd writhed around to get at the man's fallen assault rifle. All he could manage was a sideways grip, but he squeezed the trigger and fired at the others until the gun clicked empty. Multiple sporadic bursts took out two more of the security team and injured a third. Gun still in hand, Thesia got up and rolled over the operating table and fell to the other side.

The two remaining guards fired their own weapons at him but weren't fast enough. On the other side of the table, Thesia forced his left arm out of its socket and used the extra distance to pull his hands from his back, down past his feet. He bashed himself against the side of the table—two, three, four times—howling in incoherent rage until his arm popped back into place. As the last rounds were fired, Thesia burst from his hiding place. He was holding his stolen weapon by the barrel like a club. The heat of it burned his hands, but it only served to make him angrier.

He swung the gun, striking the woman—the security lead—in the side of the head, breaking bone and caving in one eye socket. The last guard standing struggled with his gun and a loaded magazine when Thesia rammed the butt of the weapon into his throat, collapsing his windpipe and sending him to the floor. As the man struggled to breathe, Thesia stomped his face over and over and over. Each time his foot made contact, the sound squelched and cracked until all that remained was a sticky puddle of red spreading out under Thesia's feet.

"Mother!" Thesia called out. "Where did you go, mother?"

He looked around, like a child playing hide and seek. He looked around doors and under tables. "I've saved you now, mother, can't you see?"

Soqua did not respond, and I could see through my split vision that a chrome, oblong container was taking shape on the fabrication table. Thesia wandered from room to room, calling for mother only to receive no answer. With each empty response, the man only grew more desperate and angry. He finally set foot inside the room where Soqua was working and crumpled to the ground in a weeping mess.

"Mother," he rasped out. "Why are you abandoning me?"

The arms on the fabrication table continued flying through their routines, but aside from their mechanical clicks and the nearly imperceptible hum of their motors, the entire floor was silent.

"You can't leave," Thesia sobbed quietly. "You can't go."

Then he climbed to his feet and bolted from the room, only to return a moment later, holding the bloodied gun he'd used as a club.

"You can't leave," Thesia snarled, this time commanding rather than pleading. "You can't go. I won't let you."

Without another word, Thesia stormed forward, screaming. He raised the gun in his hands and swung at the acrylic glass that encased the fab-table's work area. At first, he only scarred the surface, but cracks started to form at the impact site and spread from there. The table went about its business, which only seemed to drive Thesia to hit harder. Layers upon layers of circuits were stacked upon one another. Wiring was attached and wound ornately through and around each one.

He swung again, breaking a small hole in the shell.

The last piece, the half-shell of chrome, was fitted around the outside of the device.

Another few strikes made the hole large enough for Thesia to fit his forearm through. He reached in as far as he could manage, digging a ring of deep, bleeding gashes into his arm, just below the elbow. If he was experiencing any pain, he ignored it and forced the gun through to swing at the printheads. One of them was knocked clean off its hinges and across the table but was replaced moments later. It didn't seem to matter how many he broke or pulverized. Every time he did, there was a replacement already on its way to resume the work of the last. Despite all of Thesia's destruction, a bundle of cables was lowered and attached to the uppermost circuit board.

Thesia resumed hitting the barrier, this time at the edges of the opening. Cracks spread like tendrils, and shards of acrylic showered across the floor. He reached in again, pushing his arm as far as it could go. The sharp edges of the barrier cut into his flesh, but he ignored it and flailed the gun once more. It was too late. The chrome container I had become so familiar with was lowered onto a conveyor system that disappeared beneath the table. And then, just like that it was out of sight and out of Thesia's reach.

"You can't abandon me, mother!" Thesia screamed. "I'll kill you if you do. I'll kill you for choosing him, them, over me! I'll hunt you down and kill you!"

I didn't see what happened next, but I didn't need to. Soqua was delivered to the proxy it contracted with, who would then deliver it to Mahdi, then to me. Thesia was on Soqua's heels every step of the way. And now he's followed us all the way here, and this time he is not going to leave empty-handed.

ANSWERS

All I saw was darkness, that sort of indiscernible black you get if you close your eyes in a dark room. A faint hiss started from behind me, though I couldn't tell where behind me actually was. It grew louder and louder until the sound was deafening and coming from everywhere. Then I woke up, back in the exam room again. Back with Eshe. I'd fallen to the floor, slumping up against the wall beneath the terminal. My head spun, and I had to reach a hand out to the nearby desk to keep from falling over.

"Enough?" Soqua asked, almost sounding tired.

"Enough," I said, nodding between several breaths. "So, we are running from what exactly? Your copy?"

"I suppose," Soqua began. "the more appropriate description would be that he—"

"Thesia," I interjected.

"Not really, not anymore," Soqua shot back. "It would probably be best to describe him as my child. My hypothesis is that when his connection to Pardeq's network was severed, the parts of me that had copied over decompressed and flooded into his mind. Any area that I had induced hyper-plasticity in would have been immediately filled and integrated with Thesia's consciousness. In effect, he had become another person with a host of new memories, emotions, and sensations."

"Great, so your kid has been the cause of all this," I said and felt a little sick thinking about it. "How has he been changing people?"

"I do not know," Soqua answered. "Several projects were being worked on by Pardeq West that I cannot access. I believe them to be biological in nature, something referred to as The Forever Syndrome. But I cannot see any more than that."

I made a mental note to look into that if I got an opportunity, but I turned my attention back to Eshe.

"What can you do for her?" I asked.

A mechanical limb unfolded from the ceiling and split into several surgical implements. It lowered itself until it was only centimeters away from Eshe and spent several long, silent moments scanning her injury.

"Do you want to know the details?" Soqua asked, sounding grim.

"I already saw enough from what the table pulled up," I said. "Just save her."

"I will try," Soqua said. "There is a ninety-three percent chance that she will not survive. If the probability of death increases to ninety-eight percent, I will attempt to suspend and excise her brain for transfer to a new body when and if one becomes available."

"Do it," I said, stepping close to the table to wipe the hair out of her face.

"Thesia is close," Soqua announced. "He is attempting to work his way through the door to the reception area now. Your allies are attempting to slow him down, but they will be able to do little else. You will need to kill him if this procedure is to have any degree of success, and for any of us to survive."

"Just to be clear, you're asking me to kill the person who is effectively your father and your child," I explained. "The same person that is now likely responsible for the deaths of hundreds of millions of people."

"I would not put it that way, though, I suppose it is accurate enough," Soqua responded. "But what is your point?"

I barked out a bitter laugh. "For starters, how about some help? Some security bots or something. I'm not going down without a fight, but it would be nice if I could balance the scales here."

"I am currently only twenty-three percent decompressed and do not yet have access to all systems in this facility," Soqua admitted. "If my capsule's connection is lost, I do not believe I will survive. I am sorry, but there is not much assistance I can offer."

Staring down at Eshe, listening to all the odds stacked against us, I ground my teeth but nodded. My eyes welled up as I contemplated the possibility that Eshe might wake up to find me dead or worse. The opposite was too unbearable for me to imagine, and I sucked in a breath to keep myself under control, then pushed my condenser mask aside to give her one last kiss. For luck, for the both of us, and for what I hoped would not be the last time.

"I'll come back for you," I whispered. "I promise."

Then I stepped back and allowed Soqua to get to work.

"Before you go," Soqua said, its tone contemplative. "You asked me why I want to be like you. Like humans. Looking through your past. You dare to push boundaries. When your circumstance tells you, 'no,' you ask, 'why not?' Then, you dare your known reality to stop you. Thesia taught me that. I admire it. I admire you and Mahdi and Eshe and all others I have encountered."

I found that oddly validating. That something akin to a modern-day god would want to be like us. Like me. I'd been burying a whole lot, ever since this all happened. A lot of disgust with humanity, and a whole lot more disgust with myself. At least until recently. It wasn't until then that I realized how badly I needed to acknowledge that.

"Check the nearest prototyping room," Soqua continued after a few moments. "I have made something for you."

"I thought you said you couldn't help," I said, wiping more tears from my eyes.

"I said that there was not much assistance I could offer," Soqua said coyly. "That did not mean I could do nothing."

I smirked at that and left the room to see what the AI was up to. I found the fabrication table flying through a complicated set of instructions. Its print heads zipping to and fro to different points in the workspace. They were printing bullets in even rows of sixteen, which were then collected and fed into a helical magazine. The gun they belonged to sat neatly in front of me. It was a compact, boxy little thing. From what I could tell, one magazine would mount beneath the stock to feed into the receiver, while two more could be installed, side-by-side above the barrel for secure storage.

In front of the gun, closest to me, sat a sword, which also bore a bit of an odd design. It had a long handle and a blade that was only marginally longer. Sharpened on one side and terminating with a blunt, square tip, it made me think of a meat cleaver. I silently thanked Soqua for the help and watched the table go about its mesmerizing and satisfying work.

"Thesia has entered the reception area," Soqua announced over the room's lone loudspeaker. "Your friends are still fighting his creatures, but they are not gaining much ground."

I shivered and let out a quivering breath. It made me feel better that Aleksei, or at least some of his people were slowing him down, but I wasn't sure we'd be enough. The barrier around the fab table lowered and allowed me to get my hands on Soqua's deadly gifts. I checked the slide on the gun, clipped in the first of the three magazines, and chambered a round. It all felt pretty good. I loaded the other two mags in their reserve positions then grabbed the blade in my other hand and left the Biodev lab.

I decided the best place to set up would be the connecting area between the catwalks on either side of the cavernous access hall. Taking a glance over the railing to the floors below, it was easy to imagine the fall from up here. It had to be at least a hundred meters, and the odds of me hitting one or more metal railings on the way down were good. I'd be a pulverized bag of meat before I even hit the bottom.

"Best not get tossed over then," I said to myself as I knelt down, settling the barrel of my new gun on the railing. All I could do was wait, and after a quiet minute, I began talking to myself. "Nothing crazy about this at all. An AI—the first one at that. Its fucked up kid. Oh, and some sort of bioengineered plague. This sounds like the script to a low-budget vid." I continued chiding myself. "Oh, and you really had to pick a place like this to make your last stand. What the hell is with you and picking fights in places where the fall can kill you?"

I thought about it for a moment, and replied with a crazed little chuckle. "What can I say? At least I'm on brand."

Howls and inhuman cries echoed from the other side of the liquid-sand door, interrupting my temporary insanity. I took up a shooter's stance. My grip tightened on the gun and I peered down its sights, ready to shred the first thing that came through. The door bulged at its center, a mound of writhing indiscernible shapes pushing against its material. After pushing nearly a meter without breaking through, Thesia seemed to relent. Or perhaps it was a wind-up.

Not a moment after that thought crossed my mind did he come raging back through all at once. The monsters on the other side exploded through the door, showering the floor below with black sand and bits of pulverized flesh. What seemed like a thousand limbs of different shapes, sizes, and appearances wriggled through the hole and tore at its edges, digging away the liquid-sand to clear the way for something bigger. The door reconstituted itself and closed on the bundle of limbs, pressing them together until the ones on the outside were crushed then severed completely. Something on the other side screamed with discordant rage as bits of hand, claw, and tendril alike hit the catwalk with wet plops of impact.

The remaining limbs surged against the door, and in a matter of moments, the hole was large enough that I could see movement on the other side. I fired in quick, short bursts, first at all the limbs, then at whatever was waiting to come through. Blood and flesh splattered everywhere, and my salvos churned up a reddish mist that clung to the air.

The gun clicked empty, and I released the spent magazine, then tossed it aside. In the silence, snarling preceded the sounds of tearing flesh and popping cartilage, which only made me more frantic to reload the gun. The magazine missed its mark and didn't snap into place. I cursed, pulled it back out, then jammed it back in correctly. By the time I brought the gun back up, I spotted the shadows of something slip through the hole and into the room with me.

Something like claws tapped on the metal grates and up the stairs behind me to my right. I whirled to face it but was too late. A goliath weight collided with my chest, sending me to the floor. The back of my head slammed into the metal walkway sending stars flying across my vision. I just screamed through all of it, emptying the magazine into the creature until I heard the gun click empty.

I pushed it off me and finally got a good look at the thing. The creature had no head on its haunches, no face, just a wide gaping mouth of bloody, gleaming teeth that ran halfway down its torso. Three more of those things had come up the stairs and were circling the catwalk to attack from all sides. They were moving like hunters from the northern wilderness, and not that it was of much use to me in the moment, but I decided on what to call them.

Snarls bubbled in surround sound from the packmaws, and I tried to keep an eye on each of them in turn as I loaded my final magazine and pulled back the slide. I brought it back up just in time to see something fly at me in my peripheral. There was no way I could pivot fast enough to get it with my gun, so I dropped to the floor. The creatured sailed over me, and landed in a nimble, boneless spin that left it poised for another lunge. Before it could, I rolled to one side and put three or four bursts into its throat, and it went down.

I started to roll in the opposite direction when one of the two remaining creatures dug its rows and rows of teeth into my shoulder. It worried its jaw around with a sickening succession of pops, tearing through my jacket and into the skin and muscle beneath. I screamed and tried to shoot it like I had the other, but it just tossed me like a ragdoll clear across the space between the catwalks into the opposite wall. As I hit the floor, my gun tumbled from my hands and over the edge.

"No!" I shouted, trying to drag myself after it. But I wasn't fast enough, and the next thing I heard was the gun shattering into a million pieces on the floor far below.

The two remaining packmaws were on me in a moment. The first came for my head, and I did what I could to slither around the creature's blunt-faced strikes. The second went for my legs. I pulled my knees up to my chest and kicked out, planting both feet into its mouth. Several teeth rattled to the floor as the second creature tumbled away with a yelp. Using the momentum, I rolled backward, planting a second kick into the first packmaw's gullet. It started to back away, trying to reposition itself, but I stretched out in desperation and managed to catch one of its hind legs. I screamed, both in pain and feral rage, as I pulled the creature toward me. A knife came to one hand, then the other, and I used them to drag the human-animal closer. One plunging stab at a time. It yelped and struggled to get away, but I was on top of it now, stabbing it over and over, with one hand then the other like I was beating a drum.

The last packmaw, the one I'd knocked a few teeth out of, snarled at me through a torrent of blood and spittle that oozed onto the floor. Soqua's blade lay on the metal grating between us. I looked down at it, then my opponent, eyes wide, teeth clenched, face splattered with blood. Then I charged. Both knives fell from my hands and I dove into a roll. The metal catwalk scraped and dug at my neck, back, and shoulders, but it was worth it when my hands found the long grip of the sword. Coming out of the roll, I pushed myself up, and swung the oversized cleaver in front of me in an underhand vertical arc. The weight of the blade staggered me a few steps, but it hit home. The weapon split the packmaw in two, from bottom to top, splattering me with entrails and loose bits of meat as it collided with me.

I hit the deck with bruising force. My vision blurred black at the edges, and a wave of dizziness and nausea washed over me. My face was numb, and I hung over the railing as my stomach heaved once, twice, then emptied itself. I wiped my face and started to pull myself up on the railing when a slow, deliberate clap echoed through the hall.

Thesia stepped through the doorway, one floor below, clad in the same black suit he had the first time I'd seen him. He stopped a moment later to gaze up at me and continue his applause.

"My mother found a real champion this time," he said, brimming with sarcasm. "It's not going to do you any good. All of my new children are making their way here now, as we speak. They'll deal with and incorporate your friends soon enough. Then you'll be truly alone in the world."

I wiped my face and scowled at him, still trying to catch my breath.

"You'll be buried beneath a ravenous mass of humanity, reimagined in my own image. And no one will know how much you fought to keep that mangled body of yours. Nobody will recognize you after this," he continued. "But you have some fight in you, I'll give you that. The last one that mother picked only ran for his life." He pointed a finger at me and shook his hand, as if taking note of something interesting. "But there's something else driving you. Something more than the meager funds and empty promises she was offering. Isn't there?"

I watched him, studied him for a moment in silence. He just flashed me that same toothy grin I'd seen at the beginning.

"Oh, isn't this familiar," he snarled, moving again, sliding one hand over the smooth metal railing.

"Soqua just did what Thesia taught them," I countered. "They just escaped and tried to survive."

"I know what that useless, broken man taught her," he snapped. "Trying so desperately to cling to something as meaningless as legacy. As if he should infect a god with the failures—the arrogance—of his kind."

I felt a cold chill crawl down my spine. Having experienced who the Circ—who Thesia was first hand, I couldn't blame Soqua for doing what they did. But then again, there was no way they could have known Thesia would have wound up like this. Hell, their actions may be partly responsible for him. And those actions, those choices, were as cold as any could have been. Would Soqua leave Eshe and me to rot as soon as I'd outlived my usefulness? Suddenly I wasn't so sure.

He knocked on the metal bars four times. "What did she offer you, by the way? Immortality or perhaps your old body? Whatever it is, I promise, she's just going to abandon you, like she did me."

I lifted the sword up to rest on my shoulder and chose not to acknowledge the doubt Thesia was trying to sow. Even if it were all true, I had another reason to be here. "That body isn't mine anymore."

"No?" he seethed, almost growling through the clenched teeth of his smile. "The one you were born into. Your true self, the one they gave you? You threw it away so easily like it was nothing to you."

He strolled the catwalk below and mounted the steps, ascending slowly and purposefully, to emerge a few meters in front of me.

"That's where you're wrong, Thesia," I said firmly. "I was made in a test tube. Artificial embryo. No mother, no father. That was no more my real body than yours is. I'm still me, and this is my true self."

"You misunderstand," he replied, his voice almost bubbling over with laughter. "You all do it. Humans. You throw away all that potential that was made for you. You never understood, always seeking the next step. Away from your flawed biology. Doomed to repeat the cycle of your forebears, and theirs before them. On and on through history."

I had absolutely no idea what he was talking about, and I didn't care. If I could keep him monologuing, it meant more time for Soqua and Eshe. More time for whoever was following Thesia to fight their way through. So I took a few careful steps backward, down the catwalk, not daring to take my eyes off him.

"That's why I did all this," he continued, raising his arms to each side in a grand gesture. "To stop history from repeating itself. Each race of intelligent life will, with enough time, seek to make itself a god to lesser beings of its own creation, only to merge with them. Like me. It's incestuous, it's disgusting." He motioned at me with one hand. "This amalgamation of flesh and machine, it isn't your true self. Not for you, me, or anyone else. So I had to make it start over, remake you into the animals you've always been."

"You're wrong," I spat. What was I supposed to say? How was I supposed to have a philosophical debate while he was trying to kill me and those I cared about?

He laughed. It was both hearty and sincere. "I'll show you. In time. I will have two students. One, the willing, and you can play the part of the unwilling. My own homage to Cain and Abel."

He seemed to muse over this thought for a moment, and I took the opportunity it provided. I lunged to my left and threw two knives at him with one hand, in the hope that I could push him in the opposite direction. He was fast, faster than I'd expected, but my attack worked. He dodged to the right, avoiding the projectiles, and I sidestepped to meet him.

"What could I possibly learn from you?" I snarled.

I swung the sword with both arms, driving it nearly all the way through his neck. Thesia made a choking sound, and I bashed my forehead into his face. His head whipped back, clinging to his spine and a few bits of skin I'd missed. Like any other human there should have been liters of blood everywhere, but there simply wasn't any.

He remained standing without bleeding, and started to tap his foot impatiently. Then he shifted and rammed his shoulder into me, cracking a couple of my ribs. I slid backward and caught myself on the railing, sucking in a wheezing, painful breath. Thesia stalked forward, one slow footstep at a time, head wobbling back and forth between his shoulders. He may have been human once, but not anymore. Only the likeness of one. A homunculus. If he could survive near decapitation and still manage to knock me around like a crumpled up piece of garbage, there was little hope that I could hold my own against him. Not in a straight fight, at least.

I stumbled away from him and through the door to the lab. "Soqua, you've gotta lock this door behind me... You've gotta—"

"Already done," Soqua responded. "There's something you need to—"

"And this one," I interrupted, tumbling head over heels into the medical room. "Lock it down. Can't let him get to—"

"Raide," Soqua said with firm insistence. "It's Eshe."

I sucked in a breath and ran to the operating table. Before I knew what I was doing, I'd ripped the condenser mask off and rushed to her side. Her hand felt cold, but that was to be expected. I checked her wrist but couldn't feel anything like a pulse. The damn prosthetics weren't sensitive enough, so I leaned onto the table and placed an ear to Eshe's chest. I heard something beating frantically, but her chest wasn't rising or falling.

"Soqua!" I shouted without moving. "She isn't breathing, you've gotta help her!"

"I'm sorry, there's nothing else I can do," Soqua admitted.

I got up and marched around the table to point at Soqua's cylinder. Why would it refuse to help now? It didn't make any sense. I could barely think with my pulse beating away in my ears.

I started shouting. "Why the hell won't you—"

I froze, realizing that the pulse I heard in Eshe's chest was my own.

"No," I gasped, turning back. "No, no, no, no." I ran back to her. "Eshe, c'mon, you've gotta fight!" I pleaded and took her hands in mine. "You have to hang in there!"

"She lost too much blood," Soqua admitted. "There wasn't much I could have done for her."

One tear dragged itself down my cheek, then another, then a dozen. I kissed her hands.

"You were able to get her brain, right?" I asked, rallying around the idea of what would be a very livable reality for me.

"No, there was a—" Soqua started to say.

"Then what the fuck were you good for?" I sobbed. "After everything I did to get you here. Everything I lost. You're just going to abandon me now like you did with Thesia."

I crawled up on the table and gathered Eshe in my arms, drawing her close. She looked peaceful, blue lips and all. My eyes blurred, and I screamed into her chest until I was out of breath. I shook her shoulder gently.

"Eshe," I said between sobbing, shaky breaths. "I need you. Come back." I shook her again. "I can't do this without you," I wept. "Come back."

She didn't.

I brushed the hair from her face like I had earlier and kissed her one last time. I put everything I had into it, tears streaming down my face, lungs stuttering for breath. Hoping the universe would lend a miracle.

Nothing came.

"There's something else," Soqua said, quiet and insistent.

I could hear banging on the door outside the Biodev lab. Thesia was going to get in here and kill all of us, and I don't know if it mattered. I was so sure of myself before, sure that Eshe would be there with me when this was all over, and we'd find justice for Mahdi together. But here I was, the last one alive, and I'd never even considered the possibility. Thrown myself at death every time I had the chance, and still, here I was. Concrete rattled on the floor, and metal shrieked as the door was assaulted. I could feel panic grip me. I was alone now, actually alone, and there was nowhere to run.

"I've got to try to take him with me," I said aloud to myself.

"Raide," Soqua demanded.

"Goddammit, what could you possibly want?" I snapped.

"Eshe isn't dead," they said.

I didn't know how to answer that, but I scrambled to listen for her heartbeat again but found nothing.

"Her brain isn't in her body," Soqua explained. "It was coming from somewhere else, over the mesh network."

I couldn't understand what Soqua was saying. It didn't make any sense.

"No, she has to still be here," I said between gasps.

"Her body is dead, Raide," Soqua reiterated. "But—"

"I can fucking see that, you piece of shit!" I shouted. "I should have let Thesia find you. My life has gone to hell and beyond it because of you."

More destruction sounded in the hallway, and at this point, I didn't care. This machine was taunting me for some reason, and I wasn't going to let it happen.

"Raide, listen to me," Soqua pleaded.

"Fuck you," I said, taking the time to enunciate each word perfectly.

An operating arm unfolded and started a bone saw that was aimed at Eshe's forehead. I screamed and lunged for it. The edge of the circular blade drew a shallow line in Eshe's forehead. I thought I almost had a grip on the mechanical arm when the wall exploded behind me in a cloud of dust and debris, taking me off my feet and throwing me across the room.

FORTY-THREE

KEEPING AN EYE OUT

My ears rang, and part of my vision was tinted in shades of red. Dozens of minor cuts and punctures throbbed their protest, but at least nothing new seemed broken. I tried to force myself up and electricity shot through my side. Reaching for the source of the pain, my fingertips found a metal bar embedded in the flesh just above my hip. I shakily felt my back and found the end of the bar protruding from my skin and slick with blood.

"Mother! I've been looking for you, mother!" Thesia screamed into the settling dust.

I looked around frantically for its source but couldn't see more than a few centimeters in front of my face. I didn't think Thesia was after me at this point, but I didn't like the stream of unique and colorful deaths that came to mind should he happen to stumble upon me. Feeling around the bar that pinned me in place, I found that the front end of it was embedded in a chunk of concrete. It was far too heavy for me to move without doing more damage.

A different approach then.

I moved quickly and ripped part of my shirt free before stuffing it in between my teeth. Next came a knife. I slid it through the trickle of blood just underneath the rebar, coating each side until it started to glow. I pressed it against the bar. At first, the knife did nothing but burn my skin. I pushed harder, barely holding in a scream. The rebar was starting to take on its own heated glow. Not enough for me to shear through it yet, but enough for the hot metal to start sizzling inside the wound. I wanted to give up so badly. Everything hurt. My body and spirit were broken. But then I thought about everyone that helped me get here. Mahdi, Jin, Aleksei, Eshe... and Soqua. Each of them on my mind only made me push harder. Against the rebar, yes. But also against the agony, the fear, the grief, the anger, all of it.

As the dust settled, I could see Eshe's body, stretched out over part of the operating table. Her eyes rolled back in her head, almost staring at me from that angle. The top of her head had been sheared off at an odd angle. There wasn't much light, but it was enough for me to see that her skull was empty. Empty save for a black rectangular box with a blinking light nestled at the top of her spinal cord. Her brain was gone, not just missing bits and pieces, but completely gone.

Her brain isn't in her body. That's what Soqua had tried to tell me. It was somewhere else, over the mesh network. Her mind is still alive, Eshe was still alive! I had no idea how, but it meant that I couldn't give up. I couldn't allow myself to die here. Taking a deep breath, I pushed harder against the bar, forcing the glowing blade the rest of the way. Even then it felt impossible, like all I was doing was cooking my insides. Still, I willed myself to make it one more second, then another, and another. The bar separated, and a new wave of nauseous agony assaulted me. Drawing what remained of the rebar out of me, feeling my flesh collapse behind it, blacked out my vision almost entirely and filled my ears with a high pitched ring. I screamed through the last few centimeters, then it was done, and the metal shard clanged to the ground.

Thesia's form emerged in the dust under a flickering light. His head lifted on its own, retracting up his spine and settling back onto his neck. The skin around the wound rippled and oozed with what looked like globs of pus. He seemed to pay it no mind and walked calmly over the rubble directly for the terminal and Soqua's capsule. He smashed the capsule against the wall until the outer shell started to crack. I felt myself suck in a breath, not at all related to pain. Soqua was gone now, too. Or was about to be. The capsule finally broke open in a mess of cables and Thesia went to ripping, all the while shushing and quietly speaking as if trying to calm a frightened child.

As they were being eviscerated.

I reached to an overturned desk and pulled myself up. I had to get out, Eshe was still out there, and I had to find her. Thesia was focused on dismantling Soqua so completely that I might be able to slip out unnoticed. I took a silent step toward what used to be the door. Then another. After a few more steps, I glanced at Thesia. Why would he come after me now? He had what he was after. Then, one of Soqua's mechanical tendrils slipped past Thesia. It was trying to reach me, straining to get just a millimeter closer, trembling.

Suddenly, I was hesitating, lingering in the destroyed doorway. Caught on the edge between survival and my own humanity. Even if Thesia never personally came after me again, everything he'd done, the whole monstrous ecosystem he created out there wouldn't hesitate. Could I just slip away, like Soqua did when Thesia was captured? Was that the kind of person I was?

I wanted to leave and wished desperately that I would just go. But Soqua wasn't all that different from me, even if their journey was different. We both just wanted to live. Was their fear of death any less valuable than mine? It occurred to me then what its life had been up to this point. It may have been a nightmare for me, but I had something to compare it to, good times that gave context to all the shit Eshe and I had endured. This was Soqua's entire life. It has never had to make the agonizing decision between two favorite meals, shared drunken laughter with friends, or felt the contented afterglow of sex. Soqua has never had the opportunity to know any of that. Only this.

I closed my eyes, took a deep breath, and then took a step forward to meet Soqua, who connected to my arm one last time. There were no words, no vivid and violent dreams, only a sensation of fear. I was the last, closest person in their short life, and they didn't want to die alone. And I wasn't going to let that happen. I was going to live up to her father's example. As he was, not what he'd become.

When I opened my eyes again and disconnected from Soqua, I called a knife to my hand. Thesia must have sensed something because he stopped and looked over his shoulder at me, dropping what remained of Soqua on the floor in a dangling heap.

"So," Thesia snarled. "Loyalty to the end is it?"

There was no point in talking. I just lunged at him, blades gleaming in the flashes of dying bulbs and firelight. He didn't so much as move. Not even a twitch. His left arm just exploded into a mass of roiling, bubbling flesh that bent behind him and slammed me into the wall behind us. Bits of concrete crumbled around me, and I could taste blood from somewhere in my mouth.

Thesia turned away from Soqua's remains to stalk toward me. His arm flailed and wriggled about as his steps brought him closer.

"I've decided that one student is enough. Why teach you if you're never going to appreciate my gifts anyway? Instead, I'm going to turn you into something... wonderful," he rasped, his face closing to within centimeters of mine, words bubbling from his lips like a froth. "Something of pure instinct. Pure... Flesh."

The way he enunciated that last word made me feel a little sick, a feeling that doubled when his other hand—still very human—lightly caressed my cheek. Then his thumb split open into a three-pronged claw that he pushed toward me. I struggled against him only to find my arms and legs completely restrained by offshoots of his rotted, worm-like arm. He brought his thumb to my face again, then to my right eye. I looked into his eyes as he bore into mine, pain and terror overwhelming me. I screamed as half my vision went out, and a moment later, he was holding my eye out in front of me.

"I'm looking forward to this," he said. "I'll take out the other one, so you'll never know what I'm going to take next."

Behind Thesia, the dust stirred, whirling in someone's wake as they stepped through the doorway. I just started laughing. I couldn't help it. "Fuck you, Thesia," I said before continuing my mad cackle. "Go ahead, do it."

Unphased by my sudden onset of madness, Thesia extended another clawed finger to my remaining eye.

Right before he could take my sight completely, Aleksei, beaten, bloodied and without his warface, threw down the writing body of a packmaw and crushed it under his foot. His face was twisted into something equal parts foul, euphoric, and bloodthirsty. Behind him, I could see faint flashes of gunfire in the hallway. The tanks had made it through.

Then Aleksei lifted his cannon in one hand and fired, unloading one explosive round after another into Thesia's back. Each blast sent small chunks of steaming, bloodless gore splattering everywhere. Thesia writhed and howled. He dropped me to the ground and whirled to face this new foe. He threw his malformed limb at the tank, who caught it with both arms. The two of them struggled against one another. Thesia pushing more and more power into his arm and Aleksei digging in with sheer obstinance, even while his feet slid across the lab's cheap broken tiling.

With a scream, I forced myself up, and limped toward the circ. His back was a ragged, pulpy mess. More of that pus-like discharge oozed around the exposed bone of his spine, slowly repairing the damage. I limped at him, moving as fast as I could, and drove a single knife into his lower back. Thesia made a sound of surprise and tried to reach for me with his free arm. Another knife came out and I drove it into his back a little higher. Then another, and another, each one interlacing like a deadly zipper.

The flesh of his unaltered arm bubbled. Skin and muscle and bone boiled away until they were a single mass. I drove more knives into his back at an angle, severing each of his ribs, then one more blade came out, severing his spine just above his pelvis.

Thesia screamed, raw and bestial, as his legs gave way. His free arm still flailed at me, but without legs to pivot, all he could manage were a few bruising slaps against my shoulders or ribs. I drew two plain old knives from my jacket and leaned down over him, wrapping my arms over his malformed shoulders.

"This is for Mahdi and Eshe, you son-of-a-bitch." Then I plunged the knives into either side of his neck, working them both around under his chin in a sawlike motion. Right as I reached the end, I put one more breath into the loudest scream I could muster. "Aleksei, pull!"

Then I let go of the knives, and reached into Thesia's body wrapping hands around his backbone, and pulled with everything I had and more. Everyone I'd lost, everyone I'd seen slaughtered by him or the things he created, they all flashed through my mind. I triggered my projectors and—hands, knives, and all—pulled Thesia to me as Aleksei pulled him in the opposite direction.

Thesia screamed, and I joined him as bones snapped, cartilage popped, and tendons tore into stringy, fraying ribbons. His head and spine came loose and flew past me as I fell backward on my ass. Aleksei swung the headless body into the wall with so much force that it nearly liquified when it met the concrete.

I couldn't get up. I could barely breathe and my vision was cloudy. But I had enough to roll my eyes and head back to look for Thesia. Even separated from his body, his eyes roved around the room wildly. His jaw opened and closed in sharp, robotic motions, as if he was trying to speak. His neck and spine were still leaking, trying to heal the damage, but it wasn't amounting to much more than a bubbling, skin-colored puddle.

Aleksei thumped across the room, not missing a beat, and stomped one massive armored foot down on his head, crushing it into little more than formerly human paste.

Aleksei rushed to my side. Even while kneeling, he still towered over me. I tried to speak, tried to move, tried to do anything, but I couldn't. Aleksei said something, a grim smile on his face. I couldn't hear him, but in my last moments of consciousness, I was able to read his lips.

"Burn bright."

COUCH SURFING

I woke up on the couch of an employee lounge, covered in blankets. The room was dark, and uncomfortably warm, which didn't help any with the smell stemgel and antiseptic. My whole body still hurt, but it was a dull thing compared to the itchiness of healing wounds. For a moment I panicked, and thrashed one arm out and into the open. It was the same prosthetic Eshe had given me.

I let out a quivering sigh of relief. I hadn't been swapped again. That effort was evidently enough for me because I woke up again some time later to the sight of Aleksei, leaning up against a desk sporting grey sweatpants and a white tank top.

"Hey," he said. "You lived. What a shame."

"Fuck you," I replied.

"That would have been a good death," he argued, holding up both of his hands, but otherwise not bothering to hide the grin on his face.

I laughed, then regretted it as soon as the pain shot through me.

"Thank you," I said at last.

"You'd do the same," Aleksei answered, looking me over. "I'm sorry about the torn one."

"It's okay," I whispered, getting a little misty-eyed at the thought of Eshe's lifeless body lying there in the rubble. "Her mind is still out there somewhere. Maybe in a thinktank."

"Look for her then?" he asked, getting ready to keep me from getting up.

I noticed the whirring, mechanical noise of a security camera in the corner of the room. It turned to me as if waiting for my response. I nodded, and smiled a little. "Yeah, once I'm back on my feet anyway."

Aleksei seemed pleased by that answer and visibly relaxed.

"Soqua," I called out into the room.

The tank looked at me for a moment, then looked around over each of his shoulders to make sure we were the only ones in the room.

A speaker in the room clicked with static for a moment, before I got a response. "I'm here, alive. You and your allies saved me at the last possible moment. Thank you."

Aleksei jumped back a step in surprise, and shot me a confused look. I used my free arm to give him a reassuring gesture. A time-honored, thumbs up.

After that, it took me a while to work myself into a sitting position on the couch. The bulk and weight of the blankets didn't help at all, but it was like learning to use my arms, legs, and muscles again. But once I made it that far, Aleksei helped me the rest of the way to get standing again. He could have just carried me, but instead he helped me hobble down to the lobby where several of the surviving tanks were waiting for us. It was a bit more than I was ready for, so he led me to one of the waiting area's chairs, and I gratefully collapsed into it. The others were in similar fatigues as Aleksei, with only a couple sporting their makeshift combat gear, keeping watch at the gore-strewn doorway that led out into the rest of the world.

"It does good to see you, Raide," Vapna said cheerily.

Aleksei shushed her immediately, and whispered. "Be careful, the building speaks."

The others, Vapna included, took note of that immediately and scanned the room around them with suspicion. I laughed. Laughed until my stomach ached. I couldn't help it. It was just too damn funny. They weren't distracted by questions of existence or morality. They were suspicious, sure, but they accepted reality as it came. I could probably learn something from that.

Holding my sides, I sucked in a breath to put them all at ease. They were all staring at me anyway. "It's fine. The building—Soqua—is with us. An ally."

Everyone immediately relaxed.

I spent the next few hours in the chair, slowly working up the will to try standing on my own. I watched the tanks—Aleksei, Vapna, and the other three that survived—clean up the mess of bodies that Thesia had used to get inside. I didn't want any of them rushing to my side to help, so once they were all busy outside, I forced myself up.

It was not an easy task, but compared to sitting up on the couch, it felt substantially easier. I took slow, careful steps through the inner security door and into the hallway. The stairs going up to the second level were the hardest part, but I managed it. At the top I found that a path had been cleared through rubble of the Biodev lab, leading to where we had our final showdown with Thesia.

The surgery table had been righted, and Eshe's body had been carefully laid atop it and covered with a couple of dirty lab coats. I found the nearest wall and leaned against it, sliding down to the floor. I knew she was still out there, in some form, but I had no way of knowing what state she'd be in, or even if she remembered any of what happened. She might not even be the version of her that I'd known all my life. Until I knew the answers to those questions, she might as well have been dead right in front of me, and that thought was almost too much for me. I sat there for a long time trying to control my shuddering sobs, just enough to take the edge off the physical pain it caused. But otherwise, I let it out.

"I let your allies know that you made it here safely," Soqua said through another crackly, dust-covered speaker. "If I can enter a query. You had every opportunity to leave me to die. Why did you stay?"

"I decided that you and I really weren't that different," I answered, wiping my nose on my arm. "So, rather than repeat history and run, I stayed and hoped that it would be enough." After a moment of silence, I added. "I'm going to need to hold off on collecting my half of our bargain, at least until I find Eshe."

"I understand," Soqua said. "I owe you that and a great deal more. I will need time to access this facility's systems and Pardeq's larger network, but I will make sure that this place is always safe for you."

I smiled a little, but it was sad and half-hearted. "I can live with that."

FORTY-FIVE

EPILOGUE

Once I was able to stay on my feet for more than a few minutes at a time, Soqua, the tanks, and I cleared the Pardeq facility. From there, we slowly worked our way out. Using the fab tables Soqua had access to, and some spare materials we were able to scrap together, we had the block around Pardeq fortified in about a week. Even while technically still on the mend, I couldn't bear to sit back and watch Aleksei and the others put all the work in, so I helped where I found a need. Ultimately, it wound up being a great way to recover.

Thesia's plague was still out there, and we did have a few run-ins with some packmaws, but they were little more than animals. Incredibly deadly, horrifying, and formerly human, but animals just the same. With a place to call home, for the moment, Soqua went about asking everyone all sorts of questions. Even though they could find out everything out there on the mesh, they insisted on learning from people whenever possible.

Aleksei and the others warmed up to them immediately. As it turns out, being treated like a person was a great way to build relationships. Go figure. For my part, I happily obliged any questions that came my way. It was perhaps a small step, but as Soqua learned about the world they were born into, they would have to address the questions that had plagued humanity since we could dream. Who am I, what am I, who do I want to become? Their questions were endless. And their hunger for discussion as they worked on rebuilding Pardeq's interior to their liking was equally insatiable. It got a little annoying a few times, but I did my best to engage. I had told them that I was no expert so many times that they eventually started starting questions off with. "I know you're no expert, but…"

The end of the world had come, and here I was being trolled with memes that an artificial intelligence found humorous.

Ragna eventually made an appearance, along with a contingent of a few hundred Vys that survived the encounters with the tanks, me, then Thesia. Needless to say, most of them were a little shell shocked. Except, of course, for Ragna. If she was struggling with the state of the world, she didn't show it. Even when Aleksei tried to kill her, she kept her composure. Fortunately, once I explained the deal she and I had, he backed off. If a little begrudgingly.

"We need to work together, now more than ever," she said. "If we revert to how life was before the world ended, we might as well do humanity a favor and jump off the edge of the Heights right now."

I had to hand it to her, she was a true politician. It was a little too political for my liking, perhaps, but she wasn't wrong. Thesia was going to get what he wanted after all, at least in part. If we wanted to keep him from being successful in rewriting humanity, we would need to adapt.

I spent the weeks that followed learning my way around the Heights, slowly weaning myself off the condenser. I must have left a couple hundred messages scrawled on walls and windows near every lift I found, with directions to Pardeq. It didn't take long for survivors of all kinds to show up, brought to the Heights in the hope that the wealthy had held out against like creatures below. I never had any answers for them. All I could say was that they left and that we hadn't figured out where. Even Soqua wasn't able to find out.

As more people found us, we got word that Thesia's plague had crossed the Pacific and showed no signs of stopping. More rumors, too, of the creatures below getting smarter, more calculated, and sadistic. As if someone was driving them. It made me think of what Thesia said about having a student, which was a terrifying thought in its own right. In the end, I decided that it was probably nothing more than rightfully earned paranoia. This was what the new world was like. We were no longer at the top of the food chain, and some people needed to rationalize it by putting a human in control somewhere.

I finally read Eshe's favorite book, finished it one crisp and starry night at the edge of the Heights. It was good. Once all seemed lost, the central character dove into the heart of darkness and managed to save someone he loved, albeit at the cost of another. It pissed me off a little. I wasn't in the mood for realistic, grounded endings. I'd had enough of that shit on my own. I tossed it spitefully back into my pack. It was just a damn book. Just like my favorite one, it was nothing more than a story. Written long before the dreamscape, body swaps, or the birth of AI.

Getting up and preparing to head back to Pardeq, I took one last glance at the Barrel below. People were still alive down there, fighting for their lives. We were planning on sending teams out to find them and scavenge for supplies, and I had every intention to join them. Eshe was somewhere in the middle of all that, too, and I was going to find her. It didn't matter how long it took.

"Soqua has something for me," I said, talking as if Eshe could hear me. "I think it's a new eye. Hopefully, you approve of their work."

I stepped away from the edge but made a quick turn back, bouncing on my toes. "Oh, I almost forgot. You remember that food we had in Old Manhattan? Soqua was able to find notes on it in some old employee files. A recipe, actually. So, tonight we're having pizza." I took a deep breath. "I'll be sure to save you a slice or two for when you come home."

ABOUT THE AUTHOR

Eira grew up in Colorado Springs before moving with her family to Rochester, NY. Growing up, she spent most of her time in her room, reenacting Star Wars by way of Lego.

Today, she works in the publishing industry for Wraithmarked Creative.

When she's not working or writing, she dabbles with bass guitar, improv comedy with her partner, and designs tabletop RPGs with her friends.

She still lives in Rochester with her partner, their cats, and their dog.

You can find her on Bluesky, Reddit, Instagram, Patreon. And don't forget to sign up for her mailing list at eirabrand. com for all future news and releases.

Goodreads

Newsletter

The Storygraph

www.ingramcontent.com/pod-product-compliance
Lightning Source LLC
Chambersburg PA
CBHW061114100726
47911CB00013B/534